Praise for
SEA WITCH

"Prepare to be lost in these pages for hours on end."
> —RENÉE AHDIEH, #1 *New York Times* and *USA Today*
> bestselling author of *The Wrath & the Dawn*

"Henning's dive into Little Mermaid lore is equal parts dark and tantalizing. Like the sea it sings of, this story has a strong pull. I found myself unable to set it down!"
> —RYAN GRAUDIN, award-winning author of *Wolf by Wolf*

"All hail a new Queen of the Sea! Mystery, romance, and revenge sweep you in—and there is magic on every page."
> —DANIELLE PAIGE, *New York Times*
> bestselling author of *Dorothy Must Die*

"Deftly transforms a fairy tale into a richly layered exploration of culture and relationships."   —*PUBLISHERS WEEKLY*

"Readers who gobble up every watery paranormal story will certainly enjoy this angst-drenched tale of forbidden love."
> —*KIRKUS REVIEWS*

"This enjoyable read will entertain and be a great fit for collections where fairy-tale retellings are popular."

> —*SLJ*

"This spin on *The Little Mermaid* is full of plot twists and heart-in-throat action. Fans of twisted fairy tales will find plenty to love."   —*ALA BOOKLIST*

Sea Witch

Also by Sarah Henning:
Sea Witch Rising

SEA
WITCH

SARAH HENNING

KATHERINE TEGEN BOOKS
An Imprint of HarperCollins Publishers

To Nate and Amalia—
the only ships in my sea.

And to Justin—
next time there will be
more car chases.

Katherine Tegen Books is an imprint of HarperCollins Publishers.

Sea Witch
Copyright © 2018 by HarperCollins Publishers
All rights reserved. Printed in the United States of America.
No part of this book may be used or reproduced in any manner
whatsoever without written permission except in the case of
brief quotations embodied in critical articles and reviews.
For information address HarperCollins Children's Books,
a division of HarperCollins Publishers,
195 Broadway, New York, NY 10007.
www.epicreads.com

Library of Congress Control Number: 2018933269
ISBN 978-0-06-243880-5

Typography by Carla Weise
19 20 21 22 23   PC/LSCH   10 9 8 7 6 5 4 3 2 1
❖
First paperback edition, 2019

I have sea foam in my veins, I understand the language
of the waves.   —Jean Cocteau, *Le Testament d'Orphée*

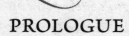

PROLOGUE

Two small pairs of boots echoed on the afternoon cobblestones—one pair in a sprint, the other in a stumble and slide. A blond girl, no older than five, dragged a raven-haired girl an inch taller and a year older down the sea lane toward a small cottage.

The dark-haired girl's lungs were sputtering, each inhale a failure.

She was drowning on dry land.

As the house came into view, the blond girl opened her mouth to scream for help but before any sound could come out, the other girl's mother burst through the door. Like she knew what had happened—she always seemed to know what they'd done.

"Evie!" the mother cried, cradling her daughter in a heap at her chest and running toward the cottage. "Anna," she said to the little blonde, who was panting from carrying her friend so far, "fetch the royal physician—"

"But—"

"Go!"

The girl didn't protest again, fine boots clacking against the cobblestones as she regained speed.

When her mother shut the cottage door tightly behind them, the raven-headed girl knew the physician's medicine wouldn't heal her.

Only one thing would.

"Gianni!" The mother called, and the girl's father poked his head out of the bedroom, his face slack with the sleep he wasn't allowed on his latest whaling trip.

"Evie . . . what—"

"A broken rib. Maybe a punctured lung." She laid the girl in her bed and ripped the girl's bodice to her navel. Blood under the skin showed black across the expanse of the little girl's ribs, fissures like spiderwebs crossed from spine to sternum. The mother tried to read her daughter's dark eyes. "What happened?"

The girl licked her lips before inhaling just enough air to speak.

"I saved Nik."

That was true. And the little girl was proud. Daring to smile despite the pain.

They'd spent the morning together—the blonde, the raven-haired girl, and their boy—running through the waves, climbing rocks, dancing in the sand. But then the afternoon came and it was time for them to part. The boy sent back to his castle, the little girls home—the younger one to her mansion, ten times the size of the other girl's tiny cottage.

Mischievous and sunburnt, they ran in protest, the boy leading the way, holding the girls' hands as they raced across the stepping-stone rocks that led into the cove. They giggled and shrieked as they hopped from rock to rock, the boy's minder chiding them from the shore.

But one rock was slick with moss. The boy slipped—falling backward, the base of his skull aimed directly at a crook of solid stone.

In a blink, the little girl made her choice.

She threw her body between the boy and the jagged edge of the rock. Her back took the hit with a huge crack. Her head snapped back, her skull missing impact by a hair. Just as she hit, the boy's head bounced onto the pilled cotton of her bodice rather than smashing into the rock.

It was a thing of magic that she'd made it in time.

They were caught then. The boy's minder yanked them back onto the beach and told them in stern tones to never do that again. Then the old woman hauled the boy away without a good-bye, leaving the girls on the sand.

As they turned for home, the little raven-haired girl stumbled, the shock wearing off and the pain beginning. It radiated up her back, around her rib cage, to the front of her dress. She couldn't catch her breath, each inhale stopping short. The little blonde said she'd walk her friend home but by the time they made it to the sea lane, the raven-headed girl couldn't stand, all her weight on the blonde's shoulders.

"Oh, Evie . . . ," the girl's mother said. As if she'd seen it all. Immediately, she sent her husband for her bottles. Her inks. Not that one. This one. She laid the girl in her bed and lit a fire with a snap of her fingers.

And tried every healing spell she knew.

It only took seconds to know none of them would work. The girl's breath withered until it was almost nothing at all.

The mother wept, wishing for her sister—the strongest witch. Healer of Kings, reviving those in power who turn a blind eye to magic when their lives depend on it, but banish it when it doesn't. She was the reason the physician might come at all—though he would be too late. As would Hansa, a day away, healing yet another noble.

The girl's father pressed his hand into his wife's shoulder and wiped away her tears. Then he squeezed his daughter's hand, already growing cold, her circulation failing.

"I'll go fetch the minister—"

"Not yet," the mother said, determination ringing in her voice. The girl's mother stood at the edge of the bed, her shoulders now pin straight, her voice calm and direct. "There is one more spell I can try."

With gentle fingers, she painted octopus ink across the little girl's cheeks, down her neck, and across her chest. Then her mother laid her hands gently over the girl's chest.

"Don't you worry, Evie."

The words she said next were old and dark, and the little girl didn't understand them. They made her blood crackle like the fire across the room. Stole the air from the cottage. Made her mother shake, violently, as she held her hands to her daughter's skin.

The little girl couldn't do anything but watch her mother,

her veins singing. Soon, her mother's palms on her skin became more than damp. They began to burn.

And then the pain stopped. Air rushed into the little girl's lungs, and her chest rose. She exhaled, long and deep.

At that the girl's mother smiled—just before her own body began to seize, her eyes rolling back in her head.

It was too much. The mother's chest compressed, a long breath pushing out—but no inhale following.

"Greta! Greta!" The girl's father placed his hands on his wife's face, his palms burning and flying away, suddenly red.

The prickle in the little girl's blood spiked with fear. She struggled to pull herself to sit, her mother's hands sliding away as her form slumped over and her pale cheek smashed into the bedsheet. The little girl didn't hesitate, reaching for her mother's potions. She turned her mother's head to face upward before smearing ink across those pale cheeks, her little fingers blistering with the touch. Her own skin was pink and warm and full of life as her mother's skin turned as white as snow, as hot as ash.

The girl was smart, though. She'd watched her mother enough. She knew how these spells worked. Magic was barter—the right words, actions, potions for the right result.

She put her hands on her mother's face and began repeating those strange words.

Words of life.

"Evelyn, no!" Her father didn't move, just screamed, fear freezing him to his spot at the foot of the bed.

But the little girl had fumbled her way through the words

enough that her own skin began to grow hot. The pain returned. Her breath became shallow. Then her mother's eyes flew open, showing beautiful hazel instead of the whites.

It was working.

Her father looked from his wife to his daughter. Those words were dark. Old. Powerful. He knew this as much as he knew his native tongue.

Her mother's lips began moving. She took a deep breath. "Gefa!" With this single command, she stole the words right from the little girl's mouth. Dark words and dark magic and all sound gone from the girl's powerful tongue.

Still, the child kept going, chest heaving—she was yelling but could not be heard. Tears as dark as night flowed down her little cheeks. Black coating her vision, the girl began to wail without sound, her whole body shaking.

And, with her last wisp of energy, the girl's mother looked to her father.

"Bring Hansa home. Tell her. Promise."

As he nodded, her mother whispered one last spell, and the little girl's screams filled the air, black tears dripping onto her ruined dress.

"No, Mama, no!"

The little girl grabbed her mother's hand, still burning to the touch, and saw the light flee from her hazel eyes.

1

THE SEA IS A FICKLE WITCH.

She is just as likely to bestow a kiss as to steal the breath from your lips. Beautiful and cruel, and every glimmering wrinkle in between. Filling our bellies and our coffers when she is generous. Coolly watching as we don black and add tears to her waters when she is wicked.

Only the tide follows her moods—giving and taking at the same salty rate.

Still, she is more than our witch—she's our queen.

In all her spells and tantrums, she is one of us. The crown jewel of Havnestad, nuzzled against our shores—for better or worse.

Tonight, dressed in her best party finery, she appears calm, anger buried well below her brilliant surface. Still, there's a charge in the air as the stars wink with the coming summer solstice and the close of Nik's sixteenth birthday.

Formally: Crown Prince Asger Niklas Bryniulf Øldenburg III, first in line to the throne of the sovereign kingdom of Havnestad.

Informally: just Nik.

But "just Nik" isn't quite right either. He's not *just* anything to me. He's my best friend. My only friend, really.

And now he's dancing with Malvina across the deck of his father's grand steamship. That is, if you can call her violent tossing and whirling "dancing." My stomach lurches as Nik comes within inches of tipping over the rail after she forces an overenthusiastic spin. I wish she'd just give it up.

Malvina, formally Komtesse Malvina Christensen, is a perpetual royal suitor. She and her father have been vying for King Asger's attention for years, hoping he will make the match. Yet despite Nik's good-natured patience for her dancing, I have my doubts there will be a royal wedding in their future.

I want to look away from the pink silk blur of Malvina, but Nik's eyes are begging me to rescue him. Pleading. Silently calling my name across the distance—*Evvvvv-vieee*.

I am the only one who can save him. Every youth in town is here, but no one else can cut in on a girl like Malvina. For the others, there would be consequences—lost invitations to galas, the oldest horse on the weekend hunt, a seat at the table next to one's senile great-tante instead of the Komtesse. For me, there are none of those things. You can't fall far in society if you're not part of it to begin with.

After another aggressive turn, I finally stride onto the makeshift dance floor, ignoring a chorus of smirks as I go—they've seen this play before. Malvina will be the victim, I'll be the villain, and Nik will let it happen. It can be a messy business, being the crown prince's confidante; enduring small humiliations is only a fraction of the cost. But I won't apologize for helping him. We all make compromises in friendships, and having Nik's loyalty when no one else will even look me in the eye is worth every criticism I face.

I tap the girl on one sturdy shoulder, screw my face into exaggerated panic, and point to the eight-layered, blue-sugar-spackled monstrosity she insisted on crafting.

"Oh, angels, Evie! What is it?" Malvina barks.

"The cake's icing—"

"*Fondant*," she corrects, as if I've spit on her oma's grave.

"The *fondant*—it's bulging."

True panic colors her features as her feet refuse to move. Torn between dancing with Nik and rescuing her masterpiece from a bulbous fate, her eyes skip to my face for a moment, incredulous. She fears I've purposely stolen her turn. It's just the sort of thing the girls of Havnestad think I would do—the ones whispering in the shadows about us now. Except in this case, they're right.

"Do your duty, Malvina. It was lovely dancing with you." Nik bends into a slight bow, royal manners on display, not a hint of displeasure in his features.

When his eyes cut away, Malvina sneaks a glare my way, her disdain for me as clear as her worry that I'm actually telling the truth. She doesn't need to say what she's thinking, and she won't—not if she ever wants to dance with Nik again. So, when Nik completes his bow, she simply plasters on a trained smile and leaves him with the most perfect curtsy before running off in a rush of golden hair and intent.

Now Nik bows deeply to me as if I'm his newest suitor, his mop of black hair briefly obscuring his coal-dark eyes. "May I have the remainder of this dance, my lady?"

My lips curl into a smile as my legs automatically dip into a polite curtsy. *My lady.* Despite how good those words feel, they're enough to earn me the ire of everyone on this boat. To them I am just the royal fisherman's daughter abusing the prince's kindness, using him for his station. They won't believe we're just friends, as we've always been, since we were in diapers. Before I knew what I was and he knew who he was meant to be.

"But of course, Crown Prince Niklas," I reply.

He meets my eyes, and we both burst out laughing. Formality has never worn well between us—regardless of Nik's training.

We settle in and begin to waltz across the deck. He has a good foot on me, but he's practiced at leaning in—whispers are often our most convenient language.

"Took you long enough," he says, twirling me through the last bars of the song.

"I wanted to see how long you'd stay dry."

He gasps with false horror in my ear, a smile tingeing it. "You'd send your own best friend swimming with the mermaids on his birthday?"

"I hear they're beautiful—not a bad present for a teenage boy."

"They also prefer their presents not breathing."

My eyes shoot to his. I can feel the slightest tremble in my jaw. Today would've been our friend Anna's birthday too. It still is, though she is no longer here to celebrate it. She was exactly a year younger than Nik. We'd each had our share of close calls in those days, the great and powerful goddess Urda seeming to want us all for herself. But we lost Anna. I glance down, feeling tears hot against my lash line, even after four years' time. Nik sighs and tugs a curl off my face. He waits until I finally glance up. There's a soft smile riding his lips, and I know he regrets pulling us from a place of joy to one so fraught. "Well, thank you for saving me, Evie. As always."

It's as good a subject change as any, but it's not enough—and we both know it. I take a deep breath and look over Nik's shoulder, not trusting myself to say more.

I swallow and try to concentrate on the party. Everything here has been borrowed for Nik's celebration—the ship, the free-flowing hvidtøl, the band, two servants, and a coal man—and it's beautiful. I focus on the miniature lanterns ringing the deck, the golden thread of my single fancy dress catching their glow.

Suddenly, Malvina hoists herself onto the dessert table, still frantically trying to control the cake's growing bulge. I expect Nik to laugh, or at least knock out a very royal snort, but instead he's looking over my shoulder, portside, at the sea. I follow his eyes, and my heart sputters to a stop when I make out a swift schooner, the familiar line of a boy—a man—adjusting the sail.

"Iker . . ." His name falls from my lips in a sigh before I can catch it. I meet Nik's eyes, a blush crawling up my cheeks. "I didn't know he was coming."

"Neither did I." He shrugs and raises a brow. "But Iker's not exactly one to confirm an invitation. Missed that day at prince school. The lecture about being on time, too."

"I believe it's called 'fashionably late,'" I say.

"Yes, well, I suppose I wouldn't know," Nik says with a laugh.

The little schooner closes in, and I see that it's only Iker—he hasn't brought a crew with him from Rigeby Bay, not that I'd expect him to. He's a weather-worn fisherman trapped in a life designed for silk and caviar. He redirects the mainsail perfectly, his muscles tensing tightly as he aims straight for his cousin's form.

Nik leans to my ear. "There goes my dancing partner."

I punch him on the arm. "You don't know that."

"True, but I do know how you've looked at him since my cake had about ten fewer candles on it."

I roll my eyes, but I can't help a smile creeping up my lips. He's somewhat right, though now isn't the best time to argue that the way I looked at Iker changed from brotherly to something else entirely about four years ago, not ten.

I clear my throat. "I'm sure Malvina won't mind—she's almost finished with your cake," I say, nodding in the direction of the blue monstrosity but never taking my eyes off Iker as he readies to throw up a line to the steamer.

Nik hugs me close and dips down to my ear. "You're such a ravishingly loyal friend."

"Always have been. Always will be."

"'Tis true." Nik grins before waving a long arm above his head. "Well, if it isn't the crown prince of Rigeby Bay!"

"And here I hoped to surprise you," Iker says, laughing. "Can't surprise a lighthouse of a man on his own boat, I suppose."

Nik laughs, standing even taller. "Not if I'm turned the right way."

Iker laughs even deeper. There is salt in his hair and few days' worth of scruff lining his strong jawline, but he strides across his deck with the elegance of a prince. He

—7

glances up at me, his eyes briefly betraying a hint of doubt about the sturdiness of my frame, but tosses the line to me anyway. I catch it, securing it with a knot I learned from Father.

Iker hauls himself up the rope and onto the ship. He manages to land on the small patch of deck just between Nik and myself. Behind us a crowd has gathered.

"Happy birthday, Cousin." Eyes laughing, Iker claps Nik on the back and brings him in for a hug, his toned arms fully encasing Nik's spindly-yet-strong form.

When they release, Iker's eyes go right to me. They're the clearest of blues—like ancient ice in the fjords of the north.

"Evelyn," he says, still retaining an air of formality from his upbringing, but he then shockingly pulls me into a hug.

I freeze, eyes on Nik as he and everyone else on the ship stares. Iker doesn't seem to notice or care and pulls me tighter, his arms wrapped around my waist. Warm from ship work, he smells of salt and limes. His shirt is freckled with water droplets, onyx on the starched gray fabric—the sea leaving her mark.

When the moment is over and he lets me go, an arm lingers across my shoulders. I try to ignore the question nagging me, the one I'm sure everyone else is asking too. *Why me?* We've known each other since we were children, but he's never shown me this kind of affection before. I'm not his type. I'm not *anyone's* type. Yet Iker continues to act as if it's all completely normal. He turns to Nik, to the crowd, and grins that perfect smile.

"Good people of Havnestad," he says, his voice commanding yet sincere. Then the grin grows wider. "Let's give the prince a celebration so hearty, he'll never forget it."

I FEEL AS IF I'M LIVING IN A DREAM.

Still warm from Iker's strong embrace, I twirl across the dance floor in his arms.

I tried to tell Iker we shouldn't, but he wouldn't hear of it. "Let them talk," Iker said. If only he knew how much they already did.

I can sense Malvina's eyes following me. *Yes, Malvina, this is what it looks like when someone dances without fearing for his life.* But I try not to think about her. I want to remember this moment, even the smallest details. Everything about him wears like oiled leather and loved muslin. His hands are rough and worn from the sea, and yet they are gentle, his thumb delicately caressing mine.

My twelve-year-old fantasies were never this detailed—hardly anything beyond me in a grand purple gown and Iker in his royal finery hand-in-hand on a stroll through the palace gardens. The reality is so different, so intense, and I'm not sure I'm handling it well. I know I'm not. Can he feel my palms sweating? My heart beating loudly against his chest?

"I saw you from my deck, you know," he whispers in my ear. "Before coming aboard. You've never looked more beautiful, Evie. And I've never begged the gods to steer my ship faster."

I don't know what to say, my voice seizing in my throat. I look around instead, trying to organize my thoughts. The sun has completely set, the last strands of light gone with our plates in a rush and clatter of tiny quail bones, torsk tails, pea pods, and strawberry hulls. And though the entire ship deck is still lit by a ring of miniature lanterns, the remaining shadow is enough that it almost feels as if we're alone.

Just a boy, a girl, and the sea.

The song ends and he hugs me tight. When he pulls back, he runs his fingers along my jawbone. "I shouldn't have stayed away from Havnestad so long," he says, capturing one of my curls between his fingers. "You have the same hair you did as a child." His gaze lifts to mine. "The same starry-night eyes."

I struggle not to look down—down to where he's still wound a lock of my hair lightly between his fingers. I bite my lip to silence the sigh there. His fingers wind tighter around the curl. It almost seems as if he doesn't know

—11

he's doing it—this boy made of smiles and grand gestures doing something so small it's escaped him.

Iker's eyes drift to the band members who have circled around a bench where someone has begun to play a guitaren. Though we can't see him, the shiny, precise plucks are a dead giveaway that the musician is Nik. He's always been the kind to pick up any instrument and immediately know exactly how to play it, ever since we were children. He's strumming the song I used to sing on the docks as a girl to wish my father safe travels on his fishing trips. Nik said it always got stuck in his head.

Iker drops the curl.

Clears his throat.

Adjusts his body so that we're not touching in so many places.

It's over. I know it. Perhaps fantasies are only meant to come true for a moment. Surely a trick of the gods.

His eyes linger on the band when he eventually speaks, but his tone has changed. "Evie, I love visiting Havnestad, but I don't like to step on my cousin's toes."

Now my voice isn't right. *Why did Nik have to play* that *song?* I swallow. "But you aren't," I say, hoping he can't hear the pleading in my tone. "Besides, I don't think Nik would mind seeing more of you, and there *is* the Lithasblot festival coming up in a few days."

"Ah, yes, when you people go nuts for Urda, throw

bread at anyone without a double chin, and run in circles until you pass out."

"*You* people?" I say and give him a jab. Iker may be from across the strait, but he's just as much an Øldenburg as Nik. Their family has ruled Denmark and Sweden for four hundred years. They know better than anyone not to discount the harvest the goddess has bestowed on us. "Don't poke fun at the games. We take them very seriously."

"Oh yes, a life-or-death game of carrying around the heaviest rock."

"Or running the length of a log. All useful skills." I laugh, happy to have lightened the mood again.

Iker turns to me. "If I stay for this Lithasblot extravaganza, you must promise you will scramble across some recently murdered tree for my entertainment."

"If that's what it takes, then I promise," I say, dipping in a mock curtsy.

A laugh escapes from my lips, but Iker's attention is locked on my face. Almost as if he can't help himself, his thumb grazes my cheekbone again, down my jaw and to my mouth. The touch of his finger to my lips sends color rising in my cheeks as I meet the glacier blue of his eyes.

"Iker, I—"

"Goooooood people of Havnestad!" Our heads whip around as Nik's voice booms across the length of the ship. He is still holding the guitaren, but now he has a crown

—13

fashioned of lemon wedges squashed on his wavy flop of hair. There's a huge smile tugging at his cheeks, and his long arms are thrust high into the air. He's actually doing quite the unintentional impression of Iker, though only after a few mugs of King Asger's special brew. "As your crown prince, I hereby issue a royal decree that we sing *for me* on this, the sixteenth year of my life."

"Hear, HEAR," yells Iker, followed by the rest of the crowd, which has suddenly crept back into the corners of my vision.

"Excellent. Ruyven has sent the signal for fireworks. But first, a so—" Nik's voice cuts out as Malvina's strong hand jerks him down so her lips can meet his ear. The other hand is gesturing behind them, toward the cake. Nik stands back up slowly and resets the guitaren. "The lovely lady Malvina has informed me we are at a loss for candles." Nik points the instrument's neck at me, feigned formality still thick in his throat. "Evelyn?" He raises a brow.

I raise one back.

"Come on, I know you know where they are."

And I do. Exactly where Nik left them when he "borrowed" the king's boat for the first warm day after a long, ice-filled winter.

"Yes, I do, good prince."

As much as I don't want to leave Iker's side, I step away, the warmth of him clinging to my skin for a ghost of a second as we separate. I snag a lantern that's dipped low on the line ringing the deck and move away from the crowd.

Boots clomping on the stairs, I disappear belowdecks to the captain's quarters. The space is much larger than something that should be a captain's anything—the whole place is nearly bigger than the home I share with Father and Tante Hansa. The miniature lantern struggles to keep up with the vastness, illuminating a halo barely beyond the hem of my party dress. It's utterly annoying.

Glancing up the stairs, I confirm that I am alone; no one followed me below. My back to the door, I reach a hand into the lantern. Softly muttered words of old fall from my lips as my fingers pinch the tip of the candle. *"Brenna bjartr aldrnari. Brenna bjartr aldrari. Pakka Glöð."*

The candle begins to glow with the full force of one three times its size.

It's a small act—something so subtle I probably could've done it in full view of everyone above. But even something as run-of-the-mill as a strengthening spell is dangerous here.

Women burned for far less under the Øldenburgs of yesteryear.

My relatives burned for far less.

Which means there are things about me Nik and Iker can never know.

Besides, I already took a risk tonight when I silently urged Malvina's cake to shed its sugary skin. I hadn't tried something like that since I was a child, but it worked well enough. Strengthening the candle in the open would have been pushing my luck, though, and I've never had much of that to begin with.

Now the cushion of light is more than enough. I ease my way through the vast space and toward the pair of chairs under one of the starboard portholes, a chessboard painted into the oak table between them.

I'd watched Nik stuff the ship's allotment of extra candles into the table's drawer while helping him clean up evidence of his warm-weather get-together. Not that his father wouldn't know about our little celebration—dishonesty has never sat well in Nik's royal mind—he just hadn't wanted to leave the castle's harbor crew with more work.

With rescued candles and matches in hand, I grab the lantern and spin toward the door. But suddenly in my peripheral vision, I catch two flashes of shocking white and blue. I spin back around to where a small halo of light beacons through the porthole.

My heart sputters to a dead halt as I realize I don't know of any fish with markings like those.

Like human eyes.

Lungs aching for me to remember how to breathe, I raise the lantern to the porthole, my mind churning to account for everyone onboard the ship. Yes, everyone had been there when I descended the stairs.

Yet, when the halo of light reaches the thick glass, a friend's eyes are there, deep blue and framed by luminous skin, water-darkened blond waves, and a look of surprise on parted lips.

"Anna?"

But in the instant I say her name into the damp cabin, the face vanishes, and I'm left staring into the indigo deep.

My lungs release and draw in a huge gulp of air as I race to the next porthole, my breath coming in rapid spurts as I repeat her name. But there's no sign of her beautiful face at that porthole or the next two.

I stand in the middle of the king's great cabin, heart pounding, breath burning in my lungs, as a heavy sob escapes my lips. Tears sting my eyes as I realize that even with Nik's brotherly friendship and Iker's new affection, I'm still just a lonely fisherman's daughter.

A lonely fisherman's daughter wishing that I could have my sweet friend back. Wishing hard enough that I'm seeing ghosts.

Wishing so very hard that I'm losing my mind.

3

I WIPE MY EYES WITH MY WRIST, THE CANDLES AND matches still clutched in my fingers. A couple of deep breaths, and I will myself through the door and up the stairs, my legs leaden.

"The good lady has returned with the candles!" Nik shouts when he sees me, his voice half-singing in tune with the guitaren.

"And the matches, my prince," I hear myself say in a much steadier voice than I'd have thought possible.

"My dear Evie, always rescuing her prince from his own lack of forethought."

"Someone has to, Cousin," laughs Iker, rising to his feet while Malvina snatches the goods from my arms. Immediately, she bustles behind Nik, spearing the beautiful layers of fondant with the fat ends of the tapers. No thank-you from her, even though for anyone else, her trained manners would require it.

Nik begins the song before they're all lit. His voice soars above us all, even over Iker's baritone. As usual, I just mouth along to the words—my singing voice was ruined the day I lost Anna. Tante Hansa says I'm lucky that is all the sea took. Nik has his eyes shut and isn't even facing his cake, the flames flickering and twisting behind him, manipulated by a strong wind from deep within the Øresund Strait.

My gaze follows the wind into the dark distance. Just past the edge of our wake, the indigo skies go pitch-black, the furrowed edges of an angry line of clouds moving in at a furious pace.

"Iker," I breathe.

". . . *Hun skal leve højt hurra . . .*" Nik hits the final line of the traditional birthday song and turns to blow out the candles, opening his eyes just as the first of the fireworks shoots off from the beach. Bursts of white and red stream across the sky in quick succession, illuminating Havnestad below and the ring of mountains surrounding the city proper.

"Iker," I repeat, my eyes still upon the clouds closing in. He turns, hand still set heavily about my waist, and I point to the storm line as a tendril of lightning strikes the water just beyond the confines of the harbor.

A flash of recognition hits his eyes as they read the distance between the rain and the ship. "Storm!" he yells, a clap of thunder cutting off the end of the word. "Everyone belowdecks! Now!"

But, of course, our party turns toward the storm rather than away, human curiosity flying in the face of safety. Iker, Nik, and I rush into motion as the first fat drops of rain splatter onto the deck.

Nik begins directing the crowd belowdecks. Iker is up at the wheel, working to right the ship toward the harbor after sending its previous driver—the coal man—down below to feed the steam engine.

With the rain already sheeting, the boat tips as I climb the stairs to the stern. I cling to the rail. There is no magic I can do in the open to stop this, which makes me grateful to be the salt of the sea and the daughter of a fisherman. I'm not helpless in the least.

Thunder rumbles deep and rich directly overhead. The cake's candles and the lanterns ringing the ship have been blown out by the blustery wind, and I'm thankful when a flash of lightning cracks across the sky just long enough to show me the scene.

Iker—getting the boat going in the right direction, his feet planted and muscles straining.

Nik—trudging up the stairs after barring the door down below, his crown of lemons fed to the sea by the flying wind.

The cake—tipped over and beached on its massive side as the boat lurches starboard.

Another clap of thunder sounds as I reach Iker and help him hold the wheel. Iker is strong enough to steer it by himself, but the boat's line noticeably straightens when I help him maintain control.

"A birthday pleasure cruise!" Iker yells across the booming skies as I smile at him through clenched teeth. His eyes dance even as every tendon in his neck strains to keep our course. "All clear skies and fancy drinks. Isn't that what Nik promised?"

Muscles already screaming, we both focus on the lighthouse at the edge of the harbor, still minutes away. A heavy wave crashes along the deck, taking the remainder of the cake with it. Nik manages to hold tight to the stair railing, his white dress shirt plastered against his skin.

"We're too slow," Iker yells into my ear between peals of thunder.

I nod and grit my teeth further as a gust of wind pulls the ship portside, yanking the wheel with it. "I've got it," I say. "But we won't go any faster unless—" I nod toward his prized craft, a present from his father.

Iker nods, heeding my suggestion. "Nik!" he yells over the whipping wind and angry waves. "My schooner! Help me cut it loose!"

Somehow Nik hears him and immediately pulls himself portside, where Iker's little boat is adding too much weight.

Another wave tips up the ship, sending us starboard. Boots sliding, I manage to keep us steady, pinning the wheel in place with all my weight. On the main deck, Nik has made his way over to the portside rail. He hooks one long arm around the rail to steady himself, and then works furiously with his free hand on my knot. Iker is on his way there.

The boat lurches again, and I close my eyes, willing land to get closer. When my eyes open, we might be closer to Havnestad's docks, but only by a few feet. I twist my head to the side and see that Nik nearly has the knot free.

A whitecap splashes over the side, drenching Nik. He shakes his head, wavy hair splaying out to the side. He rights himself, the slick railing and new floorboards doing him no favors in traction or leverage. With one final pull, the rope is completely loose, and slides over the side of the ship. Nik, much stronger than he looks, hangs on as the steamer's equilibrium changes with the loss of Iker's schooner.

"Three hundred yards to the royal dock!" Iker yells, making his way to the wheel. I look from Nik back to land. The lighthouse is indeed finally closing in, the blaze atop the tower looming just below the steely thatch of clouds.

But not as fast as the biggest wave we've seen yet.

Black as the sky above, the wall of water splashes hard on the portside, sending Nik to his knees. I call out for him to stay down—a lower center of gravity is safer—but my small voice is swallowed up in the storm.

He stands.

A charge of lightning rips across the sky.

The ship tips, pulled down with the weight of the wave, rocking Nik headfirst into the deep.

4

"NIK!"

I scream his name as loudly as I can. The boat rights itself, but there's no sign of him along the portside. Only wet wood and sea foam where he once was.

"NIK!" I wail again and let go of the wheel, passing Iker and sprinting toward the stairs to the main deck.

My mind moves faster than my wind-battered body, a string of thoughts running together in the murk as I dash forward, not caring or paying attention to the wind, the rain, the course, or even Iker.

No.

You CANNOT have him, you wicked sea.

Your mermaids will have to take someone else.

Nik belongs to me.

"Evie!" Iker yells. "Don't! Come back! It's not—"

"NIK!" I lunge down the stairs. The deck boards are

slick under my boots, but I race to the spot where Nik fell. The wind whips my curls about my face as I squint through the rain and night at the churning sea below. "NIK!"

I yell his name over and over, my voice becoming raw and weak, to the point where it's barely a whisper. Finally, we reach the royal dock. I drop onto the wood before Iker and the coal man even have time to anchor. I scan the horizon for any sign of a long arm, a flop of hair, or a piece of boot.

Iker heaves himself over the railing and onto the dock next to me, leaving the coal man to free the rest of the passengers from the captain's quarters. "Evie," he says, his voice much calmer than it should be—the sea captain in him overruling his bloodline. "Look there." He points to just this side of the horizon, where the stars have returned, unhidden by the clouds. "The storm's almost over. Nik's a strong swimmer."

I nod, my hopes pinned on the reason in his eyes. "But we still need to find him," I say. Everything my father taught me about the sea kicks in, and I point to a spot in the churning waves. "We were about there." I move my outstretched fingers in a sloping line in the direction of the wind, following the line until it lands on the cove side of Havnestad Beach. "Which means he will most likely be . . . there."

I don't look to Iker for confirmation—I just take off

down the dock, tear onto the sand, and race across the shoreline in that direction.

"Nik!" I choke, my voice still raspy and hopeless against the wind. Iker is on my heels for a few strides and then ahead of me in a few more.

Havnestad Cove is part jutting rock, part silty beach. There's a rolling W shape to it, and a few large boulders form footstep islands toward its center, before the waters become too deep. In good weather, it's a beautiful escape from the rest of the harbor. In bad weather, it's a hurricane in a birdbath.

Iker points to the biggest island—Picnic Rock. "I'm going there to see what I can."

The wind is already calming, the rain tapering off. Even the lightning seems to be behind us, disappearing with the storm into the mountains. The swiftness of such a powerful storm confounds me. The magic in my blood prickles at the strangeness, but I have no time to think of things beyond this world.

I tilt my chin toward a mass of rocks farther along the shore, the point that makes the W by jutting deep into the middle of the cove. It's just tall enough that it blinds us from the remainder of the beach.

"I'll climb up there and take a look on the other side."

"Wait!" Iker says, his face weary. For once, he doesn't seem to know what to say. He reaches his hand through my hair and pulls me close. My heart is pounding.

"Iker, we ca—" The words are whispers on my tongue—that we can't delay, that he shouldn't slow me down—when he tips my chin up and his lips are on mine.

I breathe him in, long and deep, and for a moment we're not on a gritty beach, soaked to the bone, searching for Nik. We're somewhere far from here. A place where class, title—none of that matters. Somewhere that surely doesn't exist outside of this instant. Another trick of the gods.

He pulls back, and I'm stunned still, staring into his cool eyes.

"Be careful," he says.

Shaken back to reality, I pick up my waterlogged skirts and run along the coastline to the wall of stone. The swift clouds have almost reached their end, their tail nearly directly above the cove entrance. Starry night reigns above the massive sea beyond, calm waters with it. My eyes are constantly scanning the waves, looking for any sign of Nik.

But there's nothing.

I steal a glance back at Iker. He's already made it to Picnic Rock, hoisting himself up. I breathe a sigh of relief that the stormy churn didn't wash him away and turn back to the approaching boulder just steps ahead.

I've climbed this giant rock hundreds of times since childhood, as have most of Havnestad's youth. I know the placement of the fingerholds with my eyes shut; my boots automatically drift to the perfect places to wedge themselves before taking another step up. The rain has all but stopped now, and the crag of stone is mostly damp, not slick.

I lug myself on top and scan the waters again, squinting at every irregularity, struggling to use the limited moonlight to make out what is yet another coastal rock and what might be Nik. I close my eyes, dread piling at my feet as I pivot toward the hidden portion of the cove. When my eyes spring open, I have to blink again to make sure my mind isn't playing tricks. A flash of bright-white fabric swims on the distant sandy line.

My heart swells with hope. I scramble down the rock and onto the other side of the beach. My feet work overtime to propel my body forward as the wet sand swallows my boots with each step.

Lightning radiates over the mountains, illuminating the sky for a flash—long enough for my brain to register the outline of Nik's body against the sand.

And the form of a girl hovering over him.

"NIK!" I yell, my voice coming back to me.

In response comes Iker's baritone from behind, "Evie!"

But I don't wait for him. I don't even turn in Iker's direction, keeping my eyes only on Nik and the girl leaning over him, her body still mostly submerged. Without another stroke of lightning, I can't make out much more than her long, long hair—so long it drapes over the white of Nik's shirt.

The girl's head tilts up in the moonlight as if she's just now noticed me running toward her at full speed. The lightning returns in a burst, and though my legs keep moving, my heart skids to a stop.

Large blue eyes. Butter-blond curls. Creamy flush of skin.

It's the girl. The one from the porthole.

Anna?

No, it can't be.

Recognition seems to fill the girl's eyes, and her features skip from contented calm to a pure rush of panic. Panic that sends her straight into motion. A gust of wind pushes her hair over the curve of her shoulder as she takes one hasty and last glance at Nik's face before heaving herself fully into the water.

"Wait!" I yell as best I can, but it's useless with her ears deep under the waves.

In less than a breath, I get to Nik and crash to the sand next to him, pulling his chest to mine, my ear to his mouth. A rush of air from his lips touches my cheek as Iker yells both our names from behind.

Nik's lungs work in great rasps, but they work. His eyes are closed, but he seems to be conscious.

"Evie . . ."

"I'm here, Nik. I'm here."

A ghost of a smile touches his lips. "Evie . . . keep singing, Evie."

Confused, I begin correcting him. "Nik, I'm not—I don't . . ."

My mouth goes dry. I scan the waters for any sign of the girl. The girl who looks like Anna all grown up. The girl who must like to sing the way my friend did as a child.

At first, there's still nothing. Just ever-calming waves and starry night, backlit by the summer solstice moon.

But then, just at the edge of the cove, I see it.

Blond hair gone silver under the clear moon, peeking up for a swift moment before the girl dives back underwater. A trail of sea spray flies up in her wake—and with it comes something more.

The perfect outline of a tail fin.

FOUR YEARS BEFORE

The sun was out, as fierce and as hot as possible in Havnestad. It wasn't as fierce or hot as it is in other places, but memorable to those in the mild-mannered Øresund Kingdoms, much more accustomed to Mother Nature's cold shoulder than her steamy smile, though it was the height of summer.

Two girls, one with waves of blond, one with curls of black, pranced along the shoreline. Their voices lifted toward the naked June sun, carried aloft by a deep wind from within the strait.

A boy, already as tall as a man, trailed them, piccolo to his lips, writing a tune for the girls' merry lyrics.

Despite the sun, the main beach was clear, the majority of Havnestad hauling fish and hunting whales at sea, the bustle of a modern economy weathering a boom. They would flood the shores with catch and tales soon enough, returning that night for the days-long Lithasblot festival and the midsummer full moon. For now, the whole stretch of sand belonged to the two girls and their boy.

The waves, heavy and exuberant, churned in the strong wind, tossing themselves at the girls' ankles—bare without anyone there to correct them. The boy's boots were on—his feet were gangly and hairy in a way they hadn't been last summer, and he didn't want the girls to see. He stayed on dry sand, just beyond the waves' reach, coal-dark eyes pinned on the girls' delicate toes, which also seemed to have changed in a year, but only maybe in the way he couldn't look away from the flash of skin beneath their skirts.

They went on like that until the girls suddenly stopped—singing, prancing, everything—so suddenly that the boy bumped into the raven-curled girl's back. She laughed it off, but both girls' eyes were locked on the sea. Watching the whitecaps with wonder, adventure flashing in their eyes.

The one with the blond waves and ocean-blue eyes spoke first. "She's angry—foaming at the mouth."

"Are you calling the sea a rabid dog?" asked the raven-haired one. "She wouldn't like that much."

"I suppose not."

A black brow pitched above eyes blue like midnight. "Touch the sandbar and return to shore?" She smiled, lips pinned in a slight twist. "Dare you."

The blond girl considered it, chewing on her lip, reading the waves. Finally, in answer, she began unlacing her dress's bodice.

The boy sat on the sand behind the girls, playing the piccolo so they'd think he was distracted, not paying an inch of attention to them as they stripped to their petticoats. Even in surreptitious glances, their shoulders and arms were things of beauty, smooth as the marble statues his mother had commissioned for the tulip garden. So beautiful they made his cheeks hot. He knew he should not look—it wasn't right, not at the age they were getting to be—but still, he watched.

The blond girl watched back, her eyes finding him, cheeks pinking as her clothes fell to the sand. The raven-curled girl thwacked her on the shoulder, dark eyes big and knowing. No secrets between friends, except those in plain sight.

When the girls were ready, they stood, dresses neatly folded, and pointed slim fingers toward the sea.

On the count of three, they were gone.

5

I DON'T BELIEVE IN MERMAIDS. I DON'T. THEY ARE JUST an abomination ancients like Tante Hansa dream up to keep children from doing especially dim-witted things. *If you touch that hot pot . . . if you eat that whole cake . . . if you take that candy . . . the mermaids will steal you away.* We're superstitious, children of the sea, but we're not gullible.

Mermaids don't exist.

But I know what I saw. I know *who* I saw.

Nik, for his part, doesn't seem to remember much. He thinks I rescued him. He thinks I sang to him.

It's been more than a day, and I still haven't told him that he's lost his mind if he thinks that's what happened. Mostly because I don't have an answer to what really did. None of it makes any sense.

No, I don't believe in mermaids.

But I do have a strong belief in friendship—more than anything in this world.

I believed it with Anna.

And I believe it with Nik.

Iker—I don't know what to think of Iker, though he's standing right before me on the royal dock, borrowed crew packing a borrowed ship behind him.

"Come—the sea calls." Iker brushes away a few of my curls and cups his hand about my ear as if to amplify the sea's ancient voice. He leans down, his cheek brushing right against mine, his lips warm next to my skin as he whispers, "Evelynnnnn."

His enthusiasm makes my heart skip, and I wish I could go, but Father is leaving this morning as well, and he hates the idea of me being aboard a different ship while he is at sea too. He's superstitious to a fault, even if it's just for a quick trip up the Jutland and back before Sankt Hans Aften and the opening of the Lithasblot festival. Iker is enchanted by sightings of a large whale—one that would feed Rigeby Bay for weeks in both meals and trade. I hate it, but I know Iker must go—the seafaring season waits for no one, not even a prince.

"I'm so very sorry to disappoint," I say. And I am. This time with him has been strangely magical, even if all we've done is sit with Nik, telling stories to make him smile as he recovers.

"Too late, the sea is already disappointed—your skills during the storm were top-notch. You're a sailor she needs upon her waves." His eyes flash, the curve of his mouth serious. Vulnerable, even, as strange as that is. But I don't—I can't—let myself think that it's he who needs me and not the sea. Reality doesn't work that way.

"The sea will have to wait."

"And so will I." He bends down to kiss me then, and though it's the second time, it's still a shock—a deep dive into ice-capped waters.

"You don't have to go," I say when we part, my voice small and slurred.

"What's that?" he says, pretending not to have heard. "You don't have to stay?"

He grabs my hand in both of his and begins to tug me toward the ship, full of crew waiting for his instruction. "Splendid, let's get going—you steer; I'll sip portvin and keep an eye out for the whale."

I laugh and let him tug me a little farther up the gang-plank than I should. In my heart, I don't believe in Father's superstitions. And yet I have superstitions of my own. Nik is still recovering. I can't leave. What if he took a turn for the worse while I was gone?

No, I must stay.

Iker will come back. He says he will.

I know he will.

Something changed that night on the steamer. More

during the storm than in the huddled moments before—we'd seen each other in our element. The salt of the sea, the both of us. And despite choosing to stay, it is the very last thing I want Nik to know about. Most especially the kissing. But it shouldn't be too hard to keep a secret from my best friend—after all, I've been keeping my magic from Nik his whole life.

I step down from the gangplank and onto the dock. With a wave and a shout to his crew, Iker is off, taking our secret leagues away as I tuck it deep within me. I watch as he leaves the harbor, standing there just long enough to glimpse him turning back, my hand ready to wave. And then I set out for one more good-bye and my daily duties, Tante Hansa's amethyst heavy in my pocket.

No, I don't believe in mermaids. But I am willing to believe in whatever it is that happens when I kiss the amethyst to the bow of my father's ship before an expedition. What happens when I cast the spell I created using centuries-old magical wisdom.

It's only been a few weeks, but already it has worked, bringing in far more catch than by this time last year. I smile when I see the fishermen celebrating on the docks now. After four years of suffering through the Tørhed, a barrenness so severe the town's fishing fleet decreased by half, these hearty cheers are welcome sounds. I haven't heard them since before Anna's death; the grumbles from tired fishermen coming ashore to restock on salted meat and limes have filled our ears instead.

After three years of the Tørhed, King Asger knew that praying to the gods was no longer enough. Havnestad had to find a new way to stay afloat. The royal steamship was ordered, and any man not at sea was put to work building the boat from late summer to first frost, shaping wood, and fitting sheets of metal to the smokestack.

But even that ship, hammered together by the strength of this fine town, was not enough to keep all of Havnestad's bellies fed. The steamer was a one-time measure. Even the crown can't afford a new ship every year.

I had to do something.

So, as I've done since the summer of Anna's death, I stole into Tante Hansa's room while she was off playing her weekly turn of whist down at Fru Agnata's shack. Hansa's bedroom is a stifling place, with the fire lit every night, even in the summer. Dried roses line the walls in a ring as high as she can reach—the hundreds of them a testament to her belief that their scent and beauty are superior to the tulips so popular throughout the Øresund Kingdoms.

Beneath the line of roses, in a corner opposite the flue, there's a sea chest draped in shadow and an ancient moose hide. Inside is everything the Øldenburgs fear, all they have banished by law: gemstones, age-stained books, cobalt bottles sealed with pinches of cork and wax. The very same items Tante Hansa used on me when I resurfaced in Nik's arms four years ago, Anna nowhere to be found. When I'd been in bed, nearly dead myself, watched over by Hansa and spoon-fed elixirs tasting of perfume and age. And aged they certainly are, passed down in shadow generations for centuries. Someday they will belong to me, I suppose.

That day I took a purple stone—one so small that I hoped it would escape Hansa's notice, but big enough to have an impact. I snagged one of the tattered books with crumbling spines, too, fishing it out from where it was packed under a cake of beeswax and a marble mortar and pestle.

Hours after lights out, I crept down to the beach, but well beyond Havnestad Cove. As the shoreline thins, becoming one with the rocky mountain, sharp boulders jut out from the sea. The water is deeper there and the waves choppy, but in between the shadow of two large rocks is a swath of sand. Overhead, stone from the edge of Havnestad has formed into a perfect arch, the result of Urda coaxing the sea into this crevice for thousands of years.

This place doesn't have a name, as far as I know. I've never seen anyone come here, and it's hidden from view on the beach and by the boulders from the sea. I've taken to calling it Greta's Lagoon, after my mother. She would have liked a place like this. Deep in the shadows of the lagoon is a small cave barely large enough to fit two, but it's plenty big to store the few tinctures and inks Tante Hansa has entrusted to me.

I moved away the few small boulders I use to hide the entrance and lit a candle. With the amethyst stone cradled in one hand, I slid the book under the meager light. The words were ancient and yet familiar, recalling our great goddess, Urda, and the power she bestows on the land and sea. As the waves splashed against the rocks outside, I read the scrawl over and over, swirling the spells across my tongue. It took until nearly daylight, but finally I could feel the magic tingle in my blood.

After nearly three months of practice, I spelled Father's boat for the first time.

Three days after that, he came home with his first whale in more than two years. It was thin, but fat enough for all the joy that came with it.

Now the spell is a must.

The need to keep Father safe and prosperous is thick in my veins each morning when I wake, jamming my heart with anxiety until I can do my job. My part.

Even when I've done my duty and he's away for days, I come to the harbor and spell any ship docked and still. The fishermen are used to seeing me daily now. They don't seem to find it strange that I'm always there, letting my closed palm trail along the salt-worn bodies of ships, old and trusty.

And today is the day I begin to do more. Along with what I *cannot* claim, I have been working away on something I *can*. Something all of Havnestad will recognize as helpful and not some fate of Urda.

"Evie, my girl!" Father is hauling a crate up to the deck of his whaler—*Little Greta*, also named for my mother. There isn't a single crate of supplies left on the dock beside the ship. I've only just caught him. "I wasn't sure you'd come."

I laugh lightly, fingers tight over the gem in my palm. "Just because I want you to stay doesn't mean I'll miss you going."

Father's mouth settles into a tart line, the sun spots marring his forehead crinkling up to his black hair—he's Italian by birth, though he's Danish through and through.

We walk up the gangplank together. He drops the crate two feet from the innovation I know will make these desolate seas that much easier to fish—a permanent cure my magic cannot provide. Mounted proudly to the mainmast, half-harpoon, half-rifle, my darting gun looks as shiny and perfect as I'd hoped.

Father hugs me close. "My Evelyn, the inventor."

"It was nothing," I say, though we both know that's not true. It took me the whole winter to create one from an old rifle and modified harpoon, but if my calculations are correct, the contraption will send out both a bomb lance and a tether harpoon, narrowing the chances of a whale escaping. If all goes well with Father's maiden voyage, we might be able to transform the way Havnestad snags its whales.

"It's not nothing. It'll be a revolution."

I tilt my face up to his, brow raised. "It'll still be a

—41

revolution if you wait a week."

Father bristles at the sore spot between us. He's not the only fisherman headed out during the festival, though far more are staying than leaving, bolstered by their recent luck—my recent help. But he's the only one I care about. And, as the royal fisherman, he's the only one King Asger cares about as well.

"There will be other Lithasblot festivals, Evelyn. If you've been pelted with bread once, you've been pelted with bread a thousandfold."

"But—"

He cuts me off with rough fingers on the point of my chin.

"But nothing. I have to seize my luck while it's there." Father's grizzled old thumb settles on my bottom lip. "I'll return for the close of the festival—the ball."

Despite my disappointment at yet another good-bye, I form a tight smile after his words. "If you've seen me once in my only nice dress, you've seen me a thousandfold."

He leans in and gives me a quick kiss on the cheek, his beard both soft and rough against my skin.

"Take care of Hansa, my dear."

I hug him to my chest, the cloying scent of pipe tobacco catching in my lungs.

"If only she'd allow such a thing, I would."

He releases me with a single squeeze of my forearm. I turn for the gangplank, one last look at both him and my first stab at whaling innovation. When I'm back on the sun-ruined wood of the dock, Father yells for his men to hoist up the gangplank and anchor.

Before he's gone, and with the sailors distracted by departure duties, I take my chance and press my little stone to the ship, right under my mother's name, painted in block letters across the stern. My eyes flutter to a close, and I whisper my spell into the breeze coming in off the Øresund Strait.

6

IT'S A PERFECT NIGHT FOR BURNING WITCHES.

That's what Sankt Hans Aften is, after all. A celebration in the name of ridding people like me from this earth through flames, drowning, banishment—whatever seemed right at the time.

Today, thankfully, witches are only burned in effigy. It's the traditional opening of Havnestad's version of Lithasblot. Ours is the earliest in the Øresund Strait, but we're also the longest festival, five whole days, drawing people from all around to watch the games, sing songs in celebration of Urda, and taste plates of tvøst og spik: black whale meat, pink blubber, and sunny potatoes. Even through the Tørhed, the people of Havnestad have always been willing to sacrifice their limited food supply to honor the goddess.

As the bonfire grows hot, shooting tendrils of flames high into the salmon-toned sky, the festival is ready to begin. First is King Asger's speech of love and games-manship.

Now Nik's speech of love and gamesmanship.

For on the night of that treacherous storm, Nik, thank-fully, still came of age. And as tradition demands, he must take the reins of the festival—near-drowning is not an excuse.

Thus, since regaining most of his strength, he's been shut away, pacing the halls of the palace with his father's words on his lips. I've heard him run through it twice—before his birthday and after, and both times he was excellent, if not a hair too fast. Still, that's just because this is new to him. I know he'll be amazing.

But Crown Prince Asger Niklas Bryniulf Øldenburg III, first in line to the throne of the sovereign kingdom of Havnestad, does not share my assessment.

Nik is nearly white with nerves. His long fingers shake as he tugs his hair flat. This day is already hard for the both of us—the fourth anniversary of Anna's drowning—and with the pressure of the speech added atop that, Nik looks as if he might keel over.

I don't hesitate to snag a hand and press my fingers around his. Somehow, seeing him so nervous calms my own reservations—about my innovation's trial run with Father, about the fact Iker has yet to arrive. I squeeze Nik's fingers. "You've done nothing but practice for the past week. You'll be just fine."

"But I'm not cut out for this, Evie."

"Of course you are! You're cut from the Øldenburg cloth. Kings for a thousand years." I lean in, my face consuming his vision. "This speech is in your blood."

Nik turns red and averts his gaze. "I think that particular blood spilled out of me when I bashed my leg on that rock at ten."

I nearly laugh, thinking of Nik passing out at the sight of his own blood. Right in the middle of a trail leading up Lille Bjerg Pass. Anna and I stripped off our stockings and tied them tightly above the gash across his shin before bracing him between us and hobbling down the mountain.

"Think of your birthday. You didn't seem at all nervous while you sang on a bench with lemons in your hair."

"That wasn't the whole kingdom. This is."

"So? What's a few more faces?"

He lets out a very royal snort. "Since when does a 'few' mean a hundred times more? And maybe my disastrous birthday is not the best image to calm my nerves."

"Oh, don't be dramatic."

Nik cocks a brow. "Oh, but you're not plenty dramatic when you make moon eyes at the harbor, scouting for a certain sailor from Rigeby Bay?"

I say nothing, my wit tied to a stone in the pit of my stomach. Despite myself, I squint out at the water, my heart willing Iker's boat to appear. But the sea beyond the harbor is clear, all the visiting ships and off-duty whalers already in port.

Nik sighs, and I know he's beating himself up for such a quip—and again I'm thankful he knows nothing of the kisses Iker and I shared. He squeezes me close again, the nervous tremble subdued. "He'll be here. Iker makes his own rules, but he never breaks his word."

That was the last thing he said to me before Queen Charlotte pulled him away for his final speech preparations. I sink to the sand and sit, a little doll in my lap dressed in black and white. Ready for the ashes. I can barely force myself to play along. And without Nik by my side, this year I play along alone.

I suppose I *could* join the castle workers—I've known them since I was a small child. But I'm not truly one of them. And the other girls my age? Well, they're never really an option—they've made that much clear over the years.

Maybe banishment wouldn't be such a bad thing—I could just break out my magic as we burn our little witch dolls and leave this place for good. But then I'd leave Nik for good too. And implicate my entire family.

So, I sit alone—the secret witch, the prince's friend who doesn't know her place.

I am well within eyeshot of Nik as he readies to speak—in the event that his courage has retreated up Lille

Bjerg Pass—but far enough to the side that I have a clear view of the sea in my periphery.

He will come.

He said he would.

You shouldn't care anyway.

I turn my attention back to the royal family. And to the flames I must face before Nik's big moment.

There's a traditional speech honoring this "celebration" too. And though the king may have ceded his duties to Nik, Queen Charlotte would never give up her chance to speak out against the horrors of witchcraft.

The queen is a beauty by any measure, all fine bone structure and swanlike grace. Her hair is curled and coiled atop her head, a deep blond halo around a crown of sapphires and diamonds. When she steps forward in the sand, she looks every bit a painting in the firelight.

In her hands is her ceremonial first doll—clothed in blood red.

As if the death of every Dane in the past six hundred years was the fault of a witch.

As if the Øldenburgs hadn't burned hundreds of women with flimsy proof.

As if "the witch hunter king," King Christian IV, hadn't been proud of the name he earned and of the lives he ruined.

"Good evening, dear ones." Queen Charlotte smiles to the crowd, and it's like ice cracking under pressure. "On this night, we not only celebrate the beginning of Havnestad's Lithasblot, but we remember the hardships endured by our ancestors."

In the shadows, my knuckles turn white as I clench the doll in my lap. This part is almost worse than tossing a replica of myself into the fire.

"We live in safety and harmony in the Øresund Kingdoms because of the courage of King Christian IV. We live in safety and harmony because of the laws he put in place. Witchcraft has no place except in the depths of hell."

The queen hoists the red doll above her head so hard its little witch's hat falls, the fire sucking it into the flames. "Shall there be any devils on our shores, know you do not belong here nor in this world." I swear her eyes find me in this moment. "The light will win, and you shall be swallowed deep into the flames and returned to your horned maker."

The crowd erupts, and Queen Charlotte spins on the spot, tossing the witch into the bonfire—royally ousting us because our power is a threat to her own.

We are to form an orderly line circling the fire, but I can't do that. I won't do that. Instead, I stand and toss my doll over the heads of those charging forward, eager to murder little wooden models of me. My mother. My aunt. My father's family.

I look for Nik then, who follows suit with a smile on his face. Somewhere Tante Hansa is laughing, her distinctive cackle hitting my ear. I know it's a ruse to protect us, but I don't know how she can pretend to enjoy it so much. She even goes so far as to have the most colorful doll, meddling with pastes and dyes until she can ensure its little outfit will be the brightest on the beach. This year, hers is a stunning orange, thanks to a customer who unknowingly added to her fun by paying her in turmeric.

It's ironic: the same townspeople who come to her when they burn their skin, grateful for her ancient medicinal treatments, turn little wooden replicas of our ancestors to ash each year on this date. And she just laughs in their faces like it's nothing. As hundreds rush the fire, I sink back down to the sand and wipe my hands on my skirts. It's just sweat, but it almost feels like blood.

When every last witch has been tossed, the crowd retreats. Nik has stepped a measure in front of his parents to the most prominent spot on the sand, the bonfire at his back. Even in the ochre light, his skin is unnaturally pale. I make my gaze as heavy and focused as possible, not even so much as blinking until he catches my eye. I give him a smile and a nod.

You'll be splendid.

His lips curl up, and he clears his throat with a deep breath.

"Good people of Havnestad, welcome to the opening night of Lithasblot, when we honor Urda and give thanks for her blessings and bounty, be it from the sea or from land."

The fire crackles happily behind him, the tallest flames licking at the stars. Despite the crush of people, only that crackle and the lapping of the sea fills in the practiced pause in the traditional speech. We all know it by heart—and could join Nik in its recital, if it were appropriate. Most days, he's one of us. Just Nik. But tonight he's our crown prince, and our duty as subjects outweighs our familiarity.

So we are quiet.

Nik glances up at his pause and meets my eye again. I nod him forward even though his color has suddenly returned.

"These next four days are a celebration. Games, races, songs, and feasts in our goddess's name. Let us not forget that it is all for her. It is fun. It is merry. But it has a utility—a reason. Urda."

There is an audible gasp in the crowd—Nik has gone off script. He's speaking from the heart, and I couldn't be prouder.

"Last year, we did the same as we will do this week," Nik goes on, his voice gathering strength. "We pelted our thinnest with bread. We sang to Urda. We watched as I carried the heaviest rock down the beach."

At this, he flexes a bicep and flashes a smile—all his

nerves replaced with bravado. A few chuckles carry through the crowd, but there is only one heavy guffaw—issued by Tante Hansa, from her corner at the table reserved for the ancients.

Nik rounds on her with a pronounced grin and then pulls his brows together. His tone swings back to serious. "Yes, I am aware my scrawny feats of strength are quite hysterical. But those are on display daily"—he grins again—"and they are not why we do this year after year. We do this for Urda. And some years she teaches us a lesson and reminds us of her power."

Nik pauses, the air heavy and silent. Not even the bonfire dares to crackle.

"My father stood on this exact spot a year ago and recited the very same speech he has said for thirty years. Which his father before him recited for thirty years before that. Yet we were in the thick of the Tørhed—the third year running. And did it improve when we came together to sing songs about Urda until our voices were rough and fingers bleeding on our guitarens? No. Did it improve when I defeated all you weaklings in the rock carry? No."

Only Tante Hansa is brave enough to cackle this time. But no one turns her way. All eyes are on our crown prince. Even the king and queen are hanging on his every word.

"Let us remember that though we celebrate her, Urda owes us not a morsel. Just like the tide that laps our shores—her tide, her shores—she can take as swiftly as she can give."

Nik pauses, his coal-dark eyes on the harbor over our heads. I realize he's referencing Anna too. Honoring her as something Urda claimed for her own, the sea doing the goddess's bidding.

"So, let us honor Urda this week, not just celebrate her name, but truly honor her. She is our queen—forgive me, Mother. The land that gives us bounty. The sea that brings us our supper as much as coins in our pocket. She is more than a goddess—she is us. Havnestad. And all the people within it. Without her, we are nothing. No magic can trick her. No words can ply her. No will can sway her. She is queen, and we are simply her subjects."

He comes to a full stop, eyes on the waves beyond the crowd, posture firm and tall—regal.

Perhaps stunned by his originality and honesty, it takes the whole of Havnestad a few moments to process that he's finished. I stand and begin to cheer and clap. Nik's eyes find me, and there's a wink of relief that brushes across his features before my view of him is blocked—every last person leaping to their feet, hoots at their lips and applause gone wild. And somehow it feels as if he's leagues away.

7

It's impossible to see him after that.

All the people want to shake his hand. Tell him how awed they are by his thoughtfulness. About how poised he was. How kingly he sounded. How impressed they were and are.

Nik is swallowed by their affections.

And though I wait on the beach for him to resurface, he doesn't. Whisked away for the night in a crowd of his subjects. Every other creature eventually peters out for the night too. A rush and then a trickle in exit until it's just me, a hot pile of kindling, and a few poor souls who have lost the battle of alertness to free hvidtøl and a patch of soft sand.

I stand, legs stiff in my boots, eyes toward the harbor, breathing in the sharp, salty air. My throat tightens and tears threaten my eyes.

He's going to be king, Evie.

I want to laugh at my foolishness for thinking I'd always have him. Of course everything is going to change.

The moon is so bright that I can see the length of the beach without any other aid. Too bright for my dark mood, but maybe a walk will do me good. Clear my head. I should be happy for him, after all.

I make my way down the docks first, taking the worn planks in careful steps as ships large and small clank and bump at the sea's discretion.

Naturally, the royal dock is the largest in the harbor—with room for the king's giant steamer, my father's craft, and a dozen other royal ships, boats, schooners, and skiffs. There's a pole at the end that is empty, though—the spot where the king's steamship should be.

I stare at the water there for a moment, wishing for the second time tonight that his boat would materialize among the gentle rolling waves. Just suddenly appear with Iker aboard, a shine in his eyes and laughter on his lips. That he'd jump off the bow before anchoring, not able to hold himself back from me a moment longer. That he'd pull me in deeply into his arms for another kiss.

I blink and the thought has vanished.

The pole is still untethered.

There is not a single ship on the horizon.

I step off the dock, my back to the waves that took Anna, my head and heart throbbing with the wish that she would return, too. That I'd have my friend back. That I wouldn't feel the need to pin my hopes on boys who I should've known all along would only care about me until they hit that invisible line in the sand—blood—and then let me down. Though maybe, being highborn, Anna would've felt the same way.

I am too restless to run home to bed. To nod and smile at Hansa's drunken tale of her grand evening with her grand friends—as if those friends didn't just burn thousands of *us*. So I walk along the water to the cove side, the moonlight guiding my steps, catching on the shimmering flecks of sand to create a brilliant path along the shoreline.

I don't have a plan, and I don't need one. I just need a chance to wear myself out enough that I fall asleep unencumbered by the sadness dragging my heart down to my ankles.

I do have friends who aren't royal. I do.

I have the kids from school who tolerate me for Nik's sake, but only really when their prince is around. But for the most part, all I see when I greet their faces is the disapproval reflected in their eyes.

That girl—couldn't save her mother.

That girl—lived while her best friend drowned.

That girl—thinks her father's job gives her keys to the castle.

That girl—thinks herself more than a passing fancy for the playboy prince.

I meet the first rocks of the cove and stand there, letting the salt air toss my curls about my face. The wind here always seems so cleansing—like it sweeps away grime both physical and mental with one exhale from the Øresund Strait.

Tonight the cove is calm. The waves lap gently about the shore, kissing both the sand and the rock formations with the same delicate precision. There is no one else in sight, and this dress isn't anything special—nothing I have is special—so I yank off my boots and stockings and place them carefully on a patch of beach not likely to be touched by the tide. The sand sticking to my toes, I hop onto the first footstep island and leap from stone to stone until I make it to Picnic Rock.

Though it's damp from the recent high tide, the slab isn't so wet it's uncomfortable. I gather my skirts, pull my knees to my chest, and sit there with my eyes closed, letting the sea's charge wash over me.

Finally, my heartbeat slows, and I can feel exhaustion creeping in. But I can't sleep here. I force myself to stand on stiff legs and grab my things. There's barely a breeze, but a tingle runs up my spine. I cross my arms over my chest, but I can't get rid of the cold. I squint into the night, at the shadow where the sea meets the rock formation splitting the cove, when I swear I see a flash of white skin.

"Hello?" I call, my body shivering.

Only the wind answers, gently gaining strength from well past the harbor and deep within the sea.

I am suddenly awake, and I turn my attention again to the rock wall. But there's nothing to see but shadow and waves.

Maybe it was the octopus who's made the cove his home, taunting me the same way he taunts Tante Hansa, who would like nothing more than to bottle every last drop of his ink.

But probably not. My eyes are playing tricks on me again.

Just as they must have on Nik's birthday.

"Perhaps you need to avoid the cove when the moon is strong, Evelyn," I mutter. The moon can do funny things to a witch.

I can hear it now, another strain in the chorus of pity: *That girl—seeing apparitions in the moonlight.*

FOUR YEARS BEFORE

The boy heard the splashes, one right after another, and stood, piccolo forgotten, eyes only on the sea. He held his breath, waiting for the first one to surface. They were both strong swimmers, but the raven-curled girl made a habit of winning.

It was a hundred yards to the sandbar. A worthy swim on any day, but as the boy surveyed the sea again, he knew this was not just any sea. These were not just any waves.

The sea was angry.

The boy held his breath and took a step toward the water, careful not to get too close—his mother had often lectured him on the damage salt water could do to his fine leather boots.

The blond girl surfaced first. She pulled in a deep breath and then went back under, the sandbar in her sights, still seventy-five yards away.

The boy scanned the water for dark hair. Took a breath. Squinted right at the spot where she should've surfaced. Still nothing.

The blonde bobbed up again. Now ten yards closer to the sandbar and not looking back.

No dark hair to be seen.

He took another step forward. A wave took full advantage and marked his foot. On reflex, he glanced down. Yes, the leather was completely soaked. But he didn't care. Eyes imme-diately back on the sea. Heart pounding. The wet boot already coming off.

There. In the distance, thirty yards out. Not the crown of a raven-haired head.

A single hand, reaching for air.

The boy dove in, full breath cinched in his lungs, and opened his eyes. Nothing but the murky deep and the sting of salt.

Thinking of the girls, of the hand, he surfaced early. He would keep his stroke above the waves, his head close to the sur-face. He was a strong swimmer, and his new height had not diminished his natural strength, but the undertow was fiercer than he'd ever felt, constantly tugging at his pant legs. A force from the deep pulling him toward the harem of mermaids all Havnestad children were told lived at the bottom of the sea.

At the surface, he saw nothing. Not a strand of hair, nor a flash of hand. But he knew where they were. He knew where he must go.

Twenty more yards and he opened his eyes to the sea again. Looked down. Where the undertow had pulled him.

Black hair curled up like a cloud of ink, pale fingers stretched toward him. Her face hidden. He dove, hoping it wasn't too late.

Lungs burning for air, he surfaced, one arm hooked under her shoulders. The force of the swim had pushed the curls from her face. Her features bordered on blue, and he couldn't tell if she was breathing.

All he knew was that he had her.

"Come on, Evie. Come on." He prayed to the old gods as well as the Lutheran one when he had the breath, his body fighting the tow for them both, the shoreline distant but in his sights.

Moving forward, he turned his head as much as the weight and struggle would allow, hoping for a flash of blond safely at the sandbar.

He saw nothing.

On the shore, he called as loud as he could for help. He set Evie on the sand, brushing back her curls, ear to her mouth.

No breath.

He rolled her over and pounded on her back. Salt water streamed from her lips and nose, dribbling onto the beach.

People came then. Men from the docks, women from the sea lane. They crowded around, speaking in whispered tones about the girl. They never had nice things to say about her, even with her this way.

The boy told the men that there was one more. Pointed them toward the sandbar and empty waves. Barked orders of rescue. The men listened. Because of the boy's name.

The boy blew air into the girl's lungs and pounded her on the back again, moving her hair out of the way to make more impact. More water came forth, this time in a great gush, along with the rasp of a breath.

Her eyes blinked open, dark and worn.

"Nik?"

"Yes! Evie, yes!"

Smiling briefly, he hugged her close then, even if it was inappropriate, with her bare-shouldered in her petticoat and him a prince. But he didn't care because she was alive. Evie was alive.

"Anna?" she asked.

They turned their eyes to the sea.

8

HAVNESTAD THRUMS WITH ENERGY.

The brightness of summer and the thrill of Urda's festival combine to create the kind of charge one usually witnesses with a coming storm. It has me up early, feeling light and free after such a black night.

As I walk down to the harbor, amethyst in my pocket, I see Nik's carriage pass by. I wave my hand, but I can't tell if he's seen me. He's surely headed into the valley to visit the farmers in his father's stead, a Lithasblot tradition. We give thanks to Urda but also to those who work our fields.

The ships in port are empty, but I run my closed palm along their lengths, spelling them though they won't be headed anywhere this day or the next. On a morning as glorious as this one, it is not hard to conjure the words for Urda, yet I can't help but think back to Nik's speech. *No magic can trick her. No words can ply her. No will can sway her.* Is my spell a trick? A panic suddenly seizes me. My heart beats fast and my feet feel like lead. The dock begins to spin before my eyes. Is this my punishment? I close my eyes to right my balance. I'm being silly. My magic is not meant to deceive. My words are intended to honor Urda, honor her sea. Bring life. Surely she knows that. My heart rate starts to slow and I leave the docks. I need a distraction.

Nik isn't supposed to return from the farms until midafternoon, and while the streets will soon be alive with festival visitors, the real party doesn't get started until suppertime, when Nik will have to judge the livestock. So I walk down Market Street and gather a late breakfast, paid for on Father's account—fat strawberries, a stinky half-wedge of samsø, a jar of pickled herring we call slid, and a crusty loaf of rye bread so dense it could pass as a sea stone—and return to the Havnestad Cove.

It's quiet here, just a few couples trailing along the rocks, none taking any notice of me. I remove my shoes and stockings and place them in the same spot as yesterday, and I hop between the smaller footstep islands to the big one, Picnic Rock earning its name yet again. The strong sun and calm tide has made the rock almost completely dry, so I lie on my back, face to the sky, and shut my eyes.

Though I don't want it to, my mind shifts to Iker. He still hasn't returned. I am already anxious, and the same panicky feeling quickly returns.

What if something's gone wrong?

What if the steam stack exploded?

What if the whale crashed into the ship's hull upon capture?

Am I at fault?

I know I'm being ridiculous, but worst of all, we would never know. All of us are here, for once our eyes inward instead of turned to the sea.

That sends my mind into a downward spiral about Father, and then suddenly a shadow falls across the backs of my eyelids, the direct sun blotted out by a passing cloud. It's as if the weather worries too—

"Excuse me, miss?"

That voice.

My eyes pop open, searching for the face of a friend who I know in my heart is long gone.

But there, leaning over me, is the girl.

The girl from the porthole.

The one who rescued Nik.

Yet that can't be right, either. I really am losing my senses today.

I sit up and rapidly blink my eyes in the sun, but when they refocus, the same girl remains. She shifts back, long blond hair swinging.

Her face is like the singsong of her voice—so much like Anna's, but more mature. The smattering of freckles around her nose is familiar too. She wears a gown that's nicer than all of mine put together, and her shoes shine with new leather.

Shoes. Feet. No fin—she can't be what I saw. My stomach sinks, but I don't know why.

"This is quite embarrassing, but . . ." The girl's eyes fall to the strawberry in my hand. "I haven't eaten in more than a day."

I'm so stunned, I just hand over the strawberry. She isn't ready for it and bobbles it in her fingertips before taking a bite. I shove my whole meal toward her.

Anna loved cheese and fruit.

"Oh, no, you don't have to, I—"

"I insist," I say, and I'm surprised that's what comes out because there are so many other words on my tongue. So many questions. But I'm almost terrified to ask them because I know what word will fall out—*Anna*.

The girl eats, and I try to figure out what to say next.

Did you save Nik?

Were you a mermaid?

Are you Anna?

Don't you remember me?

All would make me run if I were her. So, as she chews a hunk of rye bread, I open the jar of slid.

"Do you feel better?" I ask.

"Yes, much. Thank you. I'm so sorry. I'm done."

I shake my head and tilt the open jar toward her, the

little herring bobbing in their brine. "Eat, please."

She sees the fish and recoils, waving her hands in front of her face. I pull out a herring and eat it myself, yanking the bones out by the tail before discarding them into the cove. She looks at me as if I've just bitten off her ear.

I used to do the same thing to Anna. She didn't like slid either. I smile, but on the inside, the sadness is suffocating. I have to stop looking for the dead in the living.

"Are you sure you aren't still hungry?" I try. "There's more cheese."

"No. I'll be fine." A sob swallows the word *fine*. Her brow furrows and the skin under her lashes reddens; there are no tears, but she looks exactly like she should be weeping.

My hand flies to her shoulder to comfort her. When the girl catches her breath, she begins talking again, her voice almost a whisper. She doesn't seem to mind me touching her. "I ran away from home."

"Oh, Anna—"

The girl's eyes fly to mine. "Annemette. How'd you—"

"I didn't . . . I just . . . you remind me of someone I used to know."

She coughs out a sob-laugh. "I wish I were that girl."

"No you don't," I say quickly as this girl—Annemette— wipes her nose.

"Was her father a liar? Weaving tales about where he's

been and what he's done, selling off all our livestock and not bringing a coin home?"

I shake my head because I don't know what to say.

"I've had to sell half our fine things to pay his debt and put food on the table. I couldn't take it anymore. I took off running over Lille Bjerg a day ago."

Her words are off. They seem forced. I can't help it—I stare at her face. I've seen thousands of faces since Anna failed to surface, but I've never seen one so similar. Never heard a voice with the same timbre. If I hadn't touched her, if this girl weren't clearly made of flesh and bone, I'd think she was a ghost.

She scrubs her face with her hands, nails clean and shaped. Her eyes blink open and then she takes my hands. "I'm terrible. Here I am, barging in on your breakfast, stealing your food, dumping my problems in your lap, and yet I haven't even asked your name."

"It's Evie," I reply.

"Evie," she repeats, testing my name out on her tongue. "British?"

"Evelyn, yes. My mother fell in love with the name in Brighton."

"I can see why." Annemette smiles, her teeth clean and straight, like that of a princess or a dairymaid.

I tell myself again that she's not Anna. She's not even the girl from the porthole or the beach or anywhere else. She's a farm girl from the other side of the pass. My cheeks grow hot. Annemette squeezes my hands. "Thank you for your generosity, Evie—it's a gift. Truly." Her eyes sting red again and her lip trembles. "I doubt I'll be so lucky again."

I don't know what to do with this openness. This odd feeling blooming in my stomach. "You really have nothing and nowhere to go?"

Annemette waves her hands across her body. "Only my clothes and my pride."

I can't explain this girl or my feelings or why I have the need to believe her, but I do. And I want to help. "Come with me."

9

THE LITTLE HOUSE THAT MY FATHER BUILT ISN'T THAT far from Havnestad Cove—it's practically waterside itself, the cottage at the end of a lane in the shadow of Øldenburg Castle. It backs up to a thatch of trees that buffer it from a rocky cliff jutting out into the sea.

"It's so quaint," Annemette says.

"It's home," I answer, and push through the front door. It's been a long time since I've introduced someone to our tiny cottage. When I was little, we'd often take in children while their parents were away at sea. But that stopped after Mother died.

At the hearth, Tante Hansa is stirring something—by the smell of it, most likely the ham-and-pea concoction she brings to every Lithasblot to place beside the roast hog we have on the second day of the festival. Because "there can never be enough swine in this sodden fish market."

Hansa's back is turned, and I feel the need to announce that we have company—it's never safe for a witch to have no warning.

"Tante Hansa, I'd like you to meet my new friend."

Hansa wipes her hands, and I know by the set of her shoulders she was stirring the soup without a spoon. Domestic spells aren't spectacular, but they're her favorites because she'd never planned on having a family of her own—and Father and I are more work than she'd like to admit.

When she turns, her face is pulled up in a smile, clear blue eyes flashing with the delight of catching me at something remotely unusual. Hansa is my mother's older sister by almost two decades, the time between them filled with brothers who lost their lives to the sea's moods much too young. She is as old as the grief of burying all her siblings suggests. But I have never been able to put anything past her.

Which means her reaction to Annemette is the same as mine. Only she actually says what she's thinking.

"Why, Anna, returned from the deep, have we?"

Annemette's mouth drops open as if she's lost her tongue, her jovial attitude gone as well.

"*Annemette*, Tante," I correct. "She's from the valley. A farm."

Hansa takes a step forward and raises a brow—quite the feat given the blood-drawing tightness of her hairdo.

—71

"Is that so?" Hansa looks her up and down. "Those hands haven't seen a day of hard work in all your years. That fair face hasn't seen the sun. And that dress is worth more than the best cow in the valley." She takes a step forward and grabs Annemette's smooth hand. "Who are you really?"

"Tante, please, leave her be, she's had a rough trip—"

"Hush. You only see what you want to see." She turns back to Annemette, staring at the girl as if she could bend her will as easily as she tamed the soup. "So, again I ask—who are you really?"

Annemette's eyes have gone red around the rims again, but she doesn't cry. If anything, there's an edge of defiance in the cut of them. Like she's accepted Hansa's dare for what it is. But when she speaks, she says the last thing I'd expect.

"Your soup is boiling."

But the soup is more than boiling. The pea-green liquid hisses as it rolls in violent, unnatural waves over the iron pot's rim.

"Ah!" Hansa cackles. "I've seen your type before."

I'm stunned. *Her type?* Is Annemette a witch?

I stare at her.

Another witch. My age. Next to me.

Of all the things I can't believe about Annemette, this might be the most unfathomable.

Something cracks open in my chest as the secret we've

held so tightly as a family flies into the soupy air. I stare at this face so familiar and yet so strange, and my mind whirls. Anna was not a witch, but Annemette certainly is.

Annemette nods, and the liquid returns to a gentle simmer.

My aunt's spotted hands grasp Annemette's again, but this time there's a funny light in her eyes, all her skepticism gone. "Evie, child, you've made quite an interesting friend indeed."

~

It's a long while before Tante Hansa allows us to escape, having thoroughly quizzed Annemette on her family. In the funny way of things, we both claim lineage to the town of Ribe and Denmark's most famous witch, Maren Spliid. Tied to a ladder and thrown into a fire by King Christian IV 220 years ago, she became as much a lesson as a legend. Her talent was inspiring, but ultimately her audacity was her undoing. Her death and so many others under the witch-hunter king scattered Denmark's witches like ashes in the wind. And our kind never recovered—our covens fractured, magic kept to families and never shared.

Given the time and distance, it shouldn't be a surprise that there's more than one magical family in Havnestad related to Ribe and Maren, yet I still can't believe it. We've been alone for so long.

After Hansa is finally satisfied with her family tree, Annemette and I head outside. We walk into the woods behind the cottage, where we're shaded from every angle, including from Øldenburg Castle and its sweeping views, and start to pick our way down toward the sea.

The ground is covered in gnarled roots and branches, a danger for anyone not looking where they're going. But I know this steep path better than anyone, and I use this moment to steal another glance at Annemette. Her family may be from elsewhere, but her face still belongs here.

Anna did not have any magic in her blood, at least as far as I know. She had two "common" parents and a grandmother who loved her more than the sun. Her parents left shortly after Anna's funeral. Took their titles and moved to the Jutland—miles and miles from this place and the daughter they lost. Her grandmother is still here, but she's gone senile with grief, the loss of her family too much for her mind. I see her at the bakeshop sometimes, and she calls every person there Anna. Even me.

"What?" Annemette says, catching me looking as we pass between twin trees, slick with sap.

I can't tell her what I'm thinking, but I do have questions for her. "It's just . . . how did you know we were witches? If you'd been wrong, we could've reported you. You could've been banished."

She dips her head to avoid a branch. "I could just feel it."

Like Tante Hansa did.

"I must not be much of a witch," I say. "I couldn't tell. I

mean, now my blood won't stop singing, but an hour ago? No." There's so much I don't know about the magic in my bones.

"I'm sure you're a fine witch, Evie."

It's a nice thing to say, I suppose, but not necessarily true. Tante Hansa teaches me only the most mundane of spells. But I read her books and Mother's books, and I know there is so much more. With a few words and her will, Annemette brought out all that possibility into the open.

"How did you do that? The soup, I mean."

Annemette just shrugs and hooks a hand on a tree, swinging around it like a maypole ribbon. "It was just an animation spell," she says as if impressing Tante Hansa was nothing.

The ease, the comfort, the understanding she has about her magic makes my blood tingle with envy. It's so much of what I want. It took me months of studying and toying to create the spell to combat the Tørhed and even then, I'm not sure it actually works. My evidence is only anecdotal, and Fru Seraphine has taught me better than to use anecdotes as true measures of success.

In a few more steps we reach the sliver of rocky beach blind to Havnestad Cove, my own shortcut to Greta's Lagoon. I try to calm my heart from beating so loudly, but I've never gone to the lagoon in daylight and I'm nervous. I steal a glance up the beach. It's deserted as far as I can see, everyone off preparing for tonight's festivities.

"Careful," I say as we reach the end of the beach and the two large rocks. "The water is deep here."

I take off my stockings and shoes and wade in. As I reach the sand, I turn around, but she's still standing by the rocks. "Here," I say, wading back out and extending my arm. "Take my hand. I'll help you."

With tentative steps, she walks forward and grasps my hand tight. I smile at her. "Come on. It's okay."

Once we're in the right spot, I push aside the small boulders that obscure the entrance and steer her inside. Although it's daylight, the cave is still steeped in shadows. I light a candle. Various mundane tools hang from juts on the wall, and on the floor, oysters sweat in a bucket—my latest failure. On a ledge in the rock wall are my tinctures, bottles full of octopus and squid ink, jellyfish poison, and powdered crab shells.

"You've made a lair."

I laugh. "'Secret workshop' might be a more accurate term."

"Oh no, this is a lair." Annemette's hands move automatically to the ledge. She holds each bottle up to the light, admiring the slosh or swoosh of the contents.

Her boot nudges the oyster bucket. "And what are your plans for these little fellas?" She scoops one up and holds it in her hand as if it's a baby bird and not an endless source of frustration for me.

"They're barren, but I'd hoped to spell them into

producing pearls to be crushed for—" Annemette stops me cold with a wave of her hand. She mumbles something I don't understand under her breath, her eyes intent on the oyster in her palms.

Within moments, the oyster swells to a pink as vibrant as the sunset and springs open. Inside is the most gorgeous pearl, perfectly round with an opalescent shimmer.

"It's beautiful," I say, though the word doesn't do it justice. It's otherworldly, unnatural. I want to touch it, but I'm frightened of it all the same. It seems . . . alive.

Annemette's grin grows mischievous. "Too beautiful to crush, I think." With a simple Old Norse command—"*Fljóta*"—she sets the pearl afloat over her palm. Then, without saying a word, she commands a few lengths of thread—repurposed and therefore unspooled—from the nails on the wall. Next, she covers the thread and pearl with both hands, shielding from me the magic she's clearly working with her mind, her eyes set on her work. Seconds later, her hands part to reveal a perfect pearl necklace.

"Turn around and pull up your hair," she says.

I do as she says and she draws the thread around my neck, draping it so that the pearl lies at the base of my throat. I don't own any real jewelry and have never even tried any on, save for my mother's wedding band—Father keeps it tucked away in a little chest, along with letters and drawings and other tokens from their life together.

I touch the pearl and look up at her, but she is busy

working on another oyster and more string. After a few moments, Annemette ties her own pearl necklace around her throat.

"And now we match," she says.

My throat catches. I remember Anna saying those words to me that time we made necklaces from wooden beads the tailor was giving away. They were crude and childlike, yet still special. We promised to never take them off, but I couldn't bear to look at mine once Anna was gone. It's now in a small box underneath my bed.

I force a smile at Annemette. My pearl sits in cool repose against my neck, pulsing with vigor. It's a curious feeling that is not altogether pleasant, and I wonder if the pearl will always beat like this. Oddly, I find myself hoping that it will.

"Can you teach me?" I ask, the words spilling from my lips.

"What is there to teach? You're a witch, aren't you?"

"I . . . Tante Hansa hasn't taught me anything like that. Everything I know is like a recipe to make cheese—fail one segment and the whole thing falls to curd."

Annemette scrunches her nose. "It shouldn't be that hard." She picks up an oyster. "Here. Try. *Fljóta.*"

Annemette sees the reluctance cross my face and tilts her head. "It's just a command. Say it with confidence and you'll have the magic do the work."

With hesitant fingers, I take the oyster in my hand. It's

78—

as gray and barren as ever, and stinky, too, a tinge of rot to it. *"Fljóta."*

The oyster shakes in my fingers but doesn't lift. I can't seem to make that connection like I do when I spell Father's ship. There's something missing.

"You control the magic, Evie. It's yours. Take it."

There's a note in her voice that's like a jolt—like pushing me off the dock and into the water.

I square my shoulders and stare at the frustrating, rotting little thing. I feel my mother's blood deep inside me. The blood of Maren Spliid. The blood of the stregha hiding within my father's "common" façade. I feel the spirit of Urda, outside, inside, all around me, creating the natural energy we draw from. I spin these feelings with all the want inside me—the want to have the sort of power that could've saved Anna and my mother. The kind that can truly end the Tørhed for good, not just mask it with a daily spell. The kind that Annemette seems to have.

"Fljóta," I say with all that want. With the wound that lives deep in my belly from the day I lost Anna. The day I almost lost Nik too. When I wanted more than anything to use my magic to make it better.

The oyster hovers.

"Líf," Annemette whispers. Life. I should give it life.

"Líf," I command. The oyster begins to change colors, its gray shell warming to pink and then to the burnt orange of dawn.

—79

The oyster grows hot. Hot enough to match its new lively color. Its warmth licks at my palm.

In a moment, the oyster pops open, the most perfect pearl at its center.

It's beautiful. Again, it's almost too beautiful to crush for the magical poultice I'd planned, but there's so much magic I now want to make with it.

Annemette laughs. "And that, my friend, is how you command the magic."

Although the spell is over, I can still feel the magic pulsing through my veins, a blue fire so hot, it's cold. It's unlike anything I've ever felt before. I don't want it to stop, but I know there's a danger in sipping from this feeling too long.

I set the oyster on the table I use for my inventions, fashioned from a piece of driftwood I found on the beach. It's littered with more bottles and vials, but I clear some space and hold the pearl in my fingers. Unlike the pearl Annemette made, this one is still warm to the touch, not icy hot. The magic responds differently to the two of us, I suppose—I don't know. But I want to learn.

It's time I really embrace who I am. Tante Hansa has kept me in the dark for too long. My mother was an established healer by my age.

"Annemette, will you stay and teach me?" I ask.

"I can't," she replies quickly, her mouth drawn tight, but trembling. She turns and braces her arms against the cave's opening, watching the tide come in and out.

But I don't understand. Why is Annemette so upset? Why must she suddenly leave?

"You *can* stay," I insist. "You're safe here from your father, and we have more than enough room. And you'll be with us. With a family that cares for you and *understands* you. You don't have to run away to find that. To be yourself."

Annemette meets my eyes with a look I know, and with every force of a Viking spell, she says it again.

"I can't."

She bends down and runs her hands through the sand, letting it fall between her fingers. "I can't stay here."

It's her. I can't deny it now. She's not trying to deny it either. The look she gave me is the one I saw on the beach. The one that I saw on the girl's face as she loomed over Nik. Before diving into the water and disappearing, only a tail fin popping up from the waves.

"You can't stay," I say.

She nods, her eyes nervous.

"You're not a witch, are you?"

She shakes her head no.

"You're a mermaid."

10

"How is he—the boy?" Annemette swallows hard and takes a step toward me.

I instinctively take a step back, bumping into the table behind me and knocking a corked vial of octopus ink on its side. I'm not sure if it's Tante Hansa's old wives' tales telling me to run or the fact that Annemette is clearly more powerful than any folktale could have ever described. My hand reaches out and grasps the vial before it rolls and smashes to the floor. The pearl at my neck throbs. I want to leave, but her face looks pained, and I can see now that she's been holding this question in since she arrived.

I realize she's not here for me or my magic. She's here for Nik.

In my stunned silence, Annemette goes on. "Is he all right? He was breathing when I brought him ashore, but I didn't have time to—you came and then that man, and I had to go. I need him to be alive, Evie. Please, say something!"

I nod. "He's fine. You saved him." My throat tightens and tears sting my cheeks. If it wasn't for Annemette, I'd be dressed in mourning clothes. "He's totally healthy. Strapping. Probably milking a goat at this very moment!"

Annemette practically collapses in my arms. "Oh, thank goodness! When he fell into the sea, I caught him, but the tide and the storm was so strong, I—"

"Stop. I shouldn't know," I say. "You shouldn't say any more. It's too dangerous for me to—"

"But you aren't any more welcome here than I am," she says, pulling herself upright. "Your magic is just as forbidden as mine." And when my eyes meet hers and they're clear and hard, I realize we've made an exchange. A dangerous one.

I know her secret and she knows mine. Breaking this trust would ensure our mutual demise. I slip the vial of ink I'd been clutching into my dress pocket.

We will only survive our secrets together.

"I promise I won't say a thing," I assure her, a hint of regret in my voice.

"Thank you," she says. "My lips are sealed too." She weaves a slim finger through her blond hair, twisting a long wave into a curl. "What's his name—the boy?"

"Nik. His name is Nik. And he's my best friend. I'm so glad that you were there. I saw the wave too late, and he was gone." I realize for the first time that after saving Nik over and over again, even if it was only on the dance floor, there was nothing I could have done that night. That he'd have saved me from the sea, but I would have failed him. My smile falters and I look down to the gray oysters at our feet. "I wish I could repay you with more than a few scraps of food and a pearl necklace."

Annemette loops a finger in mine. It feels strange, too close, but I don't want to push her away. "I didn't do anything special," she says. "Mermaids are not the monsters you humans think we are. I could not just let him drown."

Drown. Like Anna did. Like I thought Anna did.

At this moment, Annemette looks so pretty. So innocent. She raises her eyes to meet mine.

"Would you like to meet him?" I ask.

"Please," she says.

We leave my "lair" and make our way back through the rocks, Annemette still nervous as she heads out first. So strange and sad to see a mermaid afraid of the sea. As I go, I pause in the water for a moment—I want to take a last look at the cave to make sure all is hidden—and that's when I feel them. At my feet, three dead minnows bounce between my ankle and the boulder—surely knocked out of the sea by a wild wave and smacked into the rocks. I shake my head, remembering the last time such fish floated at my feet, but I can't think of that day. Not now.

On the shore, Annemette and I dry off and put on our shoes. Then we head back up the trail through the forest. Once the trees spread out enough and we have room to walk side by side, I feel as if I can finally ask her more. "So, have you always been a mermaid?"

Annemette gives me a look. "Have you always been a girl?"

"Yes," I reply. "But you're no longer a mermaid. At least, I don't see a tail. Perhaps you weren't one from the start."

She laughs, and I almost draw back because she sounds just like Anna again. Our elbows bump as I check myself, wishing I'd just asked her directly what I wanted to know.

"Sorry to disappoint you," she says. "Born a mermaid, hopefully not forever one." She dances gracefully into an arabesque pose.

I stop walking. My brows pull together. My courage rises. "But is it possible, for a human to drown and become a merperson?"

She shakes her head and I reset.

"How long can you stay like that?"

Annemette glances down for a moment and then her eyes are up and locked with mine. "A few minutes," she says, her back leg still high in the air.

"No, I mean, how long can you stay *human*?"

Her eyes shift at the word. She stands up straight and stretches. "Not long," she says after a pause. "At least not as I am. But it depends."

"Depends on what?" I push back.

"I promise to tell you," she says, though I can see in her hesitation that she doesn't quite trust me. Her face turns pale and she almost looks scared—lost, even. "It's just that I have to see Nik first, or none of it will matter."

The little pearl pulses against my neck—*lif.* Her magic is strong, but good. She saved his life. The least I can do is make an introduction. I glance quickly at the sun on its descent toward the mountains. "We should get going. The Lithasblot festivities will start soon," I say. "It's our harvest festival. People come from all over. They've even heard of us in Copenhagen, I swear."

"Sounds fun," Annemette says. "And Nik will be there?"

I nod yes. If she tries anything, I have Tante Hansa's and my mother's magic in my blood. She grasps my hand tight.

"Let's go."

~

When we come upon the beach where tonight's festivities are, the palace staff and some local villagers are still setting up. We're a little early. The livestock stage is being nailed together, and a hundred or so people are milling about fixing decorations, laying out food, and tending the bonfire, where soon a giant hog will be trussed up on a spit.

"It's not Copenhagen, but it is a kingdom, I suppose.

As the sun goes down, the beach will be so full you can barely see a grain of sand."

"We have some pretty good parties on the sand where I come from too."

I laugh. "I'm sure you do."

Suddenly Annemette walks up to the fire and holds out her hands. I forget that she's never seen fire like this before.

"Whoa there, young lady," says Herre Olsen, the tailor, pushing Annemette back before I can get to her. "Any closer and you'll soon be roasting with the hog."

"Thank you," Annemette says with a curtsy. "I'm sorry."

"Who are you here with?" he asks.

"I'm visiting for the festival with—"

"Me," I interject, steering her away from the scowl on the tailor's face. "Thank you, Herre Olsen.

"We need to give you a better backstory," I whisper, guiding her toward the castle grounds.

The townspeople like to talk, especially about me, but the king and queen will need something substantial if their son is going to be seen speaking to her. A lowly girl without a house name is not good enough; I would know.

We decide to give her the title of a baron's daughter, the same title Anna had: *friherrinde*. A friherrinde from far away—Odense—come to see our unusual Lithasblot. Her chaperone has fallen ill, and Tante Hansa is tending to her.

—87

I'm filling in as her chaperone and guide. Yes. It'll work. Another lie added to the list. I suppose there's some truth behind the town gossips whispering that I spread falsehoods, saying the prince should not trust me. But telling the truth to gain their approval is not a risk I'm willing to take.

"When will we see Nik?" Annemette asks, tired of reciting her story to me.

"Don't worry." I point to the giant stone monstrosity on the hill. "He's waiting for me up there."

Annemette follows my finger.

"Øldenburg Castle," I say. "Five hundred years old and as drafty as a sailboat."

I guide her to the queen's garden, which is rich with tulips of every color. Annemette proclaims each one the most beautiful thing she's ever seen until she gets to the next one. And the next. "I love to garden," she says.

Her mouth drops with a gasp when we get to the queen's pride and joy—statutes of her family, each taller than a horse, circled up among the tulips. The king and queen are fashioned as they were on their wedding day, the marble smooth and glistening from the years. And there, next to them, is the latest version of Nik—eleven feet tall and chiseled as if lunging across the bow of a great sea vessel.

"Is that . . . *him*?"

She stands on her tippy toes, fingertips not even getting so far as his tastefully unbuttoned collar.

"Yes, yes, that's him."

"He looks different than I remember. Drier, I guess."
She laughs.

We crest the steps and there, already waiting and
watching Havnestad Harbor, is Nik. He's freshly washed
after his trip to the farms, the light crown he's forced to
wear for festival days pressed down over his wet hair. I
always think he looks ridiculous all fancy in Havnestad's
customary blue-and-gold suit, but Queen Charlotte is
from the fjords up north and very traditional. She insists
he emulate his official portrait for the high holidays of the
Old Norse.

"Evie, there you are," he says, catching me first in his
line of sight as he turns from the view. When his eyes land
on Annemette, his face freezes on her features. All except
his lips, which are still moving ever so slightly. "And you've
brought a friend . . ."

I smile and guide her toward him. "Your Royal Highness, this is Friherrinde Annemette. Annemette, this is
Crown Prince Niklas."

A light zips through Nik's eyes as he meets Annemette's
gaze. At first I think that he recognizes her—that he
instantly realizes she's the one who saved him. Or that he
sees the old friend we lost, the first half of this girl's name
ringing in his ears.

But almost immediately it's clear that he's thinking of
neither, because he does something I've never seen before.

He blushes *hard*. Honest-to-Urda heat is rising in his cheeks, and it's so intense that he has to glance at me before looking down.

He thinks she's beautiful.

And she is—she's gorgeous—but this . . . this is unprecedented.

I'm ashamed to admit the pang of jealousy radiating in my chest. So often, I'm the only one who has Nik's attention, and he's never looked at me like *that*. But I suppose if he had, we wouldn't be friends. Is this how he feels when I'm with Iker? Ugh, I do not want to think about Iker. I smile at them both, standing awkwardly between them, wanting to run away but afraid for what might happen if I did.

"Enchanted," he says when the words finally kick in, the blush still hearty along his cheekbones. "How do you know Evie? I thought I knew all of her friends."

I cut in to answer him. "Her chaperone became ill on their trip from Odense. Tante Hansa is seeing to her. Annemette very much wanted to attend a proper Lithasblot festival, so I've become her guide." I touch her arm. "And meeting the crown prince is quite the way to start, isn't it, Annemette?"

She grins. "Yes, it most certainly is."

Nik's color begins to normalize, his training rushing in on a white horse to rescue him. His humor, too. "Well, I am quite the carnival show. Over six feet tall and solid muscle." He raises a wiry arm and pats the bicep. "I have a gaggle of followers trailing after me like ducklings, just so I can open sticky canning jars."

I wink at Annemette. "It's true; I'll have no one else open my troublesome jars." *There*, I'm being a good friend. To them both. I'm okay with this. Really, I am.

Annemette continues to smile but looks a little confused. She knows a lot about this world, but not so much that she might know a canning jar from a regular one. I smile at Nik and do my best to save her. "So, are there jars on the agenda at the moment, Crown Prince Niklas, or shall we go gawk at some livestock?"

"You really don't have to call me Crown Prince Niklas—just Nik," he says, eyes on Annemette. "Evie's just joking. I don't care much for titles." He touches his crown and then blushes again. "Crowns, either . . ."

Annemette nods. "What do you care for?"

"Music, mostly."

"I love to sing." I swallow as she says this, my eyes unable to see anything other than the friend she insists she's not. The girl who had the voice of an angel—ask anyone in Havnestad.

But rather than looking heartsick, Nik begins to blush again. A sheepish smile spreads across his face. "Then I shall use my princely power to borrow an instrument later and accompany you."

My stomach churns. This is perfect. Just perfect.

We stroll down the steps and into the garden. I see him duck away for a moment and pluck a pink tulip from the end of the row, where the queen won't notice it. Annemette dips down to smell her favorites.

I step away and watch as he strides up to her lowered form, flower behind his back. When she stands and turns, he pulls the pink tulip from where it's hidden and lowers into a slight, princely bow.

Annemette's mouth drops open into a wide smile and her eyes snap to his.

"Really? I can have it?"

"What good is being a prince if I can't pluck a tulip from my own garden?"

"Oh, thank you! This one is my favorite."

"You are most welcome, Annemette." Her fingers snatch it away, and she lifts it to her nose, inhaling deeply.

When her eyes open, I catch them and smile. "To the festival, shall we?"

11

Nik chokes down what must be his tenth spandauer, the flaky sweet pastry sticking to his lips. As we walk around the festival, Nik is stopped at practically every turn to taste each table's offerings. Whether it's cheeses both old and stinky, berries and stone fruit from the valley orchards, crusty breads of rye and barley, split-pea delicacies attempting to rival Hansa's famous soup, or the tables and tables of desserts, Nik is required to try them all. He assures the vendors that whatever he's just shoved down his gullet is the best in all of Havnestad, possibly in all of the Øresund Kingdoms.

"Save me, Evie," he grumbles after his last bite.

Why don't you ask her? I want to say as Annemette walks next to me, but instead I hand him my mother's handkerchief. "Take small bites and then use this."

My mood hasn't much improved, though I'm trying.

It helps that Annemette's porcelain face has gone gray, the seafood our town is known for churning her stomach. We pass by tables selling pitch-black whale meat and pale-pink blubber, lobster bright red and still warm from boiling, soft-fleshed crab, salty salmon roe, even slices of slow-roasted eel.

At the next table, Annemette grabs my hand and leans into my ear. "Why do you kill all the sea life if the other options are so vast?"

I shrug. "It's our way of life. Havnestad lives and dies by its nets and harpoons." I suppose I should be sympathetic, but it's hot, and all this stopping and going has made me even sourer.

Her brow furrows. "But there is so much else to eat."

She leans in, her whisper growing softer as Nik tries to shake off yet another local culinary wizard. "My father always tells us to stay far from the surface, scares us with tales of our kind being split in two by harpoons, talks about humans as the scourge of the seas, always hunting and killing. But this . . ."

"It's the way it is, Annemette," I say as gently as I would to a child. In some ways that is what she is, even if she's my age. The time she's been in my world can easily be measured in hours. "We are all surviving as best we can. We don't mean harm to the sea life, or the pig, or anything else."

"I was unprepared."

"I was unprepared to meet a mermaid today," I whisper, my words just an inch from her ear. "But I did."

She laughs into the falling night. Nik glances over at us, and I raise a brow at him and purse my lips. He grins at Annemette but then catches my eye again and I know he suspects I'm feeding her girl talk. And I'll just let him go ahead and think that.

Nik tears himself away from the latest onslaught, a plate thrust into his hand, fried torsk dripping with fresh fat, heat rising from its body, head still on, beady little fish eyes staring vacantly into space.

"Fru Ulla insists this is the best torsk in all of Havnestad—possibly all of Denmark, to hear her tell it. If you seek a true Lithasblot experience, Annemette, this is where to start."

I touch the plate and press it toward his chest, where it is safely out of the way. "She doesn't eat fish."

Nik laughs. "Who doesn't eat fish? We're Danes—"

"Allergy," I say. "If she has fish, she'll blow up like one of those French flying balloons."

"It is terrible," Annemette says, coming to life and puffing out her cheeks.

The questions die on Nik's lips. Without hesitation, he drops the plate into the open hands of a chubby little boy, who grins wide-eyed and then hurries after his family. "Then it will be my sworn duty to protect you from Havnestad's affinity for sea life."

Annemette's eyes skip to mine and then back to Nik's in one swift motion. "The brave crown prince you are, indeed."

~

Long after the fire has died down and the largest bull from Aleksander Jessen's farm has been crowned this year's winner, Nik, Annemette, and I sit on the end of the royal dock, eyes on the ocean and music in the air.

Nik plays a basic rhythm on the guitaren and Annemette chooses the words—picking old sailors' songs that they apparently know under the sea as well as we do on land. This one is their play on "Come, All Ye Sailors Bold."

"The king trusts to his sailors bold, and we shall find them as of old—for father, mother, sisters, wives, we're ready now to risk our lives . . ."

I sit beside them with my eyes on the waves, surprisingly enjoying the clear quality of Annemette's voice. It's as beautiful as Anna's ever was, rich and high, with a lovely air of innocence built into the base of each note.

"For Danish girls with eyes so blue, we'll do all that sailors do. And Dannébrog upon our masts, shall float as long as this world lasts . . ."

They are sitting so close together that the fold of her skirt is touching his trousers. Neither seems to mind, and if anything, they drift closer as the minutes pass. I am on

Nik's other side, and with each song, laugh, and snippet of conversation, the gap of roughhewn dock grows between us.

While I'm glad that Nik is happy and that Annemette seems to have found what she was looking for, I can't shake this gray cloud of self-pity, engulfing me like a fog descending on the harbor. It was so easy for Annemette to make that connection with Nik, and no one thought anything of it. There were smiles all around as they walked arm in arm, each townsperson remarking on her beauty, how nice they looked together. I stalked beside them. The chaperone.

I know in this moment that I will never find what they have if I stay in Havnestad. I merely speak to anyone outside my station and there are calls to lock me up in the brig. I wish Iker were here, but it's clear that even if he is by my side, it'll always just be a childhood fantasy. He may not care what the others think when he's with me, but when it comes down to it, he'll marry a highborn daughter, and that will be that. I will be alone again.

If only Anna were here. The true Anna. Maybe things would be different.

The tune comes to a natural end, Nik and Annemette falling into each other in a fit of laughter.

"You have the most lovely voice, Mette," he says, using a shortened version of her name I didn't know she preferred. I wonder when she told him to call her that. Or maybe he just did it, feeling an instant familiarity with her that I don't have.

"Much obliged, Nik." She bends at the waist. A sitting curtsy. That's a new one.

"We must do this again tomorrow, Mette. Please tell me you will be here tomorrow."

"Yes, yes, of course I will be." Annemette's face beams in the moonlight.

"Excellent. Shall I send a coach round to your room in the morning? Where are you staying?"

"With me," I say, the lie we planned ready. "Her chaperone is quite ill."

Nik's brows furrow with concern, or maybe it's doubt. He grows quiet for a moment, and I'd wish he'd speak.

"But then Mette might grow ill," he says finally, and I release the breath I didn't know I was holding. "And you too, Evie. You both can stay at the palace. I insist." He turns to me, grin in place, though my face must reflect sheer shock. We're best friends, but the line in the sand between us has always been the palace. I've never stayed there—Queen Charlotte even sent me home the night he nearly drowned. "I'll message Hansa and have your trunks brought round."

No. That won't work. Because then he'll know Annemette has no trunk—she has nothing but the clothes on her back. "No worries, I'll get them!" I blurt. "Hansa is too busy to pack her things."

Nik nods, having gotten what he wanted, the trunks a mere formality.

Annemette grasps my hands and looks me in the eye. "Thank you," she says. There's a sincerity in her voice, tinged with desperation that I haven't heard since she first asked if Nik was alive.

Right. She saved him, and she came here to see him. She had her reasons.

I could kick myself for being so petulant and bitter all night, even if only I noticed. But at least I, too, have achieved my aim. Repaying her good deed with their introduction. And it seems to be worth a lot to her. To both of them. Yet still my stomach flutters, the dock moving as if I'm adrift past the strait, alone on the open sea.

12

I DON'T WANT QUESTIONS. I JUST WANT TO GET UP TO the castle before the queen finds out about Nik's invitation. Our lie about Annemette's noble heritage passed Nik's scrutiny, but he wanted to believe us. His mother, well, I wouldn't put it past her to know the name of every noble this side of Prussia.

At the cottage, I blow through the entryway like I'll hurtle through the back window, through the trees, and off the cliff, but at the last moment, I veer down the hall and into my bedroom.

My grand entry does not escape Tante Hansa, despite the fact that she was surely deep in her thoughts as she distilled octopus ink by candlelight.

"Was that a tempest or my sister's child bursting through the house?" she asks, coming down the hall.

I ignore her, shutting my door before plowing through

my chest of drawers for all the proper pieces of a wardrobe—stays, undergarments, stockings, boots, dress. I shove in the latest book of magic I stole from Hansa's library—*Myths of Maritime*—too. There might be something in there about mermaids that would be worth a look.

Within a minute, Hansa opens the door. Immediately, her arms cross and her brows pull together. "You aren't going to smuggle your entire closet out in that trunk, my dear."

"Who said I was smuggling it?"

Tante Hansa takes a step forward, lips drawn into a perturbed line.

"The bloomers poking out the front."

Sure enough, the ruched ankle of an undergarment is sticking out of my trunk like a dead man's tongue.

Hansa tilts her head a bit, one brow now impossibly raised. "Are you going to tell me why you are rushing in and out of here with enough clothes for an entire week at sea? It wouldn't have to do with your new friend, would it?"

The thought skips to the front of my mind to tell her. If anyone would believe that Annemette is a mermaid, it would be Tante Hansa. But I can't tell.

"Well, child? Have you formed the perfect bluff in your pretty little head? You've had more than enough time."

"It's not a bluff. Nik's asked me to stay at the castle—Annemette, too."

That earns me an ancient Hansa chuckle. "His festival

duties have the boy in such a tizzy that he needs to sleep with moral support down the hall, does he?"

"Something like that," I say, though I know Tante Hansa isn't buying it.

The brow arches higher. "Are you certain that cad from Rigeby Bay hasn't arrived with promises on his lips and a night's lodging at the castle?"

Heat creeps up my cheeks.

In my dreams.

"Iker still hasn't arrived." *I'm not sure he will at all*, I add in my thoughts, but I manage to keep my features plain despite the pang I feel in my chest. "And Nik has requested my—our—presence tonight in his stead."

"Oh, he's *requested*, now, has he?" Tante Hansa peers down her long nose like a blue heron. "So princely after one canned speech that he's now *requesting* the presence of his little fish-rat friend?"

"You know Nik's not like that. Besides, *you* come when you're called—'Healer of Kings,' is it?"

"Don't make this about me, child. I know what *I'm* doing." She laughs again as I lug the chest toward the door. Annemette will be nearly finished with the grand tour by now. If Nik's been ratted out by a member of the staff, the queen won't go to bed without addressing him.

"Are you finished with me?" I take a step toward the door she's blocking.

"No, I'm not finished with you." She crosses her arms

for a moment, looking stern, but then backs away from the door, leaving a sliver for escape. "But you are just as stubborn as your mother, and if you fight me as long as she would have, I'll be in this doorway until dawn."

I take another step toward her and lean in as much as my belongings will allow, planting a kiss on her papery cheek.

"Good night, Tante Hansa."

I stride past her, past her smelly inks, and out the door. I'm not one step beyond the threshold when I hear her call, "Don't grant all the prince's requests, darling girl. Men are always asking for more than they should."

Though I'm not with Father on one of his fish deliveries, it seems too strange to walk through the main entrance of Øldenburg Castle. There are some things that are just not for me as a commoner. Malvina Christensen and her ilk might think I don't know my place, but I do. It's evident every day.

I'm angling through the tulip garden, the trunk dragging along at my feet, when I hear my name.

It's nearly midnight, but Queen Charlotte looks just as regal as ever, still in the full evening gown she wore at the festival, crown nestled in her perfectly styled hair. I catch Nik approaching behind her.

"Evelyn," says the queen, the distaste in her voice not hard to miss. "Niklas told me you'd be joining us." She eyes her son, and I know he had to fight for me to stay. "It was gracious of Friherrinde Annemette to suggest you stay in the same room."

"She's very gracious indeed, as are you for having us, Your Highness," I say. The queen nods as if I've passed a test—I know how she prefers to be praised.

"My pleasure," she says, and steps away. But then she pauses and turns. "Please stay within this wing."

I nod. Yes, I know my place.

Once the queen is gone, Nik rushes to my side.

"Let me help you."

"I've got it." But just as I say it, he's snuck a hand on either handle and hoisted the thing to his chest, as effortless as can be.

"You shouldn't. You're still recovering!"

"I'm fine. It's practice for the rock carry—I have to defend my title."

"Since when do you care about winning so much?" I goad him so we don't have to talk about his mother.

"Turns out a taste of victory is all I needed to care."

"Or the need to impress a girl. Speaking of . . . where is she?"

Nik takes a step toward the door, and I rush ahead of him to open it. "Mette was so enamored with her room; it was so sweet, I didn't want to disturb her. Besides, Mother . . ."

His voice trails off as a guard comes to help, taking the

trunk from Nik's hands. Nik grabs the edge of the door above my head, relieving me of my duty. For a moment, I stand there trying to read his face, because it's not as clear and open as I'm used to seeing. His emotions are all muddled, like Hansa's magical ink swirling across the surface of water.

Nik looks over at the guard. "Take her trunk to the Baroque Room, please, Oleg."

Oleg nods, and Nik pulls me back outside and onto the steps. He sits down on the top step, and I follow. His shoulder nestles next to mine and his voice is low.

"Apparently coming of age means more than giving speeches," he says without preamble, his eyes on his hands.

My heart starts pounding and my hand finds his shoulder. "Nik . . ."

"Mother is pleased because Annemette is the first of her 'girls' to arrive."

My mouth goes dry. I should've seen this coming—among so many other things these past few days. Annemette must have passed the queen's scrutiny, my aid unneeded.

"She had her ladies send letters to every high house in Denmark, inviting every princess, komtesse, and friherrinde to the Lithasblot Ball and God knows what else. Now that I'm sixteen, I should be courting, but Mother thought it wise to bring the girls to me."

"Oh, Nik—" I start, but then he stares up at me, and

the look in his eyes makes my throat catch.

"Lured them in with Iker's presence, too . . ."

Of course: the playboy prince, two years older, with brave tales of the sea. I bet every last girl with a title is on a steamer right now.

"Two princes for the price of one—we're the market special," he says. "No wonder Iker's still at sea."

He's careful to smile at his joke—he's trying to save my feelings. But I can't grin back, not even a little bit. I want so badly to turn to stone like the statues in his mother's garden. There must be a spell for that, no? At least then I wouldn't have this rot of disappointment creeping up inside me. It turns out knowing better doesn't always help. It makes it worse.

It's funny, though—maybe *funny* isn't the right word, but Nik and I are both trapped. I'll forever be the fisherman's daughter, caught in a web of whispers and lies spread by those too scared to open their eyes and see beyond what's in front of their faces. And Nik—he'll be locked in by royal traditions, forced into a loveless match with someone only out for the crown. Nik will always be in the shadow of the castle. And nothing I can do will save him from that.

Except, if the queen already believes Annemette's story, surely Annemette is better than these komtesses flocking to our shores. She does seem to make Nik happy. I know it's only been a day, but even I'll admit that I've never seen Nik smile as much as he has with her. It's not everything, but it's a start. And she's not after his crown. That I know. She genuinely cares. She *saved* him. Besides, it might serve us all well to finally have some magic in the palace, to perhaps bring an end to Queen Charlotte's brutal warnings and doll burnings. Maybe as a trusted friend to both the crown prince *and* princess, I wouldn't be relegated to the kitchen door. My family would not have to live in secret. If Annemette makes Nik truly happy, we can both be free. *Stop, Evie. You're getting ahead of yourself.* But a smile pulls on my lips all the same.

"Let's go inside," I say to him. "Everything will be okay. Annemette is waiting."

I WAKE IN THE BLUE LIGHT OF THE MORNING AND SIT straight up. I thought a night in the royal wing, on the most comfortable mattress I've ever slept on, would do me well, but it hasn't. I'm anxious.

I've smuggled a mermaid into the palace, for Urda's sake!

In the bed across the room, Annemette sleeps, a ruffle of blond waves piled about her face. One foot has escaped the bedspread, five toes stretching lazily toward the ceiling.

It's easy to forget that she's never slept in a bed before. I throw off the covers and tiptoe to my trunk, left by Oleg next to the double-sided wardrobe. And there, beneath my underthings, is the book I threw in at the last minute. Though the name isn't too suspect—*Myths of Maritime*— I suppose it's lucky we arrived so late in the evening that the maid couldn't unpack the trunk. I should've been more careful, though.

I crawl onto the plush red window seat and hold the book up to the new day's light, thumbing through the pages for anything about mermaids. I know all the lore from childhood, of course. I can still hear Tante Hansa's voice reciting the tales over the campfire.

Mermaids call sailors into storms, their siren songs and beauty too difficult to ignore. Probably a myth. Annemette is beautiful, but she didn't force Nik into the sea, and I'd be able to tell if she was using magic on him now. I think.

Then there's *Mermaids can conjure storms with a blink, sacrificing sailors to please the all-powerful sea.* I hope to Urda that this is not true. A shiver runs up my spine as I think of Father and Iker.

But the one that always made me and Anna scream was: *Mermaids steal naughty children and feed them to the sharks for protection.* Ha! I'll let Tante Hansa have that one. It kept me from making lots of unwise choices, though I suppose not nearly enough. If only Anna and I had truly listened.

None of this lore is easing my rattled nerves. The only positive mermaid tale I know is the one I saw with my own eyes: *A kind mermaid may swim you to shore.*

But there has to be more written about mermaids than a few childhood warnings.

After much reading, I finally find a section on

mermaids, following an intensive discussion of the kraken. It doesn't say much—there's just slightly more detail than the descriptions I know by heart. I focus in on one paragraph.

> *Accounts of mermaids at the surface often come with tales of rescue—the saved sailor opening his eyes just as the mermaid dives back into the waves. The maids are always described as staying within the water, unable to leave the sea completely.*

That was exactly how it happened. Maybe there will be more on what happens next. I turn the page, expecting a section on a mermaid's ability to change into human form. But there is nothing. No description, no account, no guesses at all.

I stare at Annemette. She can't be the first mermaid to change into a person. She can't. It just must be so rare there's not an accurate tale to pass on.

Possibly feeling the weight of my eyes on her, Annemette shifts, her arms stretching high above her head. Her eyes blink open and she sees me watching her. I expect her to startle, to forget where she is and what she is, but she doesn't. Instead, she just yawns.

"I could get used to this." She rolls fully toward me. A slim finger points to her calf. "But is it normal that this part just aches? Burns. And my toes are . . . tingly."

"Pins and needles?" I offer.

"More like knives," she replies without hesitation. "But I'll be fine." She pushes herself up a little and yawns again.

I set my book between my nightdress and the windowpane. "Maybe it's a side effect. You know, of your transformation," I say. And now's my chance: "Have other mermaids ever turned into humans before?"

"I'm not the first," she replies. She stands and turns her back to me as she opens the wardrobe, revealing a closetful of dresses.

"Where'd those come from?" I ask, my mouth agape as I walk over to the wardrobe.

"I conjured them last night while you were sleeping."

I want to scold her for doing something so reckless, but they're incredible. Silk day dresses in pink, cerulean, and deep purple, each with little white collars and pearl buttons. I clutch at my necklace and wonder if those pearls pulse like mine. The evening gowns are even grander. Full skirts and long trains, gold embroidery, and even beading. They're going to think she is the wealthiest friherrinde in the whole region.

"Do you like?" she asks. "Hopefully they will do the trick."

I nod eagerly. "What trick?"

"Allowing me to stay," she says, clutching a Havnestad-blue dress with mother-of-pearl inlay. "Don't you want me to stay?"

"Of course I do, Mette," I say, trying out the nickname for the first time. And I realize I mean it. Not only so she can save Nik from his mother's misguided intentions, but to have a friend who knows magic, who knows the real me. I didn't know how much I wanted that until I met her. "How long do you have?" I ask, hoping she'll give me a real answer this time. "I want to help."

"The magic lasts four full days," she replies. "I have three left."

My face falls. "That's it?"

"But three days becomes forever if, before midnight on the final day, my true love has fallen for me, too."

Too.

Nik.

Forever.

"I love him, Evie. I really do." Annemette flops on the bed, no longer the shifty girl holding everything back. More like the girl I used to talk with about boys and gossip in her own grand room. "He's why I came back. I know he can love me. Didn't you see us last night?"

"But what if he doesn't?" I ask. She turns and stares out the window, out at the sea far below.

"What is it?" I come to her and sit on her bed. "Tell me, Mette."

She shakes her head and buries her face in her hands. When she responds, it's as if she's repeating something she read in a book—and maybe she is.

"To come to land in human form a mermaid must complete a magical contract—her life as a mermaid for four days on land." She pauses and shudders, her chest heaving slightly. "She may not return to the sea after those four days, for she can never again be a mermaid."

My stomach practically tumbles to my feet. "Wait . . . you *die*?" What kind of dark magic did she do? Nik is wonderful, amazing, the best guy I know—but to risk her life for someone she barely knows?

She sits up and nods. "I know. It's crazy. But you don't get it. He's what I've been missing. I knew he was mine when he fell into the sea. Into *my* arms. And to be human? Evie, you don't know how lucky you are."

I don't even know what to think. Of course I want her to live, and I want them both to be happy, but how can this work? Falling in love in four days seems . . . unrealistic, to say the least.

I temper my words carefully. "How can you tell when he truly loves you?"

Annemette's face goes dreamy again. "True love's kiss is all I need."

I almost laugh. Now it's unrealistic *and* ridiculous. So much so, I'm completely incredulous. "A kiss, really? Your life for a kiss? That's it? That's some magic."

"It's the feeling in the kiss. I'll know. The magic will know."

I think of Nik on the steps—enchanted, yes, but in

love? No. Not yet, anyway.

I walk back to the window seat. I need space to breathe, to think. If Annemette hadn't risked her life on this, I don't know how I'd feel if Nik really did fall in love in three days. The whole thing just feels wrong—her life depending on Nik somehow awakening powerful magic, simply by having enough love in his heart for a girl he's only just met. One I like, one he likes, one I'm forever grateful to. But I just don't know . . . there has to be another way to keep her alive without forcing Nik to *love* her.

When I look up, Annemette is rushing toward me. She squeezes onto the window seat beside me and takes my hands. The color has drained from her face.

"Evie . . . I'm not encroaching, am I?" Worry furrows her brow. "You were searching for him that night . . . he was waiting for you at the palace last evening. He isn't . . . ? You don't . . . ?"

"I'm not in love with Nik, and he's definitely not in love with me." I've had to say this exact phrase many times, most recently to Malvina. "We're just best friends."

She breathes out a sigh, hands fluttering as she smooths her hair. "You seem so close, and I didn't even question . . . you must think I'm horrible."

"Not at all! Nik and I have been inseparable for years." I struggle to make eye contact here, her closeness again overwhelming. "It's a common mistake."

Relief washes over her, and she sinks back against

the window seat cushions. "Do you have someone, then? Someone who makes your heart beat so hard you think it'll pound itself out?"

Iker's face flashes in my memory, a wide smile reaching the ice of his eyes. I bite my lip. "I do—I did. I don't know." Annemette is staring at me for more, so I reluctantly go on. "You saw him—the other boy on the beach that night." She nods in recognition. "Well, he's Nik's cousin, the crown prince of Rigeby Bay. But it doesn't matter, Mette. He's away at sea, and we have more pressing things to consider. *Three days . . .*"

"Oh, Evie, you're such a good friend," Annemette says, pulling me into an embrace.

Three days to fall in love. Three days to live. Three days until the ball every noble lady in the Øresund Kingdoms will attend. I shake my head. Finding true love is hard enough without the competition.

14

I DON'T KNOW HOW SHE ACTS SO CALM AS WE WALK down to meet Nik for breakfast. It must be the sea in her veins, flowing against the tide no matter what the weather. My entire body might as well be one giant bundle of nerves tied up in a sailor's knot on her behalf, but Annemette walks out onto the sun-drenched balcony off the third-floor ballroom looking as enchanting and confident as anyone could, her blue dress casting her eyes a deep ocean hue and her butter-blond hair shining in the sun.

We blink into the bright light and are met with a spectacular view of the harbor. I know our corner of the sea so well, but it's different from this angle, nearly the whole coast in sight. It's an empowering view, to be able to see all that you rule over. The current is moving faster than usual for this time of year, and I turn my back, not wanting to dredge up old memories.

"Good morning, ladies. Won't you have a seat?" Nik stands and pulls out the chair to his right. "Mette?"

Annemette blushes and takes the coveted place. I push my nerves down and greet him with a wink as he pulls out my chair. It's then that I see he's a bit red himself, that blush from last night back again at the sight of Annemette. Nik, the romantic. A good sign for sure.

True to his word of protecting Annemette from the evils of our seafaring diet, Nik asked the palace kitchens to avoid the traditional breakfast herring and traded up for summer sausage, sweet rolls dripping in fresh butter, and raspberries flush with dew. Served with it is black tea, hot and fragrant.

My stomach growls at the mere vision of all this food. It had been churning all morning, my anxiety getting the better of me. I am starving.

"Goodness, Evie. Do you have a tiger hidden in your bodice?" Nik laughs into the delicate china of his teacup.

"You know me, always smuggling wild animals to breakfast," I joke.

"I'd expect nothing less from your dark magic." Nik laughs again, and he has to put the cup back into the saucer to keep from spilling it over his shirt.

Meanwhile, Annemette can't hide her surprise. She stares at me, confused. After all that fuss I made about how we must keep our magic a secret here, the crown prince, of all people, is laughing over it.

"Nik should know better than to spread dangerous rumors like that." I gently elbow him. This is a game we play, Nik and I. Joking about the "magic" in my family—even if his joke is closer to the truth than he knows. "My tante, Hansa—"

"She turns men to toads and makes a soup out of them," Nik says, brows shooting dramatically under his hair. Annemette laughs, which only encourages him. "It's a great bit of luck you didn't have her pea soup last night."

Annemette's lips drop open.

"It's green for a reason." I wink at her.

Nik and I burst into a fit of laughter, and it feels good to relax. His fingers scramble to touch the bare skin at her wrist. Maybe this will work.

"We kid, Mette," Nik goes on. "Tante Hansa is a marvel of a medicine woman—she's saved my father a few times when our own doctor failed, and I'll never forget it. She'll take great care of your chaperone—but she can't turn men into toads." Annemette nods, a quizzical grin pulling up against her pink cheeks. Nik lowers his voice, conspiracy thick in his tone as he turns his back on me. "Though I wouldn't put it past the old bat to have curbed my cousin's playboy ways so that he might fall for her niece."

I elbow him again, this time quite hard, and both he and Annemette laugh. "If she has that magic, it's certainly gone awry, considering he didn't come for the festival," I say.

"Surely that's Iker's mistake," Nik says, snagging a sweet roll.

"I don't make mistakes, Cousin."

We glance up. Iker is standing in the threshold, his back propped casually against the doorframe. His skin is tan from days spent on deck in the high sun, making his hair seem more bleached than usual. He absentmindedly rubs at the scruff blurring the cut of his strong jaw, something I'm sure Queen Charlotte will insist he shave. I hope he declines.

My heart is beating in my throat as he looks over at me and our eyes meet. He grins.

Don't smile. Don't get up. He promised *he'd return days ago. Stay strong.*

I cave. A small smile creeps up on my lips and, in turn, his grin blooms larger. He strides over, and suddenly I'm afraid he's going to kiss me right there in front of everyone. In front of Nik. He pauses before me and bends down, his fingers grazing my chin as his face moves closer to mine.

Please don't.

Gods, I wish he would.

His lips land softly on my forehead. I breathe out a sigh, whether it's relief or disappointment, I don't know.

"Hello, Evelyn," he says, standing upright again. "I'm sorry I'm late."

Before I can say anything, he strides over to Nik, stealing the sweet roll straight out of his fingertips. "Hello,

Cousin. Glad to see you're looking so well," he says, then takes a bite of the roll.

Nik stands, and the two embrace. "Mother has been in a royal tizzy over your tardiness—I hope you found that king whale you were looking for."

"I wish," Iker replies, frustration echoing in his voice. It's unlike him not to get what he wants. "We chased him past the tip of the Jutland, but he's a slippery bastard."

"I suppose that's why he's named 'king,' Cousin."

Iker grins and claps Nik on the shoulder. "We are a slippery lot, aren't we? Always running to and from the call of duty."

"And you are forever running late in both directions."

"Nothing that can't be fixed with a grand entrance and a daring story."

I raise a brow. "That certainly is your life's motto." The words come out harder than I'd planned, and his smile stiffens in answer.

"I'd say it's worked well for me so far."

"You would," Nik says. He's now standing next to Annemette's chair, his hand grazing her shoulder. "But let it be, Cousin. I'd like you to meet Friherrinde Annemette."

Annemette stands and steps toward Iker. She holds out her hand like she's done this hundreds of times before. He takes her fingers in his and kisses them. "Lovely to meet you, Annemette. I daresay I would've remembered such a gorgeous girl from my travels in the Øresund. Tell me, where did you wash up from?"

My heart in my throat, I meet Annemette's eyes. He's just being kind, I know he is, but still.

"Odense," she says, clearly comfortable despite my heart flaring out my nostrils. "Evie and I met yesterday, and she agreed to show me around. Nik was game enough to join us."

"Who wouldn't be?" he replies. "I'd say yes in an instant." Iker smiles at her, but there's suspicion in his eyes. It's just a flash, but it's there—he doesn't even try to hide it. Nik and I both notice it before his cultivated manners return and he bows at Annemette. "I've traveled everywhere, and there are no two prettier girls in all the world than on this balcony."

Both Annemette and I immediately flush scarlet, the compliment the perfect Iker level of grandness. And, when I glance over, Nik is fiercely blushing too—his eyes have never left Annemette.

Iker's attention spins across the three of us.

"What?" I ask.

Then he shakes his head. "The lot of you won't survive your youth if you don't learn to take a compliment or ask for what you want."

Iker turns to Nik. "Cousin, clearly you can't keep your eyes off the girl. Why don't you ask the fine friherrinde to accompany you as you explore today's festivities? I'm sure there is plenty to learn about her."

Annemette turns to him, a lock of blond hair twisted around her finger. Nik lets out a nervous laugh.

Iker, not paying attention, goes on. "While you're doing that, Evie and I can walk through the gardens."

"Really?" I say. "Don't you think you should ask me first?"

"Forgive me, Evelyn. Would you do me the honor?"

I should say no. After all, what is the point? In a day's time, he'll be dancing with half the komtesses invited to the ball, one of whom will surely become his bride. But I can't help wanting what I want. I look up at Annemette, whose eyes are urging me to go. She needs this time too. Two magical creatures and two princes. I want to laugh. Maybe it's time I stopped accepting what all of Havnestad has deemed appropriate for a girl like me and started acting like the girl they already think I am.

"It would be my pleasure, Iker," I say, getting up from my chair.

Nik suddenly stands, looking very uncomfortable, ears turning red too. "Iker, I don't think that's a very good idea."

Iker's eyes brighten and then drop into the same suspicious glance he gave Annemette. He reads his cousin's face and posture, clearly trying to discern if this is about him being alone with me or about Nik being alone with Annemette or something else altogether. His words from the ship ring in my ears: *I don't like to step on my cousin's toes.*

"I'm not going to defile the girl, cousin, we're just going to have a kiss and catch up." Nik practically scoffs, but Iker just smiles. "Nothing we haven't done before."

Nik's eyes shoot to mine, and I know he knows. It doesn't take much for him to picture all of it—to picture me kissing Iker like all the other girls he leaves in his wake.

I glance down—I wish it wasn't like this. I just can't take Nik looking so hurt.

Iker makes it a point to raise his brows at Annemette, everything in the move suggesting Nik take his girl and be fine with it. A hope I have as well. The girl only has three days. Iker's arm slinks from my waist and hooks about my elbow. He leads me toward the door.

"Follow my lead, Cousin, but don't follow my footsteps."

The late morning light is blinding when we step out of the shadow of the castle and into the queen's tulip garden. We blink ourselves down the stone path, stumbling a bit until our eyes adjust, arms and legs momentarily touching—whether by accident or on purpose, only Urda knows.

It's sinking in. Iker is here.

He came back. And he immediately wanted to be with me.

All the disappointment and fears about what was keeping him seem to drain from my body. I try to push thoughts of Annemette to the side, too. *Not everyone is your responsibility, Evie*—Tante Hansa has told me this a thousand times. Annemette is alone with her prince, and I'm with mine.

After years of daydreams, my childhood fantasy is somehow now my reality: holding hands in a garden with Iker. Despite my status. Despite his. Despite the lives that are meant for us. A flash of heat runs up my neck, and my cheeks flush with embarrassment. Iker can never know how often I've thought of this.

But is this real? Am I stuck in dream? Or have I lost my mind completely, and Annemette is a figment of my imagination? Iker, too?

I wouldn't think him real at all if his arm weren't still slung about my waist, drawing me toward him, the two of us walking toward a stone bench beneath a shady oak.

Stop questioning, Evie.

Enjoy the spell while it lasts.

He smells of the sea. Of escape. And I want to be there with him, watching his skin go pink and then brown, whales in our sights and free wind in our hair. He turns to me, both hands about my waist now, face angled down toward mine. A smile curves at his lips as he reads my eyes.

"You were worried I wouldn't come," he says, and brushes a curl from my cheek.

I don't deny it.

"I ran into a problem of sorts," he says, eyes in the

middle distance, voice softening. "I lost one of my men. The sea snatched him overboard in broad daylight after we docked in Kalø. Spent the rest of the day and much of the next searching."

My breath catches. It's awful, though not unexpected on a whaling expedition. The resolute set to Iker's jaw mirrors that—disappointment but also acceptance. But then his gaze brightens and he goes on. "Eventually, we found him, floating unconscious between two rocks. Can you believe it? Barely breathing and beaten up, but alive. It was so strange, finding something you doubted could be possible."

A teasing note then enters his voice. "Just like you shouldn't have doubted me."

"I didn't doubt you. I doubted my expectations."

Iker raises a brow and his eyes are on my mouth. "And what were your expectations?"

"That you wanted to be here as much as I wanted you to be here."

At this, he draws me in until his chest touches my bodice and I can feel his legs through the layers of my dress.

"Don't doubt this."

He presses his mouth to mine, stealing my breath. He is gentle in that first moment, but then sweeps us down onto the bench.

The scent of salt and limes swirls about me as my heart

begins to pound hard enough that I'm sure he can feel it through my bodice and his shirt.

His hands move to my face, thumbs sweeping the curve of my jaw. He holds me there for a second before gently pulling away.

"Proof enough, Evelyn."

He says it as a statement, not a question, a sly little grin returning.

I purse my lips in thought. "Honestly, I'm not sure I've had a large enough sampling to be certain."

Iker's face breaks that sly little grin into something toothy and wolfish.

"I'm free for sampling all afternoon. Nothing princely planned until supper." He forces his features into serious composure. "Will that be enough time, my lady?"

I lean in and dust a quick kiss onto his lips. "It's certainly a start."

FOUR YEARS BEFORE

The visitor stood on the dock, parents fussing behind him, weary from travel, though the journey hadn't been far. Just across the Øresund Strait—a trip he could make with his eyes shut and in his own boat, if given the chance.

And he was planning to take that chance within the year, permission or not.

The day was clear, sun beating down, drying the wooden planks of the dock faster than the sea could make its mark, the waves angry the entire way from Rigeby Bay.

Footmen filed down from the castle, whisking away the visitor's parents, trunks, and duties, leaving him alone with the beach and his thoughts. At fourteen, those thoughts were mostly of girls.

Brunettes.

Blondes.

Redheads.

All of them swirling in his head despite what he knew to be true about his station—his mother and her metaphors constantly in his ear.

"Tulips wilt no matter their beauty; jewels of the crown shine forever."

"Blood lasts longer than a whim."

"The royal vase has room for but one flower, no matter the harvest."

His feet led him to the sand, eyes snagging on two girls prancing along the beach, slim forms moving in time with a song that barely reached his ears.

A few yards more and the girls stopped, eyes and fingers pointed toward a sandbar, belly up in the swirling waters. That's when he recognized them—two girls from the village, best friends always up for an adventure, just like he was, though he got the feeling the blonde was rather difficult to impress. Trailing behind them was a boy, his cousin. Another prince.

Then the girls began to remove their dresses, petticoats suddenly catching the sun's rays in all their angelic white.

He couldn't look away.

Not when they folded their dresses and laid them on the sand. Not when they sprinted into the waves. Not when he realized the current was as strong as it'd been in the strait, though he was too distracted by daydreams of their petticoats to warn them.

It was only moments later, when the prince dove in behind them, that the visitor was rudely awakened.

The visitor's feet told him to run. To help. Neither girl had surfaced—it had been too long. He took five steps and halted. His father in his ear this time, another Øldenburg ruler in a land full of them.

"Do not be a hero, Iker; you are already a prince."

His own kingdom needed him alive. If something were to

128—

happen to him, the future of his home and his family would be in danger. Yet still, another voice, his own, knocked around in his ears.

"But Nik . . ."

His cousin had grown tall of late, at least six feet already, but he'd seen tulips thicker than his arms, harpoons wider than his legs. The visitor was the same height but built with all the vigor of the Vikings. He was strong. He could help.

Still, he stayed rooted to the spot. Holding his breath as his cousin finally surfaced, a black-haired rag doll drooping in his arms. Strong and steady, Nik swam for the beach.

As the two landed in the sand, the visitor breathed again, watching in awe as the boy of twelve did all the right things to expel water from her lungs. Citizens gathered around their prince now, Lithasblot preparations halted, all of them getting a good look at the latest near tragedy in a history full of them, the sea well fed in the whale-wild Øresund Strait.

All the relief he'd felt fled the second his cousin began barking orders to the men standing around, their inaction frustrating him. The men finally dove into the water, but Iker knew his cousin. Knew his heart. Knew what he would do. He was going back too.

These girls had been a part of him for years, one the left arm, one the right. They were both beauties—even Nik had admitted it during his last visit. The raven-haired girl was more his cousin's style, but the visitor knew the blonde was the one who saw Nik in that way—it was obvious.

The visitor watched the prince dive back into the waves, and then he ran, all the strength of his Viking blood carrying him as he tore across the sand.

He yelled at the men swimming back to shore empty-handed, soggy from their attempts at finding the girl. "You there, men, don't leave your crown prince to do the dirty work alone. Back in the water with you—your hope does not fade until Prince Niklas's does."

Immediately, the men turned for the waves, diving in, hope the last thing set in their features. Every cut of jaw locked with the knowledge that this was just how things went in the Øresund Kingdoms. The sea took as much as she gave.

But he wanted them there in case Nik faltered. These men were insurance for the prince. Their shared family could not suffer this blow, no matter how heroic.

"Evelyn, are you all right?" He crashed to her side, palms cupping her elegant shoulders.

"Iker?" She blinked at him as if he were a ghost, those midnight eyes of hers dark with terror. "Anna. Nik—"

"I know," he said in his best prince voice, the one he'd been perfecting in front of the looking glass when stranded in the castle, his heart yearning for the sea.

Iker turned back to Evelyn. Tears welled in her eyes, gratitude in the curve of her lips. He knew enough about the girl to know how she felt about him, how she wanted to kiss him right there. He knew enough about her class—the fishermen, the worker bees—to know that she wouldn't.

Instead, her fingers tightened on his forearm as if she were still fodder for the undertow and he'd rescued her himself.

"It'd kill me to lose either of them."

She glanced down at her hands as if the answer were there, hidden in the web of lines—heart, life, and fate.

"There is so much I wish I could do," she said, her voice still so weak.

That was it. There was so much he could do. Nik was his cousin, true, but he had always felt like a brother. And no matter the correct name for their relationship, he was family. And family did what had to be done.

Iker squeezed Evelyn's shoulders for the barest of moments, and then he was gone, yanking off his boots as he ran toward the foaming undertow.

15

"OH, EVIE, IT WAS WONDERFUL," ANNEMETTE SAYS after half falling into the window seat in our room. Her blond waves are as wild as the tide in a storm, spilling at all angles around her shoulders. The cream of her face is flushed with pure joy, deep-blue eyes sparkling.

I'm so happy to see her like this. Iker and I spent the afternoon swirled together in a rush of touches and sweet words, two pebbles in a whirlpool, and I can only hope that she and Nik did as well.

"*Nik* is wonderful," I confirm, but she grabs my hand.

"More wonderful than I could have ever dreamed, but so are you. There is no way I would have had the day I just had without you." Her eyes swell, the skin there growing pink.

I squeeze her fingers. "It's nothing," I say, though I can't imagine the last few hours with Iker would've happened without her either. I can't picture him arriving at the castle and then hiking into its shadow to find me in the tiny house at the end of the lane. It's difficult to imagine grand Iker confined by a home smaller than this entire palace bedroom—even when he's on his little schooner, his personality still has room to burst into the open air of the sea.

"Do you think he's falling in love?" I ask as I change dresses for tonight's Lithasblot festivities.

"I think so," she says. "I hope. More time would help." She smiles weakly.

"The sooner we get going, the more you'll have. Almost ready?"

She fastens up the last few pearl buttons on her pink silk gown. "Almost," she says and then looks at my worn navy dress. "Is that what you're wearing?"

I nod. I could probably conjure up a range of dresses too if I put my mind to it, but that would really send the town chirping. Everyone knows what's in my wardrobe.

"No, no. Wear *this*," she insists, and hands me a deep purple gown embroidered with golden tulips. "I made it for you. Iker will love it."

I take the dress, running the lush silk between my fingers. "Thank you," I say. "It's beautiful, but I couldn't. Can you imagine everyone's faces? Me in *this*? What will the townspeople say?"

"Maybe something nice, for once," Annemette replies with a smirk.

I know she's wrong, but I can barely take my eyes off the dress. It's stunning, the workmanship so intricate, it truly could only have been achieved with a spell. And then it hits me. *We have magic.* "Annemette . . ."

"Yes?" she says, weaving her golden strands into an ornate bun.

"Can't you use your magic . . . on Nik? I mean, only if things don't go as planned. He can love you; I can see it. It's just . . . *three* days—now almost two—there's no t—"

"No," she says, sticking the last pin in her hair. "It has to be real when the clock strikes midnight after the ball. That's it. Magic can masquerade as love, but none has ever satisfied Urda before. These little things, dresses and such, are as far as I'll go. He has to love me as me. No tricks. Promise me you won't do anything to interfere, Evie."

I nod, my lips closed tight. Of course she's right. I don't want to manipulate Nik's feelings either, but the consequences are just so steep.

I step into her gown, the cool fabric sliding over my skin, its shape fitting me perfectly. I barely recognize myself as I stare in the mirror, looking so much like one of the nobles. Perhaps a costume is all I ever needed.

"You look like a princess," Annemette says, giving me a kiss on the cheek. "Let's go. Our princes await."

I grab her hand, and we walk down through the palace and out the gates. This night, the third night, is what everyone always mentions when Lithasblot comes up.

When it is perfectly normal, possibly even a compliment, to toss a slice of rye or a dense roll at your neighbor.

Predictably, Malvina Christensen lives for this night. It gives her a chance to show off, and gods know she would never shy away from that. Not one for needlepoint or whatever komtesses are supposed to learn, Malvina chose to take up baking instead, always underfoot of her cook as a girl. I'll admit, she became rather good, that blue monstrosity aside, though I'll take partial responsibility for its demise. She's eager to tell anyone questioning her that baking is a hobby, even though it's beneath her, an activity more befitting someone like me. "If you feed a man right, he'll be true to you for life," I've heard her say many times. It's strange, she so wants me out of her way, too crude for her class, and yet here she is parading her lowbrow achievements. I guess when you have power, you can be whoever you want.

Though the sun has yet to set and the townspeople are still wandering the offering tables in search of their suppers, Malvina has snagged herself a prominent spot by the bonfire. Around her is a literal sea of treats—petits fours, scones à la Brighton, out-of-season fried aebleskiver, and crusty rolls of rye and soft rolls of sweet Russian wheat, both in the shape of the sun wheel. There's a massive blueberry pie as well, juices glistening from under a golden lattice crust.

"Malvina, my, you've outdone yourself yet again," Nik

says with a royal smile as we come upon her.

The girl beams at him. "Why thank you, Nik. It would be an honor if you enjoyed something before the throwing begins."

Nik waves her off. "That's not—"

"I insist. Please take something, there is more than enough here for Urda."

Training and practice with Malvina's forcibly charitable nature are enough to keep Nik from fighting her one word more. "If that is the case, then yes. Something small would be greatly appreciated."

Her still-beaming smile grows larger as she dips to the blanket and chooses a petit four, done in perfect French style. "There's plenty for your friends, too," she adds as an afterthought.

I'm shocked. Malvina has never offered me anything, and then I realize, she may not recognize me. It's the dress. It must be sewn with the most powerful sorcery to deceive a shark like Malvina.

"How kind of you," I say, taking a scone and watching her pewter eyes for recognition. And then there it is, a slight snarl.

"Oh, Evie," she says. "My, that's quite a dress. Where did you—"

"It was a gift. From me, Friherrinde Annemette," Mette interrupts while plucking a sweet roll. "For being a good friend and the most gracious host." And then she does the unthinkable—she links her arms right through mine and Nik's, pulling us close on either side.

Malvina smiles so tightly I can see the veins in her neck. "Well, from a komtesse to a friherrinde, a word of advice. If you treat your help to such finery, they'll get used to it."

"I hope so," says Annemette. "I have plenty more where that came from. Thank you for the sweets."

And then we walk away. Just like that. Nik seems a little stunned, ever the proper prince, but even he can't help but laugh. "You really do look lovely, Evie."

"Seconded," Iker says, grabbing my hand.

I thank them both for probably the third time that night, and then we walk the boys to the platform for tonight's celebration of the grain crop. Annemette and I take our seats in the little white wooden chairs reserved for the nobility—another new view for me, having only sat on the sand before. As the sky darkens, Nik begins to speak, but I can't focus, my mind on so many things. The Lithasblot festival was always something I knew so well, every year the same, and for a time, I didn't go at all.

The Lithasblot after Anna drowned, I never left the house. Nik, Tante Hansa, and Father all tried to draw me from my bed, sure that a measure of festival fun would go a long way toward cheering me up.

But song and dance cannot close a wound like that. More like it pours salt on it—watching other people sing and dance like nothing had happened, all the while blistered with grief.

I didn't go. Not that year nor the next.

I'd tried to spend the time reading Tante Hansa's spell books—the only thing that'd kept me sane in those days—but even that took too much effort. All the strength I had went to shutting out laughter and song.

It was only last year that I agreed to go with Nik again.

He'd lost his friend too but had to make a show of being at the festival immediately—the day of her death—duty and title forcing him to walk around in his nice clothes and accept the people's offerings to Urda. He didn't have to speak as he does yet again tonight, but it was still painful enough just to stand up in front of everyone while so broken.

We are far from that now—not healed, of course, but with just two days left, this festival has felt like the last one we attended when Anna was alive. Iker came that year, arriving with his parents from Rigeby Bay, fourteen and suddenly very tall. Anna and I mooned over him every night, whispering about his eyes and laughing while huddled up in her mansion bedroom. It would be a year before she told me that she actually preferred Nik to Iker and my mind filled of dreams of us as twin queens, the friherrinde-to-princess and the pauper-to-princess loves of Øldenburg kings on both sides of the Øresund Strait.

Of course, Annemette is not Anna, but I can't shake

the feeling that this is what we could have had. I glance over at Annemette as she watches Nik speak on the platform in front of the bonfire. Rosebud lips slightly parted, she follows his words with the precision of a predator, so intent on remembering everything he says. I never saw Anna look at Nik like Annemette does, but eleven-year-old girls can hide their feelings as much as any of us.

Suddenly, Annemette's lips pull up in a smile, eyes sharpening to something hard, and I follow her gaze up to Nik. He's watching her back, but then looks to me, doing his best to concentrate on the words. Still, his ears begin to blush. Then Iker hands Nik the ceremonial first loaf of bread—large as a cannonball, crafted of dark rye, and braided in the shape of the sun wheel. Nik holds the loaf above his head.

"And so, let us give thanks to Urda with the staff of life—bread. Let us share our gifts of grain with our neighbors. Let no person in need go without. Let the loaves fly to them with the gentlest of care, a blessing from Urda by way of a neighbor's hand."

Nik tears a hunk of bread off the loaf and hands it to King Asger. Another piece goes to Queen Charlotte, and a third to Iker, whose parents stayed home this year. Together, the royal family lines up in front of the fire, bread in hand.

Nik lifts his piece above his crowned head.

"Let the sharing begin."

With that, all four of them toss the bread in the direction of the crowd. Nik's lands gently in Annemette's lap. She laughs, and I'm so busy laughing too that I'm not paying attention when a crusty hunk of rye thwacks me square in the chest, bouncing off my bodice and into my lap. I glance up and see Iker with a vicious grin, hovering over the royal table, snatching more.

I grab a loaf from the table next to me and stand. I rip it in half and give the remainder to Annemette. "Aim for Iker."

Her brows pull together with a moment of confusion. "I thought the bread was for the less fortunate?"

I gesture toward the sky. "It's raining bread. No one will go hungry, I promise."

Annemette looks up to see that, yes, bread of every make and shape is flying through the air. She ducks as a sweet roll screams in from Malvina's direction. It bounces off Fru Ulla with a honeyed thud before a toddler snags it with two chubby hands.

"It's all in good fun," I assure her, and chuck the bread Iker's way. He puts his arms up to shield his face but drops them too quickly and gets clobbered right in the nose by Annemette's piece.

This only serves to make him grin and seize two cherry tarts from the table. He thrusts one into Nik's hands, and they advance on us, eyes glinting.

"Run!" I screech, and grab Annemette's hand.

We snake through the crowd and onto an open stretch of beach. Twined together, we run along the shoreline. But the boys are faster, and tarts whack us each in the back. We fall to the sand in hysterics—something I haven't done in four years.

The boys pull us up—Iker hooking one arm under my knees and the other at my shoulders. He runs a finger along my back until my once class-defying gown is slick with beach-ruined cherry filling and aims it toward my mouth. "Sandy tart for the lady."

I seal my lips and shake my head.

"For Urda, you must."

The absurdity of the look on his face pulls my lips apart, and he seizes his opportunity to drop the filling onto my tongue. I gag and buck, coughing with laughter, and tumble out of his arms and into the sand.

Iker goes down too, landing beside me. His eyes seem to glow as he leans over my body and lowers his lips to mine. I enjoy the kiss, his newly shaven skin baby soft against my chin. I guess Iker doesn't defy all royal protocols; Queen Charlotte won this round.

"Mmmm," he says, licking cherry filling from his lips. "Delicious, though a bit . . . gritty."

I laugh. "Sandy tarts always are."

"Odd bit of cuisine, you Havnestaders."

"Eat up. Nik will expect you at full strength tomorrow," I say.

Iker raises a brow, mischief on his lips. "What if I told him I was saving my strength for you?"

I push him away from me and stand, my back to him, arms crossed.

"I was kidding," he pleads. "Are *all* the games tomorrow?"

I nod, dusting myself off while he still lies in the sand.

"Does this mean tomorrow is when you will shimmy across a log?"

When I don't respond, he stands and wraps his arms around me from behind, trailing two fingers across my navel, having them mimic a stiff jog.

"As promised, my prince," I say, laughing a little. *Why do I always give in?*

"Yes—"

A scream cuts off Iker's answer. *Annemette.* Both Iker and I whip our heads toward Annemette and Nik. They are closer to the crowd, Annemette crouching in the sand, Nik staggering a bit before falling to his knees, clutching his stomach. Standing before both of them is Malvina, hands in front of her body as if they'd just released a dagger.

Iker stiffens, his whole body suddenly rigid with tension. "Cousin?"

Nik staggers to a stand and raises a hand to wave him off, turning toward us. His white shirt and dazzling royal coat are a mess of black, like the tears I've cried twice before.

Iker takes a step toward the scene, fists forming.

But then Nik points toward his boots. Toward the pie plate lying facedown in the sand.

"Urda has been quite generous with Malvina's blueberry pie. The goddess must have decided that my wardrobe and the beach were in particular need of nourishment." With that, Nik begins to laugh.

Immediately, Iker joins him, and I catch Annemette's eye as she rises from her crouch. A little chuckle bubbles from her lips, growing into a full laugh when her attention turns to Nik's doubled-over form. I'm almost too shocked to laugh, having been holding my breath this whole time, but then I join in too.

The only one not finding humor in all this is Malvina, embarrassment but not regret in the set of her jaw. She doesn't apologize as she storms past Annemette—clearly her intended target—and snatches the pie plate from the sand at Nik's feet.

She stands to face him. Nik attempts to compose himself enough to look her in the eye but fails miserably, laughter still wryly present in his features as he lets the blueberry glop and sugar crust slide off his gold-threaded coat and onto the beach.

"I hope you will enjoy this gift in the name of Urda,"

Malvina announces, nose in the air, before pivoting on her heel as best as she can in beach sand, blond hair flying.

When she's gone, we gather around him and survey the damage. The shirt, coat and even his pants are all unsalvageable.

But true to his nature, Nik just grins and presents his sopping clothes.

"Pie, ladies? Urda does insist."

16

I WAKE WITH THE SUN THE FOLLOWING MORNING, STILL warm with feelings of belonging from the night before. Yesterday was a daydream from start to end, and I wanted to never wake up. But in the white morning light, reality becomes stark and my mood shifts quickly.

Annemette is still fast asleep, toes stretching toward the ceiling, arms thrown above her head, tangled within her waves. I lie there for a moment and listen to the gulls before I realize my opportunity. I know a way I can do some real good today.

On silent feet, I head to the wardrobe and tug it open. The first dress on the right is one I wore two days ago when I met Annemette. I can't believe that's all the time that's passed, but in the same breath, I can't believe so much of our time has vanished. Today and tomorrow until midnight, and then it could all be over in the most horrific way possible—or it might be the happiest ending of all.

Annemette still seems confident, and I'm obeying her request that I not intervene, at least not magically, but the thought of losing another friend to the sea is almost unbearable. First Anna, then nearly Nik, and now Annemette, who's only been in my life for a short while, but who's helped open my world in ways I'd never imagined. She's the friend Anna never could be to me, that Nik can't be, either. She's the only one who knows my secrets. Well, most of them.

I've been pushing these feelings down, telling myself this is her decision, that I should instead try to appreciate the life around me, as I'm sure she is, but I don't know how much longer I can feel so helpless.

At least I can still use my magic for one thing. I fish through my dress pocket. My fingers brush past the vial of ink from the other day and curl around the little amethyst, safe and sound where I left it. I can only hope that my morning away from the docks led to just one day of poor fishing, or maybe none at all—the magic is new enough that I don't know what happens if I *don't* do it.

I dress quickly, and, minutes later, I make it to the docks without seeing a soul. The cobblestones are littered with dew-covered crumbs, orphaned the night before, and so far neglected by the Øresund birds.

The docks are quiet too, no ships coming or going, though that will change in a few hours. Today is the favorite among the festivalgoers. The gluttony of the previous nights draws some, the final day of sailing and dancing attracts others, but not nearly as many as those lining up to participate or watch the games today.

Our games aren't exactly as sophisticated as the ancient Olympics Fru Seraphine taught us about in school, but they are more than enough for the people of Havnestad.

Palm out and full, I close my eyes and run the amethyst along the docked ship hulls one by one, mumbling aloud the words that seem to work, mostly because, with no one around, I don't have to say them in my head.

"Knorr yfir haf, knorr yfir haf, sigla tryggr, fanga prír.
Knorr yfir haf, knorr yfir haf, sigla tryggr, fanga prír."

The words hit my ear as childish, so much more sophisticated when spoken only in the space of my mind. I suddenly wish I'd trusted my magic enough to create a simple and strong Old Norse command—like something Annemette would do. I'd do it now but I'm afraid of what the change will bring.

My words are like a nursery rhyme—but they will do.

When I'm finished with every ship in port, I stand on the edge of the royal dock—the longest pier in Havnestad Harbor—and face the strait.

"Urda, if you will, bring my words to Father, wherever in the Øresund he may be. Keep him safe; leave him to me. You do not need him. Please don't take him simply because you can."

Anna's face crosses my mind, open and free with laughter before she was taken by the waves. But I push it down as far as it will go, along with my dark thoughts of the morning. I need to live like Annemette, like Iker, and enjoy the day to its fullest.

I turn and head back to the castle.

I don't see him at first, my eyes on the clouds the sun has tinged pink with the rising dawn. But then I hear the soft plink of a guitaren being strummed ever so lightly in the tulip garden. That song again, from the party.

"Nik?" His chin tilts my way, eyes swinging away from the sea. He is on the stone bench under the shade tree, the wrinkled version of his strapping statue across the garden—muslin nightclothes rumpled, unbrushed hair shoved out of his eyes with his fingertips. "Did you come out here this morning to let the birds clean the last bit of pie from behind your ears?"

"I ran a bath last night, but thanks for noticing."

"Then you must have risen early to meditate on a plan to best Iker in the rock carry."

Nik raises an arm and pats his lean bicep. "The only plan I need, my lady."

I punch him on the arm, and we sit quietly for a few moments. The pink of dawn has shifted to salmon, the tone already rumbling toward the golden yellow it turns just before the classic blue sky wins out and the sun is fully over the horizon.

Fingers scrabble Nik's hair back again from his brow, and his face turns toward the stones at our feet. After a breath, he raises his eyes to mine, and I have a feeling I might learn the real answer to his morning meditation.

"Evie . . . ," he starts, and my heart sinks at the mournful tone. *Oh no.* "Evie, have you really kissed Iker?"

My heart skids to a halt and I sit there, jaw tense. I don't know what to say. I'm not ready to talk about me and Iker. Not to Nik, anyway.

I laugh and elbow him in the ribs, hoping a joke can mend whatever is in his voice. "The real question is, have *you* kissed Annemette?"

I hope he'll turn red. Say yes. Admit to it so that maybe Annemette has a chance to stay—to live!—and fill the hole in our hearts.

Instead, his face squishes up as if he's smelled something spoiled. "Of course not. I'm a romantic, but I'm not a cad—I'm not, not . . ."

"Iker?" My voice is angrier than I intended, but there's something in the pit of my stomach. Something hot like disappointment, not only at him for his clear disdain for Iker but for anything *I* do with him.

He stops and starts, and I can tell he doesn't know where to begin. It's rare that I ever get angry with him. Rare that he can't bring order with a princely smile or a knowing glance, his only tools of conflict the royal formalities his mother has ingrained in him.

"I realize it's stupid," he says finally. "I'm sixteen and a prince to boot—I should be having fun. Mother would never let something wrongheaded get so far along. She has plans for me, besides. It's just . . . I like Annemette. But it's not . . . it's not"—he looks at me, and there's something else in his eyes—"as it is in the storybooks." Then he glances up at me, the change in his focus clear in the set of his jaw. "And for *him* to kiss *you* . . ." Nik shakes his head, his posture withering. "God, I must sound a mess—"

"No," I say, air rushing into my lungs just enough to get the word out.

He laughs softly under his breath. "Yes, I do. I sound crazed."

"You sound confused. You can find 'crazed' in those lovesick books we read as children. Those princes who lock girls up in a tower to get their way—those are the crazy ones."

Nik nods to himself. "Yes, Mette is a nice girl, lovely really, and beautiful, and I regret that she'll have to return to Odense, but I don't think I'll ever love her enough to be . . . to be . . . her fairy-tale prince."

My stomach practically collapses. But Nik is just speaking from the heart. He doesn't know there is no Odense for Annemette. No . . . nothing. She's just another girl his mother has forced upon him. What if I told him the truth? Maybe that would change things. *Evie, what are you talking about? Tell him she's a mermaid?* But maybe he'd see how wonderful she is and would want to save her, just like he tried to save Anna. But then this truly would all be on his shoulders. All that guilt. Can love spring from guilt? Is that true love? I don't know . . . how should I know what true love is? No, if I told him the truth, it might ruin any further time she has to win him over. This is all my fault, for trouncing around with Iker while Nik spends precious time worrying about me, taking his mind off Annemette. I have to try something else.

"She reminds me so much of Anna . . . ," I say, feeling as if the words are tiptoeing out.

"Her coloring, yes," he admits, but doesn't go further. Not the response I was hoping for.

"And her features. Her singing voice."

He shrugs and leans back off his knees and straightens. "But you know what's not? The way she looks at me—Anna never would've allowed herself to think of me as handsome."

"That's so untrue! She had a huge crush on you, and you know it." I knock his shoulder, though it feels strange to speak of Anna's private feelings as a joke. I'm quiet for a moment, and then I say, "Give Annemette a real chance, please. For me."

"But what about you and Iker?"

"Stop thinking about Iker, Nik! I'm happy, but I won't let him ruin me, like I know you're so afraid of. I'm smarter than that." He blushes red for a moment, but I keep going. "The only happiness I want you to worry about is yours."

FOUR YEARS BEFORE

The boy dove back in. He couldn't just leave it to these other men to find his friend. He'd saved one; he needed to try to save the other.

Drowning was common in Havnestad—the sea took as much as she gave—but this, this could not be.

Immediately, the water clawed at the damp length of him, the undertow a thousand hands ripping his body toward the swirling sands below.

His father's constant refrain crept into his head. Do not be a hero, Iker; you are already a prince.

He'd said it anytime Nik had done anything particularly reckless. A compliment swaddled in a reminder: You are not just a prince, you are an heir. The lone heir.

And here was his father's voice, nagging as fiercely as the waves.

He crested the surface and shook it all off—the words, the water—and filled his lungs. All around him, men thrashed in the waves. Not a single one held Anna.

The boy dove down again, forcing his eyes open against the salty sting.

Blue. Blue everywhere.

He blinked, letting his vision adjust.

Shadows on the ocean floor became crops of seaweed, moving in dark time. Algae, debris, and the tiniest of sea horses floated across the blue, a mosaic rather than one solidly flowing body.

His eyes swung left, right. His entire body spun around.

She's here. She's here. She must be here.

He surfaced again, not far from the sandbar now. No men yelling. No one sagging under the weight of a blonde in a petticoat.

Back down again, deeper, deeper, the undertow greedily guiding him on.

Eyes open, he scanned the bottom. Lungs burning for breath, he dove.

And there.

One hundred yards away. Down in a crevice. A flash of white. A foot, bare against a huge tangle of seaweed and coral.

Eyes pinned on her location, he shot to the surface—he'd need air to get her. Eight great, heaving breaths.

I can do this. I can get to her.

Down he dove again, eyes open as he plunged, pinned to the sliver of white. So far away. So far down.

The boy's lungs burned. His ears popped. Darkness crept into the corners of his vision.

And still the slip of white was there. But not getting closer. It never seemed to get any larger, any more attainable. It just flashed on the seafloor, so much a star he could not touch.

His mind began to slow, as did his legs and arms, which no longer struggled against the undertow.

—153

You do not need to be a hero, Iker; you are already a prince.

You are not just a prince, you are an heir.

The lone heir.

Breath beating against his lungs, he made his choice.

The prince pushed himself deeper.

His life didn't matter more than hers. He was the one with the chance to save her, and that chance shouldn't hinge on the blood in his veins.

Legs burning, he kicked, no breath left in his lungs to propel him. But he was so close. He could make out actual toes now. Head pounding without air, blood spiked with pressure, he kicked again, his arms pulling against the water.

But then came a pressure on his foot. Yanking him back—up. Pulling him until, for a heartbeat, the weight was gone. As soon as it disappeared, it was replaced with elbows hooking under his shoulders. A chest at his back. And force, so much force, propelling him to the surface.

In that moment, his lungs finally sputtered for breath and he involuntarily inhaled, water still surrounding him. A deep mouthful of the sea hovered above his windpipe for a split second before he spit it back into the water.

Out of breath, out of time, water closing in, he broke the surface. The air was so fresh it burned; as his lungs heaved, his tongue swelled from the salt he'd inhaled.

Coughing, breathing—finally breathing—he opened his eyes again, water streaming into his eyes.

He couldn't see well, but he knew the face before him.

"No! Iker—" he began, coughing. Coughing so hard. More salt water streamed out of his mouth. Dribbled down his chin. He wiped at his mouth with a sleeve so wet, it just smeared the water around with more water.

"I've got you, Cousin. I've got you. Don't worry. You're safe."

"I—" He coughed again and took a breath, long and deep. "I have to get her."

With air in his lungs, he tried to shrug off his cousin.

"She's gone, Nik. She's gone. And you were going to be too."

"No! She's down there. I saw her. You had to have seen her too. She's right there, right down—"

"Don't be a hero, Nik." Boat-strong biceps pinned the prince in a hug—his arms stuck at his sides, his only recourse to kick, but that just propelled them closer to the beach. Farther from her.

"Iker, please. She needs us. Anna needs us. We can rescue her. We can—"

"We can't." His cousin's newly deepened voice cracked as he said it, and there was a hitch in his kick. "We can't."

"We can! We can get her!" He was yelling, even though his voice was rough and sloppy.

His cousin only squeezed harder. His lips came to the prince's ear, his voice smaller than seemed possible. "If you die rescuing her, it won't give solace to your parents or your people. It will only give Havnestad another body."

"But she's not a body. She's not. She's there. Right there." But even as he said the words, he knew it had been too long now. Ten minutes, though it felt like a hundred.

And then he started to cry. Salty tears running down his cheeks and into the harbor. He didn't wipe them. He let them run. Let them join Anna at sea.

17

THE ANNUAL LITHASBLOT GAMES BEGIN IN THE SWEL-
ter of noon. Havnestad citizens and onlookers from across
the Øresund Strait spill onto the main beach, ready for
games of skill and sport to take place from the mountains
above to the seas below.

It's the first time in days the boys aren't properly gussied
up in public. To be sure, they're both clean-shaven—the
easier to show off their game faces—but they are also
wearing simple cotton work pants and shirts rolled at the
sleeves. This change of dress is tradition too.

Today is about demonstrating skill. I wasn't lying
when I told Iker our games were useful—they were indeed
born out of utility. Rock climbing and trail running in the
mountains. Log running in the stream that feeds into the
harbor. Swimming in the mouth of the sea. Vital to life,
every one of them. Useful—right down to the rock carry

along the beach, which mimics laboring to bring cargo ashore.

And each citizen in Havnestad has an equal shot to compete. Be you ninety-five or still flush with baby fat, if you can walk, you are allowed to have a go—with the royal family cheering you on, or possibly acting as your competition.

After plates of samsø, rye bread, and peaches, Nik is instructed by his father to oversee the mountain events first. Those sports have the fewest competitors, and King Asger would much rather view the action on the beach.

And King Asger gets what King Asger wants—even from his son.

True to his nature, Nik bows—no crown atop his head—before grabbing another peach and a flask of water and tugging Annemette toward Lille Bjerg Pass.

I side-eye Iker when he doesn't make a move to follow.

His strong hand gently cuffs my wrist and pulls me close. In a breath, I'm an inch away from his lips. The depths of his eyes are striking in the high sun, clear and merry after a good night's rest in a real bed and not a ship's dank quarters. "Let's just stay here alone."

I shift my eyes to the beach. "Alone—with five thousand of our closest friends, including your aunt and uncle."

Iker laughs and gently fingers the curls that have blown forward over my shoulder. "So many people that not a one of them is watching . . ."

No, they're watching. I can feel it. He's just used to it.

I pull away, shifting the arm he's snagged so I'm grabbing his wrist as he clutches mine. I tug him toward Lille Bjerg Pass. "There are many side trails along the pass, thick with brush."

He raises a brow and finally takes a step forward. "It would be a shame if we were to get lost."

"Such a shame. Nik would be so disappointed."

"Only if he's lost in the same brush we are."

It's true. Nik returned a different person after our early morning conversation, focusing on Annemette with a renewed intensity.

With tangled hands, we march up Market Street. We are several lengths behind Annemette and Nik, though they are moving at a snail's pace—Annemette has yet to see much of the town outside of the festival, and she's poking in every doorway and picture window to see the wares. The sweetshop man already handed her a lollipop, which proceeded to turn her tongue a grisly shade of red. She dared to show us a block back, sticking out her tongue nearly down to her chin. It was quite the picture, a bloody maw beneath the face of an angel. Of course, she thought it was the funniest thing. I thanked Urda that Malvina wasn't around to see it.

Nik laughed too, endearment written all over his face. He has no idea how far she's traveled to see these things we walk past every day, to stroll down the street with him.

"I have been to Odense," Iker starts, sun lines crinkling around his eyes, "and it isn't Copenhagen, but it isn't a one-horse village either. By the way she responded to the sucker, you'd suppose she'd never had a candy in all her life."

"Showing delight isn't a crime, Iker." And it isn't, though I know that answer won't atone for Annemette's fierce sense of wonder. Thus, I turn it back on him. "Not everyone is as difficult to amuse as the salt-worn prince of Rigeby Bay."

His lips turn up and his eyes flash my way. "I laugh deeper than anyone and you know it—whether I've lived on only salt herring for three weeks or not." His fingers squeeze mine and I kiss his shoulder. "What I mean is, there's just something unnatural about her level of delight."

My heart starts to pound and my temples grow hot. This line of thought is no good. No good at all. I change tactics.

"Imagine it her way." I sweep my free hand out in front of him. "She arrived at Havnestad with a chaperone green with illness, knowing not a single other soul. And despite it all, she's been taken in, given a bed in a beautiful palace, and the dashing prince she's come to meet clearly believes her to be something special." I swing up our tangled hands so they're within view. "That is a whirlwind of delight, is it not? The curl was nearly blown out of my hair just by being a bystander."

He gives me a courtesy laugh and snags a wayward lock of hair with his free hand, tugging it completely smooth. He lets it go and watches as it bounces back into a spiral. "That would've been disastrous. Even the salons of Paris would not have been able to reproduce these."

My cheeks run scarlet as we reach the end of the cobblestones and the trailhead of Lille Bjerg Pass. Annemette and Nik have already disappeared around a bend. I step in front of Iker onto the single track, and our hands drop.

"I'm just saying," he says, "what do we know about Annemette? How do we know she is who she says she is?"

I laugh, trying to make it seem as if he's being ridiculous, and not appropriately concerned. "What, do you think she's some con artist on the run, stealing crown jewels one Lithasblot at a time?" It's the most absurd thing I can offer, except for the truth.

"No. No. She's a sweet girl . . . there's just something about her I can't put my finger on. And I don't like that feeling—especially when it involves family."

"I know what it is," I say, hoping to finally put this to rest—for Annemette as much as for myself. "She looks like Anna."

His step hesitates behind me. "Your friend who drowned?"

"The very one."

"Sure. She had blond hair."

"Yes. And blue eyes. And creamy skin. A heart-shaped

face—all of it. The resemblance about bowled me over." And I can't help it: tears well in my eyes. "I'd thought I'd seen a ghost."

He stops moving forward. I turn around and he's watching me, brows pulled together and serious. It's just as he was on the balcony, suspicion slinking across his skin as fierce as the sunlight.

"Are you sure there's no way this girl could have known that? Picked the name Annemette on purpose? She could be preying on the both of you—using your memories against you."

The slope of the trail puts us face-to-face, and he presses his thumbs to the corners of my eyes, wiping away the tears that have welled. I place my hand on his chest. "Who are these scoundrels you meet on the high seas? Does anyone in the world really do such awful things? Do you not have any faith in your fellow man?"

"Evelyn, I am aware that you are not naïve, but I feel as if I should remind both you and my cousin that people aren't always who they say they are."

"You're not wrong." I take a step toward him and touch my forehead to his, our lips a breath away, our eyes locked. "And while I find your concern incredibly endearing, I'm through talking about this. Annemette may not be Anna, but she *is* my friend. I have not been duped."

I close the distance between us, our lips meeting. He

sinks deeply into me, hands wrapping around my back, fingers in my hair. We stand like that for several moments, but it isn't until he's so taken he closes his eyes that I know I've finally won this round.

"Taking the long way up the mountain?"

I push away from Iker and see Annemette standing a few feet from us, Nik surely around the bend. Her brow is raised, but there's a smirk on her black cherry–stained mouth.

"Haven't you heard? I'm never on time." He grins a bit at his own self-effacing jab, but I swear I still see a skeptical look in his eyes as he stalks past her.

Annemette grabs my hands, and we both burst out laughing. It really does feel like Anna is here.

We make our way up to the games, but by the time we reach them, Nik and Iker have already been plied into competing in the mountain run portion of the games. Royal duty and gamesmanship mean Annemette and I have been left behind to hold court on a fallen log. Normally, I'd run too—I'm swifter than I look—but Annemette's feet are already bothering her, the burning she felt yesterday more painful than before. Instead, we'll watch the rock climbers from afar while waiting for the boys to rumble back down the mountain, sweaty, dusty, and full of new tales.

"How do you do it?" she asks quietly.

"What do you mean?" I reply.

"Get Iker to kiss you like that?" she says with more than a hint of exasperation lining her voice. "It's silly, but I was watching you—"

"For tips?" I want to laugh—the idea of someone watching me for my alluring abilities is ridiculous, and I still have my doubts about whether there's actually any love behind Iker's kisses, but Annemette seems so desperate. She *is* desperate.

Annemette's cheeks flush, though the pink is tempered by the mountain light. "I've done everything I can to show him how I feel, and still no kiss! But I do think he likes me."

"He does. I know he does!" I push this morning out of my mind entirely. Nik has heeded my words. I know it. It's going to be all right.

She is quiet for a second, her features mellowing with thought. "My father, the sea king, says that when everything is as you hoped, you are blind to the imperfections."

Somehow, I'm stunned silent that the sea king in our childhood tales is as real as the mermaid before me. Finally, I nod. "Your father is wise."

"But I'm not blind. His wise words ring in my ears when I should be enjoying every moment. Instead, I look past the perfect couple we are on the outside and see all the reasons why Nik isn't in love with me."

"I know what you mean," I say.

"No, Iker loves you."

I shake my head. "I would like Iker to love me. But Iker has a reputation for kissing any girl whose knees go weak at the sight of him—and I'm not the only one in the Øresund Kingdoms with trouble standing. Iker and I are not forever, and I'm trying to be all right with that."

She looks at her feet. "So, he has other girls he treats like you?"

"Yes. Or he did. I don't know." I can feel my face flushing. "The point is, Nik does not! There is only one fish in his sea and it is you . . ."

"That is a ridiculous analogy, Evie."

"And here I thought it was clever, given your situation."

Annemette squeezes her eyes shut, and I regret making a stupid joke at a time like this. "My situation. Yes." She huffs out a sad little laugh. "Such a situation—love at first sight with a boy who won't even kiss me. I was so sure he was going to lead to a lifetime of happiness, not . . ."

Neither of us wants to say what her life will be otherwise.

18

WHEN NIK AND IKER RETURN, THEY ARE EAGER TO prove who is the strongest, the fastest, the most agile, their egos sorely bruised after both losing the mountain run. It seems the tailor's son, little Johan Olsen, is not so little anymore.

"I've never seen someone run like him," Nik admits as we make our way over to the Havnestad River, which slices through the mountains before emptying to the sea. "It was a sight to see."

"You want to see a sight?" says Iker. "Challenge me to a log run, Cousin. I could beat ten of that Olsen boy, and you, too."

I look over at Annemette, who has plastered a smile on her face and is laughing along with the boys. And, because I'd love to see Iker dunked in the Havnestad River, I am totally encouraging it too.

Nik chuckles—a royal chuckle, but an actual chuckle nonetheless. As we reach the riverbank, he's still contemplating. He props one foot up on the tail end of the right log. There's an open one to his left, ready for Iker.

"If I'm not mistaken," Nik says, "I heard you came to this Lithasblot extravaganza with the promise of a certain raven-haired girl scampering across a log, and it wasn't me, Cousin."

Nik! How could he? But I laugh an Iker laugh, head thrown toward the sky. Nik is losing it too—chortling so hard that his foot has slipped off the end of the log and he's nearly squatted to a sit on the thing.

Annemette, though, has her wits about her. I right myself just as she glances my way with a wicked little grin and a gleam in her eyes. "How about this compromise? Nik and Evie race. The winner faces Iker."

Iker's brows climb his forehead and his eyes sparkle, clear and thrilled. He claps his big, strong hands together. "Yes. That's it. The lady has the perfect idea!"

I shake my head. "Yes, the perfect idea to keep herself dry."

Annemette shrugs and backs into the small crowd that has gathered, lined along the rocks and logs. "I'm just a spectator."

Nik laughs and manages a long lunge to nudge her sweetly with his elbow. "That's what I thought, too, my dear, and now look where it's got me."

—167

I cock a brow at him. "Yes, as my first victim."

"Hey, now, what makes you so sure you'll win?" Nik says to me, a smile playing at his lips, though his tone is attempting to sound indignant.

"Sometimes you just have a feeling, my prince. You're sure to be a loser, Asger Niklas Bryniulf Øldenburg III."

As the spectators and competitors chant Nik's name, he plants a foot on the log across from me. Both logs are suspended just above the current, tied by ship ropes on either side to keep them straight and somewhat steady—to keep the competition fair, not to create ease.

It is twenty-five feet from one end to the other. We must race to the other side, touch the bank, and then make a return trip. The first one back or the one to stay out of the water wins. If we both wind up in the river, then it's a draw, no matter who fell first.

Our classmate, Ruyven Van Horn, squashed ginger hair, elephant ears and all, is there between us, the official start on his lips. "On your marks . . . get set . . . go!"

We lunge onto the logs. Nik's legs are much longer, and he's ahead after a step, but his center of gravity is much higher, and he immediately wobbles.

"Unsteady so soon, Cousin?" Iker laughs in the background.

I can't see him, but I'm sure Nik is smiling right back. "Jeer me, and you only serve to anger me."

In the time it's taken him to steady himself and answer Iker's ribbing, I've already made it five steps. The logs are slicked over, but mine is the perfect size for my feet. Planting each foot in a turnout à la the French ballet, I can move quickly to the center point with shallow steps. Beside me, Nik hasn't altered his stride, daring gravity to take him with every long step, but using his strength and coordination to stay steady.

I make it to the end of my log and tag the ground on the other side, earning me a flag raise from Ruyven's counterpart.

"Excellent, Evie!" Annemette cheers.

I get both feet back onto my log just as Nik lunges off the end of his and safely into the dirt.

"Mette, you traitor," Nik yells, mounting his log a bit too quickly. His arms windmill through my periphery in a grand arc—the crowd gasps.

"Less jawing, more movement, Cousin. Evie's smoking you!"

"You only root for me because you're stupid enough to think you can beat me in the next round. Against her you won't have a chance, and you know it."

I'm still in the lead but just barely, my steps slower and more careful now. Over the years, I've seen many a competitor fall in the river a yard from the finish because his mind was already on land. I could easily whisper one of

Tante Hansa's spells and dry the log without any notice, but I won't do that. I'm not a cheat. So my heart stills as I concentrate on the log before me, the sound of rushing water the only thing in my ears.

Nik is beside me, but my tunnel vision has drowned him out—if his arms are flailing or if he is steady and slowing too, I don't know. All I know is that when I touch dirt, Ruyven raises my arm, and when I look over, Nik is there too, hands on his hips, breathing at a good clip.

"The lady, by an inch!" Ruyven says. Annemette is clapping and Iker, too, though his game face is already sliding into place. The rest of the crowd is mostly silent until Nik raises his hands above his head in thanks—then they go wild.

"Well done, Evie." Nik squeezes my shoulder. Then he leans in, for my ears only. "Ignore them. They only cheer because they have to." Then, to the crowd, he says, "Let's hear it for Evie!"

Slightly heartier applause chases his exclamation, but—not shockingly—also some boos. And then all eyes swing to Iker. His gaze is locked on my face, the glee in the blue of his eyes already hardening to concentration. If Iker competes in the grand way that he does everything else, I'm going to need much more than an inch.

I turn and place my foot on the log.

"Are you sure you're ready to exert yourself again so quickly, Evelyn?"

"Quit stalling, Romeo. Let's go."

I glance over to Ruyven, who is having a fine time laughing at our expense. Ruyven meets my eyes, his normally dough-pale face now plum red, and raises his flag for a start. Iker is still a step or two away from his log, turned around, playing to the crowd. I settle my footing, calf muscles tense beneath my dress.

"On your marks . . ." It takes Iker almost a second too long to register the words. Ruyven is onto the next part before the crown prince of Rigeby Bay has time to turn. "Get set . . ." Iker is a yard from his log. "Go!"

I dash onto my log, keeping my chest low, hips square and knees bent. I'm five feet in front when Iker finally mounts his log, but in true Iker form, he takes the lead with just two grand steps.

The surrounding wood is alive with voices, so strong that they rise above my concentration and the babbling of the stream—Iker is always one to bring out the rowdiness in any situation.

"Go get him!" Annemette yells.

"You've got this, Evie!" Nik cheers.

But I don't have it. Iker is already a yard from touching down on the other side of the log, his bold steps risky but not without reward. I am still at least ten careful steps from the bank and the chance to turn around. When Iker's feet hit the dirt, he immediately spins and points to the flag-man on the other side and then raises his arms, grand and proud as he addresses the crowd.

"Will no one cheer for the first-place horse? Am I so hideous?"

At this, every girl in the crowd, save Annemette, screams his name. It's the same chorus that I picture when he lands aground anywhere in the Øresund Kingdoms.

Iker's grandstanding costs him, though, and I touch down on the dirt just after he's mounted his log. He calculates that he's made an error in timing and immediately sprints for the other side, half leaping to stay in front of me.

I'm tempted to speed up and take longer steps, but I hold back, the log even slicker than before.

So I take my time. Quick steps, eyes only for the log, breath steady and calm.

I'm in the lead at the midpoint, a second victory in my sights. And that's exactly when someone in the crowd decides a prince can't lose yet again, and a branch whizzes through the air, catching me across the neck.

The pain is sharp, and I lose my balance. I'm falling toward the water and Iker's log before I can do anything physically or magically to stop it. As I'm falling, I think for a split second of Annemette's floating spell, and I almost say the command, but I can't do that here. Still, I hang in the air for the slightest of seconds before I catch Annemette's eyes. I see them shift to the look of concentration I saw in Greta's Lagoon. *Don't do it,* I glare. *Not here.*

I fall into the river and am pushed under Iker's log by

the current. There's shouting above the rush of water in my ears, but I can't make out what's being said. Then comes a flash of white and navy followed by a great whoosh and water droplets splashing upon my face.

The crowd is making a hearty noise, but it's not until strong fingers tuck into the back collar of my dress do I realize Iker jumped in the water. He's clinging with the other arm to the log, in an attempt to keep from rushing downstream.

"Are you okay?"

I nod, somewhat shocked by the water as much as by the fierceness of his voice.

Iker gives me a gentle push, and I swim the final yards to the edge, working hard against the downstream pull of the current. Annemette is leaning over, reaching for me, her beautiful dress hemmed in mud.

Nik is on the bank, yelling. More than that—he's yanking the boy who threw the stick out of the crowd and tossing him from the competition. I've never seen Nik so angry.

Annemette tugs me up the slick bank. Iker follows, hoisting himself up, hands sinking in the mud. We're a mess, the two of us, dripping water and globs of mud everywhere.

The crowd is silent and so are we. Nik joins us and we turn without a word toward the trail. Not even Nik says anything, the anger still simmering off him.

As we walk away, Nik keeps glancing back at me, muttering to himself. He almost looks as if he wants to grab my hand, but Iker's arm is around my shoulders, and so all he says is, "I'll see to it he never competes, never attends again."

I don't know what to think—Nik isn't one to throw around his royal power like this, but I won't deny it feels good. Of course, it'll only make the whispers continue. More reasons for the townspeople to say I don't know my place. I rub at the bruise forming on my neck, a parting gift from the stick, and look over at Annemette. Her expression is withdrawn, her mouth in a line and her brow furrowed. She's walking a few paces from Nik's side, giving him room, leaving him be.

I've done it again, though, haven't I? Found another way to distract Nik from what's important. I just want to be alone, let everyone go on without me, but when we make it to town, Iker tugs me back, taking a moment to scrape the mud off his boots on the jumbled edge of a cobblestone. Boots clean, and Nik and Annemette out of earshot ahead, he grabs my hand.

"Why did you stay here?"

I blink at him. "What do you mean?"

"When I left to go whaling a few days ago—why did you stay where you knew people would throw sticks and say awful things about you?"

Iker could give Tante Hansa a run for her money in the

observation department, but his words also ring hollow. "It's not anything different from before," I say. "Besides, your offer wasn't real. You and I both know that."

He shakes his head, his eyes fierce. "That's not true, Evie. And it's real now, whether you believe me or not. The moment my duties at the ball end, let's leave. Just you and me on my boat. And if we catch a whale, all the better."

It sounds perfect. My dreams flash before my eyes—of freedom, of Iker, of the sea we could conquer together, one whale at a time. But it's too perfect. I can't go, even if it's only for a few weeks—why can't he see that?

But at the same time, Annemette fills my thoughts—she's risked everything for the one she loves and I've risked nothing. Even if she dies—and it hurts just thinking that—she will have lived more in these few days than I ever have.

I look up at Iker. My imperfect Iker. The right choice couldn't be clearer.

"Let's catch ourselves a whale," I say.

Iker pulls me in for a kiss, and I sink into him, my mind already thick with dreams of days on the sea and nights snuggled together with my cheek to his chest.

FOUR YEARS BEFORE

The raven-haired girl couldn't stay on the beach. She couldn't just lie there while the people she loved like family were in the water.

She pushed herself upright but felt as weighed down as if the tide still held her. Her feet stumbled and her lungs seized, and she fell back into the sand.

The townspeople who watched didn't help her up, didn't rush to her aid. They whispered into their hands but weren't quiet enough. She'd heard it all before, and the words played in her ears like memories.

That girl—she's allowed access to the castle and she's dull enough to think she lives there.

The prince isn't your brother, girl.

Wouldn't put it past her to be behind this whole tragedy—social-climbing cow.

The raven-haired girl forced herself to her feet again, eyes on Iker's form, swimming deftly through the water. Her fingers flexed at her sides. There was so much she wished she could do.

She took a step forward. And then another. Moving under her own power, breathing deeply to push herself along. Her heart pounding in time with the names of her loved ones— Anna, Nik, Anna, Nik, Anna, Nik.

And Iker. So strong. He had to save them.

Her toes splashed in the water and she stopped. Fingers flexing again. What she wouldn't give for her mother's inks and crystals, for her aunt's books and knowledge. For a world where she could use their magic—and not burn or be banished for trying.

Iker surfaced. He threw his head back, pulling in a long heave of air, and then dove, his feet splashing over the top of the churning waves.

He'd found one of them. Maybe both of them. How long had they been under? Could it be too late?

The girl looked to her toes, to the minnows swirling about her ankles like the worst thing in the world wasn't happening right then in their slice of the sea.

Like her friends weren't dying and it wasn't her fault.

Though it was. She'd been the one to suggest to Anna that Nik might be impressed by her bravery. That he always seemed thrilled with hers—why wouldn't it work for Anna? Anna, who had such a crush.

It was the girl's own fault. She'd suggested the race. She'd planted the idea of bravery in her friend's head. And now it was all so wrong.

Anna. Nik. Anna. Nik. Anna. Nik.

But she wasn't powerless, was she? A memory crashed forth in her mind and suddenly the words slipped onto her tongue. Old and dark. And worth a try. She didn't have inks or potions or crystals. But she had these words. They were a breath of life.

And they were all she had.

And so, the raven-haired girl stood in the shallows, reciting the last spell her mother ever cast.

Immediately, her skin grew hot, the seawater there evaporating into dry salt streaks. Her blood sang with magic, her back to the people who would have her burned or banished. She knelt into the waves, put her hands in the water—the more of her touching, the more power there would be.

She shut her eyes.

The words continued and she began to shake. Violently. Steam rose from the waves lapping at her petticoat.

A splash. A large splash. Male voices.

Her eyes opened and looked to the faraway surface.

Nik.

Iker had Nik in his arms.

They were yelling at each other, both full of life. Nik's voice cut through the splashes, a single clear word rising above it all, enough to be heard.

"No!"

The girl's stomach dropped. The words stopped. She was too late. They were all too late.

"Oh, Anna. I'm so sorry." She began to cry, the spell dead on her tongue, her skin cooling.

She blinked and saw black. Swirls of dark viscous liquid pooled in her eyes. Startled, she shot to her feet, thick black tears dripping down her cheeks and into the water.

Not again.

The girl scrubbed at her eyes, wiping her hands on her petticoat. And when she could see clearly again, she looked at her feet. Dead minnows floated on the tide's surface, seaweed shriveling black.

She stumbled backward, onto dry land. The magic gone from her lips, one best friend swimming for land, another lying with her tears in the sea. Tears that had killed the life at her feet.

The girl turned to face the crowd, black streaks staining the heels of her hands as she rubbed her eyes again. The magic sinking into the skin.

The collective gasp was unmistakable.

"Oh, stop, it's just sea grit. She nearly drowned!" Tante Hansa. The old woman came toward the raven-haired girl and pulled her close. Whispered in her ear: "We must leave. Hurry, your life is more important than seeing those boys to land."

19

"ARE YOU SURE YOU'RE ALL RIGHT?" ANNEMETTE ASKS as we leave the palace, a bundle of strawberries in our hands. We went back to change so I could put on dry clothes and Annemette less muddy ones. I suggested a snack and a walk so I could clear my head. Everything was just feeling so muddled—did I actually just agree to run away with Iker? But I can't talk to Annemette about any of that.

"I'm fine. It wasn't a big deal. Really."

"I just don't understand why these people are so horrible to you," she says. "You're generous and smart and beautiful and best friends with their prince!"

I sigh and pull my hands away from my eyes. "That's exactly why. You see, I'm poor, but that's okay because nearly everyone is. But in Havnestad, and probably everywhere else, too, the poor do not befriend the royals. They serve them. Being friendly as children was fine, but it should have ended long ago."

"So why didn't it?"

"Tante Hansa. She saved the king when he was a boy, cured him of some terrible illness, and then again years later after a boating accident. My family was rewarded. My father was named royal fisherman, and Nik and I were allowed to remain friends. No matter how much Queen Charlotte protested, even after my mother died in the way she did." Annemette doesn't push further on that topic, and I go on. "The great irony is that Tante Hansa has never approved of my friendship with Nik, either, but she knows me well enough to criticize yet never to bar. But the people, they just think I'm using Nik to act better than them, to be more than them. They hate me for it. And it'll never change."

We walk by a row of brick cottages, each with a small garden out front.

"Anna? Anneke?" someone calls from behind.

Annemette blinks and I twist around.

Standing there in the lane, weight on her wooden cane, is Fru Liesel—Anna's grandmother.

A crooked finger points toward Annemette, and a smile crosses the old woman's lips. "Anneke, come, give Oma a hug. It's been too long."

Annemette glances at the old woman and then to me.

"Fru Liesel, this is my friend, Annemette. She is here from Odense."

The old woman ignores me. As she always does. "Anneke, come, give Oma a hug. It's been too long," she repeats.

Annemette takes a step toward Anna's grandmother.

Just as I've felt so many times this week, it's as if I'm glancing through a looking glass at another present. One where Anna is alive, well, beautiful, and singing about boys and strawberries before embracing her beloved grandmother in the street.

But for Annemette, this is not a reunion scene.

"Fru Liesel, my name is Annemette, it's so lovely to—"

Stronger than she looks, Fru Liesel ditches the cane and hauls Annemette to her chest with the force of both knotty hands. Annemette goes along without a fight, her face buried against the old woman's heartbeat.

"Anna, my Anneke, why haven't you visited? Where have you been? Your father is worried sick—I'm worried sick."

Annemette pulls herself up and places her hands gently on the old woman's shoulders. Kindness wraps her features. "I've been away, Oma. I'm so sorry. How have you been?"

My throat tightens as I watch Annemette give the old woman what no one in Havnestad ever allows her— compassion.

"Oh, I'm trying to be good, but at my age, I'd rather fly with the witches."

"A safe bet, Oma."

Fru Liesel is still clutching onto Annemette with both hands. Annemette bends a bit and picks up the woman's cane and holds it out for her.

"Here you are, Oma. Now, where were you off to?"

Fru Liesel grabs the cane with her right hand but stays grasping Annemette with her left, all her weight pressed into the girl's side.

"Home, dear. I was headed home."

Annemette catches my eye. "Let us help you, Oma."

I walk a few steps behind as Annemette and Fru Liesel walk arm in arm down the sea lane, up to the castle and around to a row of grand manor houses on the sunny side of the Øldenburg Castle grounds. Fru Liesel is surely guiding Annemette, the way home being one of the few things she likely hasn't forgotten, but Annemette seems so at ease, it's hard not to think there's something else calling her forward.

Anna's childhood home is three down to the right— red brick and clean lines. It was Fru Liesel's childhood home, and she refused to leave it when the rest of her family fled to the Jutland. I watch Annemette's face as Fru Liesel points to it, and I tamp down the little flutter inside me that hopes she will recognize it—that this girl born of the sea really is my old friend in a shiny, impossible package. But if Annemette recognizes the grand lines of the home, it doesn't flash across her features.

"Here we are, Oma." Annemette's voice is clear and

sweet as they maneuver the foot stones to the front door.

"Thank you, child, my Anneke." She rests her cane against the threshold and opens the door. "Let us have some portvin and talk of your travels. I want to hear it all, especially about the young men queuing for your hand."

Annemette laughs gently. "Yes, Oma, we shall. But can we do it later? I have plans with Evie."

"Oh, you and Evie, always running around. Only two fish in your school. Asger's boy always did try to join, but even a crown can be a third wheel." She chuckles to herself.

"That's right, Oma." Annemette pats Fru Liesel's arm, finally freeing herself completely from the woman's grasp in the process. But that freedom lasts only a moment before Fru Liesel snags her hand yet again.

"But you be careful with that girl, Anneke. Bad things follow her. Black death. Minnows floating at her feet." Annemette catches my eye, and I don't know what to say. "That little witch will be the death of you if you're not careful."

20

WE ARE NOT EVEN OUT OF VIEW FROM ANNA'S HOUSE when Annemette stops me short by grabbing both my hands, tugging me to a thatch of trees just outside the queen's tulip garden.

"The first time you saw me, you called me Anna. And Tante Hansa mentioned an Anna too. Now this woman insists I'm her grandchild. Who is this girl? How do you know her?"

"Knew her. She's dead."

Annemette's gaze softens.

I swallow but hold her eyes. The tug-of-war in my heart has ended—the little voice in my head has received a chance to be heard.

"She's the person I think you were before you were a mermaid."

She pitches a brow. "What do you mean before I was a

mermaid? Like my soul? What is it that they believe in the spice lands . . . reincarnation?"

"No, not reincarnation—the *person* you were before, the person you were made from."

"I was only made of my mother and father," she says with certainty. "There's no other way to make a mermaid."

"But what if there is?" I flip our grip, and I'm now grasping her wrists. "I know it's crazy, but my best friend, Anna Liesel Kamp, drowned four years ago. She resembled every inch of you but younger—blond hair, deep-blue eyes, freckles across the bridge of her nose. Beyond looks, she loved to sing. She was spirited, she was—"

"Evie, how many blondes have we seen here these past few days? A hundred? A thousand? I'm sure that Malvina has three blond sisters of her own. There are more blondes in Havnestad than under the entire sea. How many girls have blue eyes? Like to sing? Give cheeky answers?"

"I know, but—"

"That's not evidence, it's coincidence." Annemette shakes out of my grasp and points in the direction of the hordes on the beach. "All these people must remember Anna, but except for that ancient woman, your old tante, and you, not a one has mistaken me for her this entire time."

"Because they think you're *dead*!"

Annemette throws down her arms, clenching her fists. Frustration has gotten the best of me, too, and I feel as if I have no measure for how loud my words are. I don't know if I screamed them or whispered them. All I know is that Annemette's face has shifted from annoyed to concerned. I open my mouth to say that Nik and Iker see the resemblance too, but she's already speaking.

"You think I'm her—you have this whole time . . ."

"In the beginning yes, and then, no. It was you I became friends with, Annemette, but has a part of me hoped—*believed*—you were always Anna? Of course!"

The second the words are out, I realize how strongly that belief has been driving me. I haven't just been imagining what an alternate future would have been like with Anna; I really believed it was happening. And is happening now.

I lower my voice and turn my back to the tulip garden. "Anna drowned. Her body was never recovered. And then, suddenly, you pop out of the same water, the spitting image of her. What am I supposed to think?"

Annemette's face is completely buttoned up. Her lips are screwed shut, her eyes closed; a wall of hair shields her ears. I realize she's preparing to answer me, but I can't take the silence.

"How well do you remember your childhood?" I ask. "Do you remember it at all? What were you doing five years ago? Ten? Who is your oldest friend?"

Finally, when she opens her eyes, there is anger there, though her tone is subdued and her words completely ignore my questions.

"I am sorry for your loss, Evie, but I am not your friend. I am not her. I am Annemette." She lowers her voice here, her voice cracking with pain. "Besides, your dream isn't possible for almost the very reason why I'm here."

"What do you mean?"

She's now in my face, the set of her jaw is angry, her nose at a subtle flare. "Mermaids don't have souls, Evie, not like you humans. I couldn't be created from someone who did. Your friend Anna is in a better place, not in this body that will become nothing but sea foam."

Her crushing words hit me one by one, diminishing nearly all my hope. Then one of Tante Hansa's sayings floats across my mind: *The only thing magic cannot do is know its bounds.* Anything is possible. I open my mouth to say more, to argue this one more point, but Annemette puts up her hand.

"Stop, Evie. Just stop. You're only hurting yourself."

I look at her closely. Is she really Anna? And then I hear her words echo from a moment before: *Your dream isn't possible for almost the very reason why I'm here.* My blood begins to rise.

"Why are you here?" I ask, my eyes squinting at her every inch.

"What do you mean? I love Nik," she says.

"No," I shake my head. "You're here for a soul. Aren't you? Any soul will do. So is this your plan, you get Nik to love you, kiss you, and then you steal his soul? Is this all some kind of dark, sick game?" My heart is beating so loudly I can barely hear myself speak.

Her eyes go soft. "No, Evie. You've got it all wrong. I love Nik. And yes, if he loves me and kisses me, I get a part of his soul. I get to live on as human, and then when I die, more. But Nik's generosity is no different from you giving a piece of yourself to him and to all the people you meet and treat with kindness, making them better. I don't have that to give, but I don't think wanting it is a crime, either."

My heart rate slows, but I'm breathing like I've completed the rock carry. How could I have said what I just said? It was horrible. Annemette grabs my hands and pulls me into an embrace, the smell of the sea on her hair, calming me down. I look up when I hear boots clicking on the cobblestones. Iker and Nik are walking down the path. I pull away from Annemette, and I'm sure my face looks like hers, cheeks flushed and eyes red.

"Smile," I say, wiping my eyes. "Our princes await."

Annemette clasps my shoulder, a smile already blooming on her lips. "Thank you, Evie."

With that she turns and runs past me and into Nik's arms, squeezing him close and taking a pink tulip from his hand when it's presented. He's changed too, his mud-splattered boots and sweat-worn clothes switched out for a nearly identical, crisp, clean edition.

"When you weren't where we'd left you, we'd thought you'd run off with some other sailors."

Iker winks. "Well, *he* thought that. I knew you'd find none better."

He hands me a red tulip, and I immediately sink into him. Impossibly, this new shirt smells of salt and limes and the sea despite being freshly clean and scratchy with starch.

Nik glances up the path to the court homes, Anna's house prominently standing at the end. His eyes settle on the sharp red brick, and then move to me.

"That was our friend's house, once," Nik says, his chin nodding in its direction. "Has Evie told you about Anna?"

Annemette nods. "We met her lovely grandmother just now. Poor thing thought I was her."

His thumb grazes her cheek in a delicate arc. "I must admit that you do resemble our old friend, but considering Fru Liesel has accused everyone—including me—of being Anna in the years since, I'd tell you not to worry about what she thinks."

Nik and I allow ourselves a small laugh with the others despite how hard it is still to speak of Anna. And while my body is drained from arguing with Annemette, I can't let go of the hope that somewhere inside of her is that old friend. I can feel it in my bones. In my heart. I'm right about this.

I'm right about her.

Tomorrow cannot be her last day, and if Nik can't or won't help me achieve what she needs, I will find a way do it myself.

FOUR YEARS BEFORE

The hero was too big for the room. That had been happening often of late, his new height making trouble with any door-frame or ceiling outside of the castle. Belowdecks on his father's ships was definitely the worst, ironic considering the Viking blood thick in his veins.

It had been a week, and he had to see her again. She'd missed the entire Lithasblot festival that year, swallowed in blankets and despair. He'd visited her every night before his duties, entering a room cluttered with bottles and incense, Tante Hansa's famous healing skills at work. He'd never been to this room before—she'd always come to him. Her house felt like another world—and it was.

It was weeks later now, August bearing down. And still she kept to her house, heartache confining her to her room.

That afternoon she'd improved a bit, sitting up with her back to the wall, reading some dirty old book in the low light. She glanced up as he ducked under the threshold, sitting at the end of her bed—his proper mother and her opinions about boys and girls far from here.

"How's the world outside?"

"Still moving?"

She flinched. He didn't blame her, he'd nearly flinched too.

Whenever anyone called him a hero for saving the life in front of him, his stomach curdled with the knowledge that he wasn't quite heroic enough. Everyone had seen Iker pull him from the water. He'd been stopped, but everyone assumed he'd failed. Everyone, including Evie. He saw it in her eyes, wells underneath them as dark as this room.

Guilt was there too. It filled the space where Anna had been, just as large and unwieldy as an eleven-year-old girl. His guilt lay in his failure to save her, her guilt in the fact that she'd put Anna in danger in the first place. In some other part of Havnestad's world, there was disappointment there too—that he'd saved the fisherman's spawn instead of a friherrinde. He was a hero, but in dark rooms and hushed conversation, he was a traitor to his class as well.

"As are you, Evie. You're here. There is so much outside these walls."

To put a point on it, he took a tentative step forward into the tiny room. She watched him as if he might bust through the roof. But he made it carefully to the window, pulling back the curtain she had draped there, letting a sliver of sunlight stream in, blinding and white. The girl blinked so hard, her eyes stayed shut. He waited to speak again until she had the will to open them.

"The world is out there. It misses you."

"That's a lie." And it might have been. But he didn't care about the world. He missed her.

It took four more days of those visits, but he drew her out.

They avoided the beach and the cove, sticking to the market streets—at first. Even though he was there to shield her as much as he could, buying honey buns and the sweet man's fresh saltlakrids with all the joy of a summer day. It didn't stop the stares. Judgment radiated out of every street corner and doorway.

"Acts as if she were the one who drowned."

"The sea takes as much as it gives; it's just the way of things, young lady."

"Saved by a prince and still can't put a smile on that lucky face."

Evie's eyes kept to the cobblestones. There was no way she could enjoy the sun with those stares—even with him by her side.

So he took her away.

He tugged her wrist toward the mountains. Up and up they hiked, the trail twisting toward Lille Bjerg Pass.

There, in a clearing, a mile from the cobblestones, he'd found a sturdy log. One with a particular view of the farmlands sprawling out in the valley below, the sea and its troubles at their backs. They'd never truly been alone like this. Not since they were children, and even then Anna had been there nearly every moment.

Paper bag rustling, he offered her saltlakrids and a smile.

"Salty licorice for your thoughts?"

She didn't touch the bag.

"I knew that was how they'd react." She gestured aimlessly behind her, the entire town in a sweep of her palm.

There was no use in denying it—he'd seen and heard it too. He nodded. She went on.

"They were the same after Mother died and Father would take me to the market, unaware of how to buy for a household with Tante Hansa still away."

She was six at the time, the hero knew. Old enough for memories to truly settle. She looked away from him then, out to the summer-burned pastures below.

"I just want to steal a ship and leave it all. I just want to be me—" She almost said more, but then he snatched her hand in his and gathered the treats in the other.

"Come, then, to the docks. Let's go."

She skipped along beside him, her joyful urgency closer to matching his with each step.

"Where shall we go? Copenhagen? Stockholm? Oslo? Amsterdam? Brighton? Name the place you want to be!"

"Anywhere but here."

"Then anywhere it is."

～

The hero and the girl made it across the strait and to Rigeby Bay that day. The hero's aunt, uncle, and cousin greeted them first with surprise—both at their arrival and that they'd come alone—and then with dinner.

His mother was the angriest when he arrived back at the castle two days later, wearing his cousin's clothes—loose at the shoulders, short in the arms.

Still, his mind wandered to the time they'd had—Evie, Iker, and himself, across the strait—even as his parents dressed him down in the royal apartments, far from where any servant could hear.

Beach walks with hvidtøl (his first taste), his cousin's seafaring stories, and Evie's hair blowing over her shoulders in the bay's famous wind. It was the first time they'd all been together since the day Anna died. His cousin drank enough hvidtøl to become wobbly on his feet; the hero stopped short of a full glass.

"You are twelve and an heir, what were you thinking?"

The three of them collecting sap for syrup in the deep forests, the shadows thicker than clouds under a knot of pine.

"You have duties in Havnestad to your people and your father. You are too old to be running off. Too smart, too important for such whims."

Her grin, crumbs on her lips, at the queen's insistence on butter cookies at every meal to fatten her up.

"Evelyn is a sweet girl, but you care far too much. Believe me when I say you will only get hurt."

His cousin escorting the two of them home, ordering his minder down below as the three of them ran the sails, capable hands all.

"Nik, listen to me. I was young once. I know what it's like to love someone you cannot have."

The hero blinked then, eyes focusing on the queen. "She's my friend, Mother," though he knew the words sounded flat, not at all how he felt.

"I don't think you should see her anymore. It's for the best. It's the only wa—"

"No!" the hero shouted.

"Let him be," said his father, moving out from a shadow in the room. "She is a good girl, Evelyn. Neither I nor Nik nor you, my dear wife, would be here were it not for Hansa. They can be friends. Just friends. Isn't that right, Son?"

The hero nodded. "Yes, Father."

21

THE SUN HAS NEARLY SET, TENDRILS OF GOLDEN LIGHT spraying the beach, when it is time for the close of today's games. The crowd is thrumming with hvidtøl and excitement for the finale—the rock carry championship. The brine of sweaty bodies mixes with the musk of the king's summer wine and the fatty scent of fresh-fried torsk.

Annemette and I pick at the remains of a fruit-and-cheese plate—grapes, a few slivers of rye left alongside crumbles of samsø and Havarti that somehow escaped our lips. We share a cup of honeyed sun tea as well—something I badly need to help calm my nerves.

Iker and Nik are warming up in the inner circle, jogging paces down the course, a hundred yards long. With them are six winners of earlier heats, ready to run one more time today after winning two earlier eliminations to get to this point. The princes, of course, get to run just in the final round. Nik hates the special treatment, but it makes the people happy to see him run, so he complies.

The rocks that they must carry are all beached at the end closest to where we're sitting. They are heavy, each roughly five stone in weight, though they vary in shape.

Little Johan Olsen is getting ready to compete again too. Nik was right: he is a sight. He's so large, he rivals Nik in height and Iker in strength. The oldest of the finalists is Malvina's father, Greve Leopold Christensen. His daughters sit across the arena from our side, Malvina ignoring us, her attention either on her father or the hand pie in her fingers. The other four competitors are fishermen I see on the docks in the morning—in their twenties and thirties, the lot of them.

"What happens if they drop the rock on their foot or some such thing?" Annemette asks, watching Nik practice his start by repeatedly hauling the rock to his right shoulder from a dead lift. She's been nearly silent since the boys left us.

"They pick it up."

"And then what? Drag themselves home on a broken foot?"

"Most likely." I laugh, though it's cruel. "Don't worry, Mette. Nik has done this before. He won last year, in fact. He'll surely have two good feet to dance with you tomorrow night."

He'll also, unfortunately, have two good feet to dance

with the suitors who arrived an hour ago on a steamer so large it could rival the king's. The docks were full of girls, their chaperones, and some parents. Every mark of Øresund nobility was accounted for from equal kingdoms to landholders of each shape—hertug, markis, greve, friherre, and the like.

It's overwhelming, and now that they've filled the rooms of the castle with their trunks and demands, they've crowded around the king and queen on the royal platform. King Asger's expression is unreadable, but Queen Charlotte is soaking up the attention, flitting among the ladies as if each is a tulip lovelier than the next. And Nik, as usual, is being a gentleman, repeating their names, kissing each hand, but still managing to steal some glances our way. Iker is being Iker—loud, grand, princely—but I can see in his eyes that his heart is not in it.

I turn away, finally, after this afternoon feeling confident in what Iker and I have. Annemette, though, continues to watch the chatter. Especially the queen's.

"What do you think the queen makes of me?" Annemette's eyes shift to mine. "She's been friendly with me . . . but then she is just the same with all of these girls." She lowers her voice to just above a whisper. "And she can't be so high that gossip hasn't reached her ears—Malvina's surely not the only one to notice Nik's time with me."

At this I nearly smile from experience. *Everyone's noticed, trust me.*

With the race almost ready to begin, Queen Charlotte has moved to look down upon the competitors, but I know she is only truly seeking Nik for one last wave of good luck.

"She has eyes only for her son. And she wants to see him properly matched."

Annemette's hand presses to my shoulder. I turn to her and find a flash of anger in the depths of her eyes.

"Properly matched? I know we fought earlier, but there is no need to be cruel, Evie. I have as much of a chance as those other girls."

"I didn't mean it to be cruel, Mette. Really. I meant it as a truth. In order to win him, which you know I hope you do, you must know what he is up against. She is quite an opponent." I move into a whisper. "Your father is a king; would he be pleased if you came home with just any boy?"

The anger recedes. "Well, no—" Annemette's face drains of color. "So, it doesn't matter if I stay . . . she'd find out eventually that I can't claim the title I've told her. . . ." She eyes the suitors, all in fine silks and hair ribbons. "Not like those other girls."

"I didn't say it was her choice." I wait until her eyes meet mine and then hold them with a smile. "If Nik is in love, he will fight for you. But it wouldn't hurt to impress her some more. You'll need to show her and these girls at the ball what kind of friherrinde you are."

Annemette laughs. "Oh, I can definitely do that."

The stiff call of a conch cuts off any further conversation, and the race begins. Our heads whirl around to a rush of sand and bodies, lunging down the course. Iker is already in the lead, Nik and Johan right on his tail. Amazingly, Leopold Christensen is fourth, experience making up for his lack of youth.

My heart is pounding as they get farther away, striding one in line with another until they are so far and so in step that it's impossible to discern from our angle who exactly is in the lead.

We leap to our feet along with everyone else, our hands twined in a clasp of nerves, our faces taut with yelling above the din and cheer.

"Go, Nik!"

"Come on, Iker!"

And from my right, "Johannnnnn!"

Across the way, Malvina and her sisters have their hands above their blond heads, chanting, "Papa! Papa! Papa! Papa! Papa!"

As they cross the line, first there is silence. Then a cheer goes up, and the king and queen are applauding. Nik's arms are above his head. He hops atop his rock and claps and waves.

The victory is his.

The other competitors circle around him, slapping hands and patting him on the back with hearty-enough claps that he must check his balance. Iker is the last one to congratulate him, pulling him off the rock, pinning his arms in a bear hug, and running him back to the start line.

The girls on the platform shriek, and the crowd laughs. And the crush of people is so great that it takes several minutes for us to meet the cousins. Both are still breathing hard, sweat slicking their brows, hands on hips. Iker catches my eye and his breath quickly enough to set his future intentions. "Next year, I'll take him. The scoundrel."

Nik's breath is still coming fast enough that he can only shake his head.

"It was close," Annemette concedes, flush with excitement.

"I think your beauty must have made the difference, Annemette. Needed to impress you, the rat."

I wince, though only a little. "I suppose that means we've come past the point where you work to impress me."

"Hardly." Iker leans into me, breath warm in my ear. "I was just planning to impress you in other ways this evening."

Before I can roll my eyes—or better yet, slap him— Nik tugs Iker away from me and regains his voice. "Iker, if you want a night to ourselves, I suggest we leave now." Nik points his chin up at the stairs, where a flock of beribboned girls and the queen are working their way down.

"Well spotted, Cousin." Iker grabs my hand and nudges Nik forward. "Let us away."

22

I LOUNGE UPON THE SAND OF HAVNESTAD COVE.

Above, the stars twinkle, the Lithasblot moon full on this, the fourth night, the shimmering light strong only thanks to the reflection off the smooth waters of the cove. But it is the perfect lantern for the night—bathing everything in a pool of silver.

Iker is lying beside me. The cut of his stubbled chin, the laughing light of his eyes, the sun-kissed pieces of hair curling at his temples fill my gaze. All of it in close relief and profile—my view coming from where I'm snuggled against his chest. It's a perfect moment, and yet my mind drifts to the other side of the cove's rock wall. Where Nik and Annemette are. She is singing, her ethereal soprano lifting toward the stars.

Please Nik, just kiss her.

I don't want it to, but her voice takes me back to that

day Anna drowned, the song we were singing before we dove into the sea. Fru Liesel's words play in my mind: *Bad things follow her. Black death. Minnows* . . . No. I stop myself from falling deeper into that hole. I've come too far from that day to take the blame for it and everything that followed. I have enough to live with.

I shift my attention back to Iker. He's talking about our whaling trip. The cities we'll dock in; the sea life we'll catch. Apparently, I haven't been the only one fantasizing.

"What do you think?" he says, his hand tilting my chin so our eyes meet.

"What's that?" I ask.

"Hirsholmene or Voerså Havn?"

"Oh, whichever you think best," I say.

"Where are you, Evie? Don't you want this?" The vulnerability in his voice is a shock, but strangely comforting to hear.

"Of course I do!" I say, and I mean it. "I'm just thinking of how to tell Father and Tante. You know how they can be."

"Tell them a prince wants to sweep you away. That should suffice." Iker's lips lower until they hover a breath from mine.

"If only," I whisper. He closes the distance and I sink into him, all of him. The pad of his thumb runs the length of my cheekbone and he shifts again until both hands are holding my face to his, our breath mingling and eyes closed to anything but this kiss.

~

Annemette falls into bed in a shower of blond waves. Flecks of sand fall too, bouncing mildly into the air, just forceful enough that I can see them leap and settle in the candlelight as I shake the beach out of my own curls at the vanity table. But something is off. Her eyes are red and her face has gone pale.

"What's wrong?" I ask. "We left when things grew quiet on your side. I thought maybe . . ."

Her shoes are off, her hands running the length of her feet, her face wincing in pain.

"Can I get you anything? Is there a spell that can ease the burning? I may have found something in Hansa's book. Here, I'll show you—"

But when Annemette looks up, I can see that her feet are not what truly pains her.

"I've failed, Evie. I'm going to fail. I know it!"

I swallow hard, because deep down inside, down in the snake pit of my belly, I fear that I know it too. I've been carrying it with me all day. "But there's still tomorrow," I offer, holding out hope. "You can't give up, Mette."

But she shakes her head, almost as if I've made it worse with my insistence.

"We're not supposed to come to land. I should never

have done this! How could I have been so stupid?"

I start to cry, the tears pouring from my eyes. I hold my throat tight so the maids won't hear my sobs. I look up at her—a lost expression on her face, her eyes puffy and dry. And suddenly I realize that she can't cry.

No soul. No tears. No way to truly feel. How is that a way to live?

But if we don't succeed, she won't live at all. And time is running out.

One day left.

FOUR YEARS BEFORE

The one who survived was starting to feel as if she had life left in her.

Most of that was thanks to the boy dragging her out into the sun, to school, up into the mountains.

But there was more to the change of things.

Time. People. Herself.

Winter was at the door, the whaling season at an end, her father home for good, drinking coffee and reading in his chair. They would talk sailing, the young survivor's head spinning with ways to make it easier, ways to make next year more prosperous. Ways for her future self to be successful on her own ship in her own time, far away from the memories of this place.

She spent time with her tante too, soaking up every bit of magical knowledge the old woman thought to share, and stealing any she didn't—tiptoeing into her room and taking one book at a time from her well-worn chest. The lessons could not come fast enough for all she wanted to know about what she would eventually be able to do.

Sometimes she found herself staring at her hands, wishing, as she had that awful day, that she could've saved her lost friend with magic. The failure still ate away at her.

Still, even with Havnestad's archaic rules against

magic—set in place by the same generation of Øldenburgs who'd sent witches fleeing from Ribe more than two hundred years before—the survivor felt it necessary to arm herself so that she would never feel so helpless again.

She knew that with power, the bravery to act would come. The right magic would come at the right time.

And so she read all she could. Begged her aunt for more lessons, more spells. That winter and beyond, her magical education deepened anew, propelled by a desire not just to know herself and her power but what she could do.

The girl even tried to find her mother's words and the history behind them. Digging through the chests for books her father had put away for years. Her tante eventually found out about them and added them to her extensive collection of magical tomes. And then the girl stole them back, one at a time, their dusty covers warped enough that they could easily be hidden within the wrinkles of her sickbed sheets.

And so she studied. And at night, she practiced quick spells with her tante as they made dinner. And then, cozied before a roaring fire, she listened to tales at her father's feet.

23

THREE HOURS LATER, ONLY THE SILVER MOON AND I are still awake. Midnight came and passed long ago, but sleep remains elusive, my mind churning like the angriest of seas. Less than twenty-four hours remain until Annemette's time is up, but I refuse to stand by and watch her become more foam in the sea. I will not be left powerless again.

I slide from the sheets and tiptoe over to my trunk. I open it slowly, revealing my petticoats. Tucked underneath are the amethyst and the vial of black octopus ink. They were in the pocket of the dress I wore at the log race, and I stashed them in here so the dress could be sent to the maids and cleaned—Nik insisted. I gather the two items and close the trunk, dress quickly, then snatch up my boots by the door. Rather than put them on, I pad out into the hall, feeling the cool marble on my bare feet.

I shut the door as quietly as possible and head outside to the tulip garden. Despite the full guest wing, not a soul passes me, and Nik, Iker, and the king and queen are thankfully two wings away.

Outside, the air is warm, but the sky is black, clouds now covering the moon. Up ahead a guard stands watch at the archway. I can't let him see me. I don't even want to think of the rumors that would spread if word got out that I left in the dead of the night, so I've come prepared. With my hand clasped around the amethyst in my pocket, I focus inward, letting the magic rise in my blood. When I'm ready, I take the octopus ink and pull out the small cork stopper. The smell of the sea fills my nose, and I pause before bringing the vial to my lips. *Greíma*, I think, then pour the vial's contents down my throat, the briny liquid making my tongue tingle.

I stand as quiet and still as possible, waiting for the spell to take hold. But nothing happens. *It didn't work.* My stomach sinks. I spent the whole night in bed going over and over this spell, trying to do it just the way I know Annemette would. And now I've drunk the whole vial of ink, and I can't try again. I turn to go back inside, but now my body won't move. My heart begins to pound, and I feel a great pressure crushing my chest. My legs go numb and my vision blurs. When the sun rises, Nik will surely find me lying here dead, another friend gone.

Then, in a split second, it all stops just as quickly as it

started. I suck in a breath of air and bring my hands to my face to collect myself, but I realize I can see right through them. *It worked!* I wiggle my fingers before my eyes, but all I see are the queen's tulips on the other side. I'm invisible—or rather, I'm blending in, my body and clothes camouflaging with the world around me.

I hold my breath and walk as quietly as I can past the guard and out the gate, not risking a glance behind me. Once I leave the castle grounds, I head straight toward my lane, only pausing to put my boots on, a satisfied smile resting on my lips.

At home, I slide off my boots on the stoop, bare feet yet again much more efficient for what I must do. On tiptoe, shoes in hand, I step over the threshold and into the house. Familiar smells of coffee, Tante Hansa's pickling brine, and remnants of boiled octopus ink greet my nose. From Tante's room I can hear her thunderous snores. Father's door is open, his bed still empty until tomorrow night. My room is opposite his, the door shut tight, but that is not where I need to go.

I press myself against Tante's door, the scent of dried roses seeping out with an even heavier round of sound. The knob turns, and I push the door just wide enough for my body. I place a foot soundlessly on each side, sandwiching the door open for a crevice of light.

Eyes adjusting, I step into the room. Tante Hansa is lying faceup toward the heavens. Her eyes are closed and her snores unchanged, so I turn my attention to the reason I am there.

Her trunk.

For Annemette to stay, I must give the magic and Mother Urda something in return—words, gifts, or the perfect combination of both. I just need the right knowledge to guide me.

Tante's trunk is in the corner, ancient moose hide over the top, exactly like it was when I found my amethyst—if she's noticed the stone missing, she's kept it to herself. Just as she has since Anna's death, most likely aware that I've tiptoed in nearly every week, borrowing books to educate myself on all she has refused to teach me.

With careful fingers, I lift off the hide and lift open the trunk. The hinges squeak with a yawn, and the snores hiccup off rhythm. I freeze for a moment before slowly turning to check Tante Hansa. She shifts a bit toward the wall, the weak light from the doorway catching the silver strands of hair braided tightly against her crown.

When the correct rhythm returns, I move again, opening the trunk farther until the lid leans against the wall.

The contents are just as I remember them—bottles of potions on the right, gemstones piled high to the left. And below both of them, what I need.

Magical tomes.

I pick out the bottles one by one, placing them on the hide, then the gemstones, too. As the trunk empties slowly, the books come into view.

I'm unsure which one may have the wisdom I need to keep Annemette here permanently, but I have a decent guess—the one Tante Hansa keeps tucked away at the very bottom. I pull out four books on potions—all near the top, given Hansa's proclivities—before the books with the older, more delicate spines appear. I lean into the trunk from the shoulders on up, my nose a few inches from the covers so that I can read their titles.

The Spliid Grimoire.

I pull the tome onto my lap and I can feel its dense weight on my thighs. It is heavy with pages, but also with power. Inside are hundreds of spells collected through generations. I run my hands along the cover, grazing over the flowers, plants, and symbols that have been etched into its surface. I close my eyes and breathe in deeply, the smell of aged leather, parchment, and ancient inks filling my nose. There's a rush of white-hot heat up my neck, and it's the same delicious feeling that pulsed through my veins when Annemette taught me to spell the oysters—*lif.* The book is pulling me in, calling me, taunting me to open it, when suddenly, I realize the room has gone silent. Tante Hansa's snoring has quieted.

I steal a glance behind me. Tante Hansa has rolled to her other side but is still sound asleep. I don't know how long the masking spell will last, but I'm wasting too much time. I tuck the volume down the front of my bodice, right up against the flat of the ribs under my arm. It bulges, but the darkness should hide it if I become visible. Then I return the other books in order and go to work on the bottles and stones.

I'm just replacing the last stone when I feel a warm dampness against my ear.

"You wicked, insolent child. Stealing from me in the middle of the night."

I pull back, so stunned that my heart is refusing to beat, but Tante Hansa moves her face closer to mine. Her brows are arched down, and her lips are pulled into a sour scowl, the regal lines of her Roman nose and strong jaw made terrifying by an anger I've never seen.

"I'm just borrowing. How can you see—"

She grabs my wrist hard, and I drop the stone to the floor. "Borrowing *is* stealing in the eyes of an owner left in the dark."

In her aging hands, my skin flashes in and out, visible to invisible, until finally my pale arm and my whole body stand out from the darkness as stark as the moonlight. The spell has lifted.

"A witch can always sense the magic that stems from her own blood."

Guilt tugs at my throat. Her room and things aren't a sweetshop, and I'm old enough not to presume so. "I would never steal from you, Tante. I'm just trying to do good—to use your knowledge for good."

"If there's good to be done, I will do it myself. Pride and ignorance cannot learn a spell and save the world; they can only combine for damage." Her fingers twist the skin at my wrist as she goes on. "Why are you here? What are you trying to do?"

I can't tell her. I know she'll believe me, but that's the problem. I promised Annemette I'd never tell anyone who she is. "I told you, I'm trying to do good!"

"No." Tante shakes her head. "This has to do with that girl. The girl who smells more of dark magic than a sailor smells of fish. Annemette, is it?"

I don't say anything. I don't even breathe because it would feel like a betrayal.

I try to stand, but she resists. "You are not blind, child, nor idiotic—though I still believe you to be wicked and insolent in plan tonight. And I believe it has much to do with her. Who is she?" Her eyes crinkle at the corners as she self-corrects. "*What* is she?"

"I—"

"You cannot hide much from this old witch, Evelyn."

No, I can't. But I can deflect. "I just don't want her to go."

"Loneliness is the weakest excuse for magic there is, and it mixes horribly with pride and ignorance." I wince. She nods at the stone by my side on the floor. The one that dropped. "Just because you believe you've stolen from me before and had success does not make you a witch; it makes you a lucky thief."

I should be reeling from her knowledge of all the magic I've done—and the fact that she knowingly let me do it—but my mind is stuck on a single word in that sentence.

Success.

What I've been doing at the docks has actually worked! It was true magic. My magic. Made without anyone's lessons.

I did that.

And I can do it again.

My heart swells. Confidence zips through my veins. The grimoire burns against my skin.

I can do this.

I can save Annemette. If I can reverse the Tørhed, if I can go invisible, I can do anything. I just need the right means.

I press my lips to Tante Hansa's dry cheek and place the fallen stone in her hand. "Tante, I'm sorry. I promise I won't treat your things with such little respect ever again."

"Oh yes, you will, child. They are familiar. One cannot hold respect with the familiar. We forget our boundaries." She moves both hands to my face, snatching my cheeks and forcing me to look deeply into her eyes. "We forget our boundaries with familiar people, too."

I nod. "I am sorry."

"As am I, child."

She lets me go, and it's not until I'm slipping on my boots in the moonlight outside that I realize she didn't mean only herself when discussing the familiar.

She meant everyone familiar at play—Iker, Nik, and, most especially, Annemette.

FOUR YEARS BEFORE

Deep under the splashes at the surface, where the men came in one after another spurred by the boy's orders, five girls with golden hair circled 'round a curiosity from above.

A little girl, tall but with no telltale signs of womanhood, floated between them. Eyes closed. She was beautiful. Just like they were.

One of the five, the oldest, had snagged the girl by her foot as the tow brought her under. There was no way to bring her up safely. Not with the men above. Not with the chance of being seen.

She could only bring the girl down.

The commotion rallied her sisters. Soon, their father would follow. And it would take every one of them if they were going to save her.

"Lida, you must take her back up," the second oldest said. "The sandbar is just there and—"

"It's too dangerous."

The youngest didn't understand. Mermaids could not shed tears but this one tested the boundary, her small hand wrapped around the girl's finger. "You brought her here to die?"

The oldest shook her head in her determined way. "She is already gone. I brought her here to live."

"Oh, Lida," their father boomed, disappointment in his voice. All the girls turned. "We cannot—"

"We can save this one. Please, Father." He didn't approach. "Just look at her face."

Her tone, her face, his gut—all of it forced him swim forward, a king ruled more often than not by the whims of his daughters. So like their mother in spirit, like his Mette, may she rest in the tide.

The king peered at the girl's face. Creamy skin. Blonde hair. Her eyes were closed but her lashes were full and dark, and he knew that open they would be enchanting, no matter the color.

He looked upon his daughters, each of them pleading, each of them touching the girl in some way. Their spirits lifting her up, keeping her from becoming bones in their sweet blue sand. He didn't want to disappoint them but he knew the limits of his magic. He'd reached them when he'd made their mother, Mette, and he hadn't been able to save anyone since. But maybe, with the girls' help, they'd have enough energy for success. Maybe.

He hoped they would.

With a sigh, he nodded.

The girls, all but the youngest, cheered. Those closest to him used a hand to pat his arm or shoulder with approval, but never fully let the girl go. The youngest was confused. She kept her attention on the girl, nearly the same age as she, watching the stillness.

"But how?"

Her father smiled. "Magic."

The littlest didn't blink—long accustomed to the tricks of the older girls. She knew what her magic could do and it was not this. "Magic?"

The oldest answered for her father, already moving to space the sisters at equal intervals along the girl's body. They had to be just right. They had to do this perfectly, or the girl would turn to bones despite their effort. Despite the fact that all but the youngest knew the story of their mother and the gift she was from a great storm many years ago. She was worse off than this, but not by much. "Yes, come here."

The oldest moved to the girl's head, pointing her father to the girl's feet. This made him laugh again—the sea king, taking commands. His daughters did not appreciate it, their serious faces unwavering from the difficulty at hand. They didn't see how much they were like their mother.

When they were set, the oldest finally yielded and he gave the order, gave them the command to say: verða. Then he turned his triton upon the girl, touching the tip to her toes. Immediately, light sprang forth, crawling up her legs to her torso, climbing until it reached the crown of her head.

And stopped.

The light blitzed out like it was never there at all.

The sea king sighed. The girl's pale skin had begun to turn gray. There wasn't much time. If this was to work, they had only one more chance.

"Let us try again." He looked to each of them. Tried to put confidence into his features. Though he knew how the magic worked. *Barter meant a life for a life unless there was just the right amount of magical energy. If he could complete the transaction by himself so long ago, he could do it with his girls. Surely. Maybe.* "Concentrate."

Again, he touched his triton to the tip of the girl's toes. Stared until all he could see was the girl's graying face. "Verða." The girls repeated it, all of them touching the girl, their eyes squeezed shut. Power in their voices.

And again, a light sprang forth, crawling up her legs to her torso, climbing until it reached the crown of her head. Then, as it climbed her cheeks, something dark and old seemed to seep into the water around them, like frigid air hitting the surface and forming ice. The sea king's triton wavered.

But then it came—a flash of light so crisp and bright that it would've been mistaken for lightning up top. And, for the first time since Mette, it was done.

The girl's chest rose. Her eyes blinked open—blue and beautiful as the sea king suspected. She lifted her head just enough to see their faces, her new body, before confusion and exhaustion took her and she fell into a deep sleep.

The littlest knew she was no longer the youngest. That this girl would be a sister. She ran her fingers along the girl's tail, marveling at the fresh turquoise scales, shimmering in the deep water.

"What shall we call her, Father?"

"Mette," he said without missing a beat.

The girls knew what this meant. It made the oldest's spine

tingle and fingers shake. She had to say something.

"On the surface, they call her Anna. The men are yelling her name over and over."

The sea king read the faces of his daughters. Glanced down at the sea's newest mermaid. The littlest of his girls. He smiled.

"Annemette. Let us call her Annemette."

24

THOUGH SOFT AND SUBTLE, THE BLUE LIGHT OF THE morning stuns me awake, and the sound of the sea echoes in my ears. *The sea.*

My eyes fly open. Candle still flickering. Book splayed pages down in my lap. My back propped against the rock wall.

I fell asleep in my workshop. *My lair,* I think with a smile. But quickly I snap back to reality. That was not part of the plan.

I grab the grimoire and carefully flip it toward the right page, the parchment delicate and thin. I'm looking for the one with the triton. I thumb through all the pages, but on my first try, I don't find it. It's too dark in here. With a frustrated huff, I grab the book and the candle and pad across the dirt floor to the cave's entrance.

Dawn is just minutes away, the indigo night reaching

past Havnestad to the west while a shade a tick lighter licks at the horizon. Between the coming light and the glow of the candle, I calm myself and read with eyes bleary from a lack of sleep.

Luckily, I found what I was looking for before my body gave in to rest last night. I can almost recite it—but I don't want to take any chances, recalling the panic I felt earlier when I thought the masking spell had gone wrong.

In the brighter light, I focus my eyes on the flipping pages, attention on the upper right-hand corner.

Where is it?

After a few minutes, there it is—the triton. Etched into the page, the symbol of the sea king. I huddle over the page and read.

The sea is forever defined by its tide, give and take the measure of its barter. In magic, as in life, the sea does not give its subjects lightly—payment is required, the value equivalent, no matter the ask. A shell, a fish, a pearl of the greatest brilliance—none can be taken without a debt to be paid.

I know magical barter. I've known it my whole life. I saw it in my mother's eyes the moment before she died, giving her life for mine. If there's a way out of the spell Annemette used to come to land, I'll find it.

I look up at the sun rising.

In eighteen hours it will be midnight.

In eighteen hours, Annemette's time is up.

I can't lose her again.

Blowing out the candle, I hide my book in a crevice in the wall and slide the crate of oysters in front of it.

My fingers dab at the pearl at my throat—*Annemette's pearl*—the light that showed me the way to my own magic. I'm grateful to Annemette, and now, hopefully, I can return the favor.

I make my way to the docks, the winds from deep within the Øresund Strait airing out the crowd of ships with fresh breeze and salt brine. Every spot is full, and half the boats will be leaving in the morning. Half the boats, including Iker's—with me on board. A warmth grows in my heart when his little schooner, towed in and repaired from the storm, comes into view, tied in place to the royal dock.

I press the little amethyst to the hull of Iker's boat for double the time I do any other ship. But I do touch them all, moving swiftly, repeating my words. This magic needs to be done before I test the kind that will keep Annemette home.

In an hour, I've finished. Dawn has risen completely, scarlet and salmon painted in wide swaths about the horizon. It's just bright enough that I squint into the light as I stand on the edge of the royal dock, the one that leads deepest into the harbor.

My heart begins to pound, a nervous twinge climbing my spine. *Seventeen hours.* I know how to exchange words for what I want, but not items, so now is the time to work it out. I place one hand on the pearl and hold my amethyst in the other. My two most prized material possessions. Items I'd fight for—though it's a toss-up as to which one I should use. I squeeze my eyes shut and make my choice.

Then, I summon Annemette's confidence. Mother's magic. My own stubbornness.

There's no reason why this won't work.

I can do this.

I can do this.

"Skipta."

From the tips of my toes to the crown of my head, the oldest of magic crackles through me like Nordic ice ripping through a ship's hull. The sea pours into my veins.

I toss the amethyst into the waters, and I watch it sink.

Then I wait. My heart thuds in my ears, fear mingling with the magic's chill. At my throat, the pearl throbs, frozen. I tell myself to be patient. Remember last night. This is how it works, but after five breaths, the panic is so great in my heart that I drop to my knees.

Fickle sea with nothing to give.

I haul myself over the side of the dock, fingers straining against the weather-beaten boards as I get my face as close to the surface of the water as possible, vision straining for any sign of my precious gemstone.

But all I see is my reflection. Pale and nervous, exhaustion and worry coating my features.

"What have I done?"

Shame bites at my heart. Heat rises in my cheeks, but a chill runs the length of my spine. I whip my head up and fall back onto the dock, curls snagging in the boards. My fingers dab at the pearl.

Tante Hansa was right—I was a lucky thief, but with cheap parlor tricks. I'm not a witch yet—not like my aunt, my mother or Maren Spliid. I'm just a—

Sea spray cuts off my thoughts, shooting straight up from the water like a whale spout just below the surface. My eyes widen as they scan an object within the stream. I struggle to sit up fast enough to cup my palms into position as it begins its descent.

When it lands, I close my grip, protecting it. Protecting the hope that has risen in my heart.

I take a breath and open my hand.

A stone as blue as the noontime sky and smooth as glass sits there, the same weight and size as my amethyst.

Just as sure as the tide, it worked.

I gave. It took. It gave. I took.

Just as I'd hoped.

Clutching the blue gemstone, I hop to my feet and meet the sea's gaze.

"*Skipta.*" *Exchange.*

I drop the gemstone back in the water and hold my

breath, thinking about my amethyst. Hope piling in my heart that I can haggle with the sea to get the exact exchange I want.

"*Skipta*," I repeat, and then whisper the only Old Norse word I know that's close to what I want. "*Bjarg.*" Stone.

Cupping my hands, I stand there, eyes on the horizon. Two gulls play on the water's surface, dipping, splashing, and rising in tandem.

As they soar just above my head, another spout shoots up from the deep. Bigger and stronger, it sprays the royal dock and me with it, but I hold my ground, hands outstretched.

Another item lands in my hands. Palms still together, I run one wrist over my eyes to clear the seawater there, blink the blurriness away, and then reset. Breath held, my fingers bloom open and reveal not my amethyst but something even more radiant.

A stone of deep crimson, jagged crystals a crust on its surface like rock sugar. Its heart is as bloodred as my own, seemingly lit from a fire within.

It is not what I had in mind, but it's blinding with beauty—much more so than my amethyst. But can it do what my amethyst can do? Or will it wreck the spell?

I can't worry about it now. It's clear from the magic's response that it will only trade like for like. The exchange will be the same when Annemette is in place of the stone. And I do not have a body to give the sea.

This *is* a problem.

But maybe the solution has already come to pass—four years before. Perhaps now I can foster the final trade.

"What is it with you and me and mornings?"

Nik.

I turn, holding the gemstone against the folds in my dress, wishing I had the right angle to drop it into my pocket without being obvious.

The twinkle in Nik's eyes doesn't let on to how long he's been standing there. He's fully dressed and clean-shaven, shoulders square and hands on his hips.

"I promise I didn't stalk you to hassle you about kisses again."

"Mm-hmm, that's what they all say."

A blush rises so quickly on Nik's cheeks that I know he's immediately wishing he hadn't shaved before the sun. "I truly am sorry. It's none of my business."

I smile at Nik. "Of course it's your business—you're my best friend."

He takes two steps and sinks to the dock, his boots kicking over the side and dangling. I find a dry patch of wood and sit next to him.

"Some best friend I am," he says. "Always ditching you for duty. And you can't even talk to me about boys—one word about kissing and I become a beet-red gargoyle."

I put my hand on his elbow and use the other to squir-rel the stone into the pocket hidden in the gown's folds.

—229

"To be fair, we are talking about your best friend kissing a cousin you treat like a brother."

He nods. "It's true. Why couldn't you go for someone a little *less* close? Say a Ruyven or Didrik or Jan?"

I can't help it: my nose scrunches immediately. "Because Ruyven or Didrik or Jan . . ." *believe I think I'm too good for them.*

"Aren't Iker?" Nik cocks a brow.

Now it's my cheeks that flame up and I point to them, laughing. "This is how you look when we talk about kissing."

Nik laughs, and just the word *kissing* makes him blush too. When our eyes meet, something about his face softens. He brushes a wayward curl away from my cheek—not in the romantic way of Iker, but in the loving way of family.

His thumb and forefinger linger in my hair, and I laugh again because I'm not sure what else to do. After the sound dies, I can't draw in a breath. I can't do anything but hold his eyes.

"Moving in on my territory, Cousin?"

We whip around and there is Iker, fully dressed but not clean-shaven, a ship rope spooled about an arm.

"I can't help it if my best friend is the prettiest girl in all of Havnestad."

Iker doesn't laugh. His voice is as sturdy as his ship. "Wouldn't say that too loudly—I have it on my own authority that you never want to anger a blonde."

I force my features into an overdramatic pout. "Did someone get burned once upon a time?"

A devilish grin spreads across Iker's lips, and that familiar joyous light winks in the icy depths of his eyes. "Yes, and it still hurts." Then he hooks a brow. "My mother always told me a kiss can make it better."

I get to my feet. I can still feel Nik's fingers in my hair. "There's plenty of time for that later."

"There is," Nik adds, putting himself between me and Iker. "Now, let's get back to work. Your ship won't prepare itself."

"That's rich, given you were the one to walk down the dock and not come back."

"Where are you going?" I ask suddenly, worried that Iker might be about to leave without me.

"Father wants to take the castle workers on the steamer for the Celebration of the Sea today."

In my sleep-deprived state and my focus on the ball, I'd forgotten about the Celebration of the Sea, the afternoon party on the harbor before the grand event. It's fun, everyone in Havnestad with their boats anchored a little way out in the water. It manages to bring us closer to our cherished sea, and yet, looking back to the coast, we can see how beautiful our home truly is.

"Anyway," Nik goes on, "Mother plans to have all her special guests and their minders aboard the old three-sail. And Iker doesn't want our party to go with either."

"Stupid as a plastered horse, that would be," Iker grumbles.

"So we made the royal decision to take the schooner."

It's silly, but my breath catches. "Just the four of us?"

"Indeed." Nik nods. "As long as we can ship off before my parents get wind of what we've done."

My heart rises. Just the four of us all day on a boat. Laughing, singing, eating, before dressing up and dancing the night away—a fitting end to our Lithasblot and a fabulous beginning to the new way things will be. The weight of the gem in my pocket tells me this is right.

"Perfect."

25

ANNEMETTE IS AWAKE AND DRESSED WHEN I RETURN, standing at the window, looking out to the sea. Despite the sky and sun pouring in, there's a weight to her silhouette, as there should be. This day—the next sixteen hours—means life or death.

If she hears the door and my footsteps, she doesn't turn. Doesn't ask where I've been. After a moment, she finally speaks. "It's so beautiful, watching the sea from this view," she says, now facing me. "But I'll never be able to go back, and I can't stay here. Oh, Evie. I shouldn't have come!" A sob squats in her voice as she buries her head in her hands.

There's not time for talk like that. No time for wishes and should haves.

"I know what to do," I say.

"No." She lifts her face, furious in the new light even as her voice cracks. "I told you. You can't use love magic,

Evie. You don't understand how this works! What I've done. What I have—"

"Yes, I do." I take a step closer, stubbornness squaring my shoulders. "And if Nik doesn't have the answer, I do. I've found the right spell. Between the two of us, we can keep you here. I know it. I have it figured—"

"No. You. Don't." She lunges toward me and grabs my wrists. Her angelic face blooms with pockets of deep red. "Whatever little spell you've created doesn't matter. The magic won't take anything else. It won't, it won't, it won't . . ." All the fight drains out of her in a flood, and her body sways and then begins to sink. I catch her on the way down and try to soften the blow as we hit the stone floor in a heap of silks and gold thread.

Her head dips into my lap, her shoulders heave in wracking shakes, and she moans. No tears, of course. I know that now. I place my hands gently on the back of her head, combing my fingers through her hair. I take a deep breath and let my voice settle, calm.

"We're spending all day on a boat with Nik. Just the four of us. And then there's the ball tonight. Balls are the most romantic venue in all the world—true love is practically a decoration."

Annemette tosses her head from side to side in my lap, but she doesn't say anything.

"If after the last dance, the magic still hasn't been

satisfied, we'll do it our own way." I wrap my arms around her shoulders and lay my head upon hers. "I won't let you go."

⁓

Annemette's nerves are as obvious as her freckles as we appear in the sunlight.

She's nervous about the time remaining.

About Nik's feelings.

And, almost more than any of that, she's nervous about being on the water. I know now that when she transformed, she had to let the sea go in every way possible, and it won't take her back, not even to indulge her to enjoy a day gliding on its back.

I grab her hand and give it a squeeze as we spot the boys by Iker's schooner. Iker and Nik each have a tulip in hand—pink for Annemette, red for me.

"Ladies," Iker says, "you're so beautiful today, the mermaids will be fuming with jealousy."

I do a little curtsy, and Annemette bobs with me. "Convenient, then, that we have two dashing princes to keep us safe from their clutches."

Iker cocks a brow and draws me in for a kiss on the cheek. "You're meant for my clutches, not theirs." His arms squeeze my waist in a bear hug.

Blushing lightly at the ears, Nik rolls his eyes. "Is this how it's going to be all day with you two?"

Iker meets my eye. "Probably."

Another roll of Nik's eyes, and then he tugs at Annemette's arm. "Let's go, before it gets so crowded we can't leave the dock." I lift my brows in encouragement at Annemette, mouthing, "You'll be fine." She turns a nervous smile toward Nik.

Iker and Nik hop onto the schooner first and hold out their hands to us—no gangplank available. I step into the boat next and immediately regret not waiting to help Annemette. Her coloring has not improved, and now she stands alone on the dock, both hands gripping her tulip with white knuckles.

"Are you all right?" Nik asks, stepping forward.

Annemette nods, but there's no credibility in it.

"She's a tad nervous—boating accident when she was a kid."

The kindness in Nik's face makes me melt. "I know what that's like. I haven't told you about my recent incident, have I? It was scary, but the best way to beat the fear is to get back on the water. And you're with an expert sailor today, Mette," Nik says, slapping Iker on the back. "The best there is. You're safe here. I promise."

Annemette nods but doesn't move to come aboard.

"Here, jump to me," says Nik. "I'll catch you."

Annemette takes a deep breath. After several seconds, she leaps into his arms.

I stumble back out of the way just in time to give them more room. Nik's excellent balance keeps them upright, and

Mette lands as gently as possible on the little schooner's stern, a grateful smile at her lips as she beams up at him, scooped against Nik's chest. Exactly where she needs to be.

~

"Summer wine, Mette? It calms the nerves," Iker says, sitting down on the bench next to me. Annemette shakes her head at his offer.

I meet Nik's eyes. "Perhaps some water?" Nik nods for Iker to retrieve it from the chest he filled with chipped ice.

We'd made it to the mouth of the harbor with ease and were now pleasantly floating. Well, pleasant for everyone except Annemette, who can barely look over the rail.

Iker returns and slips the canteen to Nik, who uncaps it for Annemette.

She takes a greedy pull. "Better?" Nik asks, and she gives another unconvincing nod.

Iker grabs a large jug and fills a tin cup with the contents—from the smell of it, hvidtøl.

"Starting early, Iker?" A glint rises in Nik's eye, and he takes a swish of Annemette's water.

"Starting right on time. And who do you think you are, second-guessing the captain on his own boat?"

"Someone who is often in charge and remains sober for his duties."

"This is a festival, and there has been entirely too little drinking for my taste. I am eighteen and a prince. I can enjoy myself on my own ship as I please."

—237

"Iker, may I have some water?" I ask, because they can't continue this way. Not that I'm sure I can stop them, but I'll settle for distracting them as a means to turn this around. It's *supposed* to be a romantic jaunt.

Iker plops down on the bench and takes a long swig from his tin cup.

"If your sober prince wants to share, of course you may."

I eye the flask—most likely Iker's personal water jug and no more. It sits lightly in Nik's hand, a third gone with two measly glugs.

"Not to second-guess the captain, but is that all you brought to drink?"

Iker shakes his head into the cup. "Like I said, there's summer wine," he says before raising the jug in his hand. "And hvidtøl too. I'm not an idiot—I know it's hot."

I roll my eyes. "What about to eat?"

Iker stands and flips open another chest of ice, plunging his free hand into the depths. "Ah, yes, cheese and fruit and not a single thing more. What is this? A garden party? There's not even a herring."

"Mette's allergic," Nik says. He was in charge of packing the food.

"Well, I'm not. And allergy, my arse. She's just being particular to watch you fall all over yourself to accommodate her."

Annemette winces and heat grows in Nik's cheeks, a true argument brewing in his veins. While I'm pleased to

238—

see fire from Nik regarding Annemette, it does nobody any good if the boys toss each other overboard.

I place my hand on Iker's forearm. The bickering is too much and almost as bad as the lack of water and food. If it goes on, this day will truly not go as planned. He turns to me and I give him a calming smile.

"We have the sun and blue sky and each other. We have enough."

Iker draws me in to the flat of his chest—the scent there more than salt and limes, a sour note from the hvidtøl ruining the balance. Nik glances down.

"Evie and her quick mouth. Always right, even when she is very wrong," Iker says.

"I *am* always right." I smack him on the arm but let him hold me against his chest, his heartbeat slowing as the fight drains from him.

"Don't trip on that pride, Evelyn. It'll hurt even more when you take a tumble," he jokes.

It takes several hours, but Annemette is eventually at ease enough to unplaster herself from Nik and, dare I say, *enjoy* our time at sea. She stays close to him, to be sure, but she becomes comfortable enough to share some berries and cheese with me, and conversation with us all.

Iker and I sit with our backs against the hull, facing Annemette and Nik at the mainmast. Nik has drifted off to sleep, having had a little too much wine, comfortable with Annemette at his shoulder. Iker has yet to slow on the hvidtøl, and it hasn't made him sleepy as much as it's made him more of a cat, enjoying a sunbeam with his claws out.

"Are you feeling better, Friherrinde Mette?" Iker asks.

Annemette responds with a regal nod.

"Good. Over your fears, then? A changed woman now that your prince is asleep?"

I elbow Iker hard. "Enough," I say. "I don't know why you're being like this. So . . . impolite."

"Forgive me, Evelyn. It isn't polite, it's true—I am a prince, and though I don't prefer it, I follow social norms most of the time. But my family is another matter." His eyes flash, ice blue and hot. "When it comes to them, I am never polite. It is worthless to be polite when something so important is on the line."

Annemette swallows, and I'm fairly certain all three of us steal a glance at sleeping Nik.

I should speak up and stave off Iker, but I can't. Nik is just as important to me as he is to Iker, and an ill-timed defense of Annemette would come off as wrongheaded. It also might put more strain on this day—enough to carry over to our whaling expedition. With a coward's heart, I shut my eyes and let him attack.

"So, yes. I want to know everything about you, Friherrinde Mette. Starting with how you came here—and why you arrived ahead of all the other invitees. And just as much as I want to know those things, I want to know even more how you knew to befriend Evie to get access to Nik."

I wince. Because he's right. But I'm too afraid to open my eyes and see Annemette's reaction. Both to his drunken questioning and to my cowardly silence.

"Thank you for your concern, Cousin." My eyes fly open, and Nik is awake and straightening himself from sleep. Annemette huddles against him while Iker's teeth are bared in something of a smile—but the intent is much fiercer. "But interrogating our guest isn't the way to go about it."

"She hasn't been properly vetted."

"Who are you, my mother? When did we stop taking people at their word?"

"*You* never have that option."

Iker shoots to his feet, and Nik is right after him. They lean into each other, jaws tense and features reddening.

"You are the sole heir to the jewel of the Øresund Kingdoms, the richest fishing village in the strait," Iker spits. "You can't just go throwing your future at a stranger."

"How is that worse than what you do? Throwing your pole in every corner of the ocean, tossing back any girl you catch?"

"If I'm so horrible, why in the name of *all the gods* would you let me be sweet on someone *you love*?"

My heart flutters at the word *love*, though there really isn't a better word for our friendship. Nik stares at Iker for a long time before he answers. "I thought Evie would be enough to settle you down. And, considering you're planning on taking her whaling in the morning, I think she's succeeded."

My eyes shoot to Annemette's. There's surprise in them—as much as I imagine in mine at Nik knowing our plans. There's something else there too, but I can't look long because the boys start up again, hands balled at their sides, color in their cheeks, faces an inch apart.

"This isn't about Evie. This is about the fact that you are so blinded by that thing in your chest that you can't see this girl for what she is—a complete and total stranger with no proof that she is who she says." Iker takes Nik's shoulders with a firm grip. "Her story is thin and her credentials are nonexistent—that makes her motives suspect. I have met many people in my travels and—"

"The fact that *you* are well-traveled does not make *me* naïve." Nik shrugs off Iker and takes a step back, out of easy reach. "And I'd rather be ruled by the thing in my chest than the thing in my trousers—"

A peal of thunder rips through the sky, loud enough to kill the words and anger on Nik's lips. All four of us tense and wrench around in the direction of the sound, to the northeast. A cloud so big and black it appears like night with no end is heavy on the horizon. Just like on Nik's birthday, this storm has come out of nowhere—so sudden it's strange.

But it's a storm, and the three of us know exactly what to do.

Without another word, the boys and I are in motion, working around Annemette, who cowers against the mainmast pole as the boat begins to rock at a heavy clip.

There are far too many ships in the harbor, and we're just beyond it, in the strait and nearly out to sea—much farther out than we were the night of the party, and on a much smaller boat.

The three of us get the ship turned, the food and drink put away, the long oars at the ready. Finally, there is nothing more we can do other than hunker down and row forward—just what every other boat in the strait is doing at the same moment. Well, save for the king's steamer, which is puffing merrily toward the dock, cutting a path through slower-moving vessels.

Ships clog the harbor, and where progress is slow on the water, it's quick in the sky. The storm beats at our backs, wind blowing in the right general direction, but also serving as a warning call. The stronger the wind, the closer the storm.

"Evie!" Nik calls between heavy breaths as he and Iker row for it. "Help Mette."

I leave my spot at the wheel and slog to the mainmast post, where Annemette is huddled, hanging on for dear life. I sink down beside her and press my bodice against her back, shielding her from the storm as much as I can.

The rain begins to pound down, and I feel her shudder beneath me.

—243

"I just want to go home."

"I know, Anna—Mette. Mette, I know."

She doesn't react to my stumble. She just repeats herself. Over and over.

As lightning flashes, something hard and biting thwacks me on the back of the head. I shake it off and turn to where the object has fallen to the ground.

Hail.

My heart drops and I raise my head. White chunks are flying through the air, plunging into the harbor in a deluge, rocks falling as fast and knitted together as fat raindrops.

I scan the horizon. We're at least four hundred yards out, and more than two dozen boats stand in our way of safety. We're small enough to cut around the bigger ships, but even with the boys rowing at full strength, I'm not convinced we're agile enough to not get crushed in the process.

I glance to the left. To the cove—the natural shelter. It's completely open, no ships there.

"The cove! Can we land in the cove?"

Behind me, Iker's voice booms over the rain, pinging hail, and another slice of thunder. "As good a chance as any. Cousin?"

Nik lifts his head, not once wincing as two hailstones smack into his flop of wet hair. "I'm not sure of the obstructions. But it's our best chance."

Taking that as a yes, I squeeze Annemette before

running for the wheel to help steer as Iker adjusts the mainsail to change course.

We get going in the right direction, and Iker turns to me. "Evie, stay. We need you to hold course against the wind."

I take one glance at Annemette. One glance at Nik. Iker's right.

We cut around the queen's three-sail, skip around two other schooners, a sloop, and the tiniest of one-man rowboats, and zip in a line to the cove. The blind part of the beach comes into view first, then the rock wall, and finally, Picnic Rock.

We enter the cove and I take a deep sigh of relief, my arms shaking while holding our line, red welts from the hail rising on my exposed skin.

Then Annemette begins to scream.

"Turn! Turn! Turn!"

I follow her eyes, but I don't see a thing. There's nothing but rough water ahead, our boat still too far out for the footstep islands to be a hazard. "Sandbar!"

Just as the word slips from her mouth, we shudder to a halt—run aground with water on all sides.

I meet her eyes and know exactly how she knew the sandbar—submerged and hidden from sight—would be there.

She's the only one of us to ever swim so far out into the cove.

I wait for the questions to begin. But they don't come. Instead, Iker is silent as he bends over the bow to survey the situation—both how stuck we are and what the damage might be. I truly hope there's no damage. "Time to swim for it, crew."

Nik leans over and confirms. "Yes."

"No!" Mette shouts, still clinging to the mast pole. "I can't."

But Nik isn't accepting that. "It's a hundred yards. I will swim you in. You'll be fine."

Iker drops anchor so that his boat won't float away when the storm ends and the sandbar releases it. He comes alongside me and brushes a few half-melted hailstones from my hair.

"Leap together?" He takes my hand and we step to the edge of the bow. The water is alive, waves at a rough clip, revealing the octopus that has haunted the cove since the beginning of summer, plus schools of large fish and several dolphins. The cove is practically overflowing with more animals than should ever inhabit it—unusual animals. My mind flashes to my spell, my daily call for abundance.

No, it can't be. I didn't do this. It's the storm—pushing sea life out of place.

Before I can think any more, Iker is pulling on my hand to go, and we leap into the cool water.

The hail has stopped, and the thunder has rolled into the mountains ringing Havnestad. Tendrils of lightning still flare in the sky, and the rain remains steady, but the swim isn't the worst I've ever had. Rocky and rough and exhausting, but I make it to shore just seconds behind Iker, pulling myself onto the nearest pile of sand with a great heaving breath. I roll over and fill my lungs again and again with salt air, sand caking the wet folds of my dress.

He helps me up until I'm in a seated position and have a view of the cove, where I watch Nik pull Annemette to safety. He holds her head above water, her body flat against his. My heart fills with love for him all over again, knowing that not long ago, I was the girl in his arms, being swum to shore in a terrible tide.

Nik's stroke doesn't miss a beat, and they are on land soon enough. His breath is thick with effort, hers with fear. In his eyes, I'm sure I see a spark of love—something I hope tonight's ball will truly ignite—and Annemette will be home at last.

THREE AND A HALF
YEARS BEFORE

The newest mermaid simply became another royal sister, her memory in such a state that she believed she had always been there. Everyone said so. Even if she had the nagging feeling that her life felt like one big conversation entered years too late.

She was just a little mermaid, swimming in the collective shadow of her five older sisters—Lida, Clara, Aida, Olena, and Galia. Blond and fine-boned all, full of cheer and manners. Together, the six girls were the pride of their grandmother, the Queen Mother Ragnhildr, or as she preferred, Oma Ragn.

The little mermaid loved Oma Ragn with a special fierceness—she felt at home when she was with her. At home, folded into the long white waves of her hair, against the warmth of her skin, the song she hummed under her breath just louder than their collective heartbeat.

But Oma Ragn was more than a comfortable lap and soothing voice. She was their guide to life in the palace. Their tutor. Their example. Their goal. Days began with lessons in policy, lessons on how to rule, followed by the sciences and the arts. Nights were filled with music and magic, the lessons shifting with the shadows in the water, becoming less definitive, more dreamlike.

To the little mermaid, this was how it had always been. How it always would be. Until something happened that she hadn't predicted.

One morning, there was a great fuss, her third-oldest sister, Aida, at the center of it all. Her room had been done up in garlands of twisted seaweed with sparkling shells twined throughout. The little mermaid swam through, admiring every last detail, but she didn't know what it was for.

The little mermaid found the ear of her sister closest in age, twelve-year-old Galia. She settled in so that they were shoulder-to-shoulder and whispered as the others circled around Aida, adjusting ribbons in her hair. "What is this?"

Galia opened her mouth as if to speak and then snapped it shut, finding the correct words a few moments later.

"It is the fifteenth year since Aida's birth."

The little mermaid thought this might mean a celebration. Galia read the confusion on her face. Again, Galia seemed to choose her words carefully, tugging the little mermaid farther into the shadows.

"On the fifteenth anniversary of a mermaid's birth, she can go to the surface."

The little mermaid's eyes grew large. "The surface?" It had never occurred to her that this was even an option—she'd been told many stories of the dangers above, humans with their harpoons and nets a terrifying reality. It wasn't something she wanted to get close to. Ever. But Galia was smiling.

Smiling.

As were all her sisters and Aida herself. Beaming *might* have been a more appropriate word.

The littlest mermaid got the distinct feeling this was something she should've remembered—two of her other sisters would've already celebrated in this way. Instead, her mind held endless black upon black, no remembrance shining through.

Still, she waved away her own question as if she'd known all along. "Oh, yes, of course."

It did not do to make waves.

26

NIK AND IKER DEPART DOWN THE HALL TO THEIR WING in a soggy mess, tired, calling for the kitchens and a hot bath. We will see them in three hours—standing at the palace ballroom's doors, welcoming guests into the Lithasblot Ball.

It's a grand end to the festival, but it's not just for the nobles. Everyone is invited to partake in the music, dance, and great feast—all of Havnestad equals for one night.

Normally, Nik only has to choose from local noble ladies and common girls to dance with, ever the egalitarian prince, giving each girl a chance. But things will be different this year. Aside from Annemette, there will be dozens of the queen's girls waiting, fighting, and grasping at their chance to dance with him.

Those girls must still be aboard the three-sail, probably down below, protected from the hail and rain.

Protected, unlike us.

Annemette and I shuffle down the guest hall in enough of a state that I really don't want to know what I look like. I thank Urda that the queen is not here to pass judgment. But what I see of Annemette does not give me hope. Her waves are tangled; deep-red welts cover her arms, every shard of hail having left its mark; and the pre-storm sun made its presence known as well, flushing her forehead and nose as pink as the natural blush at her cheeks.

I can only hope a bath and the three hours we have to dress will improve such matters for both of us. It's difficult to have the most romantic evening of your life while resembling ghosts of the bubonic plague.

We reach our room, and Annemette immediately falls into bed, sodden clothes and all. She bounces as much as the down mattress will allow before settling in a heap of hair and rags.

"Are you all right?" I ask, sitting on my bed across from her.

She answers with a smile. "I am more than all right—Nik has asked me to open the ball with him."

I gasp. Each year the king and queen take the ball's opening dance. And now that Nik is of age, it makes sense that he would dance alongside them—something even I didn't know. Something maybe Nik didn't know until his mother's guests arrived.

"That's amazing." If that invitation doesn't show

blooming love, I don't know what does. And after a night of staring into her eyes, there's no way Nik won't fulfill the magical contract.

"It is," she agrees. "Though I am thoroughly exhausted. We have time for a nap, don't we?"

I catch my reflection in the length of the window—red spots on a pink sea and a bird's nest of curls. Iker hasn't asked me to open the dance, though surely he will dance too. Maybe he doesn't think he needs to ask me. Maybe he thinks it's implied.

"I don't know—it might take all three hours to mask this and—"

"*Ljómi*," Annemette says, and a frigid breeze flows over my head and down my arms. It's cold enough that my eyes snap shut for a moment until it blows over.

When I open them, and see myself in the mirror, I'm completely different. My hair is clean and bouncy; my skin is glowing, all redness gone. I am radiant. My clothes are still a mess, but the rest of me is better than before. And again, I'm reminded that Annemette is more at home with her magic than I ever will be. She *is* magic.

"Thank you. . . . How long will it last?"

"Not forever, but long enough for Iker to have trouble remembering." She yawns. "I'll spell you a new gown later. Now, I need to sleep."

"Mette, you can't—we have less than eight hours until midnight and I need to teach you to dance."

Annemette shuts her eyes. "I'll figure it out. Mermaids dance more than we swim."

No. No. No. What is wrong with her? "Dancing with your legs is a lot different, Mette. I mean, I know you're graceful, but do you know the Havnestad waltz? Every girl in that room will know it backward and forward. If you don't do it right, everyone will know your story is false. The king, the queen . . . Nik. It could all fall apart before your time is up."

Annemette sits up and smiles. "All right. You win. Sleep can wait until after I have his heart." She lifts her arms for me to grab her hands, and I tug her into the center of our gilded room. Somehow, she's spelled herself without me seeing, her skin glowing, her hair cascading perfectly over the shoulders of her dress, now dry. Mine remains wet, but I won't ask her to change it. Not yet. I can't distract her from this. We're almost to the finish line. And the ball is more important than any moment we've had yet.

I place her hand on my shoulder and take the other out to the side. My hand goes to her hip. I'm intensely glad Queen Charlotte never succeeded in making les lanciers the dance of choice at the ball—I'd never be able to teach a quadrangle to a mermaid by myself.

And we begin. "One, two, three . . . one, two, three."

She adjusts her hand on my shoulder, clearly bothered by its damp state. *"Purr klædi."*

My dress dries instantly as we spin around the room.

Annemette steps on my toes and corrects but doesn't apologize.

"Just you wait for the dress I'll make you for tonight. If I'd known the last one was going to get covered in Malvina's pie, I wouldn't have spelled one so fine, but I'll have to go all out on this one. Really show the town up—and the queen's girls, too. Iker won't be able to keep his eyes off you."

I smile at her as we spin in circles. "Thank you," I say. And I'm grateful. This afternoon with Iker was difficult, and I'd love nothing more than to get back to where we were this morning.

"You'll look just like a princess."

"But you've already done that once," I laugh.

"Oh, now we're getting picky, are we? Fine, I'll make you look like a queen!"

I laugh so hard, it's practically a royal snort. Then I lead us into another turn, holding her hand tight.

SEVEN DAYS BEFORE

Aida's birthday had unlocked something within the darkness of the littlest mermaid's mind. She couldn't see what was there, couldn't access it, but she'd felt the click of the key settling in. She knew something lay in the endless black, hiding. Waiting to consume her whole, like a shark in a reef.

And with this shift, she noticed something else. A fatalistic obsession.

Humans.

She knew they were dangerous. That they plagued the sea, stealing lives with abandon. Upsetting the balance of things by killing too many or too few. The natural give-and-take forever ruined by their greed, their ships, their nets, their harpoons.

If the "legend" of merpeople were ever proven, they would be mercilessly hunted by humans. Made a sideshow. Sold to the highest bidder.

Confirmation of their existence would be the death of them.

Yet, as she approached her fifteenth year, she began to daydream more and more about observing humans above water. She often left the confines of her father's castle at night, looking for ships to float next to, listening and watching for any signs of what people were like, these trips becoming more frequent the closer her birthday came.

A few days before the special day, she came upon just her type of boat. One without anywhere to go—a monolith simply floating in the tide. Even better, this one had funny little windows in the hull. She'd seen those a few times before, leading to little below-water spaces where humans played cards or stored their treasures, depending on the type of ship.

But these windows were dark. All the people were above, playing music loud enough that the sound drifted below. The little mermaid had always loved music, and she swam along to the lingering notes, swirling and rolling through the water just below the surface.

But then, after a few hours, a light appeared behind the windows. Brighter than the mermaid had ever seen. Light made by more than an ordinary candle. Maybe several candles. Or something larger—a torch.

The little mermaid stopped drifting to the music and rushed to the nearest window. She pressed her face as close to the glass as possible.

And saw into her past.

The girl beyond the window struck her like a bolt of lightning.

Suddenly, all her mind's darkness was illuminated, and she could see everything. The memories in her mind surged forth through the blackness, one right after another in rapid succession, physically knocking her back with their force.

But not before she'd made eye contact.

The girl had seen her.

The girl had recognized her.

Evie. The girl's name was Evie.

And her name—it wasn't Annemette. It was simply Anna. Anna Kamp. Friherrinde Anna Kamp.

And the king's son.

Nik.

Nik, with his sweet face and dark eyes. Stately despite being slim, elegant, and graceful. A lover of music and the arts. So kind. The first memories of him came to her in a golden cloud, as if he'd filtered sunlight itself and bathed in it.

She had to see him.

The mermaid gathered all her strength and pushed forward, back to the little window. Evie and Nik were always together. If Evie was on this ship, Nik was too. She knew it deep in her bones.

But he wasn't there. And Evie was ascending the stairs. Leaving her alone.

If Nik was there, he was above.

Where they were laughing and dancing and singing.

Without her.

And that's when the dark memories crawled forward. Burning so painful she had to squeeze her eyes shut.

That day. Evie and the heavy waves. The dare. The undertow. She would still be alive if Evie hadn't suggested the race.

The little mermaid began to sob—this time very aware that she could shed no tears as a mermaid like she had been able to in a past life. And, oh, how she craved that release.

She'd drowned that day.

Or nearly drowned—she was clearly alive, though her life had been stolen away. Her father—the sea king—must have saved her, or he wouldn't have kept her for his own.

He'd lied to her. They'd all lied to her. Told her she was one of them. Kept her in the dark.

The little mermaid sobbed again, her eyes stinging as she watched the ship float along, the life she could've been living happening above.

And then the last chunk of blackness evaporated. The last images she'd seen as a human surged forth.

Evie drifting down toward her.

Nik's lithe form racing toward her friend's limp body, drawing Evie up to the surface and away. Evie first. Always first.

Then, several minutes later, his shadow returning, his eyes landing on her own body, prone near the seafloor. Him bobbing back to the surface.

Him swimming back down but then stalling out. Caught in the waves by another boy. The one Evie liked—Iker. Another prince.

Nik could've fought, but he'd let Iker pull him up. He'd given up.

Their friendship, the way she felt about him, her life—none of that mattered.

The golden glow around her memories of Nik and her human life with him evaporated. Her fond memories of Evie, the girl who was like the sister she never had, gone. Her happy memories of Iker, always a handsome distraction, no more.

All that was left was anger.

Fury.

Ire.

She wanted to break it all. Shatter it all. Ruin it all.

She wanted retribution for all that had been stolen from her.

She wasn't human anymore because of the choices of these three. She was magic, though. A being of intense and beautiful magic. There was no place the magic ended and she began. She didn't have her rightful life, her soul, but she had her magic and her anger.

And she wanted to use them.

"Veðr."

Storm. Yes. Storm.

"Veðr," she repeated, feeling the magic surge in her veins, saturate her skin, tingle behind her eyes.

She was magic. She was the storm.

"Veðr." Above a clap of thunder rolled, loud enough to shake her waves. It was the most beautiful music she'd ever heard. Yet she wanted to see this happen. See the destruction. Endless waves, and yet she'd suddenly felt so confined.

But she wasn't. A light went on in the darkness, and she knew she could go above.

The day she'd been told was her birthday—three days from now—wasn't her birthday. It was the day she'd lost her rightful life and been reborn, but not the day of her true birth. She'd shared that day with Nik, so if this was his birthday, it was hers as well. She was fifteen. She could go above.

The little mermaid repeated her command as she pushed for the surface. Lightning was growing, the wind was picking up, and the waves were rocking. The boat's hull swayed and suddenly filled with light. People running from her power. Hiding below.

But not everyone.

As she crested the surface she saw the three people from her memories—from that day—up top. She knew they'd be there—always acting like heroes.

Except when it came to her. Their bravery had a limit.

And she would make them suffer.

The boat lurched as Evie and Iker tried to steady it. Nik took orders from his cousin—of course he did—and went to the side of the ship to cut free a little attached schooner.

It was her chance.

"Veðr."

Waves rocked the ship and the prince faltered, hanging on with all his strength. And just when he seemed to settle into his balance, the little mermaid sent the largest wave yet—bigger than the wall of memories that had struck her, bigger than any she'd seen with human eyes—right into the boy who hadn't saved her.

The ship tipped. And over Nik went, into the sea.

His eyes were shut when he appeared before her—his

head striking the hull of the schooner on the way down. No blood. Just Nik, floating before her, looking almost as if he was sleeping.

Peaceful.

The little mermaid took his face into her hands. He looked older now, the beginnings of a beard scraping against her fingertips.

"Why didn't you fight for me? Why?"

Nik answered in bubbles, his lungs failing him.

She thought to let them fail.

She thought to let him become bones in the sand. Her revenge. Yet somehow that didn't feel right. It didn't feel great enough. It wouldn't get her what she wanted back.

And so she brought him to air. Swam him ashore. Her mind churning with possibility as his chest rose and fell in her arms.

The sea king had made her a mermaid—not her choice, not what she wanted. The little mermaid wanted to live above the sea. And she would find the magic to change herself back.

Then she would get her revenge.

27

THE RECEIVING LINE FOR THE ROYAL FAMILY SEEMS TO be a mile long—it curves through the hallways, down the staircase, and out of Øldenburg Castle. It doesn't make it down the exterior stairs and into the tulip garden, but it would have if they'd waited another five minutes to open the ballroom doors.

We stand at the end of the line. Several schoolmates of mine are closest to us—including Ruyven and Didrik. Malvina is ahead of us. As usual, stares come from all sides, cold and dismissive, whispers of conspiracy on warm lips. They all think I have a plan—that everything I do is to assert my place in the palace, where I don't belong.

This time they would be right, I suppose. I do have a plan.

But it's not for me.

If a kiss doesn't do it, I will. I'll take Annemette to

Havnestad Cove and tell the sea what I want. What the magic owes me—owes us. The sea took Anna. I deserve Annemette.

And Annemette, well, she thinks I deserve some of the magic she has tonight. She spelled the dress I'm wearing—an enchanting Havnestad blue, netted with black lace at the bodice. Hers is the same color, but accented with ivory. With our matching pearls and tresses left down and flowing, we're a study in contrasts—light and dark.

I try to take a deep breath in, my nerves piling high, but my bodice is a little tighter than usual. "Pride must suffer pain," Annemette had whispered in my ear as she tied the bodice. I'd think about how tight the queen's bodice must be, but laughing would only hurt more.

People line up behind us as we move forward at a steady but slow clip, the line snaking forward in a constant motion but with the velocity of a centipede. When we wind down the hallway, the entrance to the royal ballroom is finally in sight. I spot King Asger's tall form, crown atop his dark head, sapphires glittering beneath the great chandeliers that light the hall with a golden glow.

I glance to his left and see Nik and his less ornate prince's crown. One more spot and two inches down and there's Iker, wearing, for the first time this trip, his own crown, decorated with the rubies of Rigeby Bay.

Almost there.

Up front, the visiting girls dawdle, finally getting the attention of both princes. The queen is all smiles, and so is Nik—he'd never let these people down. Not in a million years. Iker has on his Prince Charming face, playing up to his reputation with winks and bows and kisses to each girl's hand.

After another long spell, we come to our turn with the king.

"Evelyn, my, you look more beautiful than ever tonight."

"Thank you, your grace," I say, shaking his hand.

"Yes, quite beautiful," adds Queen Charlotte, her eyes narrowing. "Your gown is lovely."

I'm sure she's wondering where I got such an extravagant thing, whether Nik purchased it for me, or worse, I stole it from one of her precious visiting girls. She's too careful to say anything here, though I'm sure whatever rumor she spreads will reach me later.

I take her hand and curtsy.

"Evie, you look fantastic," Nik says when I move down the line to him, and I'm surprised his attention is on me when Annemette stands behind me, looking even more striking. As I turn to him, he takes my hand and kisses it. My breath catches.

"Yes, she does. Hurry up, Cousin," Iker says, irked.

I draw in Nik and give him a peck on one blushing cheek before squeezing his hand. He is simply dashing in his sleek black suit, hair combed and lying perfectly under his crown.

Next to us, Iker clears his throat. Nik gives my hand one last warm squeeze before we part, and he bows to Annemette.

Nik and I joke about Iker's status as Prince Charming, but Iker certainly lives up to it tonight in every way. My heart was already pounding, but seeing him now causes the blood in my veins to grow hot.

Sweeping navy trousers top high-shine black boots. A crisp white shirt peeks from underneath a pressed coat that glows with golden thread and the crest of Rigeby Bay. The sun-kissed highlights in his hair shine in a way that only serves to make the ice blue of his eyes more stunning. The ruby crown is a symbol of his status, yes, but even in rags—even in nothing at all—he would look like a prince.

Iker takes my hand and kisses it, as he's done with all the girls in line. His lips are gentle; the rasp of stubble at his chin makes my skin tingle and the flush deepen.

He straightens to his full height, broad shoulders back, a smile tugging at the corners of his mouth—a subtle movement that makes my knees weak. "I am very much looking forward to dancing the night away with you, my lady."

There's a mischievous look in his eye as he leans into my ear. "Tonight you are the spitting image of a komtesse, but you have the grace of a queen. And in your blood is the sea woman I have fallen for."

It's all I can do not to kiss him right there, in front of everyone. But there will be time for that after all of this. After tonight is the rest of our lives. Together.

SIX DAYS BEFORE

The difficulty wasn't in surviving the humans—it was in returning to the sea castle, slipping into her old life like nothing had happened, when everything had changed.

The little mermaid knew who she was. And as she swam through the sea castle's ornate coral doors, past schools of fish new to this water, she could only think of one thing.

How to get herself back.

She hadn't had magic on land. That much she remembered. But Evie had. She hadn't seen it when she was a girl, but now that magic coursed through her own veins, it was easy to spot in her friend's home, especially with that peculiar aunt of hers.

Oh, what a delicious secret that would been for Anna to have known. Ever the loyal friend, she wouldn't have told anyone.

Magic existed, but it was illegal. A danger to the balance and order of things—at least in the eyes of the Øldenburgs.

Which made the little mermaid's revenge easy. Obvious.

She'd use Evie's magic against her. Force her to perform magic in public. And even better, force the people she cared about most to lay down the punishment.

Nik was trickier. Evie's punishment would torment him, she knew, but it wasn't enough. Evie's punishment would be the start of his, but it wouldn't be all.

And Iker, well, his confidence might kill him before any-thing she did would touch him, the oaf.

But before any of her plans could fully form, she needed to learn how to go above. She knew the stories of "their" mother. She'd been human once too—a witch they tried to drown off the coast of Hirtshals. But Father—the sea king, not her real father—had gotten to her first. Made her his queen. He said it'd been something he'd never been able to do before and hadn't done since.

He'd lied.

They'd all lied.

Which meant there were more secrets. And she knew just where to look.

The day her sisters had turned fifteen, the sea king had made a big show about writing their names in the large led-ger he kept on his desk—the kingdom's official listing of every merperson allowed to go topside. The sea king ruled with order and regulations as a way of protecting his people from discovery.

Thoroughness was his safety net, and so far, it had worked.

He made note of every magical transaction. Thus, if there were a way to get topside, it was likely he would have recorded it.

And so, with the scent of Nik still upon her skin, the little mermaid returned to the castle and immediately snuck into her father's chambers. He kept his business papers in a particular parlor room, one with a view of the great reef below, the million colors of his kingdom shifting in the ocean light.

His snores drifted in from the bedroom. She didn't know how he could sleep so soundly. Not only because he'd lied but because of the chaos taking over his waters. Magic had upset the natural course of things. A spell of abundance was pushing faraway creatures into their seas, creatures who were devouring the scarce resources already eroded by a strange sickness that had attacked the waters only a handful of years ago. The black plague, they'd called it. Most believed it had been magic too.

But the little mermaid knew that soon the sea's problems would no longer be hers.

Quietly sweeping past the sea king's copious bookcases, the little mermaid pulled herself up tight to his grand desk. With deft fingers, she opened the ledger and paged to four years before.

It had been no one's fifteenth birthday that day, so there wasn't a name. Simply a few entries from the sea king about that day's regulated magical activities. On the very bottom line of that day, written so plainly it shocked her, was her birth.

> Annemette joined us on this day, her eleventh birthday. Her sisters and myself brought her to the kingdom with the same magic that brought me Mette. For the first time in thirty years, that spell found success.

If this was written, why had they lied? The truth was there and everyone in the kingdom knew it. Why hadn't they told her?

Just as fury began again to creep up her spine, the little mermaid realized exactly why they'd lied to her face.

They knew I'd want to go back.

So there's a way back. There has to be.

She skipped forward, stopping for any longer entry, hoping for details of how he'd done it.

But she found nothing. Just page after page of dull business—"brought down a ship, the tally is twenty-two men, five barrels of oil, seventeen casks of wine, and ten pallets of silk."

The little mermaid racked her mind for a better guess. Any guess.

A shot in the dark: she turned to thirty years before, looking for the entry marking the "birth" of the dead queen, Mette.

She found the passage dated February 17, 1833—an awful time to drown anyone. Hypothermia might have killed her before water claimed her lungs. In the three-page entry, the sea king went on and on about how the magic he'd used to save Mette had worked, but nearly killed him, leaving him so weak he could barely hold an inked feather to document it all. The magic had indeed been a typical exchange—he asked and he received—but the toll was so great, he'd nearly died.

And in his weakness and burgeoning love, he'd told Mette how she'd come to be a mermaid. He wanted the beautiful stranger to recognize his personal expense in having saved her—maybe that would make her love him, too. Instead, his admission initiated a flood of memories—memories that left her yearning to go back right away.

She'd been a witch. She'd known magic above. And he knew magic below.

And because he already loved her, he told her she could go.

The little mermaid's heart began to pound. Fingers shaking, she turned the pages.

Finally, after lengthy paragraphs documenting weeks of the king's recovery, she found what she wanted.

Today Queen Mette began testing a spell to bring mermaids to land in human form. In previous weeks, the queen had run tests on loyal subjects but failed to send them topside, as the magic stalled out, exhausting her and tormenting them, despite all her knowledge of the ways of magical barter. But this morning, she had an epiphany.

This spell is unlike any other. The magic needs assistance—the energy it uses is too great and deadly otherwise.

Only a life added to the exchange will fill the void. I was powerful enough to save her without sacrificing myself—and love may have pushed me through—but another try could kill me. Which means that to go above, she needs to take a life—a human life.

There were no entries for three days.

And, after that, no entries about it at all. The little mermaid paged ahead.

More than a year later, a new entry with shaky writing.

A storm brought a man into our path today. Mette saw her opportunity—though she'd come to love me, she missed home. She wanted to try the spell.

My queen could not kill a human. But this man's life was over. Laying her hands on him, she repeated her spell.

"Líf. Dauði. Minn líf. Minn bjóð. Seiðr. Seiðr. Seiðr."

The human's eyes jerked open as his lungs released. His skin glowed where she touched him, and soon the glow was bright enough that I could see neither of them.

In a flash the light was gone, the man was fully dead, and there was Mette, just as I'd found her— with legs and lungs, struggling for air. I swam her topside, found her a piece of the human's shattered boat to hang on to, and then swam her to the nearest shore. I am not sure how long the magic will hold, or what will happen when it runs out. Or if I will ever get her back. Mette is on the hunt for a witch to help. She knows of a powerful one in Havnestad—one who will keep our secret.

I fear I will lose her. I fear our people will suffer.

The little mermaid turned the page. Nothing.

She turned the page again. Nothing. The sea king must have spent days waiting for his queen to return. The little mermaid knew she had, for she was the true mother of the girls who she, herself, called sisters.

On the fourth day, a new entry.

I have heard from my dear Mette! The Havnestad witch gave her four days at most. After that, I would need to change her back into a mermaid or she'd be lost to both the sea and land. I told her I was too weak. That I couldn't, but the witch simply smiled and told me I underestimated love's effect on my magic. Mette hadn't loved me when I'd transformed her the first time, but she loved me now. And that made all the difference.

The little mermaid skimmed the rest. There must be a way to keep her legs longer than four days. That couldn't be it. If she had to kill a man, she needed to know she could stay on land forever.

She skipped ahead. Nothing. Nothing anywhere.

Frustrated, she shut the book, careful not to let it slam,

though she wanted to slam it. She wanted to throw it across the room. She raised her arm to do just that when she saw the queen's bookcase across the way. She lunged for the shelf. Thumbed through the spines. And stopped when she saw what she wanted. The queen's diary.

Heart pounding, she flipped to that year. To that day. The day the queen had returned with the sea king's help.

The queen wrote that she had known what it would take to remain on land. Love wasn't just the answer to return; it was the answer to stay. True love would break the magic, the witch had said.

But so, too, would something else—death. A sacrifice so worthy it would make the magic stand up and listen long enough to create a human life.

It was right there in Mette's looping script. The answer to the little mermaid's quest. A way to get both her life back and the perfect revenge.

28

THE BALLROOM IS BRIMMING WITH MERRIMENT.
Beyond the doors, a sea of people—young and old, of
Havnestad and not—mill about, their laughter and cries
of delight adding to the general hum as the king's band
strikes a lively jig in the corner.

For once, Nik is not with the musicians, stealing their
instruments and the show. Tonight, he does that from the
dance floor.

King Asger has just finished a speech—one he didn't
foist upon Nik—and takes Queen Charlotte's hand. "And
now, the first dance."

Nik steps forward, in line with his parents. The weight
of the room is upon him as a statelier tune starts up. Wilhelm van Horn, Ruyven's father, stands in front of the
orchestra as the king's official announcer. He reads from a
scroll, stamped with the king's seal. All of this is so formal,

so unlike us. A prince coming of age is serious business.

Wilhelm clears his throat. "Crown Prince Asger Niklas Bryniulf Øldenburg III invites for his first dance . . ." The drums kick up for a minute. Annemette grabs my hand. "Friherrinde Annemette of Odense."

I squeeze Annemette's fingers just before she steps forward into a sea of applause. Every eye in the room is upon her, this beautiful creature. Fru Liesel is proclaiming loudly somewhere behind me, "My Anneke, my Anneke."

Annemette curtsies, graceful. The queen looks pleased. The king too. Nik looks slightly embarrassed, ears red. He glances to me, but I'm not sure how he can take his eyes off her. She's the sun and the rest of us are ordinary stars.

She glides toward Nik. He extends a hand and takes hers and they stand to the side, a nearly identical image to the monarchs next to them. One generation and then the next. My heart heaves. After this exhausting, disappointing day, we might have a happy ending. For all of us.

Iker steps forward next. My heaving heart begins to pound, vibrating like a rail tie under an oncoming train.

This is the moment.

Wilhelm clears his throat yet again. I can already feel eyes settling upon my silhouette.

"Crown Prince Christian Olaf Iker Navarre Øldenburg invites for his first dance . . ." The drums begin, and I can't separate them from my own heartbeats. "Friherrinde Oda of Kalø."

My heart skips a beat.

Who?

Iker extends his arm in the direction of an icy-blond stranger.

The girl steps forward, the women around her frozen with excitement. Iker doesn't so much as glance my way. He watches the girl as if she's a prize pony, sauntering forward. The queen looks pleased. *So pleased.* For once, the rogue prince has done her bidding.

My cheeks burn while my heart and blood grow cold with stagnation. I should have known all along. Iker could never dance with me here. Just like he'll never be able to dance with me in Rigeby Bay or anywhere else. Whether our whaling trip is real or not, it won't be anything more than those few weeks. I close my eyes and let the wave of embarrassment wash over me.

When I open them, Malvina's smug face flashes before mine, as if there's a spotlight on her from across the room. This is what people like her have been waiting for ever since Nik, Iker, and I became friends—my ambition slammed down in front of them all.

And here we are.

I'm just as bad as the townspeople say I am. Always expecting something from these princes whether I deserve it or not. Nik drops Annemette's hand and takes a step forward. As if he can save me. But I meet his eyes and hope our special language spans the distance and the weight of so many eyes.

My heart is broken, but his is more important in this moment. These next moments could mean life or death.

Yet Nik is still reaching for me, until Annemette grabs his hand and whispers something in his ear. He immediately moves back in line, his eyes in the middle distance.

When the music begins and the dance officially starts, all I want to do is run away, but I'm trapped, forced to watch the three royal couples, a fake smile plastered on my face.

Nik's crown is a beacon in the very center, everyone else floating around him. The smile on his face is unavoidable, the brightest thing in the room. Brighter than the queen's diamonds. Brighter than the king's sapphire crown.

Annemette's long waves sweep around, swinging with each spin, a flash of butter-blond moving at a happy clip across the inlaid marble.

Many of the older townsfolk hang by the dance floor with more enthusiasm than even the youth, standing close enough to soak in young love at its most enchanting.

The song ends, and each couple takes a bow before other couples swarm the floor, clapping them off as a new song starts up. The royals are swallowed by the crowd, almost everyone dancing. I sink farther into the background, finally settling into a chair pushed up against the wall. Almost immediately there's a hand on my shoulder.

"I didn't give the announcer that girl's name." Iker's voice is low and hushed. Strained. "Please dance with me. Please, Evelyn."

"I—"

He takes my hand in both of his. "Let me right this wrong. Please. That girl means nothing to me."

The icy-blond girl is nowhere to be seen. She's not hanging over his shoulder. She's not anywhere. His dismissal after one song must have been more than disappointing.

I make the mistake of looking into his eyes. He's spelled me as deeply as any magic I've ever known, using memories as much as the present. But I can't dance with him. The embarrassment of rejection will double if the townsfolk see this as a pity dance. I shake my head.

"Please," he begs. "I can't bear to dance with any of these girls. I need you, Evie. Only you."

I look around at everyone enjoying the evening. Dancing, spinning, laughing. Why shouldn't I have that? *Let them talk.*

Finally, I nod, and he draws me up and sets one hand upon my waist. My hand fits neatly into his other palm. Like it's meant to be there. The band plays at a sweeping clip, and we make our way onto the floor. I feel as if the entire world has blown away and only Iker and I stand alone, pressed together in an invisible, swirling tide.

"My aunt must have put that girl's name on the scroll,"

Iker whispers in my ear. "It has to be. Yours was the one that I requested."

I want to believe him. I do. But I know his reputation. His habits. And somewhere deep in my gut I wonder if he and that girl had met before. He didn't look my way when her name was called. Not like Nik. Iker only looked at her—like he knew her.

"Please, Evie—" Iker leans back so I can glimpse his face as we sweep through traffic on the dance floor. The strain in his voice has reached his eyes.

"Iker, it's fine," I say. Even though it's not.

He twirls me past the king and dodges Malvina and Ruyven. We pass Nik and Annemette, and a prickle of magic shoots through my blood. I wonder if Annemette has used a spell to keep her feet from tripping up. For all her grace, even after an hour of practice, her legs weren't doing what she wanted, her exhaustion too great.

Iker follow's my eyes. "What?" he asks.

There's not much I can say that he'll agree with. "Nik and Annemette—they're just so . . . this is just so . . ."

"Questionable?"

That was not the word I was thinking of. The specter of his anger on the ship rises. I haven't seen him have a sip of hvidtøl tonight, but his true feelings are on display again in that single word. I smile, hoping it will soften the edge in his eye. "Romantic. That was the word I was going for. Romantic."

Iker laughs, bold, in his way. The few heads that weren't watching our drama unfold turn at the sound, and he makes a show of plucking a wayward curl off my face before leaning back in to whisper in my ear. "There is not a single iota of real romance in that relationship." His voice is light, but I know he's not kidding.

"Have you seen them?" I shoot back, my voice as cheery as possible, though there is irritation crawling across my heart. Why can't he accept that Annemette could make Nik happy—that we could *all* be so incredibly happy?

"Evie, you are as brilliant as you are beautiful, strong and ship worthy; your wit is a marvel . . . but"—and my heart drops here, made worse by the fact that it feels as if his eyes are seeing through me—"all this time with Nik, and you still don't understand that royal duty is duty to the people? We are walking symbols—ones who can dance and sing and perform. We do those things for our people, whether we want to or not—symbols do not have a choice."

We whirl around in another circle, and he moves to the other side of my face, pressing his cheek into mine. "That romance you see is just passing. It cannot stay—the crown won't allow it."

And just like that, Iker confirms everything I've known all along. He may be angry at Annemette, but his same rules apply to me. It's been sitting there right below the surface the whole time we've been together. And in each chance that I've had to walk away, I've willingly fooled myself into denial, his smiles or promises changing my mind.

But the cruelest thing is that he thinks I should just accept this, which is why the words fall off his tongue as if they're a passing phrase. He can beg me to dance, to sail away with him, be at his beck and call, be his . . . plaything. And I'm supposed to accept it because *he* has responsibility, *he* has his duty? No.

I want to break free, but we're spinning, one turn after another as his painful words swirl around me. His grip is so tight.

"Don't you see how exceptionally dangerous she is, Evie?" Iker goes on.

"There's nothing dangerous about love, Iker," I say, the heated words sounding cold.

"Everything about love is dangerous. When I look at Annemette, I see a person I don't know who has incredible interest in my cousin. Considering his status, his responsibilities, and his heart, that isn't innocent. It's predatory."

Predatory? Maybe only in the plainest sense: Annemette has to win Nik's love to stay. But considering she's invested her life in this, considering my magic is insurance, considering she belongs here—I know deep down she is one of us—predatory is the wrong word.

Fate is the right one.

This is fate. It is fate for this to succeed. For our world to be righted again.

"And do you see me as a predator?" I finally ask. "I'm a girl without a title. But I wanted to be with you."

At this he smiles, and for the first time I'm not sure if it's for me or for the couples surrounding us, swirling across the marble. Iker as a symbol—Prince Charming. His role.

"Of course not, because *I* asked *you*. And *I* know that *you*, of all people, see how this works."

He's right. I always have. And under the light of the hundreds of candles decorating the chandeliers above, there are no more dark spaces to hide away this reality.

And just like I can never truly be with Iker, Nik can never truly be with Annemette. When he finds out she's not really nobility, it'll be over, and never mind if he ever finds out what she really is. If she was truly Anna, maybe. Maybe. But Anna is dead, and no spell can fix that. I don't know what I was thinking, asking Annemette to believe that Nik would fight for her. That he'd ever be able to defy the queen. I guess I just wanted to believe it for her as much as I wanted to believe it for myself.

I look for them, twirling at the center of the room. Although she only needs true love's kiss, and not a proposal of marriage, I worry that Nik may never let himself give one without the other.

I try to catch Annemette's eye. We should go. I can do my spell and she can stay, and we can be friends. New love will eventually find each of us. But instead I catch Nik's. For some reason, he breaks rhythm and leads Annemette our way, cutting through the couples, against the tune.

"Cousin, how is the dancing?" Iker greets them, as jolly as ever.

"Magnificent," Nik answers. "Though I wondered if we might switch partners for a song."

He doesn't give a reason. Just meets my eyes again. The same weight hangs in their dark-brown depths as when my name wasn't called.

My stomach blooms with warmth for the shortest of moments before a tiny sound from Annemette breaks the hold Nik has on me. I draw myself together and look to her. Color has rushed to her cheeks, her blushed lips hanging open—it's clear the last thing in the world she wants is time with Iker.

"It's so hopeless," she says, a sob cutting into the air.

She gathers her skirts and shoulders past us, toward the balcony. Toward privacy for tears that won't come.

Without a second thought, I chase after her.

FOUR DAYS BEFORE

The little mermaid knew she wouldn't be as lucky as her name-sake queen. She knew the death of another was the only way to get her soul back.

The only way to stay.

Love wasn't an option. Not for her. Not with the hate mounting each moment in her heart. Her hate had replicated itself until there was no room for another emotion. It had become her blood and breath and flesh and bone. It engulfed her, the pressure filling up without release. If she could cry, she knew that her tears would overflow the sea. Destroy all in its path. Wash away the world's coasts in one fell swoop.

She wanted destruction—not only of the world above but of the world below.

Everyone involved in taking her from the life she'd loved deserved punishment. She would ruin them. All of them.

She had a plan for revenge—on Nik, on Evie, on even the sea royalty.

And the first step was right before her.

She'd stalked the coast of Havnestad in the days since her discovery, waiting for her chance. Her family thought she left the castle often because she was nervous about going up for the first time—that she needed to swim to clear her mind. She let them think that.

On the morning of her supposed birthday, her family saw her off with songs and merriment. Galia, the sister closest to her in age, offered to come with her for company's sake. The little mermaid told her no, she would do it by herself. Galia didn't push.

And then she was free.

The little mermaid went to Havnestad Harbor, searching for ships on the move. Easy bodies to snatch. It wasn't a matter of taking a life. She knew she could do that. It was a matter of not taking too many.

She spied Evie on the dock that morning, magic in the girl's wake, like perfume trailing a noble dressed in silk and lace.

The mermaid shook it off. She needed Evie to be alive for this to work.

But Evie's father . . . She watched as the man prepared his ship, ready to sail. And she thought it might be the answer—something else to cause Evie pain—but then she spied a better option.

Iker.

Iker, who was kissing Evie in the open. Like she wasn't a peasant. Like she had a chance.

Death finding him might be more painful for Evie than death finding her father—love was strange that way.

It was Iker who kept Nik from reaching her the day she drowned. He'd been her death.

And she would be his.

The little mermaid followed him aboard the same ship she'd stalked that night—the one with the little windows. His little ship was being repaired in the yard. It was simple to stay in the big ship's wake, following through the Øresund Strait and up toward the Jutland, waiting for her chance.

The second day, it came.

The ship docked on the island of Kalø. There wasn't much there but a ruined castle, she knew. Why would a fishing expedition stop here?

But soon she understood why.

A girl boarded, her chaperone and attendants following, carrying multiple trunks. The little mermaid's memories were full of her own noble family and kin—she knew this was the daughter of a high house. She knew the trunks would be full of clothes, something she would need once she got to land, when she'd be too weak from her transformation to cast her own.

The elegant girl met Iker the same way Evie had left him— with a smile and a kiss. Just a sweet one on the cheek, but a kiss all the same. They knew each other. The playboy prince, living up to his reputation.

The elegant girl left him to go below, looking back as if she expected him to follow. He didn't—and the mermaid wondered if Evie actually did have a chance. Instead, Iker directed his men to raise anchor.

The mermaid waited. Thought of using her powers to bring about yet another storm. She hoped Iker would get drunk. Teeter too close to the rail. Make it easy for her.

And just as she lost hope, a better idea struck.

Iker's kiss did mean something. Even if he didn't follow the girl belowdecks. It meant he'd be able to hurt Evie more alive than dead.

And Evie deserved pain.

Iker would pay later.

The little mermaid stole a trunk. She spared the ship's captain, for the moment. Then she set out to find Evie's father.

29

I FOLLOW ANNEMETTE OUT ONTO THE BALCONY AND pull her around to face me. She looks as though she's about to melt into tearless sobs. I squeeze her hands. We are close enough now that our pearl necklaces catch the same lantern's glow, and they light up like twin beacons in the night.

"Please, Evie. Go. Let me have this peace."

I won't. She knows I won't.

The distance and whispers won't guarantee us privacy, but they're the best I can do. I keep my voice quiet yet confident. "Remember, I have a plan."

Annemette rips her hands from mine and presses them to her face. "It's useless! Neither you nor I have magic powerful enough to stave off what is to come. Just go!"

My words are barely audible. "I'm powerful enough," I

say, the words coming out strong and clear. "Please believe me."

She sob-laughs. "You are so ridiculously stubborn." Annemette swipes at her eyes, but doesn't go on. I take her silence as an invitation.

"You know magic is barter—despite how different we are, we both know this. Magic with the sea is no different. We give to the sea, it returns you to land in kind." Annemette doesn't say anything, her features closing tight—trying to make sense of this. I quietly hurry into more of an explanation. "I've tested this. I know my magic is rigid and book-learned, but it's right. And tonight, on the last night of Urda's festival, our magic is strong. Stronger than any night of the year. Don't you feel it?" I touch my pearl necklace, whose throbbing has grown as the days have gone by. "We are at one with Urda; we are balanced, and that is what magic is all about—balancing our inner power with the forces around us, giving and taking. It's Urda's way, and she and the sea both require like for like. They took Anna—"

"I am not Anna," Annemette says plainly, clearly annoyed. "If you keep believing that, whatever you have planned won't work!"

I shake my head. "I know you don't remember. Maybe you never will, but this is something I can feel. I can feel Anna inside of you. But it doesn't matter, Annemette—I

—291

care for you just as you are. Our friendship can be so much more than mine with Anna's ever was. You and I are the same!

"Look," I go on, trying to keep my voice as steady as possible, "the sea took Anna from me four years ago. And even if that girl only lives on as a memory in you, the sea took her soul. You did not keep it." At this Annemette flinches. "And that's what you need to survive. Anna's soul is one portion of the exchange. The sea took from us and now it owes me—*you*—a soul in return."

But she doesn't consider a word I say. She only turns and raises her voice, and I realize both princes have followed us out—what they've heard, I don't know.

"I must leave tonight, Nik," she says.

Nik glances at me, but then returns his attention to Annemette, taking a step toward her. "Now? But the ball isn't over yet," Nik says, sadness in his voice. Behind him, Iker cocks a brow.

"I have to go. I'm sorry."

Nik is about to say more, but Iker barges into the conversation, taking a few steps until he's towering above both of us. "I wasn't aware of a midnight train to Odense, and no carriage will take you that far. Surely you aren't going to walk."

Nik shoots Iker a look of warning but doesn't say a word. Instead, he takes both Annemette's hands. "If you need to go, then go. I understand."

"So, you're going to vanish in the middle of the night? What a plan!" Iker's eyes flash and he steps away from the wall. "Break his heart but not his spirit, return again in a few months and he'll be so happy, he'll just throw himself at you—title and all? Too bad you failed at the first step—"

"Enough, Iker! If she needs to leave, she needs to leave," Nik shouts. I don't know why Nik isn't suspicious too, but I have a feeling it's because he trusts me. And I trust Annemette.

"I really have to go," Annemette says, rushing to Nik's side. "I'm so sorry." She moves to kiss him on the cheek, when Iker grabs her by the arm.

"Witches are creatures of the night. That's it, isn't it? Is your cauldron about to boil over? Do you have toads that need simmering? Brew to bottle?"

"Iker!" Nik shouts, and pushes him off her.

But Iker keeps going, turning more and more into a monster than the man I love. "Or is it simply that your broom has arrived and you mustn't leave your favorite mode of transportation waiting?"

Annemette's calm cracks wide open, her teeth bared in the moonlight. "I am not a witch, you ox!"

"Then what are you? A fairy? A ghost? Or maybe just a con artist, like Evie once suggested. Foreign trash finding an easy mark in our Nik." Iker's teeth are gritted in that feral grin as he twists the knife.

I latch onto Iker's forearm, and Nik moves protectively in front of Annemette, but neither of us can stop Iker's momentum.

"How many lonely boys have fallen for your tricks? Five? Ten? Twenty? Whatever the number, I'm sure this one here would make quite the feather in your pointy little hat. He's definitely got enough gold to retire on."

"Stop!" Nik shoves Iker away, and though Iker barely budges, I lose my grip on him and stumble into the table.

Iker stands his ground but holds out his hand to haul me up. His eyes flash at Nik. "Look what the witch has made you do." I push his hand away and get to my feet.

"She isn't a witch," I say.

"I am not." Annemette's voice is firm. She's done backing down. "And I must go."

"Doesn't he deserve to know why?" Iker says then points a hand toward Nik. "The man you've been tossing yourself at out of *love* for three straight days? If you aren't leaving in the middle of Havnestad's biggest ball for nefarious purposes, surely you can tell him the reason. At least give the man that."

Annemette doesn't look at Iker. Doesn't look at me. Or even Nik. She just spins for the door. The boys freeze in shock—the both of them unused to not receiving a reply to their questions—but I whir into motion, running after her, snatching her hand just before she opens the French doors.

"Evie, it's almost midnight! Let me go. There's nothing you can do. Nothing Nik can do!"

But I won't let her die like this, and I hang on to her arm tightly. In her struggle, Annemette gets turned around enough that I can look her in the eye. "If you won't let me help, then tell him what you did. He'll understand. Maybe he does love you and just needs a push. Isn't it worth a shot? Tell him—"

"Tell me what?" Nik asks behind me.

Annemette clamps her lips shut and shakes her head as she tries to buck away from my grip.

He places a hand on my shoulder. "Evie, what is it?"

Annemette catches my eye, pleading.

"I won't have you leave us, Annemette. I won't," I cry. Her breath hitches, but I am strong, and I know this is right. I raise my voice just enough that the boys can hear it but nobody beyond the balcony.

"She's a mermaid." I turn to Nik. "She saved you on your birthday—dragged you from the sea."

Shock registers on his face as his eyes meet Annemette's.

Iker huffs out a great laugh. "Sure she is. And I'm the ghost of Leif Erikson."

I hold his smiling eyes. "No, I saw her. Before you scrambled over the rock wall. She was on land with him. She was—"

"Singing." A smile touches Nik's lips as he says it. A smile just for Annemette, whose expression only shows a brewing anger. "You were singing. I thought it was Evie, but she doesn't sing. It was you."

"I can't believe you did this," Annemette growls at me. "We had a deal."

My stomach sinks, my betrayal tearing at my insides.

"Annemette, don't!" I shout, but fury flashes in her eyes as she turns to the boys. "I am a mermaid, it's true. But, Evie . . . Evie is a *witch*! Her aunt is a witch! Her mother was a witch! She does magic every day right under your proud Øldenburg noses!"

She wrenches out of my hands with a shove that sends me to the floor.

Nik is staring at me, his face in a complete state of shock. "A witch, Evie?"

But before I can respond, Iker moves in front of me. My Iker. Strong, protective, stubborn, loyal Iker. The look on his face is one I've never known. Then, without so much as a pause, he bares his teeth and shouts, "Guards!"

FOUR DAYS BEFORE

The ship belonging to the royal fisherman of the sovereign king-dom of Havnestad was easy enough to find. Just up from Østerby Havn—far enough from the Øresund Strait to sight the best whales, but close enough to home that the ship's captain would make it back to Havnestad by the final night of Lithasblot.

The sun was failing, twilight setting in late, as was usual for a summer night this far north. Despite the hour, there was a flurry of activity aboard the Little Greta, *the crew cleaning up after a long day. Evie's father was moving about too, not leaving the work to his crew—on a ship so small, everyone had to carry his own weight, most of all the captain.*

In the shadows, the little mermaid considered the best course of action.

She could call a large wave, as she had to claim the chest of clothes now trailing her through the water, kept in tow with a simple spell of binding magic. Or perhaps a storm more power-ful than the one she'd used to pull Nik under—wreck the ship and claim the whole crew. But no, she wanted Evie to feel the agony of her father dying when others easily survived. A sharper pain, that.

She knew firsthand.

And then, the little mermaid's attention snagged on a way

to drive in the knife even further. A way to hurt Evie the most.

Without a moment's hesitation, she reached out through the distance, sending her magic snaking through the Nordic depths.

"Hvalr. Hvalr. Koma hvalr."

In short order, the edges of her power hit upon success, and her plan began to unfurl, a fat pilot whale steaming toward her like a locomotive on new track.

When the whale arrived, it was glassy-eyed under her command. But the sailors wouldn't see that. They couldn't smell magic—they would only smell a chance at another catch for His Majesty.

She looked the great animal in the eye. Her lure. And promised it it'd be safe. Then, she gathered her magic anew.

"Rísa, hvalr. Rísa."

The whale did as it was commanded, rising to the surface like a gift from the sea king himself.

The little mermaid skipped the whale across the water, dancing it across the surface.

Tantalize. Trick. Catch the big fish.

The commotion above was enough that she could pick up the sounds of men sprinting and shouting from her spot below. Smiling, she surfaced in the shadow of the portside bow, and saw that, yes, the fish had taken the bait.

The men scurried about, readying nets, spears, and, optimistically, a huge knife—a mønustingari—for severing the spinal cord. Amid it all, Evie's father did exactly what the little mermaid expected.

He readied the harpoon gun. The innovation Evie had fashioned for a better kill. They'd discussed it that day on the dock. She was clearly so proud. And he of her.

Pride must suffer pain, Evie.

As the whale danced on the edge of her fingertips, the little mermaid called a storm with another tendril of her power. "Veðr."

The storm gathered, wind gusting over the crew as they darted about, ignoring the lightning crackling on the horizon, their sights only on the catch.

The little mermaid got in position, watching and waiting as the father worked the dart gun, stuffing the harpoon into the barrel. Hauling it around, so that it might aim at the whale.

Aim right into the storm.

And in that moment, the father shot the dart gun. The harpoon exploded into the rough air, hurtling toward the whale as it crested another leap. A rope trailed the harpoon, attached to the gun stand, so that it might be easier to haul in, whale and all.

But it would spear no whale.

With a sweep of the little mermaid's hand, the storm unleashed a gust of wind strong enough to change the harpoon's course. It skipped off the rocking water, swinging around, past the whale, through the air, reversing course until it shot back toward the ship's deck. Deadly end pointing back the way it came.

It was so surprising, so unnatural, that his reflexes failed Evie's father.

He didn't move. Didn't flinch. Didn't even cry before the harpoon speared him through the stomach.

Another wave of the little mermaid's hand, and the harpoon bucked wildly, pulling itself and Evie's father into the rumbling deep.

The little mermaid moved then, surging below the surface to catch him before his crew regained its wits and tried to haul its captain up by the gun's rope.

She pulled him off the spear, blood flooding in the water, and as she did so, he opened his eyes. Not yet fully dead, despite the gaping wound.

In them flashed the slightest hint of recognition. That he was not only nearly dead, that he was not just seeing a mermaid, but that he was seeing his daughter's dead friend before him.

"Anna . . . ," he said, his voice but a whisper and a gurgle.

"Yes," she replied.

The light in his eyes flickered, and the little mermaid reached into her hair, pulled out the coral knife she'd fashioned into a decorative comb, and plunged it into his chest, right in to the soft spot between his ribs and sternum where it would pierce his heart.

More blood in the water.

The light left his eyes.

Finally, the little mermaid felt a release. Just a small amount. A crumb could not satisfy such a hunger.

Not yet.

She gathered the corpse, called to the clothing trunk that had been floating down below as she worked, and swam as fast as she could to Havnestad.

The little mermaid arrived close to midnight, heart pounding after so many miles. She immediately ducked into the cove, placing her trunk in the shallows behind the great rock wall that divided the beach, leaving Havnestad blind to her catch. She'd search it later for the perfect gown and then toss it back into the sea.

She returned to Evie's father, whom she'd left under the watchful eye of a giant black octopus who had made the cove its home.

"Later, beast. He's mine to start."

The octopus slunk away in a puff of indigo ink to a small cave in the rock. The little mermaid returned her attention to the dead man. His olive skin was tinged white and the whole of him had begun to bloat.

She hoped the spell would still work without him being freshly dead. Hoped that because it was she who had killed him, she already possessed what the magic needed. That it was bottled inside of her with her hate, ready to explode. Ready to enact her plan.

The little mermaid took him by both hands. Shut her eyes. And asked for her life back.

"Líf. Dauði. Minn líf. Minn bjoð. Seiðr. Seiðr. Seiðr."

A warmth immediately filled her, running from her fingertips to her head to her heart down the length of her tail and fin.

It spread like the mouthful of summer wine she'd stolen with Evie on her eleventh birthday. It spread like the way Nik had made her feel in those days, his dark eyes lighting up her soul.

It spread like life. Líf.

In a flash and shock of pain, the little mermaid knew a change had been made. Where once she had a tail and fin, she now had legs again. But she didn't have her soul back. Not yet.

She dropped Evie's father and pushed her way to the surface, her arms tired no more. And when she reached for air, her lungs couldn't get enough. The fresh night flushed through her, warm and free. Knocking loose a little bit of the hatred that made up her fabric. But not much. There was so much left.

And as she found her swimming legs treading water, she spied a girl on land. Leaving the beach for the step bridge of rocks leading into the cove.

Evie.

The brand-new girl smiled from her spot in the tide and adjusted the comb in her hair, the knife's edge hidden among the damp waves.

Yes, my plan will work.

30

I BURST OUT OF THE CASTLE DOORS AND INTO THE TULIP garden, hot on Annemette's heels. I took off after Iker's command and haven't looked back, but I can hear them coming.

"Annemette, please!" I shout. I know I betrayed her, but even if she despises me for sharing her secret, she can't deny I did it out of love. Although her own betrayal felt more like spite than love, it doesn't bite. Not really. Because all I can think is how I can fix it. I can do it. I will do it.

If I can save her, we can use our magic to run away, far from here. It pains me, but it's the only choice left to make.

My lungs heave to keep up with my pace, pure adrenaline propelling me forward as I tear down the cobblestones. I take a hard right through a gateway of stiff black rocks and onto the soft sand of the cove.

The moon shines heavy here, reflecting off every

surface in a pearlescent glow. Annemette has stopped running, brought to her knees in the sand, an inch from the lapping tide. The gold thread of her dress catches the moonlight as her shoulders heave in a dry sob. She's not far from where she rescued Nik—on the beach side of the cove, the stone wall jutting over the blind side.

"Annemette," I call tentatively. The sand slows my progress, already inhibited by my heavy ball gown. She doesn't move—chin tipped down toward the tide—nor does she seem to hear me. I'm about to repeat myself when she makes it clear she knows I'm there.

"Go away."

"I'm sorry." I settle onto the sand beside her, leaving more distance between us than I ever have before. "I let hope take over my words. I thought telling Nik would help us satisfy the magic."

She doesn't look at me. "It did not. It's over. I'm over."

"We're both over if we don't go now. The guards are coming. Let me help you, please."

When she doesn't answer, I move to stand. "The sea will give me what I want. And I want you to stay."

Here, she finally glances at me. The look in her eye is all questions, but she seems relieved. I think.

I step into the water. The sea is crisp, and immediately it takes my boots, stockings, ankles, hemline—all of it—as its own. Grounding me in its power.

A shadow falls over us, and I look to the sky. Another

sudden storm has swallowed the moon, the whole cove bathed in a shimmering silver darkness—the curtain drawn before the magic begins.

I measure the clouds. There's lightning in the distance. This is good. I'll need all the energy I can harness. My heart begins to pound as that familiar crackle sparks across my veins, warming me from my toes to the top of my skull. I raise my hands above my head, feeling the brewing storm's charge on the edge of my fingertips.

"Evie, STOP!"

I turn. But only because the voice is Nik's.

He's standing on the sand not ten feet from us, all the finery woven into his jacket and the crown atop his head sparkling brightly in the moonlight. Shifting his weight, Nik lifts his chin, his stance so much like the one he uses in public appearances. It's his practiced armor, and I recognize it in an instant. The next words are not his—they're the crown's.

"The guards are on their way. Annemette, if you are not gone from Havnestad before they arrive, they will forcibly return you to the water. You are a threat to Havnestad and all of the Øresund Kingdoms."

Nik believed me. He remembered. As soon as my words tumbled out he must have seen his rescue—her tail.

And it's ruined Annemette. And me as well.

There's not a prayer of him helping us now. Even if my magic is able to keep her here, he'll want nothing to do with her anyway. But if he believed my truth about her, he should believe her truth about me. And I know he does, deep down. He'll want to protect me, but he can't.

There are boots on the cobblestones now—*thud, thud, thud*—King Asger's guards approaching. Coming for us. Annemette's eyes return to the sea. Her shoulders begin to heave again, dry sobs coming fast, but she refuses to move.

I take one last look at Nik, standing there so regal, so good, so kind, but I've already made my choice. I turn to Annemette, my hand outstretched. "Get up! Let's go! Don't you want to live?"

Nik lunges toward me, his façade crumbling. "Evie, please don't do this." He grabs my hand, and I'm pulled to face him as much by the desperation of his movement as by the look in his eyes. He knows that if he sees me perform magic—confirming Annemette's accusation—then he won't be able to protect me. We're truly on opposite sides.

But we have been all along—I was just the only one of us to know it.

"Evie, please don't do this," he repeats, and I nearly push a finger to his lips to still the tremble there, despite my frustration.

"Nik, you forced me into this magic. Annemette will *die* if I don't do it," I cry. "If you'd given her your heart, it would have been so simple—"

"Evie, you don't understand. My heart is not mine to give."

His hand tightens, and despite the want in his eyes I expect him say something next about nobility, duty—all the things the Øldenburgs hold dearer than their own feelings. But he doesn't.

"My heart has been yours, Evie—always. Since Anna's death. Since sandcastles and stick princesses." His voice cracks and tears threaten his eyes. "I have always loved you. Every day. My heart is not mine to give because it is already yours."

The truth crashes over me like a winter wave.

All this time, I've known. But the truth—the truth is always something I've struggled with, whether I'm lying to Nik or myself, or both. But his truth is the truth in my heart, too.

Then I'm kissing him.

Quick as a lightning strike, I press my lips to his hard enough that he takes a step back to keep us from falling to the beach.

In that brief moment, everything surrounding us stops—the sadness, the magic, the boot strikes on the cobblestones, the entirety of it.

His lips are warm, his hands gentle as they fold themselves over mine. He is delicate and strong at the same time, matching caress with intensity in a way I didn't know was possible. In a way I don't want to end.

I do love him. I've loved him as long as he has loved me. I've just spent so much of my life, so much of the last week, pretending it wasn't true. So that we wouldn't be hurt. That we wouldn't suffer at the hands of class and expectations.

But love doesn't work that way.

And with a sudden dip of my trembling heart, I realize I doomed Annemette from the start. I've taken her true love's kiss.

"Step away from him, witch."

Iker's voice slices through my thoughts, and it's Nik who pulls away, though the order was meant for me. Iker doesn't need proof to know what I am; still the abandonment cuts deep.

The world comes flooding back in—twenty rifled soldiers on the beach, standing at attention behind Iker. Behind the only other boy I've kissed. Iker has vengeance in his eyes and armed men who can do something about it.

Nik's hands clamp around mine again as he plants his feet to shield me from his cousin. I glance quickly to Annemette. She's standing now, in the water. New clouds tightening, the wind has picked up, tossing her hair in long tangles, the coral comb nestled within them barely holding anything in place. There's something in her face—fear, anger, urgency—that has hardened what had been just a resigned puddle.

"End your spell over him!" Iker's eyes are ice. It's as if he's already forgotten who I am. Or that he didn't care in the first place. I refuse to believe either—and twine my

fingers around Nik's so he's not just holding me, I'm holding him.

"She doesn't have a spell over me!" Nik shouts. "You
know it as much as I do!"

Iker doesn't blink. Doesn't acknowledge him. "Witch,
the king has given orders to shoot you on the spot."

I look to Annemette. I hope she'll understand what we
need to do. That she won't slow us down.

I squeeze Nik's hands, willing my fingers to remember
his touch, no matter what happens.

Then I whisper into his ear.

"I love you, Nik."

And as soon as his name hits the air, I shove him onto
the sand with all my might. I grab Annemette's hand, and
dive into the water.

"To the sandbar."

As I say it I see the shadow of a wince, but then
Annemette takes a deep breath and hurtles forward. Anna
and I never made it to that other sandbar, but I know
Annemette and I will make it to this one.

We swim out past Picnic Rock, entering the open
water of the cove as Iker and the guards pull Nik to his
feet, all of them shocked into inaction. They're slow to set
their rifles, bullets unchecked—no one was expecting a
witch hunt tonight.

I assume Annemette will cling to me, as she did to Nik

earlier in the day. But the situation has given her strength, and she has new resolve, the fear gone. She kicks her legs, swimming as if she truly knows how.

We cross the distance in a bare minute, the guards finally getting off shots, bullets pinging through the water. A single bullet grazes my shoulder, searing heat and blood draining into the water as I paddle forward.

But I am stronger than the pain.

We reach the sandbar. The moon is just right and I know we only have moments now. My heart is pounding and my left arm is awash in blood from where the bullet struck me, but I try to stay calm. I haul myself onto the thin strip of packed sand and pull Annemette up. Half the soldiers have charged into the water now, daggers in their teeth as their counterparts reload.

Placing my hands on her shoulders, my eyes go to the sky. "Ready?"

She nods, watching me, hope daring to creep into her blue eyes.

"*Skipta.*" I channel Urda and the power of the waves churning beneath us. *Exchange this life for the soul you took.*

A breeze lifts, and a flash of far-off lightning answers.

"*Skipta.*" A peal of thunder.

The charge of the storm seems to radiate from my hands, the zip of energy surging all the way to my heart.

"*Skipta.*" The wind picks up. The thunder and lightning

close in. I can feel the magic in my bones. Annemette consumes my thoughts, all of my concentration on her. On shifting the sea's hand—forcing it to deliver my request.

"Skipta."

"Child, what do you think you're doing?" Tante Hansa screams from the beach. I hear her over the guns. Over the men splashing in the water. Over the thunder. It's as if she has an amplifier aimed straight for my ears. Still, I do not turn.

Annemette. I want Annemette. I want my Anna back.

"Child! Evelyn, listen to me. Listen to my age and mistakes. Magic born of pride and spite is unwieldy. It is far too much for your little hands!"

My hands are not little—they are powerful.

I am none of those things, Tante Hansa. I come from a place of love.

Thunder pounds and the magic singes my veins with every crackle of lightning above. The magic is in my palms.

This is right—it will be enough.

From the beach, Tante Hansa shouts again, though her words no longer register in my ears. The men with daggers are almost upon us, the charging waves of the storm keeping them at bay just long enough.

I order the magic a final time.

"Skipta."

I see Anna's face at eleven. I see Annemette in my future.

I'm focused on all of it so tightly. All of my concentration. All of my power.

Everything I have is aimed at Urda. Determined. Ready.

The storm rages. My concentration is flawless.

But then a flash of lightning rips across the sky, so bright my eyes spring open.

And I see Annemette is smiling.

Not just smiling.

Laughing.

Her hands cup my wrists and pull them off her shoulders. Her strength is surprising. Her lips twist into a smirk.

"You studied, you tested, you planned, and your solution is to simply ask the magic for an exchange? Like you want a blue dress instead of a red one?"

Magic surges until it is swirling around us. It sparks and undulates. I realize it's not mine. Not all mine, anyway. The storm was never mine—it has the same feel as the storm on Nik's birthday. On Iker's boat earlier that day. The storms are Annemette.

I am blind for the briefest of moments, and then I feel her cool magic welling up from the pit of my stomach, through my lungs, and clutching at my heart. When my vision returns, a cone of water surrounds us—shielding us from the beach.

They're going to think I did that.

Annemette's grip tightens as she leans into my ear, as close as Nik just minutes before.

"You know what I think? I think you didn't really want to save me. You didn't want to save me any more this time than you wanted me to survive four years ago."

A gasp escapes my lips. *Anna.* My Anna. But there's a knife twist in her words that my Anna didn't have.

Between Nik's love and Anna's resentment, my heart stops beating for a moment.

It thuds back to life, tears stinging my eyes as I try to grab for her face, her hair, my friend. I've missed her for so long. Even with all my personal loss, I can't imagine her pain. But her grip only tightens more and I can't touch her. "Anna. Oh, Anna, I wanted you to survive. I did a spell that day, but I—"

That smirk twists into a sneer. "Failed. You failed because you didn't understand, and you wrecked that too." Her teeth are bared—I don't recognize her face anymore. The torque of her grip on my hands is cutting off my circulation. "Instead of protecting my life, you caused the black plague with that magic."

The Tørhed. The minnows at my feet, faceup and inked black, flash in my mind. Dead by my tears. My black tears. The look on Hansa's face as she saved me. The Tørhed didn't just start that summer; it started with me that day.

I did it.

She's right. I know she's right. I've known it deep down for a while now.

"I tried to fix it. This year, the sea life has returned—"

"The sea life you've ripped from where they truly belong? The spells of abundance you unleashed on the sea, killing faster than the black death? If they aren't dying in nets, they're dying of famine. Because there are too many." Her hands grip tighter, her cool magic ringing my wrists along with her fingers. "The sea can't take more of your kindness, *witch*."

"Let me try—"

"To fail again? Oh, no. No. Tonight is about success." Despite the cone of water, a swimming soldier gets a hand on the sandbar, but with a lift of her arm, Anna sends him back into the deep. We can't see the rest of the guards, but I can feel her magic surging forth, pushing them all back and out of striking distance with a mere word under her breath. She doesn't even break eye contact. Her eyes flash, and the cut of her teeth finally resembles something of a smile.

"Tonight, Anna Liesel Kamp reclaims her life."

I try to move, try to touch her, implore her, but she's done something, and I can't move my arms. My feet. Anything. Even my magic won't budge, frozen in my veins. My heart begins to sink, the only thing Anna cannot control.

"Anna, please!"

"Oh, no, you will get no pity from me." Again, she

laughs. The sound is guttural, mirthless. "You stole my life. You stole it with your dare. You stole it with that stupid hold you have over Nik. He chose you. He saved you. He failed me. Because of you."

"Anna—"

"Nothing you can say will give it back. Nothing you can do will give it back."

She removes a hand from my shoulder and thrusts it out behind her in the direction of the rock that divides the cove. Though only one hand remains, I'm still powerless to move. My magic feels like sludge under my skin. If only I knew more about how it all worked. If only I'd studied harder. Practiced more. I'd felt so powerful moments ago, and now I'm completely helpless.

The wall of water surrounding us parts, and something bursts through into our space. Not a guard, no . . . it's misshapen, gray, bloated, a dark hole through its middle.

But then in a blink I recognize it. I gasp and start to fight against Anna's restraints. I need to touch him. I need to make sure. But I know when she starts laughing again that the nightmare before me is real.

The thing before me is my father. *Was* my father.

"While your solution was an exceedingly juvenile spell, the idea was right. A life for me to be here, a life for me to stay."

I see it all so clearly now. True love was never going to save Anna—not with what she's become. If it was even a solution to begin with. There've been so many lies.

There's a rumble from somewhere in the clouds, and something surges deep within the water surrounding us. And I know my part in her revenge before I can see the outline of the wall of water.

Our sea didn't claim me that day, though Urda's choice was there. Now, Anna is giving the water another chance.

"And I'm to be the life you take to stay." I force myself to look at her as I say it. My father paid the price for Anna's vengeance and now I must do the same.

She smiles—the most soulless thing I've ever seen. "Oh, no. Your life isn't valuable enough for that."

Anna's grip releases. Suddenly, I'm aloft, next to my father, floating. I'm still immobile. My muscles, fight, magic, all useless.

With a twist of her hand, a gust as strong as a cannonball strikes me in the chest. Father's body and I shoot back through the wall of water, arcing toward the stormy churn of the cove.

As I fall, I inhale my last breath. Close my eyes.

And then I am one with the sea.

ON THE SURFACE

The little mermaid was smiling. Smiling and crying—salt water was the perfect cheat for tears.

She would be crying real tears of joy soon.

"Hold your fire!" the boy called as the guards raised their rifles to the little mermaid splashing past the footstep islands on her own two feet. Behind her somewhere, Evie had taken her last breath. The approaching guards, too, dead in the deep; she couldn't let them ruin this next part. She didn't have much time, but there wasn't much left to be done.

She just had to hold on for the final piece of her plan.

"Nik! Nik! She did it! She did it!" The little mermaid crashed onto the beach—the princes and the remaining guards were the only ones nearby but at the mouth of the cove was an entire ball's worth of gawkers. An audience. This was perfect. "She did it, and I remember!"

The little mermaid grabbed his hand. Pointed her practiced smile at his stunned face. "I'm Anna. Anna Liesel Kamp. I'm Anna!"

From the sea lane above, the little mermaid heard her batty old oma, right for once. "Anneke. My Anneke—you're sopping wet! Out of the water with you! Out!"

A few titters came after the old woman's outburst, but then

Iker's voice thundered over them all. "Cousin, step back. She's no better than a witch and you know it. She's worse. Move away."

"Not this time, Iker," Nik said, touching the little mermaid's face. Reading it. Confirming the suspicions he should've had since the moment he set eyes on the "traveler from Odense."

"If you're really Anna, tell me this: What happened on Lille Bjerg Pass when I was ten?"

The little mermaid didn't blink; rather, her answer brimmed with joy and urgency. "You bashed your right leg on a rock, you've got a scar as long as your shin bone. Evie and I had to carry you down the mountain."

Those dark eyes of his widened and he grinned. "It's you—it's really you." But then he broke her gaze, his eyes searching the waves for the girl she would never be. He couldn't even give her this moment of attention. Yes, he deserves this.

"Where's Evie? There was a wave and—" His eyes broke from hers, scanning the water.

"Niklas, what are you doing? Step away from her!" The queen—the little mermaid almost smiled again. The queen and her piety. The king and his nobility wouldn't be far behind. "What are you waiting for, cowards?" she yelled at the guards, porcelain features cracking in fury. "You have guns, use them."

The guards advanced—but Nik was prepared. "Stay back. That's an order." He turned to his mother, looking over the little mermaid's head. Holding her tight. "You too, Mother."

"Overruled," the king answered, his voice stern. "You are of age, my son, but as long as I am alive, your orders will still be those of a child." He faced the guards who were left. "Seize the prince and kill the girl."

This time, the guards didn't hesitate to advance, their bayonetted rifles pointed squarely toward the little mermaid. The prince stepped in front of the little mermaid, shielding her from the guards. From view.

The time was finally right. And with not a moment to spare.

The little mermaid pressed into his back as if cowering. Then she swept a single hand through her hair. Her fingers wrapped around her comb, the point glistening with seawater.

"Nik!" That voice. Evie—she'd survived, the little witch.

The prince turned toward the water. Looked toward his true love.

The little mermaid smiled then—the prince had yet again made the wrong choice.

It would be his final one.

With all the strength remaining in her body, the little mermaid plunged the knife straight through the prince's back and into his heart.

31

MY EYES OPEN TO DARKNESS. EVERYTHING ABOUT ME IS midnight. Sad and colorless. Time does not exist.

So this is the sea.

The true sea.

The only light from above is the moon. As my eyes adjust, it gives the blackness a little color—a hint of blue in so much dark as I sink beneath the waves onto cool sands. My father lies next to me, his eyes sunken and gone. The hole in his middle—it's the size of a harpoon. From my dart gun, surely. I want to scream as my heart aches. The cove's octopus sweeps into view, even larger than I'd thought.

Thought. Thoughts. I have thoughts.

I'm alive.

My lungs scream.

Wait.

I'm alive, and I need air.

I test my arms. My feet. Anna's magic has somehow gone—I can move.

Suddenly, my feet are kicking and my hands are clawing at the water in an upward stroke. Pain radiates up my arm from where blood seeps into the water.

I was shot. Yes, I was shot by the king's men. And I survived.

I survived what Anna had planned, too.

And now I must warn Nik. Anna isn't our friend anymore—she's something else entirely.

She is rage.

My heart quickens, pounding harder with each foot gained toward the surface. Blood clouds every stroke, my shoulder threatening to fail.

My vision breaks the surface, and with a heaving breath I'm already moving forward, swimming and then lunging toward the beach once my feet gain purchase on the submerged sand. I try to breathe in deeply, but my necklace is too tight, the pearl still throbbing. With every ounce of energy I have left, I tear at the magic thread until the pearl bursts free, landing with a plunk in the water below.

I am free now too. I can feel my connection to the old Annemette fade away with the waves. She must have had a spell on me this whole time, or perhaps I put the spell on myself.

Water streams from my hair into my eyes. *Nik.* I have to find him.

He's standing tall and regal on the beach—protecting Anna from advancing guards. My heart beats fast. He's alive. But not for long. I know now his is the life she plans to take.

He's standing too close.

"Nik!" I scream.

I get his attention. But then I also get Anna's. And the guards'.

Shots ring out, and a sudden burst of pain rockets through my chest. I flail back but manage to keep my momentum. I bring my fingers to the wound along my ribs and wince. It's hot and wet, and my breathing grows shallow, each intake bringing a fresh stab of pain. But I have to keep moving, slogging through the water, now almost waist-high.

Nik is stunned still, but Anna is not. Her hand reaches for her hair.

A knife is in that hand, the blade moving straight at Nik, who is watching me.

"NO!" *You will not take him! You will not!*

Now Iker is yelling—running. He sees it too.

Despite the blood. Despite the pain. Despite the distance, I surge ahead as fast as I can, water just above my knees. Wet, my gown weighs more than the rest of me, but that won't keep me from him. Nothing will.

Five yards away. Four. Three.

But it is too late. Annemette's blade is already in a downward arc. The sharp coral pierces Nik's back just as Iker grabs him, wrenching him onto the sand.

Nik's blood is on the beach.

Spilling in a trail from where he was to where he fell, staining the sand.

Oh, Urda. No. Not Nik.

Even after everything, I can't believe Anna has done it, but I have no pity for her. If she thinks she's the only one who will get her revenge, she'll be sorely wrong.

"Niklas!" the queen wails, and dashes forward. The king runs too, finally coming to their only son's aid.

The onlookers go still—recognition, terror, and fear frozen upon faces I've known my whole life. Malvina. Ruyven. Every member of the castle kitchen staff.

Anna's beautiful features twist as she dips her toes in Nik's spilled blood, laughing. *Laughing.* "You ruined my life, and I've ruined yours, *my prince.*"

I dive for her feet, knocking her to the sand. I move on top of her, pinning her hand that still holds the knife, red with Nik's blood. I scream for my tante. "Hansa! Nik— you must heal him!" But two guards hold Hansa back, my magic enough to condemn her, too. I reach out to the only person with the power to change their minds. "Iker, let her do her work. Please! She can save him!"

My heart stutters as Iker immediately does as I

say—family over everything. "Let the old woman go!" he commands.

The guards comply. But I can't watch her act. My heart can't take it if she fails. She's known as the Healer of Kings, but tonight she'll have to save my prince.

As Hansa works, Anna's magic tugs at the edges of my strength. Overhead, storm clouds gather. Pinned beneath my body, Anna's suddenly laughing again. I want to slap her, but I don't want to lose my grip. "Shut up!" I scream. "How could you? He loved you! *I* loved you!"

She spits in my face. This person I no longer know. This person I don't recognize. This person who tried to take Nik. This person who took my father.

The wind picks up, and lightning sizzles in my peripheral vision. Thunder crashes. Her magic rolls over us, and I do everything I can do to keep her down, my magic sparking in spurts as I bleed.

Now she's laughing so hard that she's crying. *Actual tears.*

They flee down her blood-splattered cheeks, wet and real. Terror claws at my heart as it struggles to work under the weight of the blood streaming out of my shoulder and chest.

No, she can't be human. This person doesn't deserve a soul. She can't have won. Nik isn't dead.

He can't be.

Yet her tears are there. And with them, her eyes roll

dramatically up to where I have her hands pinned to the sand. Where the knife is pinned—*no.*

No.

Screams sound from the sea lane. A mass of bodies rushes forth. The guards, too. All to a single body, prone on the beach. Knife sticking out from a strike dead center to the throat—the last of Annemette's mermaid magic used to hit its target.

Not Nik.

His father. The king, dead on the sand.

It must only be royal blood that matters to the magic— Øldenburg blood, passed down from the witch-hunter king—because before him is Iker, pulling himself up from a crouch. He'd been just low enough that Anna's blade missed. It was meant for him—the final player on the day Anna drowned, but the king would do.

The queen's voice, shrill and high, echoes above the chaos as she sinks to the sand. *"Kill them!"*

The guards spring forth. Anna continues to laugh, her human legs kicking at mine. My blood has stained her dress, her skin, her hair. It only makes her laugh harder. So hard she doesn't even try to escape—she's reveling in it too much.

Over the noise—the laughing, the lockstep of the guards, the screaming townspeople, I hear it. The voice I've always known as well as my own.

"Evie."

Nik.

He's crawling toward me with Hansa's aid. The look in her eyes tells me her healing cannot help—he'll soon be dead, like his father. Nik knows it too, his voice shaking. "Evie, I love you. I'm sorry I didn't say it until today. I'm sorry . . ."

"Tante, hold Anna still. Please. Don't let her up." Hansa's magic is strong and she uses a binding spell like Anna used on me. One I never learned.

Still, only when I know Hansa has Anna pinned do I let go. Anna is screaming at me, struggling against Hansa's magic, but I drown her out. My hands find Nik, and I bring his bleeding body to my chest. "I love you, too. And I won't let this be the end."

Confusion crosses his face. The skin there has lost its color. His breath comes in pants, his lungs struggling against my bodice. The blood from our wounds runs together, like finding like.

I shut my eyes, my mother's words coming to me. I don't need octopus ink. I don't need gems or potions or charms. I just need the words and the will.

I am a witch. I am and I always will be. The magic is in me and it is enough—I suppose Annemette taught me that.

"I love you, Nik," I repeat, and then I start my mother's spell. The words coming like I've known them my whole life, and maybe I have.

"Líf. Dauði. Minn líf. Seiðr. Minn bjóð. Seiðr. Seiðr."

My skin begins to burn, white hot, heat radiating from my bones outward, steam in the air. Tears come to my eyes, and I know they're black—Mother's eyes didn't do that, but I'm my own kind of magic. They drip onto Nik's skin as I begin to shake. My eyes roll back for a moment, and the last thing I see is color returning to his skin, his cheeks pinking like we've been together all day at sea.

I force my vision to clear. I need to see him. I need to.

His eyes flash open. He knows what's happening. He knows it like I did the day my mother died.

I will see to it that he is safe.

That he lives a long life.

That he can rule his people without fear.

I will see to it.

With the last of my strength, I leave Nik and push my failing body onto Anna's, tight as a corset. Tighter than the magic Hansa used to paralyze her. My tante steps back, tears in her eyes, and helps Nik to his feet. He's almost completely healed. He will be fine.

Anna is the only threat left, but I have plans for her.

With my last breath, I take ahold of her—this girl I loved, this girl who came back to me. Used me. Ruined me. Ruined every person who ever loved her so that she could be human again. Ruined for revenge.

I get to my feet and heave her toward the water. My hands burn fingerprints into her skin as she tries to pull away.

"What are you doing?" she shrieks. I can feel her heart beating wildly against her bodice. Against my heart—still in my chest.

The clouds are clearing overhead. The wind has died down. The lightning vanished. Her magic is leaving this world, and soon she will too.

Her blue eyes grow wide. She's realized that she'd gotten what she wanted. She's just a girl, like she was before—and it's made her vulnerable to people like me.

I smile at her, and there's no pity in it. No joy. Nothing but rage.

"This life is not yours to live."

With that, I do the only thing I can to reverse Anna's final magical act. To keep my loved ones safe. To stop her threat cold.

I return Anna to the sea.

BELOW THE SURFACE

The tide claimed the two girls, one with curls of raven black, the other with waves of butter-blond. Its water was crisp, despite the summer night. All veins of magic swirled under the surface, mixing with the blood and death that bound the girls together.

The raven-curled girl's heart was failing. Her time was up, spent on the boy above. The one she'd always loved. Always protected—even from herself.

But she would win—the blonde's lungs were seizing. The raven-curled girl could feel them sputtering and shuttering as she held tight to the girl's chest, driving them both down, down, down. As deep as the cove would allow. To the bottom, home to that bewitched octopus, her father's corpse, and the fresh bodies of the guards the blonde had killed with a sweep of her fingers.

So many dead, but the prince was alive. Her boy. Her own borrowed breath in his chest. She'd sacrificed herself for him again.

As the cool remnants of magic swirled around them, the girls plunged to the sandy bottom. The blonde's back lodged in the cove floor, the raven-haired girl's body flushing streams of blood into the water, more of her life fleeing through bullet holes.

Light was failing as fast as their bodies, the strong moon barely reaching these depths. Still, the raven-curled girl wouldn't give in to the darkness. Her heart was barely beating, but her eyes were open, watching the blonde struggle and fail to break free.

She wouldn't die first. She couldn't.

She had to know her boy would be safe—her family, her home—from the monster beneath her fingertips.

Just before the raven-curled girl's heart finally stopped, the blonde went still. Her blue eyes stuck wide, blank. Her rosebud lips forever parted, water seeping in.

The girl had really drowned this time. There'd be no coming back.

The raven-curled girl opened her mouth and accepted the ocean. Let it sweep in and claim her along with the magic still singing in her veins. Still skimming over her skin—it would live longer than she.

Then, a darkness fell across the pewter light of her vision. The end, pulling the curtains shut.

No.

The octopus. The giant one. The one that haunted the cove. Her beast—a product of her spell of abundance. A mistake. An aberration.

The animal was swift. Vengeful. Spiteful.

"Lif . . . lif," the girl started, the words dying in her mouth, drowned in salt water. She wasn't sure what to say other than to tell the octopus to go. Live. Live away from this battlefield. Let her rest with her father in peace.

But the octopus smelled the ink in her veins and the magic it held, and it began to feed. The beast's tentacles trembled with power as they slithered across her wounds, mingling with the water, with her blood, with her spell that controlled its life for the past few months. The girl's eyes rolled back into her head as fresh magic entered her veins.

"Lif. Lif."

Suddenly, a great spasm of white light shot up between them. Connected them. Magic as old as the sea itself threaded the octopus's life and hers.

The light drew the great beast closer to the girl's prone form, barely alive. Barely anything at all. The tentacles reveled in her blood. Tried to capture it. The magic between them was a magnet, pulling all of it to all of her.

"Lif . . . ," she repeated again, no breath in it. Seawater washed the word down her windpipe, pushing the oxygen out of her heart, her blood. Until she was one with the sea. Her soul water itself.

The light flickered and grew, engulfing both the girl and the octopus in its warmth, shooting past the water's surface, to the moon and the magic still hovering in the air above. With the light came an equal darkness, seeping across the cove in a sheet of black.

The people on the sand scattered then, knowing it wasn't safe. All but the boy and his cousin, still watching the water as if the girls might resurface. So many questions on their lips as the black water feathered out toward the Øresund Strait.

And down under the surface, the water roiled and turned until great whirlpools twisted from cove bottom to top. Scalding gas from deep within the earth shot up through the deadened sand, violent geysers forming between the whirlpools. The cove's sand began to rot, all the color washing away until nothing but gray remained. And when the light faded to nothing but the obsidian of the ocean, something peculiar happened.

The girl with raven curls was no longer a girl.

She still had her raven curls, her beauty, and the upper body of a woman, but where her long legs had once been were eight tentacles, onyx black and shiny as silk. They plunged from her waist, unlike anything the ocean had ever seen.

And, with magic swirling around her, through her, from her, the creature opened her eyes.

EPILOGUE—
FIFTY YEARS LATER

THE SEA KING AND HIS PEOPLE CALL ME THE SEA witch—though I'm still surprised to be anything at all.

I was prepared to die that day in the water.

I'd given my life to Nik. I knew what that spell would do.

But something happened in the swirling magic—mine, Mother's, Hansa's, what was left of Annemette's. The octopus haunting the cove had something to do with it too. All combining to leave me with the body I have now.

Not the body of a mermaid.

Not the body of anything else seen in these waters.

I am my own magic.

I spread out my tentacles beneath me: eight, shiny and black, and as voluminous as one of Queen Charlotte's gowns, each plucking a shrimp from the seafloor. I am quite the sight, though very few have laid eyes on me. I am tied to the cove, something keeping me here. Magic or memories, or both.

My lair is a sunken cave, surrounded by bubbling mire—turfmoor—and violent whirlpools. The water here is a flat black—Havnestad Cove now a sunspot on the sea.

Around my cave, strange trees have grown from the bones of Anna and the guards, though my father's bones never changed, buried gently as they are. These trees—polypi—are half-plant, half-animal, like serpents rooted to the pewter sand, a hundred heads where branches should be.

The Tørhed died in the magic that made me this way, the sea rid of both drought and abundance. And so, the whirlpools draw fish into the polypi's clutches, keeping me well fed without ever having to hunt.

Feeding on my strange forest's catch, I study magic. I've learned everything I can about the sorcery beneath the waves, though new mysteries present themselves to me daily. And so my power has grown, but so has my reputation.

The merpeople are frightened of me—time and tales building upon each other. They've been told to stay away from the witch powerful enough to ruin the sea as soon as save it. The sea king knows of the magic I've done—of the black death and then the famine—and he also knows of me and his Annemette, memories of her resurfacing when my name is spoken aloud. But that is rare. No one dares.

It, too, has been long enough that no one on land knows me as Evelyn. Evie. That girl.

They know the story of the mermaid and the witch

and King Niklas. They know of—and dare to visit—the strange cove with ink for water and sand as gray as steel. Now they forgo the bonfire and toss their little wooden dolls into the cove every Sankt Hans Aften. Presents to the witch who saved their kingdom.

But they don't know me.

My people are long gone, or so I've heard from pieces of conversation floating down from above over the years.

Tante Hansa was taken by age, having lived out the remainder of her life in Havnestad despite her magic. Safe from banishment because of her role in saving Nik on that awful day. Hansa sent me gifts until the end—enchanting her own magical tomes to be waterproof before hurling them into the deep. All the secrets that she didn't dare teach me when I was a girl, now at my fingertips. Almost as if she knew I were alive beneath the muck. And maybe she did—though I cannot surface.

Iker: lost in the North Sea. Victim to the king of the whales, who grew tired of being his prey.

Nik is gone too, but he lived out his days as he should have. How I had hoped he would. Marriage, children, a successful reign, and beloved by all.

I miss him. I miss everyone. I strangely miss her sometimes, too—Anna, Annemette, whoever she was.

Alone, there is a quiet under these waters that no one above will ever know. A quiet that makes me miss even the most painful of sounds.

But one day, I receive a visitor. Not from land, but by sea.

A little mermaid. Brave girl, with golden curls topped with a wreath of sea lilies and a complexion as clear as fresh milk with cheeks blushed at the apples. Her eyes are an earnest blue—as icy as the fjords up north.

As icy as Iker's once were.

But rather than the confidence that flashed in his, her eyes hold a determination warring with fear. For such a fearsome creature I've become.

So immediately I know.

Yes, only one thing would cause a mermaid like her to brave my presence.

I stare down at her as she approaches, tentacles mounded beneath me—a throne if ever there was one—a web of ghost-gray curls swirling about my face. Her tail swishes under the weight of eight oysters, each showing her rank. For a moment, I think she will retreat, but instead she holds out her arms, which had been clutching a bouquet of bloodred roses.

"Please accept these flowers grown in my garden, a gift for the great sea witch—"

All it takes is a shake of my head, and her voice immediately cuts off. I glide toward her, and to her credit, she stays still.

"I know what you want," I say, and the girl's eyes blink with my words. Her arms flutter down, the roses sinking to the seafloor. "You want to chase the love of a human boy on legs of your own."

Her answer is immediate. "He already loves me, this I know."

Dubious. "And do you know this boy's name?"

"Not his official name—it is long and drawn out, five names in one—but the other sailors, they called him Niklas."

Crown Prince Asger Niklas Bryniulf Øldenburg V.

Nik's grandson.

I grit my teeth and set my jaw, glancing down my nose at the girl before me. A princess. One of the sweet singing girls who perform often at the palace. Shows to which I'm never invited. I can hear the music, though—the sea king's castle isn't far. If I squint past my strange forest, I can see the peculiar blue radiance surrounding the palace grounds. It looks almost as if a piece of clear sky fell from the heavens to the navy depths of the sea and mingled with the brine.

"Please," the girl starts when I say nothing. Though she's desperate, there's a thoughtful quality to her face— both her head and heart are feeding her bravery. "You are the only one with the magic to change me—it's been banned for so long. Please, even if it is just for a day, I must see him. My heart cannot bear to be away from my Niklas."

Looking in her eyes, I am sixteen again, learning of

—337

Nik's love for the very first time on that beach. Kissing him before our lives changed forever.

But now I am old enough to know better than to listen to my memories.

And I know she doesn't know what she is asking. The price: the cost to her family, her loved ones, the magic. The pain: physical, mental, familial, magical. It is too much.

"The heart can bear many things, child, and love is one of them."

The little mermaid reaches for my hand, but thinks better of it at the last moment. As if my touch will burn. Maybe it will. "Please—I will do anything."

I again think of Nik. His laughter. His love. How long it had been there, waiting for me to see it. There in his dark eyes.

Before he passed, Nik would visit me sometimes, walking the cove's edge, fancy boots marked by my black water. Then he'd tell me stories of the world above, trusting the tide to carry his tale. Maybe he knew I was alive too. A friend, a love, to the end.

I hold the girl's stare. Her eyes are no longer fearful, determination and need filling them in a rush. It is impressive, I suppose—no one has ever braved my lair with such a request. She wants this, more than anything.

More than anything she can promise me.

But I will need something more in return. The magic may no longer require a life, but it still demands a sacrifice.

In the years since, I have learned this, and much else.

And I know what I must take.

"I must know that you will only tell the truth above," I say finally.

The little mermaid is so surprised that it takes her a moment to understand what I mean: that I will help her. When she does, her reply is immediate.

"I will—"

"Do not answer so quickly. What you ask is a serious request." The girl concedes, her lips drawing shut, thoughtfulness sewn tightly into her skin. Good. "Once you have become a human, you can never become a mermaid again. You can never see the palace again. Your father. Your mother. Your sisters. Everything you know and love—save for this prince—will no longer be yours."

The girl blanches. Her blue eyes fade to the middle distance. For all the time she spent thinking before making her request, plucking those flowers from her garden, summoning the courage to swim past the polypi and above the turfmoor, this is something that never crossed her mind. I had heard that the sea king had destroyed the ledgers with the story of Queen Mette, hiding history so that it could not become the future. This girl proves that. If she could have researched more, she would have.

After several moments, her eyes return to my face. Resolute.

"I will do it."

"Very well. But I must be paid also—and it is not a trifle that I ask."

The girl lights up. "I can give you whatever you want," she says. "Gems, jewelry, the finest pearls—please." Privilege and *things* define the life she hopes to leave.

I don't need pearls. The one from long ago had held enough false promises for a lifetime.

"I only ask for one thing: your voice."

The girl's fingers immediately fly to her throat. "My voice?"

"It is imperative that you do not tell a lie above."

"I won't lie."

I cock a brow at her. "You won't without a voice, will you? And if you write a lie while above, your fingers shall fall off."

The girl swallows hard. "If the price is my voice—*though I shall not tell a lie*—how . . . how . . . ?"

"You'll have your beautiful form, your graceful walk, and your expressive eyes," I say, lowering my intonation in the way of Tante Hansa so long ago. "Surely, if you are willing to brave my dark magic and leave your family and friends without a word, you can communicate to your true love without a word as well."

The little mermaid's lips snap shut, her mind working furiously for another way.

My brow arches higher. "Unless you fear his love is not true?"

"It is! It is. He is my true love. Take my voice! Take it! It is worth the cost!"

I slither a tentacle to her face and tip up her chin. There is something else in her eyes—not just fear or longing or love. "Do you really love him or do you love the idea of being human?"

The girl's pupils bloom and her jaw stiffens. Finally, brave thing, she speaks without looking away. "What is it like—to be human?"

I won't give her a bag of saltlakrids and tell her a magnificent story—I am not her grandmother.

If I were, I could tell her that it's like the tang of summer wine and the ring of voices as a new ship docks. Like the scent of salt and limes and the twinkle of a boy's eyes just before a kiss in the moonlight.

But I don't say that. I can't.

If she loses her voice in proving her love, then so be it.

"Very well." I slide my tentacle to her waist and pull her even closer. And suddenly it's as if the girl's voice is already gone, her lips dropped open, no sound escaping. I place my fingers to her bare throat, luminous and elegant even in the bleak light of my home—a pearl shining in the murky depths. Her pulse thrums beneath her warm skin, the first true heartbeat I've felt since Anna's faded in my grasp. "Tell me exactly what it is you love about this Niklas."

"You . . . you just want me to talk?"

"You will have your voice for only a few more moments,

my dear. Use the time wisely."

The girl swallows again and then takes a heavy breath.

"I first saw Niklas on the day I turned fifteen. It could be called love at first sight—but I'd seen his face before. In a statue I've had in my castle garden since I turned ten. Those red flowers I brought you, they grow—"

"Yes, the Øldenburgs love their statues," I say, sounding again very much like Hansa. "There is yet to be love in this story. Only coincidence and horticulture."

The girl licks her lips and recasts. "I stayed beside the boat all night, watching this boy. Then, after midnight, a great storm came, waves crashing down so hard, the ship toppled onto its side. The sailors were in the water, but I didn't see the boy." Here, her voice hitches. "I dove down until I found him. His limbs were failing him and his eyes were closed. I pulled him up to the surface and held his head above water. We stayed like that the whole night. And when the sun returned and the ocean calmed, I kissed his forehead and swam him to land."

Reflexively, my tentacle tightens around her waist as I'm reminded of Annemette, even though I've read enough to know this story by heart. A storm, a shipwreck, a savior.

"And?" I ask.

"I placed him on a beach beside a great building. I stayed to watch, hiding among some rocks, covered in sea foam. Soon, a beautiful girl found him and sounded the alarm. I knew then that he would live. He awoke, and was smiling at the girl."

"No smile for you?"

"No." The determination returns to her voice. "But I wanted that smile—I want it now. I want him to know that I saved him. That I love him. And I want him to love me."

Ah. She's lied to me.

"But you said he already does."

The girl looks away, caught. Finally, she continues. "For the past year, I've watched him. And I *know* if I could just be human, he would love me. He thinks he's in love with the girl from the beach, but I saved him. I saved Niklas."

Like Anna, this girl believes she deserves something and she's willing to risk her life and all she knows for it. But this girl doesn't crave revenge.

She wants a happily ever after.

And for that, I cannot blame her. Even after all these years, I still wish for my own.

"It is very stupid of you," I say finally, "but you shall have your way."

And so, I recall my mother's dying spell. The one she used to save me from myself.

"*Gefa.*"

The little mermaid's eyes spring open. She shirks back—getting nowhere in my tentacle's grasp, pale fingers

—343

flying to her throat. An invisible heaviness settles within my hands—her beautiful voice weighing on the lines webbing across my palms. Heart, life, fate.

I release her and turn to my cauldron, fashioned from sand and magic.

In goes the girl's voice, a brilliant white light in the dark.

The cauldron glows. I retrieve a swordfish spear from my cave, and hold it over the spring, sterilizing it. I am lonely, but I am clean. Then, leaning over the bubbling cauldron, I prick the skin of my breast, just above my heart. A life is no longer needed, true, but this dark magic still feeds on sacrifice. Like anything of power.

Blood as black as midnight oozes into the murk. Molasses slow, it slinks into the pot, slithering through the white light of the girl's voice. As they mix and mingle, they heat the pot together, pushing the temperature up until the cauldron itself is a fireball, a comet come to rest at the bottom of the cove.

Steam rises, curling above the brilliance. As it does, it swirls and dances, forming shadows like the worst of night. The polypi forest parts for the horrid shapes, wanting no measure of their magic.

I prepare the words I've learned, the ones Anna used to regain her legs and seek revenge. Ones that won't work for me, strange magic that I am, tied to this cove.

"Líf. Dauði. Minn líf. Minn bjoð. Seiðr. Seiðr. Seiðr."

The cauldron begins to tremble, the contents swirling round and round under great pressure. Coming on like life itself.

An explosion like a dying star rockets forth, rippling through the cove with such heat the water evaporates in a plume of smoke and steam. White foam settles around us in a swath running the length of my home. It all smells of sulfur, the stench heavy enough that it burns my nose and the back of my throat. When the foam and light clear, I see the little mermaid has turned away, arms flung over her head in protection. I don't blame her.

I dip a small bottle—another long-ago present from Tante Hansa—into the vat. The draught shimmers like moonglow and sunlight trapped under glass.

"There it is for you," I say, holding it out to the girl. She drops her arms at the sound, whirling around, so afraid that she didn't realize what was happening until I spoke. "Drink it down, and you will gain legs for four days. If your love is true, so much so that your prince loves you with his whole soul, you will stay in human form for the rest of your days. If you do not win his love, you will become but foam in the tide."

The girl's lips drop open to respond and her tongue begins to move. It takes a few moments before she remembers that no sound will ever come from her mouth again.

—345

Regret floods into my chest, but my tentacles float into view and the feeling immediately disperses.

Lies ruined my life as much as they ruined Anna's. Nik's.

With shaking fingers, the girl takes the bottle. Fear has returned to her eyes, but the deed is done. Only her determination and love will do.

"Take the draught in the shallows. It would be a waste if you drowned before you could get to land." The girl nods. "Go now. Visit your family one last time. You won't regret the good-bye." Again, she nods, and I know she will do it. Losing them was more of a surprise than losing her voice. Maybe even her life.

She turns to go, but then I call out for her to stop.

No one knows me, it's true, but I am still Evie. And for all my fearsome reputation, for all my years and loneliness, I'm not heartless.

I retrieve from my cave a gown from long ago—one from a trunk I found submerged in the cove after I arrived. Back then, the cool scent of Annemette's magic still draped across the wood and latches, and maybe that was why the fabric remained undamaged. I quickly whisper a spell that will keep it dry until she surfaces.

"Take this with you. It will help if you look the part."

It is all I can do.

Hopefully the magic is kind.

I know the magic well enough now not to expect a

happy ending. The fairy tales of my childhood are the exception, not the rule. It's a wonder there aren't more creatures like me in this world.

And so, I return to my cave, the new silence ringing in my ears. Somehow, it's more painful than before. As if hearing a new voice, regaining the shortest moment of humanity, has torn open the wound that is my loneliness. Leaving it gaping. Festering. Infected.

But in truth, I am not alone. No, the polypi are living and breathing in this murky place, fashioned from the spirits who tried to kill me. My dark life tied to their souls.

Lining the cauldron is a smear of shimmering light, what is left of my payment. The girl's voice. Only a drop was needed for the draught, her body paying the price for the remainder of the magic.

I scour my hands across the cauldron's belly, collecting the voice until its weight has returned to my palms. The white light dances, its glow reflecting across the cove, illuminating my forest, my cave, my own dark form.

It is truly something special.

Maybe it's the new silence or the memories that swirl in the front of my mind. Maybe it's simply that enough time has passed.

But I know exactly what I will do with this gift.

And so, I turn to the largest polypi. The one planted next to my cave. The last body to drift below.

When I give the command, I know the magic will

listen. That it will know what I want. I feel its power surging from the tips of my tentacles to the roots of my hair.

"*Lif. Lif.*"

The girl's voice sweeps forth, floating up, up, up, until it settles into the top of the strange tree's trunk where the branches shoot off into the flat black murk.

It settles and becomes one with the polypi. And, after a moment, there is a deep breath, all the heads in the branches inhaling seawater in time. And then the little mermaid's voice speaks with the thoughts of another little mermaid from long ago. One tied to me here silently, fifty years since I sprouted tentacles from my waist.

When the voice comes, it's direct and focused on what just occurred. She has centuries left to dredge up what happened when we were human.

"She will fail. He loves another. That mountain will not move in four days."

"I know." And I do. I hope she will not fail, but I also cannot forget what my mother did for me. What I did for Nik. What Anna's family would've done for her had they been given the chance. "But her family will not let her go so easily." They'll come begging for a way to save her.

When I return from my lair with a deadly length of coral, Anna understands. "Make it sharp. The blood must fall on her feet—if she will use it at all."

And so, I prepare the knife. Because though magic can shape life and death, love is the one thing it cannot control.

ACKNOWLEDGMENTS

Ever since my parents introduced me to *Cat's Cradle*, I've always been drawn to the idea of Kurt Vonnegut's "karass"—a group of people cosmically, inextricably linked together. Yeah, I know it's a term coined as part of a fake religion and sort of silly, but I do think the fates put people together for a reason. Call it a karass or something else entirely, but the following human beings are in my life for a reason, and I love them in their own ways. Without them my life would be considerably less full.

To my lovely editor, Maria Barbo, whose magical imagination made Evie's world possible. I can't thank you enough for your faith in me.

To Katherine Tegen, our fearless leader; Rebecca Aronson with her queries and smiley faces; copy editor Maya Myers for her sharp eye and grace in weathering my hatred of the Oxford comma (journalists unite!); production editor Emily Rader for her steady hand; Heather Daugherty and Amy Ryan for their beautiful book design; Anna Dittmann for her stunning/haunting/perfect rendering of

Evie; and to the rest of the Katherine Tegen Books and HarperCollins team.

To Rachel Ekstrom, my agent/cheering section/ grounding force, who always greets myself and my work with enthusiasm and guidance. And to the rest of the IGLA family, most especially Barbara Poelle, for their support, humor, and belief in me.

To Joy Callaway, my ray of forever sunshine—you've made a difference for me every single day. You know exactly when to text, call, make me laugh. Your grace and friendship are truly inspiring.

To Renée Ahdieh, leader of my pack—wisest, chicest, most altruistic rock star in the world. You're part sister, part fairy godmother, and 100 percent diamond dust.

To Rebecca Coffindaffer, who has a habit of murdering off my characters before I even realize there should be blood on my hands. To Natalie Parker and Tessa Gratton—my coven elders, who vetted my magical system with wisdom, wit, and cold LaCroix. Additionally, to all the Kansas writers I'm lucky enough to know. Our time together is like the best of college—nights spent dissecting the art of writing in the most delicate and interesting ways. Plus, you all have amazing taste in snacks.

To Julie Tollefson, Christie Hall, and Christy Little for the hours upon hours spent huddling with me in the freezing-but-delicious confines of T. Loft. To Marie Hogebrant for pinch-hitting in Old Norse.

To Kellye Garrett, my fictionally murderous sister-in-arms, always one text away. To Randy Shemanski, keeping me sane over email for twelve years and counting. To Whitney Schneider, Nicole Green, Laurie Euler, Coleen Shaw-Voeks, Colinda Warner, and my passel of Trail Hawks for the endless sweaty miles and even sweatier hugs. To Jennifer Gunby and Cory "Cass Anaya" Johnson, who awoke my imagination early and never let me get away with a boring scene.

To Ricki Schultz, Danielle Paige, Zoraida Córdova, Dhonielle Clayton, Brenda Drake, the Sarahs—Lemon, Cannon, Jae-Jones, Smarsh, Blair, Fox—and everyone else in my life, for their various cameos during this journey over the hill and through the woods. In ways big and small you kept my sanity with humor, love, and light.

To my parents, Craig and Mary Warren, for being the best dream enablers out there. You kept me in construction paper when my "books" were stapled-together crayon drawings, and never let up when actual words found their way to the page. I'd be nowhere without you. To Nate, Amalia, and Emmie, and the stories you're unfurling before our eyes. To Meagan, our missing piece. So it goes.

And, finally, to Justin. My IT department, my chocolate pretzel supplier, my kid-wrangler. My heart. Without you, literally none of this would be possible. I'm so glad you're here with me on this journey. I couldn't imagine setting sail with anyone else.

FOLLOW EVIE'S CONTINUING ADVENTURE IN

SEA
WITCH
RISING

ALIA'S SLIPPERED FEET MOVE JUST SO AS SHE CURTSIES for the boys.

"Oh, *cousins*. Don't let formalities confuse you, my lady," Will says. "Even though it won't be official for two more days, who cares? We'll be cousins for the rest of our lives." Will laughs, and I hate that I like the sound of it. "Why not start now?"

"Fine, cousin, then," Niklas agrees.

They laugh, once again too jovial as Alia looks from Niklas to Will and back, clearly confused. The joy crumbles from Niklas's face and suddenly my lungs stutter themselves shut as I comprehend what would make these boys cousins.

Blood. Or *oh, no.*

As it hits me, the boys must realize it too and excuse themselves on the pretense of wanting coffee. When they're gone, Niklas removes Alia's hand from his arm, clutching her fingers sweetly.

"Dearest," he starts, taking a deep breath almost as if he cares, "I am to be married the day after tomorrow."

Alia's face falls. Her other hand grips his arm so tight, her fingers wrinkle the starched fabric of his tea jacket. My heart feels as if it's in her vise grip, too.

"Though it's only been a day, I . . . I feel like I know you. It's strange, this kinship that we have—both of us lost as sea. Washing ashore on the same beach, some miracle, my little foundling."

Alia nods, close to him, a look on her lovely face so pure that it says a thousand of the words she cannot. Willing him to see. Willing him to know that he does know her. That she saved him. That it wasn't an act of his God that saved him from the wreck that drowned his brothers and father; it was *her*.

I hold my breath as I feel it coming. He's leaning into her and she's still clutching him for dear life, looking up to him with eyes that contain whole oceans of blue, her lips and cheeks rosy from dancing.

Yes. Kiss her. Please, kiss her.

For the magic to work, she needs true love's kiss—all the stories have been the same.

Their lips touch, and my arms give way as I slide down the pole from relief. It's short, and sweet—but I realize right away that it's not enough.

There's no magic to it. It's not transformative in the least. Whatever spell Alia has found to give her legs, this kiss doesn't have the power to keep her on two feet.

Too quickly they're apart again, all of it rushing back to Niklas—the surroundings, the people just steps away in the dance hall, what he is bound to do in two days.

"I'm sorry. I'm king now, and a king's duty is to his people. With my father and my brothers departed . . . it's up to me to do what's best. There are so many uncertain things about the world right now . . ." He trails off, and I can only imagine how the war would affect a kingdom like this. "But what is certain is that despite what's going on, I need to make the right decisions for Havnestad. And the right decision for a new king is to ensure the continuation of the monarchy."

Continuation of the monarchy. Anger singes my veins as my breath grows short. His monarchy would be dead if it weren't for the girl right in front of him.

The *king* weaves his fingers tightly in Alia's. "But please, please stay. Sofie will love you—I'm sure of it."

Sofie. I hate her name already.

He smiles softly. "Perhaps you can be one of her ladies and stay here as long as you wish."

Yes, yes, I was right—this boy just likes to collect things. His foundling on the beach. Now his dancing girl in the castle. There to entertain his wife as her own heart explodes from sorrow.

What a kind and generous king indeed.

"Your Highness," comes a woman's voice from within, "the queen mother has requested your presence in her chambers."

Niklas squeezes Alia's fingers. My sister's hand drops from his arm, obliging, as if she hasn't just weathered the biggest blow in all her life. The boy she's in love with, the one she rescued, the one she sacrificed her life for, cannot love her because his heart is wrapped up in a contract signed by his father.

"I will see you soon, my sweet foundling."

And then he's gone.

My sister's form slumps on the balcony, her head resting on the cross of her forearms against the railing, her shoulders heaving beneath her tumbling hair. I slip my fingers up through the slats in the balcony floor, thin ribbons of marble crosshatched beneath my sister's feet. I touch the toe of her slipper, as light as rain. Alia's eyes flash open, meeting mine. She immediately glances over her shoulder to the room off the balcony, clearing out from the breakfast entertainment. The guests are gone, and a few servants run about shutting the open doors.

When all the doors are closed, Alia sinks to sit on the woven floor pretending she's just looking out past the cove into the tip of the sea.

My voice is low and rushed. I swing around the pole so that she can see the entirety of my face as I bark at her all the questions I can't hold inside anymore.

"How? Did Father keep the books we thought were destroyed? The ones Annemette used? Or did you ask them—Mette's daughters? Why didn't you tell me? And what happened to your voice?"

Alia takes a deep breath and holds up her hands—*watch this,* her fingers spell. When we were younger, our oldest sister, Eydis, taught us hand signals she'd devised to communicate across the room during our daily lessons while our instructors' tails were turned.

Alia signs a single word. *Witch.* We used this to describe our voice instructor, who had a habit of burying us up to our necks in the sand so that we'd learn to properly project without the crutch of movement.

But there's only one real witch I know. Alia didn't find the magic herself through books or rumors. She went straight to the creature who doesn't need to know the old ways—the only one under the sea dangerous enough to try something like this.

"You went to the sea witch?" My tone is appalled and disgusted at once—if there's a single being beyond humans that we've been consistently taught to fear, it's *her.* I take a deep breath and I ask, though I know what she will tell me. "And she took your voice?"

She nods.

My disgust squirms and twists into blatant outrage. I'd never sacrifice a life, but *this.* It's all I can do to keep my voice down. "So you really can't tell him that you love him? Who you are? What you did?"

She shakes her head slowly, sadly.

"What about writing? Can you do that? Tell him the story that way?"

With another shake, she confirms it. She's utterly defenseless. Able only to use her smile, her shining eyes, her graceful dancing, to get what she needs. She's done well for herself to get this far, but it's . . . so superficial. Not to mention, he's about to be *married*.

"That kiss didn't do it? Didn't appease the deal? You must earn his love," I confirm. Alia nods and I continue. "It's not the kiss that does it; it's the love behind it."

Alia squeezes my fingers and then makes our sign for human—two fingers walking. Human love.

"Or Øldenburg blood?" I whisper. Alia's face blanches, and she shakes her head violently.

No. No. No, Runa, NO.

It's the only other way to satisfy the spell. We know this from Annemette's story too.

A kiss of true love or Øldenburg blood.

But this path isn't one she's entertained—not yet. In fact, given the look she gave Niklas, it's the last thing she'll entertain at all.

"Alia, listen to me. You may not have a choice. His brothers and father died in the storm where you saved him. Everyone in the sea knows that." I think of that other boy,

Phillip, but his relation to Niklas is on his mother's side. His blood will not satisfy Urda. "His blood might be the only Øldenburg blood available. And if that's what it'll take—"

Alia shakes her head violently again, pointing at me, then her ear, then toward the door where the king made his exit. She points to herself, and through the force of her hands, the signs she's using, the fury on her face, I understand her.

You heard him. He knows down deep I rescued him. He loves the mermaid who rescued him. That's me. He loves me.

"Alia," I say, hooking the pole with one arm and swirling my tail around the bottom so I don't slide. I grab her trembling hands, trying to still them. I've always been the one to tell her the truth when her dreams push the boundaries of reality. "He loves the *idea* of you—this girl he plucked from the same sea he survived. He hasn't said he believes in mermaids, has he? Or that he believes one rescued him? Or that you look just like her? No, he hasn't."

I reset my grip, harder, stronger, as she shakes her head. "You can't hang you hopes—*your life*—on a boy like that. The only person he's in love with is himself. He loves the idea that Urda swept him up and saved him while his inferior brothers sank to the deep. You were just the courier." The words feel like darts pouring from my lips, but I have to make her see.

Alia's shaking head gains speed, and she grits her teeth

hard, a red flush gathering under her eyes.

She points to me, and I know what she's going to say before she signs it. I know her nearly better than I know myself.

You don't know him, Runa. You don't. You're wrong. That's not true.

It's then that Alia surprises me, breaking my grip on her with such strength that I teeter back, holding on by only my tail, curled around the balcony base.

Then she signs a single word.

Leave.

"No, I won't leave you. Are you crazy? You have, what, three days? And he'll be married by then. Alia, won't you—"

Leave!

She stands, red in the face, so angry she mouths the words.

I don't want to see you again. If I am to die, let me die in peace.

Then she turns, because if I won't leave her, she'll leave me.

And she does, not even looking back, disappearing through the nearest French doors and into the crowd milling within.

I slip beneath the water. All the panic I've pushed down rises, galvanizing within my chest, setting my heart a-skitter and my fingers trembling. The sudden need to do something holds tight to my skin, bones, heart, and tail.

I have to stop this. This can't happen. It can't. There has to be a way to undo this. To save Alia from herself. I can't have Alia fail. I can't lose her twice.

I must visit the sea witch.

Get Your Act Together

Get Your Act Together

A 7-Day Get-Organized Program for the Overworked, Overbooked, and Overwhelmed

Pam Young and Peggy Jones, D.E. *

HarperPerennial
A Division of HarperCollinsPublishers

*Deficiency Experts

FIRST EDITION

Designed by George J. McKeon

Library of Congress Cataloging-in-Publication Data

Young, Pam (Pamela I.)
    Get your act together. : a 7-day get-organized program for the overworked, overbooked, and overwhelmed / Pam Young and Peggy Jones. — 1st ed.
        p. cm.
    ISBN 0-06-096991-1 (pbk.)
    1. Home economics. 2. Housewives—Time management. I. Jones, Peggy (Peggy A.) II. Title.
TX147.Y67 1993
640—dc20   93-17065

93 94 95 96 97 ❖/RRD 10 9 8 7 6 5 4 3 2

We dedicate this book to the American family.

The history of humanity is not the history of its wars, but the history of its households.
— JOHN RUSKIN, 1819–1900

Contents

Acknowledgments

We want to thank the two men in our lives, Danny and Terry, but there aren't words meaningful enough (not even in the synonym finder) to express the depth of our gratitude.

We want to give special thanks to each of our children: Michael, Peggy, Joanna, Chris, Jeff, and Allyson, for being guinea pigs for all of our bright ideas.

At the risk of sounding like an Academy Awards acceptance speech, we must thank our parents for raising us to believe that success comes from having a positive attitude even in negative circumstances. Growing up, we were allowed to be discouraged, depressed, angry, or in a bad mood, but Mom was always there with a timer and we had ten minutes to get through it and get on with life. The timer has come in handy during the evolvement of our new system.

Special thanks to John Boswell for his friendship over the last fifteen years. It is a privilege to be part of his flock of authors. His enthusiasm, wonderful sense of humor, and his kindness to strangers has always been an attraction to us.

Our wonderful friend, Kac Young, deserves special thanks for her daily, long-distance hotline of quality feedback. She has been a great cheerleader for this book, but, just as valuable, she has had the courage to tell us when something didn't work. We have always respected her professional advice, but her personal friendship is priceless.

Thanks go to Sydney Craft Rozen, for once again saving us from literary embarrassment. To have Sydney help us over the last fifteen years has been a real blessing. Her unique ability to edit a manuscript, without changing the voice of the author, is rare and truly appreciated.

Nancy Peske, our editor at HarperCollins, deserves special acknowledgment. She can giggle and edit brilliantly at the same time. It was great working with her.

One

What Is a Person Like You Doing in a Mess Like This?

We know what kind of a mess you are in right now. We could tell you, in detail, what your kitchen, living room, closets, cupboards, drawers, car, purse, refrigerator, and even your bedroom look like. No, we're not psychic, and no, we haven't been sneaking around your house, peeking in your windows at night. We know because we used to be in the same messy dilemma. We escaped and have helped thousands of other people get free from the vicious grip of disorganization. We can help you do it, too.

You know you are overworked, overbooked, and overwhelmed, but did you know that maybe one of the main reasons you got that way is because you were born that way? We believe that if you have struggled to be organized but still lead a messy and disorganized life, you can blame it on heredity. It's our guess that your mess is genetic, and if we're right about that, we can tell a lot more about you.

Instead of reading this book, you're probably supposed to be doing something else. Maybe you're in a bookstore at the mall when you should be picking up vacuum cleaner bags at Sears. Or maybe you're propped up on your bed reading and you should be starting dinner. One woman in a small midwestern town wrote and said that she "accidentally" ran into one of our books. She had locked herself out of her house in bare feet and no coat. It was the dead of winter and her first thought was the "warm" library that was just a block from her home. Once inside, she called her husband to bring her a key and made a decision to get organized. The librarian, able to size up the reader, led the trembling, shoeless woman to our book.

We bet you've tried to get organized in the past. In fact, you've probably gone off on organizational binges with great energy and enthusiasm, only to end up with one more discarded clutterbuster to add to your stash of gadgets and papers. We suspect that you have a lot of organizational tools around the house: filing cabinets, shoe trees, stacking bins, pen caddies, and mail organizers. But instead of satisfying your organizational needs, these tools just loom like lighthouses in a sea of clutter and chaos, beaming rays of accusation that you didn't follow through.

Maybe you also have a diary, photo albums, weekly planners, and calendars that are blank or only partially filled out. Perhaps you bought a rowing machine, stationary bicycle, NordicTrack, Thigh Master, or Gut Buster, but you're not rowing, biking, tracking, squeezing, or busting. In fact, your exercise has probably been limited to hauling all that equipment from the attic to the driveway for a garage sale every couple of years.

Speaking of exercise, do you belong to a health club that you don't go to? Speaking of health, did you invest in the Richard Simmons Deal-a-Meal cards, but the last time you dealt them, you left them in your bathrobe and they went through the wash? Is your *Meet You at the Top* motivational tape at the bottom of the bill basket? Did you buy

Pull Your Own Strings but still find yourself at the end of your rope?

Have you ever been a victim of PREMATURE EVALUATION? Any time you've tried to get organized but had to look for a pen, unload a chair, and clear a spot on the kitchen table for a piece of scratch paper, you've jumped the organizational gun. In the end, you have suffered the letdown and disappointment of premature evaluation. Embarrassed at ending up in more of a mess than you had when you started, you're left with battered self-esteem and public failure (usually logged by family and friends.)

The reason we know so much about you is that we are deficiency experts. We really do think that being disorganized is genetic. As you will read in Chapter 2, we inherited our messy genes from our dad. For more than fifteen years, we have made it our mission to help people who were born with the congenital tendency to be locked out, left behind, and overdrawn.

We think people who are prompt and efficient are born that way, too. They're those few naturally organized people who have it together. They have five- and ten-year plans; they floss, make lists, and actually do the stuff on the lists. They don't run anywhere, look for anything, arrive late, or forget birthdays. They have low cholesterol, IRAs, cash in their wallets, milk in the refrigerator, and high-fiber cereal in the cupboard ... and they were all born on their due dates! They're people like Ordell Daily, our make-believe Goddess of Order, who has a standing hair appointment on Saturday, sleeps on her face Saturday night, and comes to church Sunday morning, resprayed with Follicle Freeze and looking brittle yet lifelike.

> *Ordell Daily was an organized soul.*
> *No one could match her skill.*
> *The crack of dawn was her rising time,*
> *Her day was a routine drill.*

Showered and dressed in less than ten,
Breakfast in just under three.
Dishes cleared, the dusting done,
She knew she wouldn't be free

'til the table was set for dinner
And the bathrooms were sanitized,
And the plants in her terrarium
Were properly fertilized,

And the pile of ironing nagging her,
Just a blouse and her husband's shirt,
Were pressed to their perfection
And put away so they wouldn't hurt
The streamlined look in her laundry room,
A sight not seen by most;
With its white and shiny counters
And appliances she could boast
Were cleaned on the inside,
Polished on the out
Twice a day with the right amount
Of elbow grease and Lemon Pledge.
She'd even polish the window ledge,

Then back upstairs to make the bed,
Brush her teeth while her prayers were said.
Vacuum carpets, check the clock,
Exactly time to wake the flock.
"Get up, kids, it's time to rise."
Back downstairs to bake some pies.

At eight when the kids got on the bus,
Her day had just begun.
She didn't waste a moment,
But worked straight through to one.

At one she ate an apple
While she wrote a menu plan,
Answered several letters
Then off to the store she ran.

She never had to look for things
They were always in their place.
Her hair was always perfect,
She had makeup on her face.

She never missed appointments,
And she'd always get there early.
Tardy wasn't ever part
Of her vocabulary.

That's why it's so ironic
That when her name was in the news,
A synonym for tardy
Was the word the writer used.

The column in the paper said,
"Ordell was thirty-four."
She left behind a tidy home
From the ceiling to the floor.

Ordell never played in life,
She worked to her demise.
The writer named the funeral home
Where the "LATE" Ordell Daily lies.

Do you know somebody like Ordell? If you do, you've probably envied her ability to get so much accomplished, and you've wondered how she does it. God made one Ordell to every ten people like you. That's because Ordell does the work of ten people, and she needs people like you to create work for her. You see, it all goes back to genetics. Ordell doesn't have a creative organ in her body. Her gift is an operative left brain.

Undoubtedly you have heard or read about studies of the right and left brain. If you look at a diagram of the human brain, you'll see that it is divided in half. One half takes care of creative information such as music, color, imagination, and intuition. That's the right side, and people who are predominantly right-brained are artists, musicians, actors, writers, etc. The other half of the brain keeps track of numbers, time, direction, logic, and practical information. That's the left side; people who are predominantly left-brained are scientists, mathematicians, computer wizards, bookkeepers, and people like Ordell. *You* were born with a left brain that isn't hooked up and a right brain that is overactive and renders you organizationally impaired.

Here's what happens. You start out on a project, and with the help of your well-developed right brain you dive in with great imagination and enthusiasm. It doesn't matter what the project is; it can be something as simple as changing the oil in the car or washing the breakfast dishes, or as complex as making a dress or building a carport. The important thing to note is that, at some point, you'll hit the boring part of the project. (Every project has one.) When you come to that cheerless place, your right brain will always kick in with an alternative list of activities. It works like the remote control to the television in the hands of a husband. You just get interested in a project and, BANG, a new program. Depending on how much energy you have, you can start so many things that you could end up talking to the fruit in your wallpaper.

If you were to try to be like Ordell, you would not be happy. You would overgoal yourself into a frenzy and end up mean and cranky. We think books like *The Seven Habits of Highly Effective People,* by Stephen Covey, were written for people like Ordell, who are already highly effective. We made up our own seven habits, which are more realistic for people like us.

Seven Habits of Minimally Effective People

1. Plan your appointments around the *TV Guide.*
2. Every fourth day, stay in your pajamas and be a zero.
3. When you get the mail, allow at least thirty minutes to focus your complete attention on filling out all the Publisher's Clearing House stuff.
4. Aim low so you won't be disappointed.
5. Go to bed at nine and get up at nine.
6. Surround yourself with pets, children, and friends.
7. Dress for comfort. Before adding an item to your wardrobe, ask yourself, "Could I sleep in this?"

Once you get realistic about what you are doing with your life, you can begin to take steps to improve it and still enjoy the easygoing kind of person you are and always will be. It's also very important to keep in mind that getting organized is really as simple as breathing. You are going to discover that it is NOT the mountain you think it is.

Five Steps Out of Your Messy Dilemma

STEP ONE: AWARENESS

The first step out of clutter and chaos into peace, joy, success, and order in your life is to become aware of how your organizationally impaired mind works. Being organized really is a matter of MIND management, not time management. We have experimented with our own minds and have been able to pinpoint the exact time into a project that the right brain gets a new idea. This depends, in part, on how interesting the activity is and at what point it becomes boring. You can try this experiment with your own brain:

At the end of this paragraph, put the book down and find a boring project. It could be a load of clothes to fold or a bed to make. You could shave or peel potatoes, or, if you can find a pen and paper, you could start writing the alphabet over and over. What you need to do is see just how far into the project you go before IT happens. If you don't want to do this experiment now, remember it the next time you are faced with a boring task, which won't be long, because life is full of boring projects. It's our guess that you'll get about six seconds into the job when a conniving little thought will subtly sneak its way in and say, "MMM, there's leftover pie in the refrigerator," or "Hey, shouldn't you see if there's any mail?" or "Oh, let's call Mom and see how she is."

Once you are aware that this is what happens and that it's behind all of your unfinished business, you can be prepared for the interruption. A split second after the launch of the thought, you'll be able to intercept it before it can destruct your work.

People with our problem have reported as many as a dozen of these mental interruptions in a single minute! You will be able to significantly stifle this sidetracking trigger in your brain if you get in the habit of recognizing it. Then all you have to do is stand up to it and stop it immediately. Think of the sound of an air horn at a basketball game and, if you have to, simulate its sound with your own voice. Whenever you start to wander, give yourself a blast on your air horn. (Don't worry if people look at you as if you are weird. Just smile and say, "I hate it when that happens.")

One young mother told us that the "air horn" had made her very aware of what her right brain was doing to sidetrack her. She said that now that she is aware, at least she has a choice to stay on track or be distracted. Before, she just unconsciously ended up somewhere else in the house, doing something else. Now she is able to accomplish so much more than before.

STEP TWO: APPRECIATE YOURSELF

The second step is to appreciate your own positive qualities. Think about yourself for a minute. You own some of the most valuable qualities a person can have. You are spontaneous, creative, flexible, optimistic, and friendly. Yet with all of these wonderful qualities, how is it that you are in the mess you are in? The reason is that every virtue has a fault at the other end. In fact, a fault IS a virtue ... left unchecked.

Take your OPTIMISM, for example. You have a positive outlook and great intentions. You might put a pile of stuff on the stairs, convinced that you'll take it up on your next trip. But the next trip doesn't include the waiting pile; instead, you start a new pile at the top of the stairs, planning to take it on the next trip down. You keep adding to the piles with the best of intentions, and, before you know it, you'd be risking suicide to maneuver the stairs with even a small armload. The only way down is the banister.

FLEXIBILITY is another of your great assets. You could go down the banister just as easily as take the conventional way. You are able to conform to many molds (even when they're growing on the food in the refrigerator). You are like a good set of shocks. Your easygoing nature can cope quite nicely with all the little bumps and holes in the road of life. But the trouble is, if the road doesn't get fixed, the bumps get bigger, the holes get deeper, and the road to life turns into a pathway to CHAOS (the "Can't Have Anyone Over Syndrome").

When you can't have anyone over, you aren't happy,

because another of your qualities is FRIENDLINESS. Because you are friendly, you are popular and almost everybody loves you. Consequently, you are on the phone so much that your listening ear is flatter than the one out in the open. If you go to the store and run into one of your many friends, you can totally lose track of time and the reason you are even at the store. People love to be around you because you are playful and fun-loving. You love to laugh, dance, sing, and play with kids and animals, and you welcome interruptions from boring or routine work.

You are SPONTANEOUS. You can switch direction like an expert skateboarder. That's because you rarely have a direction. Interruptions are a signal to move on to something more interesting. You aren't ruffled by a change in plans, because your plans are usually roaming around in your right brain. Because of your hyperactive right brain, you are very creative.

CREATIVITY is a priceless commodity. It builds bridges, scripts movies, and writes love songs and best-selling novels. Creativity sets fashion trends and paints priceless works of art. Unfortunately, creativity costs a lot of money if you're disorganized. We think we know why Picasso had to charge so much for his paintings. It's probably because he needed to recoup all the money he'd spent on craft supplies before he got organized. Like Picasso, we too have gone nuts in a craft store. Once we spent over $150 on silk flowers, faux gems, ribbon, fabric paint, and beads at the Ric Rac Craft Shack, and all we'd gone there to buy was a new glue gun and some styrofoam balls.

We have often been introduced as the Slob Sisters, which has always been okay with us, except that we get quite a few letters from people who say that the word "slob" is too harsh and that it conjures up a vision of a dirty, smelly person who spends most of the time propped in front of a TV set, slugging down pork rinds and guzzling cases of generic beer. We therefore decided to make each letter in the word "slob" stand for a quality that most disorganized people possess.

> S stands for spontaneous.
> L stands for lighthearted.
> O stands for optimistic.
> B stands for beloved.

Now that you see that the main reason you are in a mess is because you are such a fine person, it's time to move on to step three.

Step Three: Find a Reason

The third step is to find a good reason to change. WHY do you want to be organized? WHY is much more important than HOW you are going to do it. If you can get a hold of WHY, we can teach you how.

Have you ever gotten an unexpected call from out-of-towners in the middle of a lazy weekend?

"Hi! We're up at Burger King on Highway 99 and thought we'd drop in."

Where does the energy and motivation come from as you dart, stash, cram, chuck, and turn your living room into a presentable place to entertain? (We call it the dance of the Seven Disorganized Dwarfs: Dart, Stash, Cram, Chuck, Hide, Hoard, and Stow.) The effort comes from having a very good reason to do it. You don't want casual and nervy acquaintances to think you're a lazy, messy, couch-lounging dog. Because of this, you can muster incredible energy to make the place look good. It sounds pretty stupid, but stupid works!

We used to think that your reason to change had to be pure and good. We now know that reasons don't have to be noble to work. What you have to do is find a reason that will be strong enough to keep you working on the goal.

If you want to lose weight so that you will be healthier, GREAT! But if you're doing it so you'll look fabulous at your class reunion and make your old boyfriend wish he'd never let you go, THAT'S FINE, TOO! If you want to stop smoking so you'll live longer, GOOD FOR YOU! But if you want to kick the Camels so your hair won't stink and your smoke fingers will get their color back, THEN SO BE IT!

If you want to get organized so that you'll be a good example to your children and be a wonderful keeper of your home, welcoming unexpected guests, preparing nourishing meals, and providing an oasis for your family after a busy day out in the world, THAT'S BEAUTIFUL! But maybe you've always felt the condescending, watchful eye of a vicious, know-it-all in-law and you'd like to get organized so you could shove it in her face and show off your pretty, clean, happy, prosperous home, making the stuck-up pillar of perfection so jealous that she would become a binge-eating, rash-scratching, pathetic pile of disbelief. THAT'S NOT PRETTY, BUT IT'S MOTIVATION!

If you've failed in the past to reach a goal, it's probably because you didn't have a good enough reason for achieving the goal in the first place. When we finally realized why we really wanted to get organized, we stuck to our resolution. Looking back, we see that our reason was pretty silly. We both wanted to get organized so we would have more free time to play and not get in trouble with our husbands. We wish we could say that our motives were purely to glorify God and serve our fellow human beings, but they weren't.

Nobody needs to know your REAL reason now. (Once you are organized and have stepped away from the pain of the embarrassment, stress, chaos, anxiety, and guilt this problem usually causes, you might want to share what motivated you ... and then again, you might not.) If you've done some soul searching and you can't find an honorable reason to change, ask yourself for an honest one. If the only way you can succeed is to picture the sneer on someone's face if you fail, then DO IT. If you would like to flaunt the new, financially organized you in front of an old girlfriend or an ex-boss, picture yourself with an expensive leather Hartman briefcase full of money, running past them on Wall Street with a really hot tip and no time to talk. GO FOR IT. Whatever gives you a jolt of energy to pull you off the couch and on to your goal, USE IT. Psychologist and philosopher William James said, "Excitements, ideas and efforts are what give energy."

Famous and successful people have been using creepy reasons to get where they are since the beginning of television (and probably before). Take the famous body builder Charles Atlas, for instance. We have read that he started his early weight training with fear and revenge as his motives. He was a tiny guy who got pushed around by bullies as a kid. He vowed to get strong enough to beat people up if they asked for it. He turned out to be a very nice man and, to his surprise, never had to clobber anybody. We think even a sleazy reason can bring good results. If your reasons are questionable next to a more noble cause, so what? Down the road, when you're healthier, free, and organized, you can do another soul search and move on to a loftier mission.

An interesting thing will happen when you get the results you want, thanks to your secret reason: It will only be fun for a while to rub it in somebody's nose or show off the new you. The longer you live the organized life, the less you're going to care what that original reason was. The truth is that any reason that is less than righteous and good is going to end up like a balloon that slowly loses all of its party air. The old reason that kept you doing a job you didn't want to do will gradually be deflated as you begin to enjoy your new way of life. It is then that a higher purpose will begin to emerge, automatically.

In *The Seven Habits of Highly Effective People* Stephen Covey said that highly effective people know what their calling in life is. He said we need to make a statement (in writing) that defines the calling. He calls it a personal mission statement, sort of like a creed or philosophy that states what you want to achieve, what you want to contribute to humanity, what your character is, and what your values are. He compares it to the Constitution of the United States of America, only it's a personal constitution. Only a highly effective person can sit down and write what his calling or mission is. That's a great idea, but we guess that most of the thousands who bought his book got it because they were **NOT** highly effective and wanted to become that way.

The thing about missions is that your mission will always be your mission. That will never change. You were born with a unique calling, which was determined the instant all your little chromosomes hooked up with each other. At this point in your life, everything that you have experienced—the joy, the grief, the wisdom, the love, the suffering, the giving—all of it has happened for a reason that has to do with your mission. But that higher calling won't be very clear if you are overwhelmed. It will come to you when you are ... ORGANIZED. Until you are organized, it could be very difficult to write down what your calling is. What is truly wonderful about life is that your purpose will come clear to you when you take care of the little things in your direct circle of control.

Our high calling has been to create happy homes for our families and to use our sense of humor to help people get their homes organized. But back when we were slobs, that higher direction was invisible. If Jesus Himself had come to either one of our front doors in those desperate and depressing days, the encounter would have gone something like this:

Knock, knock, knock?

"Yes? Uh, oh!"

"Pam and Peggy, I am calling you to go out into the world and help my beloved, struggling, disorganized children who are drowning in a sea of clutter, chaos, and confusion."

"Oh, Lord, you have come to the wrong house. You must have meant to go to Nancy's home, two houses down. She is a pastor's wife with five children under the age of five. She is very organized. She's the one you want."

"No, you two are the ones I want."

"But Lord, you haven't seen the inside of our refrigerators."

"Yes, I have, and you're the ones I want."

If you are buried and overwhelmed with your life's circumstances, it would be nonsense to get your personal mission statement down on paper, let alone be ready to receive a commission from Jesus.

That's what we found wrong with most get-organized programs we tried. They were designed by effective people for effective people. They expected us already to be successful and prepared to become even more so.

For now, just get a juicy reason or two, knowing that down the road, when the kitty litter is emptied regularly, when you're not afraid to go to the mailbox for fear it's full of collection notices, when you get to the dentist appointment on time, and when you write letters (and send them) to all the people you owe, the bigger picture will come clear.

STEP FOUR: MEET SCHMIDKY

The fourth step is to meet Schmidky. Schmidky isn't a real person; he's an imaginary character, but he has gotten in the way of our self-improvement by sabotaging our efforts to lose weight, exercise, or stick to a budget. We have discovered that he has a great deal of power in our lives. Since we met him, he has been a major influence in helping us to succeed in areas of self-improvement.

Before we introduce him to you, we want to list a few familiar sayings. No doubt you have heard or said some or all of the following:

I was beside myself.

I was by myself.

I had to talk myself into it.

I asked myself this question.

Part of me wants to do that, but part of me doesn't.

I struck myself funny.

I didn't know what I was getting myself into.

Since the above sentences prove that we talk about ourselves as if we are more than one person, the following shouldn't seem strange.

FROM PAM:

I saw a woman on television who said that she had lost a hundred pounds and had kept it off for twenty years. Although I've never had that much of a weight problem, I have been in and out of Weight Watchers since I had babies, and I wondered how she had kept the hundred pounds off for so long. I bought her book, *Alyce's Fat Chance*, by Alyce P. Cornyn-Selby, in which she explains her theory that we have "internal directors" who run our lives. She says that a person can call on these internal experts to get solutions to problems. I liked that thought, but I didn't know what I was getting myself into when I got quiet and asked to talk to the person in charge of my extra weight. I closed my eyes and pretended I was the mayor of a city that was out of control. In my imagination, I buzzed my secretary.

"Yes?"

"Who's in charge of the intake of food in this place?"

"Let me see, that would be Mr. Schmidky."

"Get him for me."

"Yes, Ma'am."

I pictured myself in a lavish office, behind a big mahogany desk. I imagined the door mahogany, with beautiful carvings and brass fixtures. I pictured the door opening and let my imagination soar as I saw Schmidky walking in. He wore a Hawaiian shirt, shorts, thongs, and a goofy straw hat. He had a tall, tropical drink in his hand, with a chunk of pineapple stuck on the edge. He was about twenty pounds overweight. He resembled John Goodman.

"Mr. Schmidky?"

"Yo, that's my name. Ask me again and I'll tell you the same."

"Sit down. We need to talk."

"Shoot."

"I'm twenty pounds overweight, and it's your fault."

"Hey, wait a minute. I'm not in charge of your mouth. You're the one who opens it and puts the food in."

"Yeah, but you are the one who makes me want the food, and I think you are the one who can help me eat less."

"Yeah? What do you want me to do?"

"Well, for instance, Peggy and I go out to lunch too often. It's really fun, but I'm eating way too much. Today I've decided I'm not going to go out with her, but I need your help, because I'm afraid I'll change my mind when I see her."

"Yeah, I can help you, but you need to know one thing."

"What?"

"The Schmidkys are everywhere. My younger brother Darrel works for Peggy, and unless you tell her what we're doing, Darrel will talk all of us into going."

After my imaginary conversation, I called my sister and told her what I was thinking. She went right along with me and said she'd have a talk with her Schmidky and we'd both have a small salad and an apple for lunch. She called me about ten minutes later.

"Guess what?"

"What?"

"I talked to Darrel and he promised to help me, too. However, once I had the talk, something interesting happened."

"What?"

"I discovered that my Schmidky has a very good friend."

"Who?"

"Truman Conniver."

"Truman Conniver?"

"Yeah. After Schmidky agreed to help, a few minutes later I found myself on the phone with Danny, seeing if we could go out to dinner! I finagled a way to get to eat out after all."

"Well, it's good to know who Schmidky's friends are."

Schmidky is your pleasure-seeker. Everyone has one. Even Ordell, although the things that make her feel good are different. One of the things that pleases her is the superiority of being the first to the curb with her can on garbage day. As an added bonus, there is always the possibility that one of her neighbors will have to chase the truck in her nightwear. When she sees that happen, she gets all dressed up and celebrates.

You know what your Schmidky is doing in your life, because if he's out of control, the effects of his work are on your hips, smoldering in your ashtray, or wrecking your credit. You name it; if it's a problem involving too much pleasure, Schmidky is at the bottom of it. No matter how much damage he has done in your life—whether you're on welfare and it's Schmidky's fault; you need to go through Betty Ford's and it's Schmidky's fault; your clothes and your house smell like the lounge at the Legion and it's Schmidky's fault; you're fat and it's Schmidky's fault— Schmidky is extremely important to you, and he can help you.

If you tell your Schmidky how certain improvements in your life would PLEASE you, you will be amazed at what happens! Once he knows that you are unhappy in any area of your life, and you explain new ways you would like to be pleased, Schmidky will set to work to make you pleased and happy in those ways. The important thing to remember is that *you* are the boss. Schmidky is your servant. It's smart to keep in touch with your pleasure-seeker, because he is definitely a key to your self-improvement. In Chapter 7, we'll talk more specifically about diet and physical fitness.

Step Five: Get a Partner

The fifth step is to get a partner. Since we are sisters, we took each other for granted and didn't really emphasize, in our early years of teaching, the importance of having a partner. We now know that our success in conquering our problem and getting control of our lives was mainly because of our partnership. You need a partner, too. In fact, when we run into a student of ours who has fallen off the program, it's usually because she tried to do it alone. Find someone in the same degree of a mess as you are. You will be able to share your successes and your temporary setbacks. Your partner will be your single most valuable asset. We know of some partners who are still best friends after getting organized back in 1977, when we started our outreach.

If you do not have a specific person in mind, such as a friend, sister, or husband, start today to find someone. Put a 3 × 5 on the bulletin board at church, in the post office, or at the grocery store, or hire a pilot to drop flyers in your neighborhood. You could even put an ad in the paper. It could say something like this:

PERSONAL: Help Wanted! Just read *Get Your Act Together!* and need a partner. Mother of three, ready to get organized, seeking someone who would like to do the same. Westridge area. Call 696-4091.

We are as adamant about your having a partner as we would be if we were writing this book about how to conceive a child. YOU NEED A PARTNER!

So now you know why you are disorganized and how it happened. You realize what a wonderful person you are. You are going to get a couple of good reasons to get organized, have a nice long talk with Schmidky, and get a partner.

Now what? Well, we aren't going to teach you anything you don't already know. If we did give you a list of things to do, like fix it when it breaks, return it when you borrow it, and clean it up if you mess it up, you wouldn't sock yourself in the forehead and say, "Whoa, you're kidding? I didn't know I should be doing that! This is great information! Thanks, I'll do it!" The truth is you wouldn't do it, because your brain hasn't been the kind that would help you follow through on things.

Your brain has brought you to this point of being overwhelmed, and it's going to take a bunch of new habits to straighten you out. If we told you to hang up your coat when you took it off, we know it wouldn't come as a big surprise that the coat would look better in the closet than tossed over the couch, with the cat sleeping on it. You have to practice putting your coat away before it will become automatic. It will take a while to program the new habit, but if you've been tossing your coat and everything else onto the couch, the dining room table, the counters, stairs, chairs, and bed for even one month, let alone a lifetime, you must go through tossing withdrawal.

Now you might be thinking, "What's the point in hanging up my coat when the rest of my house is a pigpen?" Hanging up your coat will be one less thing to deal with. If you just promised yourself not to make any more messes than you've already made, things would improve. Start with your coat and stretch from there. "But you don't have any idea what a mess I'm in." Yes, we do. As you'll see in Chapter 2, we've come through the dust of our own pigpens. To us, there is no difference in a big or little mess. If it's a mess that has become a problem, it doesn't matter how it compares to another person's mess. Somebody with an attic full of boxes might be in as much despair as a person who can't walk into his den because of piles. A person with a chronic mess in the trunk of her car could be as frustrated as the one who can't get the car into her garage.

Getting organized is a matter of realizing that the ONLY things that stand in the way are a few silly habits AND the way you've turned the **thought** of getting organized into such a big mountain. Getting organized is not a big deal.

Jesus said, "If ye have faith and doubt not, ye shall say unto this mountain, Be thou removed, and be thou cast into the sea; it shall be done" (Matthew 21: 21).

Two

The SLOB Sisters

FROM PAM:
My sister and I not only share the same genetic defect; we share the same history of disorderly conduct. We can trace it back to the summer day we moved into the same bedroom. (I get to write this chapter because my recollection of that time is far clearer than hers. I was ten and she was five! For one thing, I remember that the bedroom really wasn't one, and she thoughtit was. In reality, it was the gutted upstairs of our old farmhouse.)

A piece of plywood almost covered the stairwell hole, except for the last two stairs at the top. Dad had thrown an old tarp over the rest of the opening to seal off the upstairs and conserve heat in the winter. We had been allowed to play up there, but when I asked if we could sleep in the unfinished, unplumbed, and unheated upstairs, I hit a parental cement wall. I spent most of a year in relentless petition and, sometime in early summer, Mom and Dad caved. With the caving, Peggy and I got a double bed, two dressers, all of our personal belongings, and seven years of inspection-free living in that upstairs room.

Our born-organized mom was not willing to lift the plywood and the tarp in order to inspect our living quarters. Every morning when we came downstairs, she said, "Girls, how does your room look?"

We said, "Fine!"

Our "fine" and her "fine" were two different "fines."

For those seven years, our mess didn't cause us much of a problem. In fact, we enjoyed a kind of chaotic bliss. We have had to give serious thought to when our organizational defect really started to cause us pain. For each of us, it was when we entered junior high.

In junior high we were hit with our first long-term assignments. We were finally forced to face reality when our teachers began assigning them. They were called units and they had to have maps, graphs, pictures, a table of contents, and a bibliography that was supposed to represent all the research we had done. Since we would usually have six weeks to complete the assignment, this was our first real, hands-on experience with procrastination. SIX WEEKS SOUNDED LIKE SO MUCH TIME!

Our brains have a hard time taking a large project and breaking it down into smaller, manageable parts, so we put off such matters until we were forced to work nonstop to finish the assignment by its deadline. To this day we still have bad dreams, where we're in the classroom and everyone hands in thick, colorful, bound units on everything from Costa Rica to Frog Anatomy, and we have nothing to give but a pile of pretty pictures ripped out of *National Geographic* or some random frog drawings stapled together. The dreams are as scary as any nightmare, and our husbands know how to bring us back gently to the present.

"Babe, wake up. It's just another unit dream. You're big now."

Peggy and I have talked a lot about our "unit dreams,"

and in sharing their horror we have come to realize that the person who is disorganized and out of control is a lot like the alcoholic. The trap begins innocently enough. Remember *The Days of Wine and Roses*, when Jack Lemmon and Lee Remick started out sipping a sweet and tasty chocolate liqueur? Near the end of the movie, they were staggering, slobbering inebriates who had lost everything, including each other. Disorganization starts out innocently, too. You leave the foil from a chocolate Hershey Kiss, with its little paper tail wadded up, on the coffee table, and soon it disappears under a heap of newspapers, junk mail, banana peels, gum wrappers, cups and glasses, magazines, loose change, business cards, dishes, dirty napkins, peanut shells, stray hairs, and nail clippings.

In his book *Choices and Consequences*, Dick Schaefer addresses four defenses that the alcoholic uses to try to change reality and avoid changing behavior: denial, projection, rationalization, and minimizing. You are probably out of the denial stage (refusing to recognize or accept that you have a problem) or you wouldn't be reading this book, but it's interesting to think back to the first time you realized you were disorganized.

I can remember Mom telling us we were a mess, but we didn't believe her. We were like little puppies who played hard and then slept long. Surrounded by love, we had "enablers" like our disorganized dad and Granny, who'd say to Mom, "Aw, c'mon, let 'em play. They're so young and free."

The four defenses came into play with the units. Here's how.

Denial. For me, it started in Mr. Mattenich's seventh grade science class. After a few easy weeks, he hit us with the big assignment.

"Students, we are going to learn about reptiles. Reptiles are in the phylum Chordata. They belong to the subphylum Verbrata, and make up the class Reptilia. You will have six weeks to complete your unit on reptiles. You'll need to spend a great deal of time in the library doing research...."

The next thing I knew, I had a month and a half to research the life of the lizard. I had to find out how he sleeps, who or what he eats, what he looks like on the inside and out, what we as humans use him for, who his enemies are, where he came from, and where he's going. I could not have cared less.

Vicki Schram was excited. "Wow, I'm gonna get started tonight! I'm gonna have my mom take me to the main library downtown so I can check out some great books on lizards."

An alcoholic denies there is a drinking problem. Easily caught up in Vicki's enthusiasm and unable, at the time, to know that I was in DENIAL, I thought, *"Yeah, I'm going to start tonight, too!"*

With great concern, Vicki said, "Six weeks isn't very much time to get all of this done."

Six weeks seemed like an eternity to me. I thought, *"No problem, I've got way over a month."* DENIAL!

Vicki's concern didn't fade. "I don't want to let this go to the last minute like some people do."

"Me either," I agreed.

She continued, "If I have to have twenty-five typewritten pages, that's an awful lot of work, especially with all my other classes."

It didn't even occur to me that I couldn't type yet. *"Twenty-five pages, no big deal."* DENIAL! DENIAL! DENIAL!

Rationalization. Inventing excuses to make unacceptable behavior seem acceptable. The alcoholic might rationalize that everything is under control, that he can quit drinking any time he wants to and that he is only drinking socially. As the weeks passed, I began to rationalize that everything was under control, that I could start any time,

and that my social life was far more important than learning about Reptilia.

Two weeks passed; I had done nothing. I watched Vicki
Schram's efforts stack up. Her dad even bought her a
small lizard, and she had been charting his sleep patterns
and eating habits.

Four weeks passed. I told myself that I had two whole
weeks left. Vicki's unit was shaping up into something for
which the government might pay some serious grant
money.

At five weeks, my ability to rationalize kept me from
any conscious form of frenzy. After all, I had seven whole
days and the whole UNIVERSE was made in that length
of time.

Projection. Finding blame with others. An alcoholic
projects his problem onto other people and circumstances.
Six weeks passed, and the day came when Mr. Mattenich
announced, "Students, please turn in your units."

I had cut out a picture of a lizard and copied, word for
word, what was written in the "L" volume of our encyclo-
pedia. There was no way I was going to turn in such a dis-
graceful piece of work. I went up to Mr. Mattenich and,
with a heavy heart, I projected, "Margie Vannoy told me
our units weren't due until Monday! And every time I went
to the library, Tom Prediletto had the 'L.'"

Mr. Mattenich liked me, and he didn't like seeing me so
upset.

"Now, now, don't cry. I can give you till Monday."

From after school on Friday night until I caught the bus
Monday morning, I worked on the lizard unit. I didn't
sleep, I didn't bathe or comb my hair, I stayed in the same
clothes, I didn't get to watch TV, I barely took time out to
eat. My life was focused and dedicated to the study of
lizards ... and everyone in my family was reptilia-con-
scious as well. I had turned all of them into enablers!

On Monday, I handed in the unit, as promised. It had

twenty-five typewritten pages (Dad did the typing for me). The maps were great (Peggy had colored them with the expertise of a master colorer), the graphs were fabulous, the drawings were clever, and the cover was absolutely Steven Spielberg. Mom had let me cut up an old, fake alligator purse into the shape of tiny lizards. I glued the shells of an open and gutted walnut on the cover and had the lizards coming out of the shells and spelling my title with their little fake bodies ... *Lizards in a Nut Shell*. I got an A.

Minimization. Made to look less serious than it is. The alcoholic minimizes his drinking problem by emphasizing how little the problem affects him. With the A I got for *Lizards in a Nut Shell*, I thought, *"Hah, I got an A for something that I created in two days! Those fools spent six weeks working on their units, and I did mine in a weekend!"*

Using the four defenses didn't stop with the units; they were just the beginning. And just as experts claim alcoholism is a progressive disease, Peggy's and my problem progressed to astounding dimensions. As adults, when faced with vacations, Christmas, remodeling, moving, getting ready for a new baby, income tax preparation, dinner parties, birthday parties, or anything that required a commitment of time and more than one or two steps, we clung to our precious defenses.

I was seventeen when we moved from the farmhouse to the home our parents still live in today. When the plywood and tarp seal was removed, Mom went upstairs and into shock! She was flabbergasted to discover that her "fine" wasn't the same as our "fine."

"It's a ghetto! How in heaven's name could you ever sleep in such squalor?" she shrieked.

Mom struggled to cope with our disorderly life-style after she discovered the room upstairs. At the new house, she separated us to isolate the most Spontaneous, Lighthearted, Optimistic, and Beloved daughter. (We tied for the honor.) In desperation, Mom read a bunch of books on child psychology and found one that dealt with "the messy child." She tried to follow the author's advice and close the doors to our rooms so the chaos wouldn't drive her nuts. According to this book, in time, out of a natural desire for order, we would clean up our rooms.

It never happened. When forced to straighten up or face the penalty of solitary confinement, we'd stash the mess behind our dressers, under our beds, or in the backs of our closets. Since Mom didn't have a "stashing mentality," she assumed that when the room looked tidy, it was. She would stand in the doorway of one of our rooms to make her inspection, and, without suspicion, she always let us go free ... until the next time.

The idea of hanging something up or putting it back in its place was, to us, a complex concept akin to quantum physics. Years later, Mom finally resigned herself to the fact that she had raised not one but two slob daughters, and she regularly apologized to our befuddled and frustrated husbands.

In spite of our cluttered and chaotic childhood, units and all, we still managed to enjoy it. But our lives took a serious turn when we waltzed down the aisle into the real world of marriage, motherhood, and homemaking. It's a cruel awakening for the domestically challenged. A demanding world of in-laws, overdrafts, chimney fires, diaper rash, peeping Toms, door-to-door salesmen, car pools, pets, toddlers, teenagers, and disconnection threats. When we said, "I do!" we had no idea how much had to be done.

In the time it takes to have six children, we did. With each addition to our families, we went further down. Our homemaking was only as good as our resourcefulness. We found that a Cornish game hen would fit nicely inside a turkey if there was no other stuffing available. Late bills could be marked "Please Forward" and, when placed behind the rear tires of the car and rolled over, would give the impression that the already suspect postal service had temporarily lost our otherwise timely payments. Jogging suits could be slept in and, after a couple of days, would make the wearer look like a marathoner.

We became masters at creating the illusion that we were successful homemakers, but all too often our deeds would lead to public humiliation. There was the time the car mechanic dislodged a petrified Big Mac from under the front seat of my car, solving the mystery of why the automatic seats would not work. Peggy still hasn't lived down the time Jeff's schoolteacher made a visit and seated herself on the living room couch. She didn't know that she was also sitting on a couple of Milk Duds. While she chatted happily and sipped a cup of hot tea, the chocolate-covered caramels melted and fused themselves to the back of the teacher's white skirt and the cushion of the couch.

It wasn't as if we never tried to change. Every New Year's Eve we would vow to clean up our act, but by Valentine's Day (as we were taking down the Christmas tree), we knew that, once again, we had failed.

We even bought self-help books, including *How to Stop Procrastinating* (we never did get around to reading it); *Is There Life After Housework?* (there wasn't); *The Time Minder* (we didn't), and *Motivate Yourself* (we couldn't). The problem was that the authors of those books were born organized and seemed to have no idea how bad things can get. A highly effective, genetically organized person could not possibly address the concerns of those of us who struggle just to be minimally effective.

Stephanie Winston, the bestselling organizational wizard, would never wear her husband's Jockey shorts to work as Peggy did. Before she had kids, Peggy worked for *The Columbian* newspaper. The usual backup on laundry often left her without underwear. Whenever that happened, she simply wore a pair of her husband, Danny's, shorts. One day she got caught. Going down the stairs at work, she slipped at the top and bounced to the bottom, where her boss stood in helpless horror.

"Oh, Peggy, are you all right?"

"I'm all right, I'm all right!" She wondered if he'd seen her shorts.

"Well, it's company policy that we take you to the doctor just to make sure you're fine." He was insistent. They went straight from the bottom of the stairs out to the company car and to the doctor. By then Peggy was beginning to feel stiff and sore. An X-ray was ordered.

"Strip down to your underwear and lay on that table," a cranky old nurse ordered. The humiliation of having to lie on a stainless steel X-ray table in a bra and men's Jockey shorts defies comment.

I too suffered humiliation, but more than humiliation, I was in a constant battle with my husband, who was crotchety and demanding. Sometimes he didn't know what went on behind his back. Shortly before I got organized, we moved from Fresno to Vancouver, Washington. We drove a few weeks ahead of the moving van. My husband had told me to get some tranquilizers for the cat, because she hated riding in the car. I had forgotten to get them. Knowing how volatile he could be, especially when I didn't follow through with his orders, I had to make an emergency call on my right brain, when, just as we were leaving, he asked for the tranquilizer. I brought him a capsule. I watched him poke a Dexatrim down our poor cat's throat. During the trip, the cat was a nervous wreck, and she didn't eat for days.

On June 16, 1977, my sister and I both hit bottom. On that day, the Bekins van pulled up and delivered my stuff. I had 157 moving boxes, all marked "MISCELLANEOUS." A load of wash that had been accidentally left in the washing machine had also made the long haul from Fresno. (Mold travels quickly in a hot moving van. All of our clothes, all of our upholstered furniture, and every sheet and towel had a musty smell and a faint green tinge.)

Peggy's crisis actually started brewing the day before. What happened that day is best told in her words.

FROM PEGGY:

I knew it was wrong to go to the zoo with my sister that morning, but I did it anyway. Danny had shown signs that he was close to reaching his personal point of no return. His damp underwear had refused to quick-dry itself in the microwave, and the look on his face, as he snatched the steamy briefs from my hand, had warned me not to speak. Before he left for work, he had questioned me about my plans for the day.

"So, what's on that TO DO List for you today?"

"Uh ... I thought I'd clean up the house and get some groceries."

"Well, wouldn't that be nice, but don't overgoal. Why don't you just concentrate on one thing?"

"What?"

"GET GROCERIES!"

When my sister called to ask if I'd like to take the kids and go with her to see the first viewing of the new baby elephant, I knew I should turn her down. In fact, I did turn her down. "Oh, Sissy, I can't. Danny's all huffed out of shape this morning. We're out of everything around here, and I promised him I'd get groceries today."

"Groceries? So what's the big deal? It'll take us twenty minutes to drive over to the zoo, we'll look at the baby for twenty minutes, and twenty minutes later we'll be home. Let's go! I'll help you get the groceries when we get back."

It sounded so foolproof and deliciously devil-may-care. I couldn't resist. We piled our six kids into her station wagon and headed for the zoo, like a busload of Elks on their way to Reno. When one of our kids asked about dinner, we realized we'd stayed all day. We raced through traffic to try to beat Danny home. There was no time to get groceries, so we stopped at Bill's Burger Bucket for something for dinner. I knew if I could at least feed him, Danny would be pacified enough to discuss the grocery problem like an adult.

My sister pulled up and yelled our order into the speaker. "We'd like three Bronco Burgers, two Chili Bull Dogs, one with cheese, two Double Heifers with extra onions, a Triple Bull Dozer with everything, two large Bucket-O-Fries, seven regular Cokes, two diets, and be quick about it."

"Excuse me, ma'am, we didn't hear that order. Could you move your car up a little?"

My sister, who wasn't wearing her glasses, had ordered into the heat vent! When we got to my house with the burgers, Danny wasn't home yet, but there was a sheriff's car in my driveway, and a couple of my neighbors were standing in my yard. The sheriff came up to the station wagon.

"Which one of you lives here?"

"I do." My voice was shaking.

"Well, I hate to be the one to tell you this, but somebody broke into your house. Your neighbor over there saw 'em go out the back and run down over the hill." We were absolutely stunned with disbelief that anyone would actually do that. We'd seen break-ins on TV, but you never think it'll happen to you. "Just try to stay calm when you go in there, but I gotta tell ya, they ransacked the place ... even ate and left their plates in front of the TV!"

When we went inside, we were pleased. It was exactly the way I had left it. Nothing had been touched. When Danny got home, the poor sheriff was finishing up his report. Danny told him that he thought the reason the crooks didn't take anything was because they were totally confused in there and probably thought somebody else had beaten them to it. For a moment I was tempted to tell

Danny that there *was* one thing missing ... THE GRO-CERIES!

At that point, I did not know that things would get worse.

We would have been at the end of our ropes (if we could have found them.) Each of us had, in fact, been there many times before, but never both of us on exactly the same day. On the morning of the sixteenth, Peggy sent Danny to work with long, gray cat hair covering the back of his police uniform in a circular pattern that matched the shape of a baby's behind. Peggy had started to diaper Ally, their sixteenth-month-old, when the phone rang. Peggy left Ally on the bed, and when she returned to the bedroom, Ally was sitting bare, Vaseline-bottomed, on the uniform that had been laid out while Danny showered. Peggy flipped the shirt over, and the sticky Vaseline attracted the cat hair from the bedspread, where the cat had spent the night. Danny never knew.

He also didn't know that what he thought were the clean socks he was wearing were really dirty socks sprayed with deodorant and warmed in the dryer on "high." He didn't know that his face was tinted a faint shade of turquoise (since Peggy hadn't gotten groceries, she had secretly filled the empty Lectric Shave bottle with blue food-colored water).

Peggy listened as the Smurf-faced crime fighter delivered what she called a "mild ultimatum."

"GET GROCERIES!"

When he left, Peggy, motivated by guilt, started on a cleaning tangent. Staying in what she had slept in (one of Danny's oversized T-shirts and bottoms to a pair of his pajamas, whose top had been lost in the laundry months before), she started vacuuming. She told her kids to dump out all their drawers and she'd help them sort and store their winter clothes. Completely unaware that her right brain was a ruthless idea machine, she was a servant to every impulse. She pulled some weeds in the flowerbed, pulled out the contents of the pantry, took down the drapes in the living room, washed two windows, plucked one eyebrow, started a garage sale pile in the hall, wrote part of a letter to Aunt Viv, called Mom, and, at some point, ended up in a tent her kids had made from couch cushions and the drapes she'd taken down.

The doorbell rang. It was Danny's boss. He had dropped by to look at a travel trailer Danny had advertised on the police bulletin board. There was no way Peggy could find the key to show him the RV. There she was at noon, in makeshift nightwear, chicken hair (chicken hair gives new meaning to the traditional "shampoo set," because you shower and wash your hair late at night and then go to bed with wet hair that sets during the night in a style that depends on how you position your head on the pillow— usually the effect is reminiscent of a rooster's topknot), no makeup, 187 pounds, and a house from hell. The boss just backed out the door, giving her a look that she has never forgotten. *"How did Dan get hooked up with a deal like this?"*

After he left, Peggy called me, described what had happened, and confessed how embarrassed she was. I told her about the moving boxes and together we stepped out of denial. On that momentous day, we began our trek from pigpen to paradise. We found out that the journey requires three things:

1. A firm decision to change. (We definitely had that.)
2. A commitment for the right reasons. (We had that, too.)
3. A plan. (That we didn't have.)

We spent the afternoon at a local restaurant, mapping out a strategy and a system. In Chapter 4 we will explain that system, which has evolved over the last fifteen years—

into the perfect tool for sidetrackers as terminal as we once thought we were, to Ordell Daily types who need to lighten up and have more fun in life, and everyone else in between.

The plan involves a new way of thinking, which is just like getting a script for a play. If you were an actress and you were going to play the role of a very organized wife and mother, you would (if you were a good actress) research the character and become very aware of the way organized people act. This doesn't mean we want you to turn into an Ordell, but we do want you to become acutely aware of how she functions, because part of the time you are going to need to act like her.

The best advice we've ever heard, when it comes to learning anything new, is to copy the masters. So, if you wanted to learn to paint dancers, you might study Degas. If you wanted to become a great dancer, you might rent a bunch of Gene Kelly movies. And if you want to clean up your act, you need to mock the masters of order. To do that, we need to take you to Intercourse, Pennsylvania.

Three

Why You'll Never Meet a Disorganized Amish

Intercourse, Pennsylvania, home of many Amish families. There are no disorganized Amish. (According to a library book we checked out, they have a high suicide rate, but none of them is disorganized.) That's because the Amish live very simply, they aren't bombarded with worldly distractions, and their good habits and daily routine are infused into their bloodline. (Perhaps the printed, Monday-through-Sunday underpants were inspired by an outcast, Amish entrepreneur, who grew up with the memorized weekly plan of "Monday's washday, Tuesday's ironing," etc., and could see the need for the world to get on a regular laundry and personal hygiene program.)

The Amish Garden

The simple Amish way of life carries over into every area. Take their gardens, for instance. They never overplant or grow for show. Their neat, tended rows of thriving vegetables are bordered, in moderation, by pretty flowers, whose purpose is not to impress but to distract the bugs. Throughout the community, there are no rambling, weedy patches of overgrown salad fixings that have bolted and gone to seed. Snoopers could not find one zucchini past pan-size, let alone one as big as Schwarzenegger's thigh. There'd be no big, brown tomatos that nobody came back to pick or worm-ridden radishes the size of beets.

Unlike many secular gardeners, the Amish really do reap what they sow. They know their seeds because they gather them by hand from their own gardens when the time is right. They also know exactly how many of them to put back in the ground, in order to get out of it what they need for their table. Since they tend their gardens right after breakfast, they never dig, pick, or pull on an empty stomach. That prevents them from ever scalping their plants, as a hungry reaper might do. Nothing is wasted, and everything is done according to a precise plan, which each family follows.

We, the chronically disorganized, on the other hand, have to be careful of anything that multiplies and has to be tended. We are easily inspired to start new projects, but it's one thing to watch the Master Five-Minute-Gardener do it on cable TV and another to race down to the Rusty Hoe and fly headlong into reckless propagating. Planting on impulse, without thinking of the long-term commitment of a growing garden, is almost as irresponsible as a momentary frolic on the flatbed of a Toyota 4X4. Planting is the easiest part of the growing process; it's the weeding, watering, thinning, pruning, and fertilizing that come afterward that take all the time. The Amish would never let their pole beans choke the tassels off the corn stalks because they had neglected to set up the necessary poles before the teenage seedlings were itchy to climb something and crept into the corn rows. For the Amish, gardens are serious business, and the rules for planting are handed down from generation to generation.

In our second book, *The Sidetracked Sisters Catch-up on the Kitchen,* we warned sister slobs to think before they sowed, offering our own "30 RULES TO GROW BY." Some of the best rules included the following:

Start small.

If you plan to travel, don't plant at all.

Make friends with a farmer and borrow his tools.

If you can't take care of your house plants, don't try a garden.

Be patient and don't pull up carrots to see how they're doing.

Keep deer away by tying your teenager to a post outside your garden when he's been grounded.

The Amish Home

Inside an Amish home, the functional simplicity continues. The purpose of the living room is to accommodate fellow Amish for services on Sunday. Each family takes its turn hosting the regular gatherings and preparing the afternoon meal. Never on a Saturday night would an Amish mom have to fly through the house, tripping over toys and yelling at everybody to pick up their stuff for the next day's meeting. There wouldn't be anything to pick up, because they don't collect STUFF in the first place! She wouldn't have to shriek at her teenager to "Turn down that music and get off the phone!" because there wouldn't be a stereo and there wouldn't be a phone. There'd be no fights over the TV clicker, either. Nobody would have to put the cover back on the VCR or round up the tapes and match them to their jackets. There'd be no need to work at the nail polish stain on the carpet or to haul the piles of old magazines out to the trunk of the car to hide them.

In our slob days, if we had wanted to have a gathering

after church, we'd have had to make a whirlwind swipe through the living room before we left in the morning. (We'd have forgotten the night before that we had invited people over.) Each one in the family would have grabbed a grocery sack and, as if in an Olympic track event, dashed around the obstacle course, bagging up clothes, dirty dishes, newspapers, coffee mugs, slippers, dog toys, stuffed animals, craft projects, and anything else that had been used and left out during the week. Snapping at one another, blaming and making excuses, we'd have left for church in the spirit of anger. Consequently, we'd be nervous, cranky, tired, fighting Christians when the guests knocked at the door for fellowship.

It might be nice not to be invaded by worldly distractions and enticements. There would be no confusion, because you could keep your attention on what you were supposed to be doing. A friend wouldn't call to see if you wanted to go with her to the mall and get a make-over at The Mud Pack. You wouldn't spend time figuring out which shows you'd watch on TV. There wouldn't be commercials to make you feel sorry for yourself, and you wouldn't be tempted by mailers from your favorite department store, luring you into their 15-HOUR LAST CHANCE SALE!

Don't Do It! Don't be snared by materialism and get off the track like Peggy did one year. This is her story, and it contains a warning for other sidetrackers with credit:

FROM PEGGY:
Last year I charged Christmas. I didn't mean to, but as the big day drew nearer, I guess I got sucked into the notion that there weren't enough gifts under the tree. I think I can blame it on television. I saw a couple in a commercial who really loved each other, and, in the end, he handed her a pretty velvet ring box and she teared up and he held her close. You didn't get to see what he bought her,

but underneath the frame it said, "Diamonds are forever," so you knew it was something pretty good. Then I saw little children in awe over their toys from Santa. The mom and dad just smiled at them and then at each other, and then the dad pulled out his Discover card and showed it to the mom, and he winked at her like a little elf. They were all so happy.

I left for the mall, armed with a full wallet. I checked my weapon like a gunfighter checking the bullets in his pistol before a shootout. The cash compartment was empty. *Hmm* ... I looked at the splendid, well-stacked row of credit cards, some silver, some gold, some green. Then three things happened. I pictured all the beautifully wrapped packages I could put under the tree, surprising my delighted family. I heard the distant voice of my hard-working husband, warning me to let the Visa cool off. Then I bargained with the credit devil and agreed that I would only use my department store cards. (I had enough of those to get lots of nice things for the people I love.)

Looking back, I wish I had told the revolving Satan to get behind me, but he and I made a pass through the mall that Danny and I would be paying off for months to come. In the spring, when the clothes I'd charged were either outgrown, stained, or too wintry to wear and all the other stuff was forgotten, the bills were still there. I made a decision never to be tempted again. Now, there are no more deals with the credit devil. In the past I had cut up the plastic demons, knowing I could charge without them, using my driver's license as ID. This time, when the bills were paid off, I closed the accounts.

When you're all caught up in the spirit of Christmas, and the commercials are beckoning you to buy, buy, buy, remember that charging your gifts isn't a gift at all. It's a burden you place on yourself, and your family. Remember my words, DON'T DO IT!

In our experience, homes today are overloaded with

things. The objects may be worth money, but, stockpiled, they lose their value. In one home we visited, the couple collected expensive Precious Moments figurines. Each one represented a significant milestone in their lives, but jammed together on three shelves of a bookcase, there was nothing precious about them. In fact, they were depressing. Regardless of whether you're collecting teddy bears, fabric, tools, Tupperware, yarn, magazines, recipes, paints, plants, pictures, or other treasured accumulations, if you can't get to them to enjoy them, how valuable are they?

How much easier would it be to have only what you needed? How much faster could you wash the dishes, launder the clothes, pay the bills, and clean the house if you had to handle only what you actually needed, instead of what you had accumulated?

We found an interesting article in *Money* magazine a couple of years ago, about the American dream. The writer, Walter L. Updegrave, interviewed folks (rich, poor, and middle class) from all across the United States.

A generation ago, the American dream consisted of a black-and-white TV and a basic, eight-hundred-square-foot house with a carport. When summer hit, the family piled into the station wagon, like the one the Cleavers owned, and headed for the Grand Canyon or Yellowstone. When Junior tossed his mortar board into the air, he had just three short months to work to help pay tuition, until he hopped a Greyhound for college.

Today the American dream has escalated into a rat race of cranky commuters, who work fifty- and sixty-hour weeks to finance their sophisticated collection of the latest whatevers. Updegrave writes, "Clearly, the American dreamers of three decades ago reached and surpassed their goals. The past 20 years of progress came with hidden costs, however. To acquire more and better of everything, just about everybody gave up free time and amassed a mountain of debt...."

"In the past two decades, much of the stuff of dreams was purchased with the paychecks of hard-working women. In 1989, 74% of women ages 25–54 were in the labor force compared with 49% in 1969. While many wanted careers for reasons of self-fulfillment, most knew they were trading off time and home life....

"Yet the impulse to spend more—largely on conveniences like eating out and high-tech appliances—grew quickly out of the two-paycheck life-style. More begat more. Consumer credit became an addiction. Total consumer installment debt rose from $97.1 billion in 1969 to $716.6 billion in 1989."

What we think is especially interesting, in this conservative, money-oriented magazine, is that when subscribers were polled and asked to rate twenty-four elements of the American dream, the one that came out FIRST was something money can't buy ... HAVING A HAPPY HOME LIFE!

Isn't it interesting that, in our pursuit of happiness, we have ended up charging seven times more than our parents did, to buy the things we think will give us pleasure? In the end, we have had to leave our homes to go to work, to help pay the bills for the happiness gadgets, and then wish, above all else, that home—the place where we don't have time to be—is happy.

Here's a poem Pam wrote that sums up the whole problem.

DISILLUSIONED

I got a job a month ago.
Today's the day they paid.
They took out some withholding
And FICA's got it made.
When I cashed my paycheck
For the thirty days of work,
I went to pick the children up
And nearly went berserk

'Cause when I paid the person
Who agreed to watch my brood,
There was just enough left over
To buy the dog some food.

I thought that when I got this job,
My wallet would be thicker.
I'd ease financial tension
And we'd no longer bicker
Over little things like overdrafts
And disconnected phones.
We'd pay off all our credit cards.
We'd reconcile our loans
On the car we bought in '83
And trashed in '85,
And the one we're driving currently
And hope it stays alive.

I thought that when I went to work
The checkbook would be in the black.
Maybe he'd buy that boat he loves
And I could take a whack
At tennis at the country club,
Where everybody goes.
I'd buy a BMW.
I'd get some classy clothes.
We'd take that cruise to Mexico,
The vacation of our dreams.
We'd leave the kids at Gramma's,
Romance bursting at the seams.

We'd rip up all the carpeting.
The walls could use some paint.
The kitchen needs remodeling;
The sink's my main complaint.
I'd get to buy a stereo

That plays a compact disc.
I'd also get a VCR.
That too is on my list.

The kids don't like the sitter.
My life is in a shambles.
I never see my husband,
And all we eat is Campbell's.

There's never time for romance.
We're lucky if we kiss.
I don't have any leisure.
It's the simple life I miss.

All I ever wanted was
To ease financial stress.
Instead I'm hypertensive
'Cause the house is in a mess.

I guess I was mistaken
By what I thought would be.
There is no extra money,
And there's no time left for me.

The Amish don't pursue happiness; they are in the pursuit of simplicity and Godliness. We admit to a worldly attachment to our possessions, but, inspired by their simple, less-is-better ideals, we have culled the chaff from the treasures worth keeping, and we are happier for it.

We have always admired self-discipline, whether it's shown in athletics, art, religion, or just daily life. While we know we wouldn't be able to live the totally disciplined life of a Mrs. Schimelpfenig in Lancaster County, we can learn from her organized ways. She has dozens of GOOD HABITS, a DAILY ROUTINE, and a WEEKLY PLAN, and we do, too.

Good Habits

It takes twenty-one days to establish a habit in the subconscious mind. If you made your bed for three weeks, on the twenty-second day, if you didn't make it, you'd feel as if something were wrong. Organized people, like the Amish, rely on the support of their good habits, and we can, too. We have developed TEN HABITS TO MEMORIZE AND LIVE BY. They are not going to be head-slapping, light-bulb-goes-on, new thoughts, because you already know you're supposed to be doing each one. They are old ideas that we'd like you to think about with new enthusiasm. As you memorize them and then act on your memory, think of them as little soldiers, out in front of you, protecting you from feeling like Lucy and Ethel at the candy factory, shoving chocolates down their blouses in an effort to keep up with the pace.

Ten Habits to Memorize and Live By

1. Pick it up, don't pass it up; and don't put it down unless you put it away.
2. Finish what you start and keep the horse before the cart.
3. When you're on the telephone, visiting, or watching TV, do something productive with your hands.
4. If you can't talk and do something productive with your hands at the same time, put masking tape on your mouth and get your work done.
5. Eat sitting down.
6. Make your bed for your own self-respect.
7. Make sure that each room in the house serves its own purpose.
8. Do it when you think of it.
9. Don't write long letters.
10. Work faster; say No when you should and say Yes when you can. Ask yourself, "If I do this, in a year from now, will it matter that I did it?"

Peggy's two sons tell about their experiences during their first year at West Point and the Air Force Academy. When they first arrived in June, they were required to memorize not only their daily routine but all sorts of information (such as the entire front page of the *New York Times*). At first it seemed impossible, but, with practice, their brains accepted the assignment, and by fall, when the academic year started, their lives were on automatic pilot. Memorizing the basics left their minds free to think of more important things, like calculus. The rigorous demands on body, mind, and spirit brought out a slogan one of them coined. Chris said, "I just kept telling myself, 'Let your memory serve you.'"

The Daily Routine

After you've memorized the new habits, you need to memorize a daily routine. Pretend you're an Amish woman. You don't have to start milking cows or churning butter, but pretend you are a very tidy, organized woman who takes care of tasks before they develop into monsters. Draw up a daily routine that such a person would have and memorize it as if you were playing her part on the stage.

If you asked an Amish woman what time she gets up and what time she goes to bed, she'd know the answer. She sticks to her routine like a goldminer sticks to his claim, because she doesn't have to think about it. Everything can be reduced to a habit. As soon as you memorize your daily routine, it will become a habit and everything will have a place in your new schedule.

Sometimes the home front can seem like a battlefield. There is always so much to do and never enough time in a day to get the things done that we wanted to. If we can let our memory serve us, so that a routine is already etched in our mind, we won't have to waste time figuring out where we're supposed to be and what we're supposed to be doing.

A regular routine doesn't need to be scary. It also doesn't have to be a workaholic routine that would make Ordell look like an easygoing slacker. If you've never had a regular daily routine, don't go to extremes with this. Our first attempt at a schedule had us up too early, running too fast, working too hard, and, after three days, swatting at flies that weren't really there. Don't try to be on a fast-tracker's routine if you're a sidetracker by nature.

In the next chapter, we will show you our daily routine, which we put on 3 × 5 cards (see page 59). Before you read further, take some time to think about an ideal day. First plug in all the givens. Those are the things you can't get away with skipping. While you obviously can't figure in the unknowns, you can program the compulsories like eating, sleeping, working, playing, exercising, etc. If you're a night person, arrange your routine to fit your personality. If you're an early bird, give thanks for the gift and figure out the rest of your day. Above all, DO NOT TRY TO GET ORGANIZED WITHOUT A MEMORIZED DAILY ROUTINE AND A WEEKLY PLAN ... IT WON'T HAPPEN!

The 7-Day Weekly Plan

The Amish worked up the singsong limerick that kept them washing on Monday and ironing on Tuesday, etc., and because all the ladies were singing the same song, nobody felt sorry for herself. Since the grass wasn't greener in the other guy's yard, the laundry was done and the homemaker was on to another simple task. We worldly wives and mothers have the challenge of balancing work outside our homes with cooking, cleaning, finances, carpools, children's sports, vacation planning, holidays, and entertaining.

With all the demands on the modern woman, we understand that a simple weekly plan is not EASY to make. In fact, it is the single most DIFFICULT part of getting and staying organized. Most won't make one! Out of one hundred people who read this book, only five will actually take our advice and make a weekly plan. You could be one of the five, if you could just get a glimpse of the magic of it.

Think of a weekly plan as a disposable guide to focusing your life for seven days at a time. When written on a 3 × 5 card, it's also earth-friendly and can be recycled as your situation changes. Above all, don't be intimidated by the thought of failing to actually do what you said you'd do because you wrote it down on paper. If the plan is loose, you can be, too. Basically, we have learned that there are seven different elements to a weekly plan. If one element is left out, the week will be out of balance and so will you.

In a typical week, you will need to devote a certain amount of time to do housework, play, be with your family, rest, run errands, and do paperwork. Your WEEKLY PLAN should include the following:

A Play Day

This is a focus for the day, not an entire day to do nothing but play. Remember the old adage, "All work and no play makes Jack boring," but all play and no work and Jack goes on welfare. A play day is a day in which you have set aside SOME time to pursue your own interests. On this day, your free time won't be occupied doing housework, you won't be going grocery shopping, and you won't be making stew at the rescue mission, unless that is what you love to do. This is a day that has time plugged in for reading, painting, lunching with friends, etc. It's a day in which you set aside some time to refresh yourself—and you must do it GUILT FREE! (If you feel guilty about having fun because you have been accused of playing all the time when there was work to do, don't forget that this is a new plan. Now you will schedule your play and you will deserve to take the time out, because on work days you will have done what you needed to do. Remember, THERE ARE SIX OTHER DAYS TO BE CONSCIENTIOUS ... PLAYING IS GOOD!)

A Desk Day

Of the six remaining days, you will need to select a day of the week to spend time at your desk. That is not to say that on that day you will be strapped to your chair with a pen in your hand for twenty-four hours. (Don't Scrooge yourself on this day. Remember, even Bob Cratchit got to go home at seven.) It only means that you'll spend time paying bills, balancing your checkbook, answering letters, planning family activities such as vacations, holidays, birthdays, etc., making lists, entering contests, reading grocery ads, and clipping coupons that you want to use. In fact, you might want to plan your DESK DAY to coincide with the day your local newspaper features the best grocery ads. That way, you can more easily plan your menus. It won't take an entire day to catch up on desk piles, but it will require some focused attention at your desk. This is also the time each week when you will work with your card file (but that concept is one chapter away). For now, just sketch in a particular day of the week where you will set aside time at your desk. (By the way, if you don't have a desk, GET ONE!)

A Full Cleaning Day

OK, this is the day you work like an ant trying to get a potato chip off the deck and up his hill before it starts to rain. This is a day you'll need an extra swipe of Mennen Speed Stick because, for four to six hours, you are going to be an Ordell clone. Until your house is de-junked (see

Chapter 6), you will spend your cleaning time in the closet. Once everything is streamlined (and we mean 90 percent of the stuff is gone), you won't actually be able to CLEAN. When you have gutted your closets, cupboards, and drawers throughout the entire house, then you can actually spend this time scrubbing and polishing surfaces. You'll see wood look good again. You'll smell the results of Pinesol. You'll marvel at the nap in the carpet and you will Windex your face in a mirror that once looked like a sheet of aluminum. And after you've been a cleaning maniac (and everyone in the house knows it), you'll slump down in a LA-Z-Boy and feel wonderful!

A Half-Cleaning Day

This is a day for general home maintenance on a minimum scale. Without telling you exactly what you should do, let us give you a feeling of catching up, falling back, and regrouping. Take some time (two to four hours) to focus on laundry, dust, pet fur on carpets, toothpaste blobs in sinks, and closed containers in the refrigerator. This is not a day to sweat; it is a day to make the rest of the week run more smoothly. We set the timer at ten-minute intervals to keep us working fast. It's a trick we play on ourselves. Knowing the dinger will go off soon, a latent competitive spirit within takes over and makes us try to beat the clock. Try it yourself. In a couple of hours, you could get so much accomplished that you could relax for the next three days!

A Go-fer Day

On a go-fer day, obviously, you will need the car. If yours is a one-car family, arrange with your spouse to have the car the same day every week. This day is reserved, not for fun, but for buying groceries, banking, going to the dry cleaners, library, hardware store, mall, post office, or anywhere else your errands lead you. If everyone in the family knows you have a specific day to be out on a supply run, requests can be limited to once a week. Remember you're not one of those rubber balls hooked to a paddle by a long rubberband. Don't be thrown out of the house to Lumbermen's for a sheet of plywood, jerked back home, slammed over to Dick's Rent It for a nail gun, bounced back, thrust across town to The Clog Doctor for a plunger, snapped back and whacked out again to the Patch Master for spackle just because your spouse is on his back in the bathroom. Don't let people foul up your weekly plan just because they weren't organized. If a need arises before the go-fer day, the needee can do without till the following week or get what he or she needs on his/her own. This only works when the ruler of the weekly plan really does act as a go-fer when she says she will. People love regularity. Businesses thrive on it and so do families. To know that every Wednesday, for instance, is grocery day, is very calming to a hungry teenager and even more comforting to a busy mom, who doesn't need to waste time floundering at an empty cupboard or groping through a 7-Eleven at dinner time.

A FAMILY WORK DAY

With freedom comes responsibility. This is the day when each person in the family can expect to contribute to the maintenance of the household. There might be a lawn that needs to be mowed, a car that needs to be washed, clothes that need to be ironed, or special projects that would take an hour or two of someone's time. Rather than be a martyred mother, working by herself for six hours on the weekend, doesn't it make sense to get everybody to pitch in? If there are five people in the family, everybody could work for an hour and ten minutes and accomplish what one tired female could do in a day. The family work day will pay off unexpectedly when each, in his own way, is proud of where he lives because of what he has done to make his home the best it can be. Teaching children the value of having a good work ethic will serve them for life. Remember that you don't do them any favors when you do all the work yourself.

A Family Play Day

Most people choose Saturday or Sunday, which are our society's traditional days of rest. This is the day that you and everybody else in the family get to be minimally effective. You can sleep late, slop around in your nightgown or pajamas until you feel like getting dressed, and do nothing if you feel like being a zero. You can go to church, take a nap, watch football, or read a book, but, most important, you can do whatever makes you feel rested and refreshed as a family. Part of this day could be devoted to a family activity. Plan to do things together. You're all stuck with each other for a very long time, so you might as well learn to enjoy each other's company. The best way for all family members to appreciate each other is to spend time having fun together.

Take a few minutes to think about an ideal weekly plan. How could you arrange the seven elements of a balanced week into your own circumstances? If you can fit in a scrap of time for each of the seven basics in the next week, you will discover the magic of the weekly plan. Next week it may change. That's OK. That's life! Just get a focus for the next seven days and see how much easier the week is.

When you are outlining the week, don't forget that you have a family to help you get everything done. Peggy's daughter, Ally, who is seventeen, buys the groceries each week. Using a duplicated, standardized list of all the items they usually buy, together they mark the list for the week. Peggy signs a dated check, made out to the Safeway, and writes her driver's license number by the address. Ally cuts out coupons from the newspaper to turn in at the check-stand. Her reward for her time is that she can use whatever money she can get back from the coupons on magazines, makeup, or other goodies. The time and effort average out to be worth about five dollars each week, and Ally has become a very wise shopper!

When you have a weekly plan sketched out, put it on a 3 × 5 card and tape it inside the lid of a 3 × 5 recipe box. The box will become your best friend in the next few weeks, but for now the weekly plan is all you need to put in there. If you haven't made out a weekly plan, you might as well close this book and go back to your old ways, but remember, you could be one of the two who actually gets organized. All you have to do is get a plan!

You don't need to try to be somebody you weren't born to be. It's no coincidence that Providence didn't deliver us into an Amish household or Ordell's kitchen. Our mission in life is clear to us. It is to be lighthearted and happy and to simply live each day so that, at its end, we feel good about what we accomplished or what we shared with someone else. Our weekly plan and daily routine reflect our need for flexibility and our fun-loving natures. They might make Ordell shudder, but the plans work for us because they're a realistic schedule that we know we can stick to or change.

Ring, ring, ring ...

"Mmmello?"

"Hi, Ordell, this is Peggy Jones from church. Your name is on a list I have of people who clean up in the kitchen on Sundays.

"Yes, I do it every first and third Sunday."

"Yes, I see that you have been doing that for the last eight years. I was wondering if you could possibly swap with Esther Higgins and take next Sunday, since she's just had surgery?"

"No."

"Uh, couldn't you just ..."

"Peggy, dear, I don't SWITCH anything EVER."

You will find that this 7-day plan will honor your gifts of flexibility, spontaneity, lightheartedness, creativity, love of living, and optimism. By honoring those attributes, it will be much easier to stick with this new way of life and change it whenever you want to.

Four

It's in the Cards!

Working with the cruel genetic hand we've been dealt, we have learned to happily play the game of life in nervous remission and win. And thanks to that shaky state, we have stayed on the cutting edge of self-improvement movements, in search of relief for ourselves and our disorderly brothers and sisters. Breaking free from disorganized bondage ourselves, we know what will work and we know what won't.

In the fifteen years we have been teaching household upkeep to the downtrodden, we have honed our advice to the very simple rescue plan we are about to outline. It took more than a decade of trial-and-error experiments to come up with just the right dose of direction a person needs to get it together. When birth control pills first came out, the heavy dose recommended was enough to sterilize a hippo. Today, medical science has learned that only a fraction of the prescription is necessary. Over the years, we have proved that the same thing is true of our formula for good housekeeping. Our advice has changed dramatically, as we've learned more about the psychology of getting and staying organized. Like the birth control pill of the sixties, the early card file system we were on was an overdose of discipline that few sidetracked people could survive. Today, we have reduced the prescription and we take it ONE DAY AT A TIME.

FROM PEGGY:

Back in 1977, when we were trying to make sense out of our chaotic lives, Pam was surprised to learn that I had been very organized at one time in my life. Never at home, but during the five years I worked at *The Columbian*, before I had children, I was a pillar of order. The top of my desk was a clean sheet of metal each time I stepped away for my lunch hour. At night, when I left my cubicle, it was as if I had died and someone had cleaned my desk in anticipation of hiring a new employee who would come and make a reasonable mess. My fellow workers joked about it because it was odd. They didn't realize how afraid I was to leave one scrap of paper, for fear I'd disappear in a mound of unfinished work. I forced myself to stay on top of things, because I knew my tendency to procrastinate, and I NEEDED the job to help my husband get through college. I got in the habit, right from the start, of keeping my desk perfect, but each night I would leave my controlled environment at the office and step into the reality of a home fit for swine. In 1977, when my sister and I got our homes organized, I know my co-workers at *The Columbian* thought it was a scam. On the surface, anyone would have thought I was a compulsive organizer instead of a scared slob trying to cope in the working world.

In examining why I could have been so organized when it doesn't come naturally, I realized it was because there was already a system in place. Because I mind really well, all I had to do was learn the routine and establish the habit of leaving things neat.

At *The Columbian*, it was my responsibility to get advertising from businesses. Regular advertisers wanted an ad in the paper every day, while others wanted one every other day, weekly, monthly, or just occasionally. Rather than work from a master list, we used 3 × 5 cards to keep track of the clients. On each 3 × 5 we put the name of the business, address, phone number, person to contact, and how often an ad was to appear. Inside a card file box there were dividers for the days of the week, as well as monthly dividers. We always kept the current day in the front of the card file; all of the businesses that were scheduled to be called that day were filed in front of that day's divider. After the call was made, the 3 × 5 card was refiled so that it would reappear on the next day that the business had to be called again, depending on its advertising frequency.

As I thought about the simplicity of that system, it occurred to me that HOUSEWORK IS REPETITIVE—at least if you do it and then do it again when you're supposed to! Housework could be put on 3 × 5 cards just as advertisers had been. With that one idea, Pam and I revolutionized our housekeeping standards. Today, we have streamlined our own card files and will share with you some new things we have developed to make them serve our needs even better.

Think of the box as your housekeeping command center. It will contain all the central intelligence of your home. Inside, you'll need a small calendar for the year, similar to the kind on the back of your checkbook register. You'll use the calendar to schedule future activities, such as making Halloween costumes, decorating for the holidays, planning vacations, or working on income taxes. You'll want to tape your weekly plan (you know, the one you made after reading the last chapter) into the lid of the box for easy reference.

Next you'll need to purchase some dividers. Get Monday through Sunday dividers to schedule daily activities, and put them in the front of the box. Use January through

December for less frequent activities, and put them behind the days of the week. Then get a package of alphabetical dividers and put them in the back of the box. They will serve as your reference section for frequently used phone numbers and addresses, as well as a cross-reference for items you file in folders in your bigger filing cabinet later. Get rid of your ugly old address book and transfer the current, up-to-date addresses and phone numbers to blank 3 × 5 white index cards, using one card per address. We don't use address books anymore because people move and the pages get messy. If you buy a new book every few years and transfer everyone over, it is time-consuming and unnecessary. In a purse-size daily planner, which we replace at the beginning of each year, we copy just a few names, addresses, and phone numbers we might need when we're away from our card file. (Eliminate names and numbers magnetted to the refrigerator or scribbled on the cover of the phone book.) Finally, purchase some blank dividers to keep track of information regarding special interests such as gardening, camping, entertaining, etc., and label them accordingly. Mark one of them "STORAGE," so that items you pack away when you clean out your closets, cupboards, and drawers can be catalogued and kept track of on a 3 × 5 card in the back of the card file (more on that in Chapter 6).

With the basic parts of the card file set up, you will be ready to make out the cards. Although this is time-consuming, it will be the key to unlocking the door of organization and stepping into a smooth-running home. Originally, the only cards we had were work cards, and they got old fast! We also had too many of them because we put only one job on a card. Now, after fifteen years in the box, we've realized that that was unnecessary. If several jobs in one area have the same frequency, we put all of them on one card. That means fewer cards to handle and keeps us focused in one place. The biggest change we've made since we developed our original system is the addition of some cards that make life more fun! We'll explain that kind in detail in a minute.

To start using our new system, you'll need to fill out six different kinds of cards, not counting the cards you'll use for addresses, storage, and special interests. (We use six different colors of 3 × 5s for each category, but that's up to you.)

ACTION CARDS

Action cards are a pleasant way to say "work cards." In this category we have eight 3 × 5s that deal with the kitchen, one with the living room, family room, and dining room, three with the bathroom, two bedroom cards, two laundry, and four miscellaneous cards. Each card follows the same format (see example). We put the frequency of the "action" in the top left-hand corner (daily, weekly, every other week, monthly, seasonal, every six months, yearly) and the total time estimate in the top right corner. We have estimated, for instance, that we spend thirty minutes every day doing routine kitchen cleanup. On that card six jobs are listed:

Daily	30 Minutes
1. Empty Dishwasher, Set Table.	5 Min.
2. Fill Dishwasher.	As you go.
3. Pots, Pans, Serving Dishes—Hand Wash.	10 Min.
4. Clean Countertops, Surfaces.	5 Min.
5. Scour Sink, Empty Garbage.	5 Min.
6. Sweep Floor, Shake Rugs.	5 Min.

Sample action card.

Kitchen

When we began the system, we thought housework took much more time than it actually does. When we finally got around to doing it, we were so far behind that everything took longer to finish. Cleaning the kitchen when you haven't tackled it in a while takes a lot longer than doing it every day. Instead of a sink full of pots and pans to wash, you'll have only a couple. Because you know what needs to be done, you'll be able to delegate jobs to other family members.

The cards need to be typed so they don't have the personal implication your own handwriting would have. Your handwriting insinuates that you are the boss, telling someone else what to do. Typewritten, the action cards are the impersonal, factual reality in black and white that there is lots of work for everyone to do.

Continue to make out your kitchen ACTION CARDS, including a one-hour weekly or every-other-week card with the following jobs:

1. Wash the Window over the sink.   5 Min.
2. Clean the Refrigerator.   10 Min.
3. Clean Microwave.   3 Min.
4. Clean Range Top.   5 Min.
5. Wash Floor.   15 Min.
6. Wax Floor.   15 Min.
7. Self-cleaning Oven.   5 Min.
8. Wash Scatter Rugs.   2 Min.

Of the remaining kitchen ACTION CARDS, five will need to be done every six months. We group them in the following way: On one card put:

1. Wash Canisters, Knickknacks.   5 Min.
2. Clean Cutting Board with Bleach

(Then Put in Dishwasher
if It's Plastic).   5 Min.
3. Clean Small Appliances.   5 Min.

The total time estimate is fifteen minutes. At the bottom of a card like this, we put the words "Last done," with a space for marking, and "Skipped," with another space for the date so that we can keep track of jobs that have to be rescheduled. If any card comes forward to the current day with two skips logged, it becomes a priority action and must ACTUALLY be addressed before it can be refiled.

You'll also need a separate card that directs you to "Clean, Reorganize the Pantry." This will need to be done every six months, with a time estimate of one hour. In addition, make out two more cards marked "Clean, Reorganize Cupboards" and "Clean, Reorganize Drawers" (each job will take one hour). Each of these kitchen jobs will also need to be done every six months. Finally, every six months you'll find this kitchen card:

1. Clean Light Fixtures
(Put in Dishwasher).   15 Min.
2. Clean Stove Fan, Filter, Hood.   30 Min.
3. Wash All Kitchen Windows.   15 Min.

Once yearly you will have a card that tells you to:

1. Defrost Freezer   55 Min.
2. Clean Drip Pans, Coils
Underneath Refrigerator.   5 Min.

You can see that, when done routinely, all the kitchen jobs can be staggered so that your kitchen always looks good and never gets out of control or becomes too big of a job.

You'll need one card to take care of the basics in the

living room, dining room, and family room. We group those rooms together because they need to be cleaned weekly. If everything is already picked up (which it will be if you play the infraction game you'll learn about in Chapter 11), all you will really need to do weekly is vacuum (ten minutes each room) and dust (five minutes each room).

There are only three bathroom cards to make out. One you'll do weekly or every other week, with a time estimate of forty-five minutes. The jobs include:

1. Clean Toilet   5 Min.
2. Clean Tub/Shower Stall.   10 Min.
3. Scour Sink.   5 Min.
4. Clean Mirror.   1 Min.
5. Polish Counters.   2 Min.
6. Wash Floor.   10 Min.
7. Wax Floor.   10 Min.
8. Wash Scatter Rugs.   2 Min.

The other two bathroom cards have a seasonal frequency. Each card will take one hour of your time.

1. Polish Woodwork.   20 Min.
2. Polish Tiles.   20 Min.
3. Clean Light Fixtures.   10 Min.
4. Wash Windows.   10 Min.

The second card will have you:

1. Clean, Reorganize Cupboards.   30 Min.
2. Clean, Reorganize Medicine Cabinet.   30 Min.

That will take care of cleaning the bathroom!

Next, make out two separate bedroom ACTION CARDS.

One will be done weekly or every other week and will take about twenty-five minutes. You'll need to:

1. Change Sheets.	5 Min.
2. Clean Under Bed.	5 Min.
3. Clean Mirror.	5 Min.
4. Dust.	5 Min.
5. Vacuum.	5 Min.

The second card will need action seasonally. It is part of the deep cleaning that will take about two hours.

1. Turn Mattress.	
2. Wash Mattress Pad, Bedding.	5 Min.
3. Clean Closets, Drawers.	45 Min.
4. Clean Fixtures, Lamp Shades.	10 Min.
5. Wash Windows.	30 Min.
6. Blinds, curtains, etc.	30 Min.

There are only two laundry cards. One is to be done daily, with an actual time estimate of fifteen minutes per load of wash (the number of loads per day will depend on the size of your family):

1. Sort into Three Baskets (Darks/Blues,Other Colors, Whites).	
2. Wash, Dry.	5 Min.
3. Fold, Put Away	10 Min.

Note: Laundry must be sorted in the morning before anyone leaves the house. Levy an infraction penalty (see Chapter 11) for laundry left in bedrooms or sorted improperly. The last laundry ACTION CARD will take thirty minutes each week and includes:

1. Mending.   10 Min.
2. Ironing   10 Min.
3. Hand Washables.   10 Min.

Laundry only becomes overwhelming when it's left undone. Do it regularly when the card comes up in your card file and you can handle it easily, with cooperation from your family (more on that later).

The remaining action cards fall into a MISCELLA-NEOUS category. Three cards are to be done weekly. The first is miscellaneous pet care and requires approximately fifteen minutes to:

1. Change Kitty Litter   5 Min.
2. Clean Bird/Hamster Cage.   5 Min.
3. Other pet cleanup.   5 min.

The other two weekly ACTION CARDS will take considerably more time. One card will show up on your scheduled "desk day" and you will need to plan on spending about two hours finishing it. You will:

1. Plan Menus.   10 Min.
2. Make Grocery List.   10 Min.
3. Clip Coupons.   10 Min.
4. Sort, Answer Mail.   30 Min.
5. Pay Bills, Balance Checkbook.   60 Min.

The other miscellaneous ACTION CARD will also take about two hours and will probably be handled on your "Go-fer Day." On this card, type the following activities:

1. Miscellaneous Errands—time varies.
2. Banking.   10 Min.
3. Post Office.   10 Min.

4. Dry Cleaners.	10 Min.
5. Wash car, clean inside.	20 Min.
6. Grocery Shopping.	45 Min.
7. Unpack Groceries.	15 Min.

A final miscellaneous ACTION CARD will need to be scheduled seasonally so that you:

1. Clean Fireplaces.
2. Clean Furnace Vents (put in dishwasher if they fit).
Both jobs will take about one hour.

That takes care of all the housework you'll ever have to do in a year. If you cover the 3 × 5s with clear contact paper, they will be plasticized and will last forever. You can mark notes on them with a washable marker or use Post-it notes for comments or reminders. In all, these twenty action cards replace the old version of the system, which had you handling more than a hundred cards. We think the simplified card file will be easier to use and will keep you on track and help you stay focused.

Midway in our organizational odyssey, we realized that all work and no play made us mad. Aside from the ACTION CARDS, we suggest you make out "extra credit" 3 × 5s in the following categories: REFLECTION CARDS, REMINDER CARDS, FLASH CARDS, ROUTINE CARDS, and our favorite, REASON FOR LIVING CARDS.

REFLECTION CARDS

These are cards to add to your card file to help you relax. We've found that, in our busy lives, we all need to take some time to think about our blessings and our accomplishments and to focus on a positive attitude. Reflection not only brings a great sense of inner peace; it also reinforces new habits while helping you let go of the old. If your church puts out a monthly meditation booklet, you might not choose to copy the thoughts onto cards, but we have found that paraphasing a particular selection, writing it down, and putting it in the card file makes it more personal and deepens the meaning with each reading. Choose a number (thirty-one would give you one reflection card per day for a month) of special quotes, Bible verses, sayings, or profound thoughts to read and think about each day. Whenever you have a quiet moment, at bedtime, for example, select one. Read it a few times and focus on the message. Then, the next morning, read it again and try to live the theme of that reflection card for the entire day.

MY GOALS

I know where I am going. My path arches high. The spectrum of my experiences will give me strength and purpose. Life will guide me toward what truly fulfills me. Each moment in time moves me closer to the completion of my journey toward success. I know what I plan to do. It is already an accomplishment in my inner experience. My actions are a simple projection of my inner design. Already certain of the outcome, I am able to adapt to any cloud of gloom or fear of doom. Eagerly I set out on my life's journey

---

Sample reflection card.

REMINDER CARDS

These bold little gems (use a wide felt marker) remind us to do the basics. We suggest you post these reminders in strategic places where you tend to get sidetracked. For an example, we have several cards that say, "Don't Do It!" We have one on the refrigerator to stop unconscious eating, one in our purses to prevent impulse buying, and another by the phone, to cut down on long-distance calls.

The following are suggestions for additional reminders.

ORDER NOW!*

---

*This is a reminder to keep things orderly. We post it in places where we could be tempted to leave a mess.

EVERYTHING WILL BE ALL RIGHT!
(This is a nice card to run into if you tend to worry a lot.)

SPEED IT UP!
(We have a tendency to move too slowly, and this card reminds us to move faster.)

SOMEONE MIGHT DROP IN!
(This is not meant to be a stress-inducing card. It is an energy-creating tool to remind you that you could have some unexpected company, and you'd want the house to look nice.)

RELAX AND TAKE A DEEP BREATH!
(When you run into this card and do what it says, you'll be surprised at how tense you were.)

FLASH CARDS
Flash cards have a "buzz word" on one side and a rule to memorize and live by on the other. Until we knew

them by heart, our card files included the following flash cards:

Buzz word	*NOW*
Rule to live by	DO IT NOW.
Buzz Word	*FINISH*
Rule to Live By	FINISH WHAT YOU START BEFORE YOU START SOMETHING NEW.
Buzz Word	*SET*
Rule to Live By	SET A TIMER AND WORK FAST.
Buzz Word	*JUST*
Rule to Live By	JUST DO IT.
Buzz Word	*WRITE*
Rule to Live By	WRITE SHORT LETTERS AND MAIL THEM.
Buzz Word	*SHOWER*
Rule to Live By	SHOWER, DRESS, HAIR, AND MAKEUP BEFORE ANYTHING ELSE.
Buzz Word	*FUNCTION*
Rule to Live By	EACH ROOM IN THE HOUSE HAS ITS OWN FUNCTION.
Buzz Word	*EAT*
Rule to Live By	EAT AT THE TABLE.

DON'T

Sample flash card, front.

DON'T OVERBOOK YOURSELF!

Sample flash card, back.

Buzz Word   *PRODUCTIVE*
Rule to Live By   WHEN ON THE PHONE,
                                   VISITING, OR WATCHING
                                   TV, DO SOMETHING
                                   PRODUCTIVE WITH
                                   YOUR HANDS.

Buzz Word   *PICK*
Rule to Live By   PICK IT UP. DON'T PASS
                                   IT UP, THEN PUT IT
                                   AWAY.

If you did nothing more than work your FLASH CARDS, you would have peace in your home as you have never known before!

ROUTINE CARDS

Memorize the following:

MORNING DAILY ROUTINE

Get Up on Time.
Personal Grooming.*
Make Bed.
Empty Dishwasher.
Eat Breakfast.
Follow Your Weekly Plan.

EVENING DAILY ROUTINE

Happy Hour.**
Eat Dinner.
Dinner Cleanup.
Free Time with Family or Alone.
Turn on Dishwasher.
Personal Grooming.
Private Time in Your Bedroom.
Lights Out on Time.

---

*Good grooming may be so basic to you that you don't need to write it down, but from our experience it wasn't that automatic. Including it in our memorized daily routine ensured that we wouldn't get sidetracked and forget how important it is to look your best.

**We don't mean "cocktail time." We'll explain what we do mean, later.

REASON FOR LIVING CARDS

Ah, yes ... the Reason for Living cards ... they are the fiber of life that holds the card file together and makes you want to open it again! In all, there are sixteen golden cards to get up for each day. Eight cards will show up daily in the card file, one will appear three times in a week, and seven more once a week.

DAILY

20-SECOND KISS

A marriage counselor told us that a 20-second kiss can improve an already good marriage. The rule is that you must kiss and not come apart for 20 seconds.

We suggest the following daily REASON FOR LIVING CARDS:

TIME ALONE: (choose one)

Every day you need at least an hour of time by yourself. It doesn't have to be all at one time. Some suggestions of what to do with your time alone are: read, pray, daydream, write in your journal, take a bubble bath, nap, walk the dog, mess around in the garden, enjoy a cup of tea, etc.

TIME TOGETHER: (choose one)

Meet your spouse for lunch, dinner out, a movie, a walk, a picnic, happy hour, singing, etc.

INDULGENCE (choose one)

This is a reward card. (It may be used daily; however, do not give yourself the same reward each day or you will get into trouble.) Go out for lunch, order something out of a catalogue, buy a magazine, have breakfast in bed, go off your diet, call long-distance, get a massage, etc.

GOOD GROOMING

Shower, hair removal, deodorant, dress (all the way to shoes), teeth, hair, lotion, perfume, fingernails, and toenails. WOW!

20-SECOND KISS

A marriage counselor told us that a 20-second kiss can improve an already good marriage. The rule is that you must kiss and not come apart for twenty seconds, twice each day.

HAPPY HOUR

At the end of the work day, you and your spouse need at least a half hour together to relax, talk, and regroup. It's best to have something to occupy the children so your time is uninterrupted. Serve hors d'oeuvres and something refreshing to drink.

FAMILY MATTERS: DAILY

Every day the family needs to share a meal together so that each member can enjoy the benefits of having a close family. Make a list of fun things to do together and pick something from that list each day.

The next card will come to the front of the card file three times each week.

EXERCISE

Experts claim that we should do aerobic exercise at least three times a week and for at least twenty minutes.

Be sure it is something you enjoy. Walk briskly, bicycle, swim, jog, ski, dance, do step aerobics, etc. JUST DO IT!

The seven remaining REASON FOR LIVING CARDS will show up once a week, and include the following:

SELF-IMPROVEMENT
Spend at least an hour a week on personal growth. Study, take a class, read, increase your vocabulary, grow spiritually, work on faults, strengthen virtues, practice something to perfection, go on a diet, etc. All self-improvement takes planning. If you stay in the card file each day, you will be able to schedule the time it takes to be successful.

HOME IMPROVEMENT
Spend at least an hour a week on a home improvement project. Pretend you are going to sell your home or have a big party. Fix all of the things that usually get fixed only for someone else.

PUBLIC SERVICE
Volunteer at school, do church work, or be a political supporter. Open your home (once it's under control) to a child in need, visit the sick or elderly, make dinner for somebody tired, teach something you know, etc.

CHECK NEXT MONTH
Place this card in the weekly dividers on your desk day. It will always be there and, on the last desk day of the month, it will remind you to check the next month's divider for special events you don't want to miss, such as birthdays, anniversaries, etc. You will also find your occasional ACTION CARDS and will be able to incorporate them into your weekly plan.

TIME WITH A FRIEND
If you have a partner who is getting organized with you,

you can team-clean your homes. Exercise together, lunch, shop, etc.

FAMILY MATTERS: WEEKLY
Have a family meeting to delegate work, set goals, plan vacations and holidays, and discuss problems that come up during the week.

After you make out all of the cards, put all of the "Dailies" in front of today's divider. File the Weekly cards, according to the kind of activity they are, to coincide within your Weekly Plan. If any of the tasks on your printed cards will be done less than once a month, file them in front of the appropriate month in the January through December section.

Each night before bed, put the ending day's divider behind, and the next day will come forward. We like to take a look at the various cards that we will need to handle the next day. We put the cards in a flexible order so that we will do the most important things first. Then, depending on our situation at the time, we will either do them, or, if unexpected interruptions occur, we will reschedule them for another day, if necessary, marking them to reflect that decision.

People always ask us how we handle interruptions. Interruptions are a regular part of life. They will hit you whether you are organized or not. If you're using the card file, you merely change direction, and know that you are not neglecting things, you're only adjusting your schedule to fit reality.

Have fun setting up your 3 × 5 command center. Play with it and adjust it to fit your personal circumstances. Put your spouse and children in there. Fill it with your interests as well as your responsibilities. Orchestrate it so that work and play are in harmony with one another, and the card file will become your most valuable helpmate.

Fⁱve

Pigtales

One day a couple of years ago, Elaine Veits, a syndicated columnist for the *St. Louis Post-Dispatch*, called our office to get some spring cleaning tips for her column. Since we had written three books on how to get organized, it wasn't unusual to get a call like that. We were both happy to help her, only not in the way she thought we would.

"I haven't read any of your books, but several of my readers have recommended them, and I wondered if you could share some of your spring cleaning advice with us?"

"We don't spring clean," we said in stereo.

"Really?"

"No."

"I was always told you had to spring clean if you were a good homemaker."

"No ... that's a carryover from your great-grandmother's time when they used coal to heat their homes," one of us explained.

"Really?"

"Yeah, the houses back then were closed up tight through the fall and winter, and a sooty veneer gradually coated everything. In the spring, she *had* to open up the house and clean the scum off her stuff. Today we have what we call electricity and natural gas, and we have yet to find a coat of electricity or a film of natural gas on anything."

"So if you don't clean in the spring, what do you do?"

"Play, mostly. Then we clean in the fall after the kids go back to school and routines take over where the summer slough left off."

The silence was broken with our suggestion. "You know what we could help you write about in your column?"

"What?"

"Well, spring is one of the best times of the year to catch a slob. They sorta come out of their holes, like ground hogs in the spring, to get a breath of fresh air and see what's going on out in the world. You can usually spy one with a new jogging suit and shoes, starting what she hopes will be a regular exercise regime, which will probably last a couple of days."

"That's interesting. I guess I misunderstood what your books are about. I thought, since they were on home organization, you'd be efficiency experts."

"Did you know we're reformed slobs?"

"No."

"We're actually deficiency experts, and we could help you find a slob in your city and do a make-over on him or her."

"A slob search?"

"Yeah, we did one in Detroit and the results were amazing. Just write in your column that you are looking for the messiest family in St. Louis. Have your readers send photos and tell what's wrong with their house and why they want to change."

"What would the winner get?"

"We would come to St. Louis on a clutterbust and actually go to the home of the winner with our weekend recovery program."

"They'll actually have their house clean by the end of the weekend?"

"Oh, no, they'll do most of the work after we leave. The weekend recovery program is an intensive, personalized in-house meeting to map out stategies and teach the principles of our system. In return for our services, the winner would have to be willing to subject the family to the public humiliation factor. They'd have to let you, and a photographer from the *Post,* come with us to record the devastation. In six weeks, you'd go back and document the miracle transformation!"

"Transformation?"

"Yep! All we need is a weekend."

"Who'd be willing to come out of the closet and open their private lives to a huge newspaper?"

"We would've."

Elaine was intrigued by the whole idea of finding and reforming a slob in St. Louis. She couldn't resist the temptation of a make-over on her turf. She couldn't deny that a potential Cinderella story would have definite human interest, but she really didn't think she would tempt many messy contestants. That's because St. Louis is probably the worst place for an organizationally impotent person to live. Elaine told us that a large portion of the population there is known as the "Scrubby Dutch." The Dutch are famous for their cleanliness. They have Dutch Boy Paint and Dutch Cleanser named after them. We know why other countries haven't come out with paint and cleaning products in their names; the Scrubby Dutch have mopped up the market. There's just no room on the shelves for Bedouin Boy Paint or Bulgarian Cleanser.

You don't have to live in St. Louis to know a Scrubby. They stand out across the country as tense, ultratidy people, with a single mission: to glorify their persnickety existence and make the rest of us feel inferior. Their lawns are flawless, their homes are fastidiously maintained, their cars are preserved like museum pieces, they never sit down and nobody else in the family does either. If you live in St. Louis, where there's an infestation of smartalecky treadmillers, you have our condolences. To the rest of you with dirty genes, be thankful you only have to hide your affliction from a few.

Elaine had wondered if neighboring, rubber-gloved Scrubbies would intimidate the slobs of St. Louis and keep them behind closed drapes. Eighty desperately disorganized people wrote in. More than one third of the entrants' letters arrived the day of the deadline. Elaine extended it to accommodate the pathetic stragglers. Another ten came in under the extension wire, and letters and photos continued to trickle in long after the contest was over. (Those were the ones who really needed help.) Think, if eighty were willing to go public, how many shy slobs just wished they could enter, but didn't have the nerve.

Since we live in the state of Washington, we had to help Elaine pick the finalists over the phone. She called after she had waded through and eliminated fifty of the pleas for help. Her voice had lost its lilt. She was depressed.

"I do not know what to do! I was up past three in the morning, reading all these incredible letters. I have narrowed the entrants to thirty-something, and I don't know how we can pick just one."

We asked her to read the ones she'd picked. When she finished, we could see why she was so depressed. It was extremely hard not to be able to help every one. These people were all wonderful! They were great writers, with humor pouring out of their pens, pencils, and crayons. The photos were priceless. They revealed the awful truth about the bedlam that disorganization breeds. These people were so eager to receive help that they were beyond worrying about shame.

Elaine was relieved to learn we had some rules for elimination. For instance, we won't work with whiners. We can spot one in just a few sentences. They're the people who sound like John Candy when he whines. A whiner usually makes a comment like, "Well, it may work for you but ..." We know from past experience that you cannot change a whiner's "but ..."

Once we had a woman in one of our six-week seminars who continually interrupted the lecture with, "But I've got twins!" After three weeks of hearing, "But I've got twins," we were determined to put a stop to her whiny complaints. We called Karen Anderson, who lives near us. (Maybe you've read about Karen; she is the mother of quintuplets and has been written about in many women's magazines.) We asked her to come to our group and talk about how to be organized when you have FIVE babies. Karen is very organized, and we thought that her testimony would shut up the mother of twins. Not so. She continued to whine her way through the entire six weeks.

Another letter writer we eliminated was the person who loved telling all her stories. There was no doubt that the material was great comic work, but when the letter went on for six pages with joke after joke, we could see that the writer would be lost without her material.

Also, some people may really be ready to change, but circumstances and timing are not on their side. Anyone with a new baby should wait at least until the baby is through nursing before trying to reorganize her household. The mother needs at least a year to feel like herself again, and the baby requires so much of the mother's attention in that first year. (That's not to say the child won't also need it in the next twenty years.)

The other reason for eliminating entrants was the severity of the problem. Since we are not psychologists and are not schooled in helping people with BIG problems, we could help Elaine see that the woman who had an alcoholic husband, a child on a respirator, a mother with Alzheimer's and had herself undergone three surgeries in the last year was not someone we could help ... not now. Still, it was agony to narrow the remaining thirty down to one ... in fact, we couldn't. We picked eleven.

The letters that moved us were both humorous and sad. Letters like the one from Kathy, a mother expecting her second child:

Dear Elaine,
Please, please, please pick me! I'm at the end of my pregnant rope. The baby is due in two months and everything is in chaos. I almost had a miscarriage the other day. I thought I saw a mouse shoot out from under the bed and run across the hardwood floor in the master bedroom, but when cornered and inspected, it turned out to be a rather large cockroach caught in a dust ball! I've got to get organized. My husband is a lawyer and he said he would be willing to quit his practice and let me go back to my career (I was a very organized secretary) if I thought that would make me happy, but it wouldn't. I love my home and I love being a mom, I just don't know how to get control of everything and I feel so guilty that I am teaching my young son to be a slob.

Kathy was among the eleven finalists.

We decided to conduct a personal interview with the remaining eleven and then whittle them down to five. Out of the five, we would pick a winner; the other four runners-up would get to go to the house of the winner as observers. It gave all five women a built-in support group, which enforces our advice to get a partner (which, by the way, if you haven't ... PUT THIS BOOK DOWN AND GET ONE!).

When Elaine called the eleven finalists, four had second thoughts and decided not to remain in the contest. Out of the seven who said they'd meet us at the paper for the final interview, only five showed up.

The St. Louis Five

It was a Saturday morning in April. The tension was high as each finalist in the disorganized contest was checked at security and led into the conference room on the second floor of the *Post*. We sat with Elaine on one side of a large conference table. The contestants all had the same comment: "I hope I win ... I think." We passed around the photos they had sent with their letters, so that each one was able to see that she was not alone. They also could see how close the competition was.

Elaine spoke: "I have to tell you how impressed I was with your letters. You all need to know that Pam and Peggy picked each of you for several reasons. It was obvious by your letters that you are basically happy and healthy individuals having trouble with organization. They tell me that you can lick the problem this weekend. I wish each of you my best."

We had the women tell a little bit about themselves and their families, and each of them won our hearts. They were all so sincere about changing. They'd had it with their old ways, and their excitement about the real possibility that their lives were about to change drastically put magic in the little conference room.

KATHY

Kathy was quiet and rather serious. She was thin, except for her huge tummy, which gave the impression that her baby was due any minute. We were concerned about timing, but she assured us that she had well over two months before the baby was due. She told everyone the cockroach story, and, with the laughter that followed, her seriousness disappeared, revealing a very lighthearted, fun-loving mother who wanted more than anything else to be in control of her life.

DEBBIE

Debbie was also very serious ... at first. She told us that she had always wanted to be organized, but somehow it never worked. She said that for Christmas her husband gave her organized closets. He hired a bunch of people who came into her house, built closet organizers, and arranged everything for her. It took under a year for a miscellaneous array of junk to be on the floor, stuffed in drawers, and crammed under beds. Her guilt level was off the meter. She hated that her two sons were following her example.

CINDY

Cindy was a natural comedienne. She told the group that getting organized was a matter of life and death! She had contracted food poisoning from eating a salad tossed in bottled dressing (from her refrigerator) dated for expiration two years earlier. When she was well enough, she went through all the other bottles and dumped five outdated dressings. She, too, had two children and felt guilty that she was such a crummy example for them.

JEAN

Jean had moved nine times in fourteen years of marriage, and each time she thought she would get organized. It never happened. She had a cooperative husband and two children, ages seven and ten. She talked of piles on top of piles and said that when she wrote the letter to the newspaper, she lost it and had to write it again.

PATTI

Patti was a vivacious southern lady with four small children. Her youngest son was ten months old. She wailed about the clutter of toys, clothes, and papers. She and her family were very active in their church, and she confided that she had never been able to invite anyone over from their church on the spur of the moment.

We could see that it would be impossible to choose a winner. There was no way we could pick one over another. We decided to pull the winner out of a hat. Patti won. An hour later we had caravanned to her beautiful home in a lovely neighborhood. On the outside, Patti's house looked fabulous. The yard was beautiful. A weeping willow added to the peaceful setting. On the inside, it looked as if Hurricane Andrew had had his way with her.

There is something magic about getting seven happy-go-lucky, organizationally impaired people together in a mess. It seemed we'd all known each other forever. There was not an iota of judgment in any of us, and Patti was amazed that she felt no embarrassment. Elaine was so devastated by the condition of Patti's home that she turned gray and had to take medication for a migraine. What we learned that day was just the start of our advanced study of the Spontaneous, Lighthearted, Optimistic, and Beloved. Since the St. Louis slob search, we have had the privilege and honor of being invited into more than thirty messed-up homes across the country. We needed to go into about ten different houses before we could perfect our message. The priceless knowledge we have collected will truly change your life.

S i x

One Man's Junk
Is Another Man's Junk Too!

Making house calls and conducting "clutter intensives" has given us privileged information. By actually going into homes and getting to see into every closet, cupboard, and drawer, every basement, garage, and attic, under every bed and behind every cornered piece of furniture, we are this country's number one authorities on housebreaking the disorganized! The stashes we've discovered, squirreled away, behind those closed drawers and secret hiding places is the main reason any home is in a mess. The clutter factor in your home is in direct proportion to the state of your closets, cupboards, drawers, and hiding places. If you want to get and STAY organized, the starting place is there.

Before we tell you what to do, we have to harp on the partner issue, just in case you haven't found one yet. YOUR PARTNER IS GOING TO BE VERY IMPORTANT IN WHAT YOU NEED TO DO NEXT.

All the homes we've visited have shared one common denominator: TOO MUCH STUFF! We've been in a mobile home, a large five-bedroom home in a prestigious neighborhood, an apartment, a teeny-weeny house in the city, a teenier, weenier house in the country, a mansion, and many typical, three-bedroom ranchers. We have helped a senior citizen, a single mom, large families, small families, and extended families, and we've seen the same thing in every case: TOO MUCH STUFF! In our dog days, we knew we needed to get organized, but we didn't realize, in the beginning, how much we had to get rid of. Now we know that in every disorganized home, there beats the heart of a little pack rat. In all thirty homes, 90 percent of what they had, had to go!

One of the thirty messy winners had enough Tupperware under her kitchen sink and in her cupboards to serve twenty families. (We loaded her van with the plastic hodgepodge of containers and took them to her church for its rummage sale.)

Then there was the "cliptomaniac," who had clipped coupons and newspaper articles (to read later) until we couldn't see the furniture. (We arranged to have 1,500 pounds of paper removed from her living room so that she could reclaim it as a functional room.)

You might not hoard newspaper clippings or Tupperware, but maybe it's pens, fabric, coupons, knickknacks, books, or one of a million other things. Whatever it is, if the thought of getting rid of 90 percent scares you, don't panic. We will talk you through letting go, just like in the movies, when they nudge a virgin paratrooper out the door at ten thousand feet. It's not easy to let go of the things you've collected, but you CAN do it. The reason it's hard to let go is because, behind everything you have saved, there is the thought that someday you will need it. In the process of letting go, we hope to convince you that you DON'T need and WON'T need most of what you THINK you need.

The Spark

With every woman we have helped to face the clutter culprits, it has been most exciting to see her sense of humor kick in. We call it "the spark," and we have seen it ignite in all but one. (The one out of thirty who didn't spark really wasn't ready to let go. Every slip of paper and scrap of fabric she threw away was pure agony for her.)

GREAT-GRAMPA TUBERLY'S SILVER

In your mind, you probably can't see that cleaning out your drawers could ever be FUN or FUNNY, but we've found it to be exactly that. In every home, the homemaker, flanked by the two of us, has experienced intermittent hysterical laughter! We didn't know that would happen. We had one of the best times with Cindy. She was organizing her kitchen and, in the back of one of the drawers, she found a bunch of tarnished silverware, wrapped up in a plastic bag and secured with a rubber band.

"Oh, that's Great-Grampa Tuberly's silver. He was a silversmith!" She was proud and we were impressed. She watched us take off the rubber bands and unroll the plastic to expose five blackened silver-plated forks, three spoons, and a couple of knives. Upon close scrutiny of the flatware, we looked at each other, just a little puzzled.

"Sissy, doesn't this pattern look familiar?"

"Yeah, it's just like the ones we had when we were little. Mom got it by saving Betty Crocker coupons."

Cindy protested, "No, it can't be! Great-Grampa Tuberly was a silversmith, and he created his own patterns." She picked up a knife and took a closer look. "Hey, there's an 'F' engraved on this." (Her name started with an "S.") Her memory kicked in. "Wait a minute, Great-Grampa Tuberly wasn't a silversmith, he was an engraver, and not a very good one at that!" She started laughing. "I remember my aunt telling me a long time ago that he was full of it and dumber than cheese. All these pieces have an 'F' on them! This was probably one of his botch-ups, and all these years, I've been carting these stupid things around, thinking they're sterling, family heirlooms."

You are going to be able to do the same thing Cindy did with Great-Grampa Tuberly's Oneida. You are going to look at each and every thing in your possession with new eyes, and through the eyes of your partner, and you are going to see how silly it is to let manufactured goods come between you and your peace of mind.

Looking with New Eyes

For a minute, pretend that you are going on vacation and you get to stay in a very ritzy, four-star hotel. Picture being led to your very expensive and fabulous suite. Think of how wonderful it would feel to walk into your suite, where everything is streamlined and beautiful. The beds are made, the towels are fluffy and white, the decor is tasteful and classy, and there is an air of freshness and freedom. NOTHING is messing up that picture, because you haven't been in there yet. Think how inviting that vision is!

Now imagine having the bellman unlock the door, and the same suite is heaped with everything that is cluttering your home right now! The beds aren't made, there's a load of towels to be folded on the couch, the drapes are hanging crooked, and the TV is blaring. Has your picture lost its glamour?

If you walked into a hotel room that was full of your junk, you probably wouldn't want to stay there on your vacation. It certainly wouldn't be relaxing, and you probably wouldn't be willing to pay to stay there, either. Think how your belongings have devalued your fantasy!

They are cheapening your reality in the same way!

These trappings you think you have to have are causing arguments, tension, lost time, money, peace of mind, confusion, distraction, guilt, chaos, and disorder, just to mention a few of the problems.

In the past, you've probably said something like: "I'm gonna pick this place up!" What you really do when you straighten up the place is move things around. You migrate the piles to another part of the house, or bag or box the piles for a later time. It hasn't worked, and it never will work, because a pile migration always comes back in the spring or sooner.

Instead of rearranging your clogged-up closets, cupboards, and drawers and nook-and-crannying things from one room to another, we want you to try a NEW way.

Organized from the Inside Out

The first thing you need is a timer. You can use the one on the oven, as long as you'll be able to hear it when it buzzes. You need a timer because you are only going to fight this war one hour at a time. You need to think of this process of elimination in terms of time. We can look at a room or a whole house and calculate how much time it will actually take to reclaim it and put it in order. We've seen five-hour living rooms and twenty-five-hour living rooms. The house we found that needed the most time was a three-hundred-hour house with a forty-hour living room. Over a year, that's still less than an hour a day, with one person working. One family we helped was willing to cooperate with one another, chipping away at their two-hundred-hour house, and they had it perfect in three months.

Can you take a guess how many hours your home is going to take to reclaim? In our first book, *Sidetracked Home Executives,* we said, "It's the trend that counts. You didn't get into the mess overnight and you are not going to get out of it overnight." What's the rush? We can tell you what we think the rush is; you want results instantly. That's our Western culture's way. We've been programmed to go for instant mashed potatoes instead of mashed from scratch. (In fact, our kids actually prefer instant to scratch.) Our microwaves, Polaroids, touch-tone phones, remote controls, cruise controls, and all of our finger-on-the-button technology have given us more time. Yet the main complaint you hear is, "I don't have enough time!" Well, we DO have enough time if we will just stop and organize it.

If your home is a one-hundred-hour home, it took you and your family one hundred hours to get it into the condition it's in. AS SOON AS YOU CAN ACCEPT THAT IT DOES NOT MATTER HOW MANY HOURS IT IS GOING TO TAKE TO FIX THINGS, YOU ARE READY TO CHANGE.

Be a Little Bitter

Our idea of becoming a little bitter does not mean to be resentful or begrudging; it means to be able to do a little bit at a time, every day. To be a little bitter, you have to stop looking at the whole picture and stop feeling overwhelmed. You are not a quarterback who's been sacked; you're a wonderful person who has let things go for a while. That same "while" is waiting for you to take things the other way.

We received a call from a woman in tears, who confided that her basement was totally full. She said the stairs were even gone. When we told her to put the timer on for an hour and follow our rules (below), she said, "An hour won't do anything." An hour of work on a mess is an hour of work on a mess. If it was a two-hour mess, true, the hour would take care of half of it, but with a two-HUNDRED-hour mess, the hour of work wouldn't show. That doesn't mean it's a wasted hour.

With weight loss it's the same thing. If you were one hundred pounds overweight and you lost five pounds, it would not show. If you were ten pounds overweight and you lost five pounds, it would show. And yet there is no difference between the first five pounds and the latter five pounds. Sheryl Pridmore, a friend of ours in Detroit, said, "If you have a sand pail full of sand and you take a cup of sand out, it'll show. But when you have a whole beach of sand, one cup doesn't make a difference that shows." Still, a cup of sand is a cup of sand.

If you have a lot of work to do, you've got to grasp the idea that IT DOES NOT MATTER IF IT DOES NOT SHOW. IT WILL IN TIME!

How to Fight the War on Clutter

You will need the following items, which we will explain in detail:

Timer

Produce boxes

Shoe box

3 × 5 scratch pads

3 × 5 index cards

Pen

Piggy bank

Manila file folders

Cute mending basket

Containers with lids (about the size of a Sucrets box)

Card file

Start by setting your timer for one hour. We suggest starting in the kitchen. The kitchen is probably the room you and your family spend the most time in, so it very well could be a depressing dump site. The best place in the kitchen to start is the junk drawer by the telephone. Take the drawer out and turn it upside-down on the floor or on the counter, or onto a table (if there is room). Once the drawer is gutted, wash it out with detergent and place it back in its frame.

The next step is crucial. THINK BEFORE YOU FILL YOUR DRAWERS! Think about what you have to have in the drawer by the phone. We suggest the phone book, a pen and 3 × 5 scratch pad, Scotch tape, scissors, and fingernail care supplies. (Caring for your nails is a great thing to do while you're on the phone.) You also need to know that you don't have to fill your drawers. Less is better.

The next step involves using your thumb and forefinger of the hand you use the most, plenty of thirty-gallon garbage bags, and three produce boxes (ask the produce manager at your grocery store what day most of his produce comes in and start collecting orange or apple boxes). Don't settle for any medium-size box. Produce boxes are always the same size, making them easy to stack. They're made of extra heavy cardboard. They have holes for ventilation, lids with handles, and they are always available.

Mark one produce box "Give Away/Sell"; one "Put Away"; and one "Storage." As far as your thumb and forefinger are concerned, you need to use them in conjunction with one of the rules we asked you to memorize in Chapter 3: *Pick it up, don't pass it up; and then put it away.* When we say "away," we mean put it in one of the three produce boxes or into a garbage bag. You will have to make one of four decisions once your thumb and forefinger have successfully picked something up.

"Give-Away/Sell"

The produce box marked "Give Away/Sell" is for items that have value, but you no longer want them in your home. Great-Grampa Tuberly's silverware went into that box at Cindy's house. Make a decision before you start clearing out your house; will you be giving away or selling your unwanted, but still useful, junk? If you decide to give those items to the Goodwill or Salvation Army, just box them up and make a weekly run to their new home on your Go-fer Day.

If you want to have a garage sale and sell all of it, you need to price each item as you pick it up. Have a roll of masking tape and a pen handy so you can price as you go. We have seen too many mythological garage sales. If you merely pile without pricing for that someday sale, you will slowly turn your garage into an unprofitable warehouse of cullings, because the job of pricing will be too much trouble.

"Storage"

Things like holiday decorations, seasonal clothing, or anything you will need later, but do not want in the main living area of your home, will go into the produce box marked "Storage." (We'll tell you how to set up a storage area later in this chapter.)

"Put Away"

The produce box marked "Put Away" is for items that go somewhere else in the house. This box will keep you at the job site for the entire hour. When you pick something up, like a videotape, instead of taking it to the family room where you would end up watching it or you would start organizing your videos, just put it in the Put Away box. When an hour of de-junking is up, it will take approximately ten minutes to put away everything that you put in the box.

The **shoe box** is for photos. Collect them in the shoe box and write on a piece of **3 × 5 scratch paper,** "organize photo albums." Put the memo in your **card file** to do ten months from now. You'll also use the scratch pad to list supplies you will realize you need to buy, such as batteries for the smoke alarms, tape, drawer organizers, etc. Keep a 3 × 5 scratch pad by every phone, in your purse, and in the back of your card file. The pads are cheaper than 3 × 5 index cards and can be thrown away once you take action.

The **piggy bank** is for all the money you will find. The **mending basket** will have thread, scissors, glue, etc., and since it is decorative, it can stay by the phone. You'll find lots of things that need to be fixed. Put them in the mending basket and fix them while you are on the phone. The **small containers with lids** will keep items such as safety pins, rubber bands, and paper clips organized.

Write on a **manila folder,** "Desk Day." When you find letters that need to be answered, bills that need to be paid, or anything involving paperwork, put it into the Desk Day file folder, and once a week, on your Desk Day, take time to attend to your paperwork.

We have discovered that there are some things that everyone seems to hang onto, so we have made these very specific rules about what you may keep.

PAM AND PEGGY'S MOTTO FOR UNCLOGGING CLOSETS, CUPBOARDS, AND DRAWERS: *If it's something you haven't hooked up, turned on, eaten off of, covered up in, sat in or on, looked out of, at, or over, mailed, watered, or read in the last year ... dare to dump it!*

The items below are some of the typical drawer, cupboard, and closet cloggers that seem to be universal.

MAGAZINES

Ask yourself this question: When have I ever had a block of free time and used it to scrounge through a mountain of old magazines in search of some old information? If the answer is NEVER, ask yourself this: Will I ever take one of my old magazines with me to the doctor or dentist so I can read mine instead of his? If the answer again is NEVER, then you just might want to follow our rule for magazines.

DO NOT KEEP OLD MAGAZINES! If you subscribe to a magazine or magazines, you may keep only this month's and last month's issues. You may also keep any old, but special, Christmas issues. We know how hard it would be to dump all those commemorative magazines you've saved. It would be cruel to insist that you toss *Life: The Year in Pictures 1985, People: The Royal Wedding Issue,* etc. We only ask you to be very selective.

While you are bundling up the collection of unread material, consider how much of it you have really read. If you see that you have not been reading what you've been paying for, you might consider canceling your subscriptions and buying a magazine only when you know you will have the time to enjoy it (like on a vacation).

If we still haven't convinced you to chuck your treasury of periodicals, remember that there will ALWAYS be more magazines and they will ALWAYS come out every month. If you are afraid that someday the monthly flow of type will stop, remember that there is a place in your town where all the issues of all the magazines are kept, and you can go there, at no cost, and ask one of the professional keepers of information to help you dig out any issue from any year ... it's called THE LIBRARY.

NEWSPAPERS

Our rule for keeping newspapers is simple: DON'T! You may keep one to start a fire in your fireplace. Exception: If you have a teenager who relies on the newspaper for current events and school reports, you may keep back issues for one week only.

KEYS

When you clean out drawers, you are going to find keys, and you will get to keep some of them. Ask each key this question: Are you a key to the present or to the past? If it's a key to the past, and you've forgotten what hole it goes to, throw it away. You may keep all keys to the present.

Keys to the past include: any key with a symbol of a past car you have owned (what are you thinking? *"Maybe someday I'll find my old car and rip it off"?*); any key that seems vaguely familiar but you can't remember what it unlocks; any key that you haven't the foggiest idea what it ever went to; and luggage keys. (If you didn't lock your luggage on your last trip, throw away your luggage keys. If you do lock your luggage when you travel, those keys will be with your luggage and not at the bottom of your underwear drawer.)

Keys to the present include the key to your house, car, office, and anything else you know you'll need to get into. You may discover duplicates as you clean your drawers. They are good to keep in case you lose the originals.

PENS

Test every pen by scribbling in a circular motion on a scratch pad. If scribbling won't release the ink, throw the pen away. You know how hard it is to read a message that is gouged into paper with the inkless point of a dead pen. If ink comes out with the test, it's a keeper. Remember, every pen you find that works is one more pen you can put in the drawer by the phone, eliminating, once and for all, the frantic search for a writing utensil at message-taking time. Also, we caution you not to take pens from hotels. They have only enough ink for a night or two, and you will soon discover a multitude of drained instruments in your drawers.

The typical family is allowed to have a maximum of twenty-five pens.

INSTRUCTION MANUALS

Throw away your instruction manuals to simple appliances like toasters, blenders, mixers, and coffeemakers unless you think you are going to forget how to use them. Keep the rest in your filing cabinet.

TWIST TIES

If you have a surplus of twist ties, it means one thing ... you are not using them. Since you are not using them, why are you saving them? When you buy a quantity of garbage sacks, there will always be enough twist ties to seal each bag. If you are not using the twist ties, it's because you are filling the bags too full. If that's the case, and we think it is, you need a daily card to remind you to empty the trash before it overflows. You may keep six twist ties and make a conscious effort to use them. (Peggy has a twist tie fetish and insists that you may keep six ties in ALL of the various sizes.)

COUPONS

Dump all the coupons in your drawers, because they will have expired. If you find any coupons with dates more than a year old, you lose your cutting privileges until your whole house is streamlined. And don't be fooled into saving a coupon just because it's worth more than fifty cents. Five dollars off a pizza you needed to order two years ago is no good.

PAPER GROCERY BAGS

Keeping grocery bags is very dangerous! We have discovered that they have babies while they are under the sink and in between the counter and the refrigerator. We've been told that in some climates these paper grocery bags also attract cockroaches (they love the glue), which is another reason to avoid collecting them. Because they attract bugs and have a sneaky reproductive spirit, we suggest that you keep only five at any one time. If you feel anxious at this thought, try to recall a time when you had to bring your groceries home without a sack because your grocer ran out of them. As long as you need groceries, you'll get another bag. Many environmentally conscious people are investing in reusable net grocery sacks for small purchases and larger, grocery bag–size sacks are also available in some places.

RECEIPTS, CHECK STUBS, BANK STATEMENTS

We asked a friend who is a certified public accountant how long we should keep receipts for tax purposes. She said that the IRS can audit your files for up to three years unless they suspect fraud, at which time they can ask for your books up to seven years. Since you are the only one who knows if you are frauding, you will have to decide if you will save your papers for three or seven years.

BOXES YOU THINK WILL MAKE GOOD GIFT CONTAINERS

If you have a special place to save boxes, you may keep a few. Just remember that with every gift you buy, you can ask for a perfect, new gift box and usually get one.

Odd Socks

Odd socks are like lonely hearts; they need mates, and they won't find them as long as they are shut up in the odd-sock drawer. Free them so that they can get out and meet all the other odd socks in the world. To borrow words from a famous odd-sock song from *West Side Story:* "There is a place for us ..." That place is the Goodwill or Salvation Army. Incidentally, we called the Goodwill to see if they want odd socks and they said yes, but they also wanted us to know that they don't try to mate them. Instead, they use them for various stuffing projects, in which they need fiber in rather small pieces. Bag up all those odd socks you keep thinking will one day miraculously find their long-lost partners ... because they NEVER will.

Souvenirs

If you are sick of your home being a national gallery for the cowboy boot ashtray from Phoenix, the ceramic beaver made out of Mount St. Helen's ash from Washington, the mock leather moose from Yellowstone, and the tin Trump Tower bank from New York City, box up the vacation flashbacks in one of those gift boxes you don't get to keep anymore and pick some lucky guy out of your phone book to receive some unexpected tourist trap mementos. Imagine how surprised the recipient will be when he receives the anonymous, tasteless gift! It would be great if the surprise could arrive on April Fool's Day. Note: In your future travels, purchase souvenirs that can be hung on your Christmas tree. Then every Christmas, when you haul out the fake holly garlands to deck the halls, you'll be able to relive your bygone vacations.

Batteries

Chances are your bevy of batteries is worthless. We all

have a tendency to save them too long. Somewhere in our brains this message is engraved: BATTERIES NOT INCLUDED—so we buy too many in the first place, not wanting ever to be stuck with something new but powerless. It's easy to end up with the wrong size, and there's nothing more frustrating than trying to fit a "C" battery into a double-"A" hole.

Give all your mystery batteries to someone with a tester and, in the future, buy only what you need, and get the kind that come with a little tester strip on the side.

PACKAGED PARTS

These are the little screws, nuts, and bolts that manufacturers so kindly include with new products. These little packages live on long past the time you'll ever remember what they go to. Dump them! In the future, write on the package what the parts belong to and put them with the tool box.

MAPS AND TRAVEL BROCHURES

Maps get outdated, because new roads keep being made. If you find a map that is frayed on the folds and threatens to fall apart if you open it, it's time to throw it out before you get lost. When you plan a road trip, buy new road maps. You'll save yourself time and maybe even gas money in the end.

SAVED "FOR GOOD"

If you keep things for good, be sure you can define what "good" is. We have a friend whose aunt saved all gifts of new clothing for "good." When she died, her closets, cupboards, and drawers were jammed with things for "good." Our friend told us that her aunt always wore the same thing at all family gatherings and that she would consent to wearing something new only when what she had was literally in rags. She was laid to rest in something she'd saved "for good."

SENTIMENTAL THINGS

As long as your sentimental possessions are organized, you can keep them. Plan to organize photo albums, put home movies on video, bronze the baby shoes, make scrap books, etc. Memorabilia is wonderful when it is organized and depressing when it is not.

GAMES

Weed out games. You don't need Candy Land if your youngest child is sixteen. Have a closet shelf for your games and keep only the ones you play with regularity. Games with missing pieces are useless. Most games have the manufacturer's name and address somewhere on the box. Plan on one of your Desk Days to get missing parts to those games you dearly love.

CRAFTS AND FABRIC

Like grocery sacks, crafts and fabric multiply. One of the women we've been helping with her home is a very talented craft person. Her home has a wonderful, cozy feeling, due in part to her gift for decorating. However, her craft room was out of control, and she was almost afraid to go in there. We helped her organize shelves and drawers, and she gained the courage to give up over two thirds of her material. Now she has just exactly what she wants in the room.

Remember that crafts are always changing. If you do crafts, you know that cows are IN one year and mushrooms are IN the next. There is nothing more depressing than to have to finish last year's clown when everybody else is doing ducks. Be brave. Get rid of the old so that you can make room for the new.

Kids' Schoolwork and Art

The papers that your children bring home from school are enough to pack the average household. You may keep only 10 percent of the best work. Each of our kids got one produce box filled with their favorites. The rest was discarded when the little ones were not looking. The box will go with them when they leave home.

Undeveloped Film

Peggy used to have a huge salad bowl on top of the refrigerator, full of undeveloped film. She had written on each cartridge what year and for what event the snapshots were taken. She and Danny would occasionally get the big bowl down and look at the rolls. "Oh, Danny, look, Grand Canyon 1974, Chris was two. I'll bet these are good."

Our rule is, if you aren't developing, you don't get to shoot. Picture taking is a four-part process. Buy the film, take the pictures, develop the film, and put the pictures in an album. Leave any of the steps out and you will be frustrated. If you find a lot of undeveloped film, collect it in a plastic bag and, every Go-fer day, get one or two rolls printed.

Beware of the Phantoms

Without exception, we have discovered phantoms living in people's houses. We even found them in our own houses years after we reformed. We can guarantee that you'll find phantoms in your house, too. As long as you are aware that they exist, you can catch them and kick them out!

We first became aware of the phantoms after a clutter-bust in Sacramento. We came home feeling very good about the condition of our closets, cupboards, and drawers and our ability to maintain streamlined and efficient homes. Peggy even looked under her kitchen sink with a profound feeling of superiority, and that's when she discovered the first of several phantoms we have since rounded up and kicked out.

FROM PEGGY:

I looked under my sink and reveled in the cleanliness and order I had maintained over many years. A garbage can, lined with a plastic liner, was on one side and a Lazy-Susan, with liquid detergent, dishwasher detergent, scouring pads, and a sponge was on the other. Upon further inspection, I noticed, in the darkened recess of the cupboard, another Lazy-Susan that was hiding behind the one holding my dishwashing necessities. "Hmmm ..." I pulled it out into better light.

The turntable was dusty and so were the indoor plant products on it. Leaf Shine, African Violet Food, Vita Root, Blossom Boost, Mr. Mister, "Your Fern's Best Friend," and two different kinds of bug spray. As I looked at the products, I thought, *I don't use any of this stuff*. That's because I'm not good with indoor plants. The ones I have would live regardless of human attention. Why did I have all those greenhouse supplies in the back of my cupboard?

I remember buying all of it when I was at the mall with Mom. She even had two-for-one coupons for some of it. That's how I ended up loading a cart full of horticultural supplies. She was so excited to be saving, and I got caught up in her enthusiasm. I offered to pay half and we'd split the take. I spent about thirty-five dollars on the phantom horticulturist living under my sink. It was me thinking I could grow like my mom.

After discovering this space-taking figment, we uncovered a phantom gourmet who went to The Kitchen Kaboodle and bought bundt pans, ravioli presses, and an espresso cappuccino maker. We also exposed a phantom painter, intellectual, athlete, letter writer, and quilter.

When you pull the plug on a phantom, you free yourself to be who you are. Maybe you thought you'd use that yogurt maker, but if you haven't cultured in the last year, you're not going to. Maybe you used to quilt, but you little-stitched yourself into burnout. Pass on the frame and the squares. Times change, you change, and what you keep in your home should reflect who you are now. Let someone else be who you used to be. Face the fact that you can't be all the people you admire. If you keep the phantoms, you hold back opportunities for others to have what you don't need anymore.

Establishing a Storage Area

There are certain things in your home that are seasonal, such as holiday decorations, ski clothing and equipment, and hunting and fishing gear. Clothing, for most parts of our country, is seasonal. As parents of a growing family, you will need to keep things like diapers, potty chairs, and car seats until you have finished having children. These storage things need to be out of the mainstream of your household until they are actually going to be used.

Choose a storage area in the basement, garage, attic, spare bedroom, or any place that is dry and warm. The more organized your storage area is, the easier it will be to get to things when you need them. Our system requires about twenty produce boxes, a divider in your card file marked "Storage," and blank 3 × 5 index cards.

Start by filling a produce box with a specific category of things like "size 12 boy's church clothes." As you put the boy's dress shirts into the box, write on a 3 × 5 card, "3 dress shirts." When you put the sport coat in the box, write, "navy blue sport coat, size 12" and so on until the box is full and you have recorded everything that's in the box on a 3 × 5 card.

Put the lid on the box and mark the outside "C-1," for clothing, box number one. On the 3 × 5 card write "C-1," and put that card into your card file with the divider you marked "Storage."

It's as simple as that! When you have finished boxing up and writing down everything, you will have saved yourself hours and hours of searching for things when it's actually time to use them.

FROM PAM:

Recently, we created a de-junking video to show people how to clean out their closets, cupboards, and drawers. In order to demonstrate how to de-junk a house, we had to have a messed-up set. The producer of the video was open to several possibilities. We could make the video on a real television set in a studio or do it in one of our homes. In any case, the set would have to be messed up so that we could show how to clean it up. We used my home.

As soon as I knew my house was going to be the place, I had about a month to scrape together enough rubbish to recreate my past. In just a few days, I had quite a nice collection of cereal boxes, Pepsi cans, milk cartons, newspapers, dog food cans, junk mail, and more. I accumulated the trash on one section of the kitchen counter, but within a week it started to scare me. It felt sickeningly familiar. I had to move the mess into the garage to save my sanity.

I put the word out to neighbors, friends, and family that I needed toys, stuffed animals, fabric, unfinished crafts, and any garage-sale–type junk. In a month, I had enough junk to successfully reenact my ugly past.

Since we wanted the video to show before and after scenes, it was decided that we would do the "after" shots the first day and the "before" shots the second day.

Two producers came from Los Angeles and a television crew from KATU-TV in Portland came the first day to videotape my kitchen, dining room, and every drawer and cupboard. Everything was perfect. The next day everyone returned to shoot the mess.

I had totally trashed the kitchen and dining room. The sinks were full of dishes and old food. (A week before the shoot, I had started growing some molds and saving left-over meals at room temperature.) The stovetop was caked with dried pancake batter and egg yoke. Every dish, glass, and cup was dirty, and there was no spot on the counters or any other horizontal surface without a pile at least six inches high. My husband, Terry, was dumbfounded. We got married long after my slob days, and he has come to enjoy our immaculate house.

It was actually quite fun to make the mess, especially because I knew that there was money in the budget for cleanup. Incidentally, it took three people six hours to make my house look the way it did before the shoot.

No one could believe I really lived that way, and they all accused me of exaggerating. (You'll have to see the video!) Peggy was the only one to back me up. That is, until my two older children came over.

Peggy Ann was the first one to come by. (Fifteen years ago, when I reformed, she was nine.) I couldn't wait to see her reaction. I introduced her to everyone, and they all stood waiting for her response.

She walked slowly through the devastation, taking in everything with a definite look of recollection. Then she spoke, "Well, it's ALMOST like it used to be." She paused, and I knew everyone was thinking that I did exaggerate, then she continued, "but you don't have any cat food on the kitchen floor!" It so happened that I did have cat food on the kitchen floor; she just hadn't seen it yet.

Then my son Michael dropped by (he was thirteen when I changed my ways). He walked into the mess with a confused but comforted look, as if he'd just found his favorite, old ratty teddy bear. He actually liked the mess and complimented me on its authenticity!

The making of this video was quite a mental adventure for me. I had just finished reading a fabulous book by Dr. Wayne Dyer, *You'll See It When You Believe It,* and I know his title is the truth. Jesus said, "It is done unto you as you believe." Back in 1977 when Peggy and I vowed we were going to get organized, we both BELIEVED we were going to do it. At that time our houses were both caves, but we were able to BELIEVE we were organized in spite of the way things looked. After six weeks of hard work, fueled by our new belief, we got to actually SEE what we had BELIEVED.

In the making of this video, I was able to see circumstances in my home that I knew were not the truth, just as Peggy and I had done 1977. It was all pretend and I knew it, and yet I had been in those same circumstances fifteen years before and the mess was NOT pretend. There is no difference. The messes were identical; it doesn't matter if one was make-believe or not. The person I was back in 1977, who believed she was organized, is no different from the person I am today, who knows I am organized. The results were identical, too. Both messes went away.

Start believing you are organized right now, in spite of how things look. Get that feeling that comes when you really believe something. Stop saying, "I'm so disorganized," or "I'm always late," or "I can't find anything." By announcing those kinds of statements, you only postpone the results you so dearly want.

REMEMBER, IT DOES NOT MATTER IF IT DOES NOT SHOW IMMEDIATELY ... IT WILL EVENTUALLY!

Seven

Gone With the Wind

During the fifteen years that we have been conducting workshops for the disorganized, we have noticed that about 75 percent of our clientele is overweight. That has never surprised us. Collectively, we have lost 104 pounds since becoming organized. When our homes were in a mess, our dining room tables were not only our craft centers but the place where we folded laundry and the drop-off spot for everyone's miscellaneous incoming and outgoing junk.

By covering the one place where you are supposed to eat, a right-brainer will automatically expand his/her dining territory. It's our educated guess that you and your family eat over the sink (when you're worried about spills) and in every room of the house (when you're not).

If that's true, you have probably developed what we call free-range feeding, or "free-ranging." Our definition of free-ranging is: the taking in of any food (regardless of nutritional value), while standing, walking, driving, resting, working, bathing, talking on the telephone, or watching television.

FREE-RANGING IS VERY DANGEROUS! It can cause

accidents when a free-ranger drops food into his/her lap while trying to wrestle a Whopper and maneuver through traffic with one hand. FREE-RANGING IS VERY EXPEN-SIVE! An accident almost always causes an increase in insurance premiums. FREE-RANGING IS A NASTY HABIT. It is one of the causes of obesity, stains on furniture and car-peting, garbled telephone conversations, and sticky clickers to the TV. It'll stop a shopper at the door of most stores at the mall, with their rule of no food or drink beyond this point. In fact, all the litter on our highways and in our parks and waterways is caused by *careless* free-rangers.

If you make a rule that, from now on, you will eat only at your table, sitting down, we guarantee you'll lose weight, because your eating opportunities will be slashed in half. You'll also reduce the chance of hazards and cut down on the mess in your home, your car, and our beauti-ful country.

If you are a free-ranger, chances are you have free-range children. Television doesn't help. If you think about it, many of the food commercials show kids eating while they do just about everything. You see them hopscotching while eating a hot dog, skateboarding while munching cookies, and playing video games while drinking soda pop. The commercials give the impression that, unless you eat while you do other things, you are just not having much fun. The truth is, you miss a great deal of the pleasure of eating when you mix it with other activities.

If you are a hard-core free-ranger, you are probably doing a lot of unconscious eating. That means you don't even remember what you ate. Have you ever said some-thing like, "I didn't have lunch today ... oh, except for the crackers and a little bit of peanut butter ... oh, and the doggy bag leftovers ... oh yeah, and the glass of grape juice and a chicken leg"? Often you can totally reconstruct sev-eral meals you've had when you thought you hadn't eaten a thing.

Here's a poem written about unconscious eating, by a former free-ranger.

DEAR JENNY CRAIG
by Pam Young

I made myself a sandwich
And something's really weird.
The crumbs are on the counter,
But the sandwich disappeared.

I can't believe I ate it
And I won't admit I did!
I know I ate a bite or two
While I was screwing on the lid
To the gallon jar of mayonnaise,
After licking off the knife
That was standing knee-deep in there
Treading mayo for its life.

I may have eaten just a half
Of that sandwich that I made.
I know I washed some down
With a glass of lemonade
That I poured to quench my awful thirst
After eating guacamole
Or maybe it was taco chips,
Or, no, the crescent roll. See
I smeared some peanut butter on the roll
And took a taste,
When my buds relayed the message
That unless I heaped, in haste,
A glob of homemade jelly
On the butter and the roll,
The overall experience
Would leave a gourmet hole.

So I carried out the order,
Drank some milk to wash it down
And when I put the carton back,
You won't believe it but I found
A Snickers Bar I'd started
And didn't have time to finish
So I'd hidden it with forethought
In a box of frozen spinach
Which I bought for just that reason,
'Cause my kids are little snackers.
I've learned from past experience,
They'll eat you out of crackers
And anything that's chocolate
And everything that's sweet.
They're worse than ants at picnics
When it comes to finding treats.

Which brings me back to wonder
If that's what happened to my sandwich.
Did my children spy my meal
And fail to understand which
Food is theirs and which is mine?
It's hard to keep things separate.
Those sneaky little snackers
Must have gotten awfully desperate.

OK, if I did consume it
And I must admit I'm stuffed;
Then where's that little voice I have
That says I've had enough?

I guess it's pretty obvious
By looking at my hips,
That more than fruits and vegetables
Have passed between my lips.

A small bite here, a swallow there,
Just how much I can't remember,
But according to my scale,
I've gained ten pounds since last September!

Free-ranging is for cows, and, if you think about it, look how big a heifer is! Could there be a correlation? Cows get to eat on the hoof, because they have FOUR stomachs to fill. You only have one. If you decide that from now on, you are going to fill yours only while seated at a table, you will be amazed at what a difference that simple change will make.

Getting Healthy

If you have ever had a New Year's resolution to lose weight and get in shape, and then by bathing suit season, you could kick yourself for the condition of your body, you are part of the majority. We think the main reason people fail at diets and physical fitness programs is that they are disorganized. To follow a diet plan and stay on a fitness routine, you have to be organized. By incorporating our plan into your card file, you will give yourself the direction you have lacked in your previous attempts. Before you read further, we want you to take ten minutes to make two short but very important lists. We'll tell you why, later.

The first list we want you to make is a list of reasons why you want to lose weight and get in condition. Just as we asked you, at the beginning of this book, to list some good reasons to get organized, we want you to figure out some good reasons to lose weight and get in shape. Here is a sample list to help you make yours.

WHY I WANT TO LOSE WEIGHT AND GET BACK IN SHAPE

My clothes hurt because they are so tight, but I refuse to move into the next size up.

I am not going to be a fat bride at my wedding or a fat mother at my children's weddings.

I don't like the looks I get from people who haven't seen me for a while. I think they are thinking, "Wow, what happened to her?"

My feet and knees are killing me because of the extra weight they're carrying.

I sense that my kids are embarrassed.

I'm embarrassed.

I feel left out of activities, because I don't have the energy to hike, ski, run, and play with my family like I used to.

My blood pressure is high, and I'm worried.

I have low self-esteem, because I don't like the way I look.

Once you have written down the negatives of being overweight and out of shape, next write down why you are not doing anything about this facet of your life. Here is a sample list.

WHY I HAVEN'T BEEN EATING RIGHT AND GETTING EXERCISE

I love chocolate, mayonnaise, chicken skin, beef, grease, butter, you name it. If it's fattening, I love it.

By avoiding exercise, I don't have to sweat and hurt afterward.

My schedule is already cramped. By not taking time to exercise, I have more time to do other things I enjoy.

By not exercising, I don't have to think about getting proper shoes and exercise equipment. I can spend the money on other things.

By eating the way I always do, I don't have to read up on what is healthy, and I don't have to buy a bunch of food that is foreign to me.

It's hot most of the time, and by not walking, I get to stay in my air-conditioned house.

It's always raining where I live, and by staying in my house, I don't have to go out and get cold, or buy water-proof attire so that I can walk in the rain.

When I am depressed or bored, if I eat, I feel better.

I love to eat in restaurants.

Now you have a list of reasons why you should lose weight and get in shape and a list of what has been keeping you from taking action. The two lists are very important, because they represent PAIN and PLEASURE. Besides being disorganized, two more reasons why you haven't been successful in this area are the ways you link PAIN and PLEASURE to eating and exercise.

We agree with many of the human behavioralists who claim we are motivated by PAIN and PLEASURE and that we will do far MORE to AVOID PAIN than we will to GET PLEASURE. For instance, if you love chocolate chip cookies, and someone hands you a warm, fresh Mrs. Field's chocolate chip cookie and says to you, "Here's a cookie, but don't eat it because you are on a diet," would you eat it? You would probably say, "Oh, big deal, I'll just eat this one." That's because, in that scenario, you have no pain linked with the eating of the cookie. At that moment, if you chose the cookie over the diet, where would the pain be? It wouldn't be there.

Now let's say the cookie-giver hands you a fresh, hot-out-of-the-oven Mrs. Field's chocolate chip cookie and says, "Here's a cookie, but don't eat it because it is laced with arsenic." You wouldn't eat it because arsenic poisoning would be very painful. In staying on a healthy eating program, you will be faced with temptations all the time. Unless you can associate more pain than pleasure with eating all of the temptations you'll face, you'll eat them.

Until you associate enough pain with being overweight, you will not eliminate the problem. In fact, until you can associate enough pain with being overweight, you will continue to GAIN. If you are overweight now and you are not going to do anything about it, YOU ARE GOING TO GAIN MORE. That first list of reasons to lose the weight is automatically a list of the negatives in your life, caused by the extra weight. Unless it produces enough pain for you to want to take action, you won't.

If scientists say that we will do more to avoid pain than we will to seek pleasure, it's a wonder everyone doesn't have at least fifty pounds to lose. As far as exercise is concerned, getting into shape hurts. If something hurts, it's our nature to avoid it. As far as food is concerned, eating is pleasurable. There is no pain involved with eating, unless your jaw is out of kilter, you have a sore throat, or you have tooth problems. The pain of eating fattening foods comes three weeks after you ate the food and you can't zip up your pants. What you need to do is turn up the pain when it comes to eating and turn down the pain when it comes to exercise.

Turning Up the Pain When It's Time to Eat

Since it's our nature to enjoy food, the best way to turn up the pain factor is to associate pain with eating fattening foods. What if that same cookie-giver said, "Would you like a cookie?" and you responded by using your "air horn"? What if you promised yourself that, for the next week, whenever you're faced with unexpected temptations, you'll use your own personal, inner air horn?

Years ago, we read a book on dieting, in which the author told about his strategy to turn up the pain. He needed to lose a lot of weight, and he had failed in the past. He knew himself well enough that he put into his weight-loss plan enough pain that if he didn't succeed, he would be sick. He was Jewish and had lost many family members in the Holocaust. He had his attorney draw up a legal and binding promissory note, stating that if he did not lose the weight he wanted to lose in one year from the date he started his diet, the American Nazi Party would receive five thousand dollars. The thought of that hideous group receiving all that money kept him true to his personal promise to lose the weight.

You probably don't need to take such drastic measures, but you are the only one who really knows yourself. If you decide you really need to muscle yourself, perhaps you could pick an organization you absolutely abhor and promise them your first-born if you don't reach your weight goal. (Be careful with that suggestion; you may have days when you'd be tempted to gorge yourself.) For us, it took posting that first list we asked you to make (the reasons why you want to lose weight and get in shape) on our refrigerators and keeping it in our purses so that, when we went grocery shopping, we stayed on track. Healthy eating starts in your mind and can take a detour at the grocery store, if you are not prepared.

Turning Down the Pleasure When It's Time to Eat

We do not want you to make eating less pleasurable, but you will be changing your tastes so that nourishing foods are more pleasing and fattening foods are less pleasing. One of the wonderful things about humans is that our pleasures can change. You can truly learn to enjoy foods that are good for you. We live in a time when there are so many new foods that are fat- and sugar-free and taste very good. Once you get used to these foods, going back to the fattening fare is awful. A good example is milk. We were raised on whole milk. By the time our kids were born, we were drinking 2 percent. Now we drink skim milk. To go back to whole milk would be like drinking a glass of whipping cream. Soda pop is another example. Drinking regular pop when, for the last fifteen years, we've been drinking diet soda, would be like drinking liquid cotton candy. Since the change to new and different foods is relatively painful (no one likes change), that's when you need the first list foremost in your thoughts.

Turning Up the Pleasure When It's Time to Exercise

From our own experience, when it comes to working out, if we don't enjoy the type of exercise we do, we will end up on the couch watching reruns of Jack La Lanne. You must pick forms of exercise that will fit your personality. Walking, biking, horseback riding, ice skating, mountain climbing, skiing, dancing, step aerobics, football, golf, swimming, whatever sounds fun. Remember, your basic nature is fun-loving. If you try to take on a grueling aerobic program like Ordell maintains, you'll peter out on about the second set of one-arm push-ups.

Once you pick out some forms of exercise that sound fun, get the proper attire and equipment. There's nothing worse than using your daughter's "Little Tike" if you want to bicycle. The best way to kill the joy of a sport is to have the wrong equipment. Skis that are too long will send you to the lodge on a stretcher, way before the rest of the group is ready to quit. A bowling ball with holes spread too far to match your reach will keep you from being invited into the ladies' league. Golfing with your husband's clubs will slow up the game and cause a tie-up of aggravated players behind you. If you are borrowing your daughter's bike, your sister's skis, your brother's ball, or your husband's clubs, you're telling yourself one thing—THIS ACTIVITY IS TEMPORARY. Make it a priority to have the right equipment and apparel, and make it belong to YOU. You'll have a much better chance at staying with whatever you choose.

Don't Forget About Schmidky

Remember that Schmidky is your pleasure seeker. Schmidky already knows everything that you love to do and everything that you love to eat. Have a meeting with him and tell him you need to change some of your likes and dislikes. Tell him you are going to cut your intake of fat to twenty grams a day, which will make you happy. Tell him you are going to start an exercise program that will be fun. Tell him that, because of your new decisions, you are going to be healthier and live longer, that you are going to look good in your clothes, feel good about yourself, climb stairs and not get out of breath, move with grace and ease, be able to ski, run, hike, and play with your family and feel better, because you will be eating foods that are healthy. He'll start to work immediately to make sure that your orders are carried out.

Eating the Cards

Richard Simmons created what he calls Deal-a-Meal. He took a healthy diet and put the food on cards. On any given day, the eater uses the cards to direct what he/she will eat for the day. We were surprised when Simmons came on TV with his new program, because we were eating cards long before he was. In our weight-loss program we call "Gone with the Wind," we used the Weight Watchers diet and transferred the various foods onto cards. Then we incorporated them into our rotating card file system. For instance, in the Weight Watchers program, it is suggested that you drink eight glasses of water every day. We wrote the word "water" on eight blue 3 × 5 pieces of construction paper. Each day, as we drank a glass of water, we'd move one of the water cards to the next day. We used other colored cards to represent fats, protein, milk, fruits, vegetables, etc. If we'd eaten all our cards, we'd have to go to bed.

You can use the card plan for any healthy diet. The American Heart Association diet is very good, or you could use a diet your doctor recommends. List each food and the amount you can have daily (in the case of foods like red meat, eggs, and cheese, list the amount you can have weekly) and transfer the list to cards. The cards can go into your card file along with all of your other cards. It's that easy!

Exercise

Many physical fitness experts agree that, three times a week for twenty minutes, we should do aerobic exercise to raise our heart rate. In Chapter 4, we had you make out an exercise card to direct you to work out three times a week. It is important to check with your doctor before starting any physical fitness routine, but as soon as you do that, JUST DO IT!

So, there are five ways for you to be successful at losing weight and getting in shape.

1. Make your table functional by clearing it off and using it for dining.

2. Put a moratorium on free-ranging.
3. Link pain to eating the wrong foods and pleasure to exercising.
4. Find a nutritional diet plan, put it on 3 × 5 cards, and incorporate it into your card file.
5. Use the exercise card you made in Chapter 4.

If you can do those five things, you are going to be healthy and happy. Remember, though, you didn't get out of shape in a week, and you're not going to get back into shape in a week. Also, one of your traits is a childlike nature, so be gentle with yourself or you'll rebel.

Eight

The Inside Story

After all of our efforts to get organized and have clean houses, we gradually began to realize that something was wrong. True, the janitorial duties were being handled according to plan, but we hadn't yet learned how to deal with our families' tide of unconscious clutter. In the bigger picture, it doesn't matter that the oven is cleaned on a regular basis if the kitchen is cluttered with backpacks, schoolbooks, home improvement tools, junk mail, and the personal belongings of various family members. If the room is messy, it leaves a dirty impression. Regardless of the cleanliness on the inside, the outward appearance caused by a careless clan can give a clean home mistaken identity.

One of the main problems of staying organized is the challenge of getting the other members of the family to be accountable for their own tracks.

We had been receiving hundreds of letters from homemakers, pleading with us to tell them how to get family members to cooperate. With so many requests to solve that problem and our own inability to clear up our situations, we knew we had to find the answers. It took us over a year and what we learned is in Chapter 11.

Before we tell you our solutions, we want to share with you the dirty story that led up to finding them. We have to take you back in time to March 24, 1987. Hazel Dell, Washington, (a sleepy community established in a hazelnut orchard, three miles north of Vancouver), inside the home of Peggy Jones.

Six A.M. I woke up to the cheerful voices of my sister and her walking friends, as they marched past my house on their daily four-mile hike. I rolled over and looked at my mate. Danny's mouth was slightly open as he snored softly, his morning breath gently puffing into my face every six seconds. Not ready to stir, I adjusted my breathing so that our exhales matched. I stood it as long as I could.

"Time to get up, Danny," I said.

"Huh?"

"Time to get up. The walkers just went by. It's six."

"Okay ..."

"Danny, do you think we should start walking?"

"Where?" He yawned and stretched at the same time.

"With Pam's group. It sounds like they have a lot of fun. Look at us. We're still in bed. Don't you feel guilty, lying here? By the time we get up, they've done their exercise for the day. What do we do? We sleep as late as we possibly can.

"I worry about us now that we're forty. You know how high your cholesterol was two years ago ... well, I'll bet it's gone up. I'm going to make an appointment for you to get it checked. Pam says we should be drinking more water, too. At Weight Watchers, they told her everybody needs to drink at least eight glasses a day. We need to do that ... so what do you think?"

"Yeah, I'll have a glass of water."

"No, I mean, what do you think about walking? Danny? ... Danny! Danny, do you think we should start walking?" There was no answer from him, so I answered myself, "Yeah, maybe in the summer, when it warms up."

The morning started out the same as any other busy weekday. Five people, all getting ready to leave the house at the same time, caused the usual circus. The bathrooms were taken by the two teenagers, and the kitchen showed signs of a hurried breakfast, but this morning was unusually tense. I had been out of town for a couple of days, to tape some television spots with my sister, and the family was feeling the effects of my absence.

"Babe, are we out of shampoo?" Danny called to me from the shower.

"Just a minute!" I dashed to the supply cupboard in the hall. I was used to shopping in bulk at Cramco (it was really called Costco, but we renamed it because we could never cram all we bought into the car), so I was sure I would find an extra gallon of shampoo. I rummaged through the surplus inventory of products. I found three economy-size cans of industrial-strength bathroom cleaner, two gallons of Windex, a tub of Epsom Salts, six Comet cleansers (in institutional-size cans), a pound of Q-tips, a pound of Band-Aids, a quart of Liquid Woolite, two aerosol cans of hair spray (for professional use only), and a half gallon of Scope. There was no shampoo.

I flew to my suitcase, thinking there might be some hotel shampoo in there, left over from my trip. I pawed through the clothes and found nothing but an empty plastic travel container I'd used for conditioner.

"Peggy! Are you getting the shampoo or what? I'm running out of hot water!" Danny's voice was urgent.

As was often the case throughout my life, my right brain coughed up the solution. I ran back to the supply cupboard, grabbed the Liquid Woolite, and filled the little plastic bottle.

"Here you go, Babe. Use this. I guess it's time for me to make a run over to Cramco again."

I was making the bed when Danny came in with a towel wrapped around him. "Boy, does that shampoo ever suds up! I had trouble rinsing it out."

"Hmm ..." I didn't look at him. I went on making the bed. "How come you never make the bed, Danny?"

"Cause you do."

"If I didn't make it, would you?

"I don't know. Probably not. What do I have to wear, Babe?"

"I don't know. I've been gone. Did you get your clothes from the cleaners?"

"I wasn't aware you'd taken them in."

"I took them before I left."

"Well, that doesn't do me a lot of good right now, does it?" His face glared down into mine.

I was just about to say, "Now wait just a minute, pal. Who made me your slave?" when Danny pivoted to go to his closet and fell into my open suitcase. "Did you have any plans to unpack this thing, or were you just going to leave it out here on the rug?" He wouldn't accept help getting out of the luggage, and waved me out of his way. "I'm gonna be late for work. Just see if you can put an outfit together for me, would you?"

He hurried to the bathroom, and I heard the hair dryer go on. I looked in his closet and scrounged up an exhausted ensemble. It was obvious he needed new clothes. That wasn't my fault, I reassured myself. After all, he had been a uniformed policeman for the last couple of years, and his new job in Investigations had recently put him in plain clothes. Unfortunately, his wardrobe was skimpy and outdated. His aversion to fitting rooms and tailors had kept him away from the mall.

"Peggy!" Danny yelled from the bathroom. "Can you catch the back of my hair? I can't get it to stay down."

I rushed in to help him. He looked like one of the Three Stooges. Who would think that hair and wool wouldn't be the same? I took the brush from Danny and made a futile attempt to calm the coif.

"I think you blew it dry wrong. I'm afraid it doesn't want to go down."

Danny grabbed the professional hair spray and gave his head a good going-over. Then he took the brush and tried to force the follicles into place. They stuck together in wet clumps. I put the hand mirror back in the drawer.

"How does it look in the back?" It looked worse than I had ever seen it look in twenty years. "Fine," I said, hoping he'd take my word for it. After all, what were his options ... wash it over again and this time use Joy or Four Paws Magic Coat (flea and tick shampoo), wear a hat, or call in sick? There were no other options.

Danny stormed back into the bedroom. I shoved the suitcase under the bed, out of his way. He threw on the stupid outfit I had laid out for him. The slacks were about an inch too short (shrunken victims of too many tumbles in the Maytag), but he was moving so fast, it was hard to notice. I followed him as he started to leave. "See you tonight." He dutifully kissed me, a quick, off-centered smack, and started through the front door.

Our two German shepherds had been on one of their all-night digs, and there was a huge pile of dirt from the planter on the first step of the porch. Danny's long, rubberlike legs absorbed the surprise of running up and over the mound of dirt, and he recovered gracefully as he negotiated the hill like a flamingo.

"I'll get this cleaned up, Danny. You go on to work.... Don't forget to drink your water."

"My water?"

"Your water. Remember, Sissy says you're supposed to drink eight glasses every day?"

He muttered something I didn't care to ask him to repeat, and he was off to fight crime.

I went back into the house, making a mental note to get a shovel as soon as the kids left for school.

"Did you make my lunch, Mom?" Chris, my fifteen-year-old, asked. He was pouring himself a glass of apple juice.

"No. Get a dollar out of the money drawer."

"There's nothing in there," Jeff, fourteen, said. "I already looked."

"Where's my purse?!"

We started hunting. "Look under those newspapers, or maybe it's under that pile of clean clothes. Somebody go look in the car."

"Whose cereal bowl is this? Allyson, is this your bowl?"

"No, I didn't get any cereal. All the boxes in the pantry are empty."

"What!? Who keeps doing that? Don't put the box back in the cupboard if it's empty. How many times do I have to tell you guys, you don't put empty boxes back in the pantry? If the box is empty, put it in the trash!"

"Mom, will you tell Chris to quit hogging all the hot water? He was in the shower for fifteen minutes!"

"I was not."

"Were too."

"Was not."

"Knock it off, you guys!"

"Here's your purse, Mom. I found it in the car." Ally tossed it on the counter and started to leave.

"Oh, good. Here, Chris, here's a five. You and Jeff stick together at lunch and bring me back my change. Put the jug of apple juice back, Chris. Ally, come and get your lunch money. Jeff, clean up your mess in the bathroom before you leave."

"Mom, can you go on a field trip with my class next Wednesday? My teacher says the snakes aren't out yet." Ally was waving a permission slip at me.

"Snakes! Where are you going?!"

"To the Ridgefield Wildlife Refuge."

"Oh, no, Ally, I can't do that! The teacher promised me there wouldn't be any snakes the year I went with Jeff's class, and they were everywhere! I had to be carried back to the bus. It was humiliating! I'm surprised Miss McKinney would even ask!"

"Mom, there's swimming after school and I have to work tonight. Can you wash my uniform? It's on the floor in my closet."

"I'll try. You'd better bring it upstairs and put it in the hall so I don't forget. Bring up your other laundry, too. You guys need to do that every morning so I know how much there is to do. Come on, you guys, you're going to miss the bus."

When the last one had gone out the door, I slumped down onto the couch. My life was not running smoothly.

I knew what I wanted it to be like. I wanted a modern-day Walton's Mountain, only with more money, a housekeeper, and no in-laws living with me.

The children would adore each other, and honor and respect their father and me. They'd be so used to helping that I could say, "Go do your chores," and they'd know exactly what I meant by that. Our home would be clean, cozy, and filled with laughter, and we'd all look forward to worshiping together on Sundays.

Each morning I'd go to my warm, sunny kitchen and make the coffee. The children would make their own breakfast, and, one by one, they'd rinse their dishes and cheerfully put them in the dishwasher. The sink and counters would be spotless, inviting me to start preparing a few things for dinner.

The pace would be unhurried, but steady, as each one would shower and dress (in outfits set out the night before). They'd make their beds, sort their laundry, and get ready to leave for school.

As the last one stepped happily onto the school bus, Danny and I would linger over a tender good-bye kiss at the front door. Then I would enjoy a second cup of coffee in my peaceful, lovely living room, as I curled up with a good book. At the end of a chapter or two, I would check the soup in my crockpot and jump into a nice, hot shower.

I would put on a size-five pair of name-dropping jeans and a crisp, white cotton blouse, step into a sporty pair of tennis shoes, put on coordinating earrings, fix my hair and do my makeup, and, with an hour to kill before work, I'd check the 3 × 5 housekeeping cards in my card file kit. I'd set aside jobs for the housekeeper and do a bit of light housework myself. With soft music in the background, I'd rinse out a few hand-washables, shine the glass-top coffee table, set out the china for dinner, and freshen the guest room.

Then my sister would come over to work on our novel.

"MMMM ... it sure smells good in here," she'd say.

"Really? It's probably the stuffing I made for the Cornish game hens, or maybe it's the soup simmering."

"Well, it smells wonderful!"

We'd work until noon, do lunch at the Alexis, drop by our office to get our mail, and knock off at three.

I would return to my home-sweet-home, and the aroma of a delicious dinner would melt away any stress I'd collected. My happy honor-rollers would come home from school, and over a nice, tall glass of iced tea, they'd share their day with me.

Danny would call to see if he could run any errands for me on his way home from work. The children would ask what they could do to help with dinner.

At five P.M., my husband would spring through the door and hand me a small bouquet of wild violets he'd picked. He'd put his arms around me and say, "These reminded me of you. You're so delicate that a good wind would blow you away!" Then we'd sit out on the deck in matching chaise longues, and, while sipping a fragrant glass of lemonade, we'd tell each other about our fabulous day. We would enjoy our meal together as a family, and afterward, each one would rinse his or her own dishes and put them in the dishwasher, and the last one would start it up. Then Danny would insist that I relax and read the paper, while he and the children scoured the pots and pans, polished the sinks and wiped the counters, damp-mopped the kitchen floor, and emptied the garbage.

Unfortunately, Walton's Mountain was only a fantasy. The only mountain close to my house was Mount St. Helen's!

MEANWHILE ... Salmon Creek, Washington (a sleepier community about three miles north of Hazel Dell), outside the home of Pam Young.

MARCH 24, 1987:

I got back from my sunrise trudge with a heavy heart to match my thighs. My friend, Carole, and I had started walking after weighing up the Christmas pounds we put on. To date, we figured we had walked about 320 miles, and we still hadn't lost a gram. Carole had even gained a pound more than what she had weighed the night she waddled into a Weight Watchers meeting, threw herself onto the stage, and cried, "HELP ME!" She had even resorted to wearing what she termed her Watergate wardrobe. She said it consisted of several full-cut garments that covered up everything.

I had started to gradually disappear into a cushion of cellulite when I stopped dating a midlife jogger. It had been a relief to slow down from the fast lane at the athletic club. Now I was blessed with a man who had a rowing machine stored in his attic, and whose idea of exercise was bringing it down for his annual garage sale and hauling it back up afterward.

Back in January, when I had bumped into Carole in the grocery store (we were both reaching for the same pork roast), it had been like running into myself in the mirror. We were the same age, height, and weight, and we had identically proportioned bodies.

"Carole, how are you? I haven't seen you since ..."

"Since that time we had lunch and ended up going out to dinner after that."

"Gad, how long ago was that?"

As we blocked the aisle, catching up on each other's activities, there was silent recognition that we had each put on a little weight. (We confided, later, that we had both felt a rush of "grocery-cart guilt" until we realized that our purchases had been similar in their fat content.)

"Oh, Carole, I've gained ten pounds since Thanksgiving! I've just got to get a hold of myself! The trouble with me is that I'm self-indulgent. That's all there is to it. Look at the calories in this cart! I mean, please, I know I shouldn't have real butter and mayonnaise and those cookies ... I don't even remember putting them in there."

"Hey, self-indulgence is my middle name. I'll be at home all alone, minding my own business, and I'll think ... *Hmmm, what sounds good?* and before I know it, I've answered myself ... *Well, how 'bout some ice cream?* ... and then I think, *You don't want it blank! Let's put some chopped cashews, a little chocolate syrup, and Cool Whip on top!* There's a little Mr. Sweet Tooth inside of me, and he's a real hog!"

"What are we going to do?"

"Well, I started walking last week. I go four miles a day with Ann and Claudia. You oughta come along."

I joined the walkers, but here I was, three months and 320 miles later, still heavy. My only solace was that if I HADN'T exercised, I'd probably weigh ten pounds more than I did now.

As I reached my house, it didn't help my cloudy spirit to see the contents of my garbage can strewn all over the driveway. My front yard looked like a landfill. I was embarrassed, especially since I had written three books on getting organized, and I knew that this mess would delight Mrs. Dorchester, the neighborhood jogging gossip. Her network of rumor mongers always enjoyed finding any evidence to show that I needed to take some of my own advice.

As I picked up the junk in the yard, I thought about what had happened to me since Peggy and I had become organized twelve years earlier. We'd traveled all over the country helping homemakers improve their domestic affairs. Things had definitely improved for me too, but they were far from perfect. I was still plagued, and probably always would be, with the effects of my genetic disorder.

The garbage was a good example. The lid on the can had been squashed flat in the winter of '82 (it was buried under the snow when I ran over it with the car), but instead of buying a whole new can, I always balanced the useless lid on top of its overstuffed contents. Consequently, every garbage day there was a race to see who would get to my refuse first, Vancouver Sanitary Service or the neighbors' dog, Lasagna (a garbage and Labrador retriever mix).

In recent years, I'd had some drastic changes occur in my life (two of my children had gone away to college). Now, even more distressing, they both had returned home for spring break! Joanna, fourteen, my born-organized child, and I had become quite comfortable without the chaos that her two siblings could generate. When they returned, the house submerged under the clutter before I realized what had happened. With the yard cleaned up, I vowed to get a new garbage can lid (I wondered if I could buy the top without the bottom), and I went into the house.

As I opened the door, Chelsea Marie, my basset hound puppy, greeted me with what had been one of my good high heels. I lobbed it in the vicinity of her toy box, which was filled with an assortment of objects she had, out of boredom, confiscated and destroyed. It contained a colorful variety of leather shoe casualties, a fuzzy assortment of the children's prized stuffed animals that they had collected over the years, and a potpourri of things we'd neglected to put away. The mark of a teething puppy was everywhere.

Walking into the living room, I remembered there were four extra bodies staying over. Fraternity brothers of Mike's, my oldest offspring, were conked out in their clothes on the living room floor like a gathering of park-bench bums. Their party remains were everywhere. A rented movie was still in the VCR, and I cringed at the titles of the other two on top of the TV. I didn't care to know the name of the one they had fallen asleep to. I reminded myself that they were all over twenty-one.

The morning-after kitchen was testimony to a great night before. The refrigerator was stripped of everything edible, including some borderline potato salad and a bowl of leftover beans that no one had liked in the first place. The home-moviegoers had obviously enjoyed my absentee hospitality. (I had gone out to dinner and to a movie, then had slipped to bed while the Delta Upsiloners were engrossed in their video rentals.) Since it was only 8:15, I decided to let them sleep, while I took a shower and started polishing my half of an article Peggy and I had to finish for *McCall's* magazine.

On the way to my desk in the corner of the living room, I tripped on the arm of one of the sleepers. He didn't move. *If the children's father still lived here, God forbid, these people would not be sacked out in my living room like this. We would have come home last night and he would have clicked off the TV and thrown a huge fit over the mess.*

I could feel my body start to tense, thinking of the scene that would have occurred. I knew from experience that I hated confrontations like that. Still, I knew that as soon as these vacationing scholars stirred, I would have to tell them how upset I was with the way my living room and kitchen looked. I knew it would be a hassle to get them to clean everything up. Since I hate situations where I have to be the "bad guy," I didn't relish the inevitable clash.

I wish there was a man I could hire to come over and throw a fit for me. I would leave for an hour, and, when I came back, everything would be straightened out. I'd find his ad in the yellow pages: "ATTENTION, SINGLE MOMS: Sgt. Stickler will take care of all disciplinary actions in your home. I will put an end to unnecessary bickering, enforce punishments, make rules, and deliver lectures approved by the mother. Hourly rate or salary. Call 574-MEAN, and I'll wear the pants in your family!"

I looked at the rough draft of the article we were writing. The title made me squirm, "Fifteen Hassle-free Ways to Get Your Family to Help Around the House." It implied manipulation, and I didn't like the idea of GETTING anybody to help around the house; I wanted them to WANT to do their part. Besides, the fact that our article was going to be published in a women's magazine implied that it would be the woman who would be doing the manipulation; the mother would still be responsible for domestic order. *Sports Illustrated* would never think of featuring an article with that title. Why? Because most men don't feel that the house is their responsibility, and they would never read it.

I glanced back at the living room. *How can I possibly contribute to this article when my house looks like a mission house on skid row? I'd do better writing about the hazards of being a single parent. At least I'd be writing about what I know! The 15 million women like me would probably love to read about somebody else who has had to raise her children by herself.*

I had assumed full responsibility for my three kids when they were four, nine, and twelve. Their father had moved away after the divorce, and I was left to raise them without the power that comes when two parents stand together against the constant challenge of growing children. So many times I had wished that I could say, "You'll have to ask your dad," or "Wait until your father gets home." Instead, I was the only one there to help them through the tangle of thoughts and feelings of growing up.

As a single mother, I went to PTA meetings alone. I was their only parent who rooted for them when they participated in their sports activities, praised them when they succeeded, consoled them when they were upset, and disciplined them when they did something wrong. That was the hard part. It isn't fun to have to make unpopular decisions.

I remember the time when Peggy Ann was furious with me for grounding her for a month. "We'll never be friends!" she cried (as only a teenage soap opera fanatic can). I wanted to be lenient and cut the grounding period in half, but I stiffened and replied, "I have plenty of friends, and I don't need you for a friend! YOU are my daughter!" She was livid, then cool throughout the sentence. (Today we are best friends.)

I glanced down at Mike as he slept. Except for the mustache, he looked just like he did when he was a child. As I watched him sleep, I felt so thankful that I had been able to be home with all my children as they grew up. I had never agreed with the idea that it was "quality time" that was important when raising children. I think it's quantity time that counts. A child can't be expected to concentrate all the important things he or she feels and thinks into some arbitrary hour or day that a parent designates as "quality time."

When Mike was two, he had interrupted my housecleaning seventeen times in one hour! I'd counted them because I wanted to be able to justify to my husband why I could never get the whole house cleaned up. One of his interruptions was just to show me the inside of the dog's lips; unimportant by my standards, but a great discovery in his life.

In the end, the person who is there all the time is the one who gives quality time. I was glad that I hadn't missed any part of my children's lives. They had grown up so fast! I had such wonderful times with them, but there had been some hard times, too.

It's difficult bringing up children when two parents are actively involved. When one parent has the whole responsibility, it can be overwhelming. On one of our visits to the TV show "The 700 Club," my sister and I talked to the talent coordinator, Jackie Mitchum, who had reared a son by herself. She told us that there were times when she felt overburdened by the responsibility. During an exceptionally stressful time, she cried out, "Lord! I cannot be father and mother to this child." The Lord spoke to her heart and said, "I didn't call you to be the father and mother to this child, I called you to be his mother. I will be his father." From that point on, she said everything was much easier. Her son is now a very successful pastor.

I had always known that I wasn't alone when the kids were growing up. Whenever I was confused about what to do, or swallowed up by some problem, I knew that God was with me. That power has far more influence than the presence of any biological father.

I knew I could write volumes on my experiences as a single parent, but right now I needed to work on the article.

At 11:30 the guys started to come to life. The instant that the sleep was out of their eyes, I started on them to get the place cleaned up. I began with what I would describe as mild scolding, which promptly turned into moderate complaining. By the time I left to meet my sister for lunch, I was repulsed by the sound of my own voice, but at least my house looked like the kind of place where the author of a book on home organization just might live.

As Peggy and I stood in line at the Ron Det Vous (one of Hazel Dell's finest restaurants), we were both out of whack and preoccupied with our domestic state of affairs. Normally we would both be in whack, so the mood in the air was gloomy.

"You're awful quiet."

"Awfully quiet."

"Well, *pardone*, grammar queen!"

"Oh, I'm sorry. I'm just tired, I guess. I think I've got jet lag."

"Sissy?"

"Yeah?"

"We stayed on the West Coast. I think you only get to lag when you change time zones."

"Well, then I've got trip lag, and I didn't sleep very well either. I had a bank statement dream."

"A bank statement dream?"

"Yeah, I kept trying to find the mistake, but I never did. I spent the whole night looking for missing checks and deposit receipts. When I woke up, I needed a nap."

"When I go out of town, everything falls apart, and it takes me two or three days to get things back under control. Stuff really piles up fast. You can't see the top of my dresser for all the mail and Danny's junk on it ... and the laundry! While I was gone nobody did a thing ... No, I take that back. Danny had each of the kids wash and dry a load, but do you think they folded any of it? Of course not! It's all in a pile on the couch. It's like they think some laundry fairy will come through in the night, fold their clothes, and put them neatly back in their drawers! They don't even bring their laundry to where I sort it. I get so sick of having to drag everybody's dirty clothes from their rooms to the washer. I've lost my feist."

"Why do you do it?"

"Because if I didn't, it wouldn't get done."

"That's disgusting!"

"I know it is! And you know what else? This morning, Danny had the NERVE to criticize my sorting procedure!"

"Huh?"

"Yeah. He said I shouldn't put the dirty laundry in piles in the hall. That's where I have to sort the clothes."

"Well, it'd be a little hard to do it in a laundry room with a batch of eleven German shepherd puppies in there."

"Nine. Rosie's *first* litter was eleven."

"Oh."

"Where was I?"

"Dirty laundry—piles in the hall ..."

"Oh, yeah. Danny's no laundry expert! He wouldn't need ANY place to make piles, because he doesn't know you have to separate the colors! He'd throw 'em all in together, like the time I had the flu and he washed the pink throw rug with his black Dockers and underwear. He even threw in his tie!"

Finally it was our turn at the cash register, where Ron's wife took our order. We got a booth and waited for the hot pastramis to come to us.

"Sissy, do you think people who read our books picture our houses just immaculate?"

"Sure, they do."

"That makes me feel bad."

"It shouldn't. We've never claimed to be perfect. We've always admitted that we have a problem with organization. Besides, we were gone for three days. Why should we feel guilty for getting behind on the house, when we weren't even there?

"I hate the pressure of everything in the house falling on the woman's shoulders. Give me a break! It's not women's work inside and men's work outside! It's people-who-live-in-the-house work!"

"That's true, but a lot has to change in the male brain before it'll show up in the laundry room. Remember when we were at the vet and Dr. Slocum asked if we were working on a new project?"

"Yeah. I told him we were putting together a class to get

husbands to do half, and he said, 'Half of what?' When you said, 'Half of the household management, cooking, and child care,' he looked at you like you'd told him he needed to gupvail and fleckhammer his vendecrod more often. Your words did not compute."

"Yeah, but I'll bet those words would draw a blank with most men. Course there is that ... what's his name ... that preacher on television ... he does everything!"

"I wish there was a way to keep the house under control without nagging. I get so frustrated with everybody. When five people each leave out a few things, the place looks a mess even if it's clean. I mean, who cares if the blinds are dusted and light fixtures shine, when there's junk everywhere you look?"

"I'm just as guilty as the next guy. I left my makeup and curlers all over the bathroom counter, and I haven't even unpacked yet! But I feel like I'm responsible for everybody else, too, and that's not fair.

"You should see the house right now! It's a cave because, ever since I got home, my energy's been on the *McCall's* article. I haven't had time to do the breakfast dishes, so the kitchen's a mess; there's a huge pile of laundry to fold; we're out of groceries, and everybody's finger is pointed at me!"

"Well, I left my house clean, but everybody's MAD at me. Last night, before I went out with Terry, I threw a fit over Peggy's messes everywhere and she finally cleaned them up, but then Mike and his friends came over and made new ones. All I do is nag. I'm sick of the sound of my own voice."

We ate our lunch and talked about how we'd like things to be different.

"You know what I'd like? I'd like it if everybody just automatically cleaned up after himself, that's all! If they'd just take care of their own messes. Doesn't that make sense? If you trim your beard over the sink, clean up the whiskers before you leave the bathroom."

"Yeah, and if you take a bath, you clean the ring."

"And the last guy out of the bed makes it."

"Right! How about when you use the last square of toilet paper, you replace the roll?"

"Absolutely! Who buys the toilet paper?"

"The one with the most time, but the guy who shops doesn't have to haul the stuff from the car or put it away."

"That's fair. Who cooks?"

"I love to cook. But I shouldn't have to do the dishes."

"Of course not! Each eater should do his own dishes!"

"What about the pots and pans?"

"You don't touch them! If you cook the meal, they clean up after it!"

"Whoa, that would be interesting."

"What do you mean?"

"Think about it ... they're used to being served and cleaned up after. They wouldn't like that."

"Well, it's only fair."

"I know that, but just because it's fair doesn't mean they'd like it. How would you like it if, all of a sudden, we came here and ate our lunch and then found out we had to bus our own dishes and help out in the kitchen before we could leave? You'd hate it! Ron would be out of business in less than a week!"

"I see what you mean. But here, we're paying for the service. At home it's all free."

"That makes me wild. My time is not free!"

"Maybe you should start charging for meals and kitchen work."

"Yeah, or maybe I oughta go on a strike like that lady in *People* magazine did."

"What ever happened to her?"

"I don't know. Nothing, I guess."

"When I remarry, you can bet my husband will take care of himself! I won't be waiting on him hand and foot! He'll have to get up out of that recliner chair and do his half."

"Yeah, but he'll be used to it. He'll know what it takes to run a home because he's been on his own. Danny was twenty when we got married. He went from being taken care of by his mother to being waited on by me."

"You were a fool to get that started."

"Yeah, but I thought it was fun for a while ... and then we had the three kids all in three years 'cause you told me you can't get pregnant if you're nursing, and we got a bigger house and German shepherds and a cockatiel and three cats and I started a business.... I don't know when, exactly, but waiting on everybody and picking up after them stopped being fun."

"What are you going to do?"

"I'm going to go home and throw a fit! I'll line the kids up, and, through clenched teeth, I'll demand that they take an interest in having a clean house! I'll look Danny in the eye and tell him exactly what's wrong, and I'll insist things change! I'll tell him the days of "Father Knows Best" are over!"

"Schwooo ... I love it!"

"I'll say, 'Look, Danny, while you're propped up in your easy chair reading the evening paper, I'm sweating over a hot stove!' "

"Oh, that's good."

"Yeah. I'll say, 'You expect me to wash your clothes and have them hanging in your closet, all starched and ironed, and what thanks do I get? ... none!' "

"Yeah!"

"I'll say, 'Who balances the checkbook? Who picks up the boys from swimming practice and tennis classes? Who takes Ally to horseback riding lessons, and who takes the dogs to get their shots? Me! I mean, I!' "

"Ooo, yeah, watch your grammar."

"Yeah, I don't want him correcting me on anything! I'll say, 'Danny, the time has come for you to bond with the dogs!' "

"What'll he say?"

"He's a reasonable man. He'll see that things have to change. He's always real open and receptive to whatever I need. I'll just sit down with him and explain how I feel, and everything'll be fine."

We finished our lunch and, grateful to stand up and distribute the weight of the pastrami, went to our office to proofread the article. Our fifteen "hassle-free" ideas were merely Band-Aid tips that would cover up the real problem ... lack of willing cooperation. We wished there were some way to cause the whole family to become aware and accountable for their share of the load, because we were trying to do it ALL, and we were being swamped by the backwash of people, places, and things.

Nine

Can This Marriage Be Saved?

I went back to my cave after Pam and I sent the article. I felt as if I needed a nap, partly because I was regrouping from the trip and partly because I felt stress over the house. *"I'll start in the kitchen and get that under control."* I walked onto the porch, up and over the pile of dirt. *"No, first I'll get the shovel and dig out the entryway, and then I'll do the kitchen."* I went into the house. It could have been my imagination, but it even smelled messy. I know a meal tastes better when it looks good. I wonder if it's the same kind of deal with a house. Maybe a home smells better when it's neat.

"Hi ..." I called to Jeff and Ally. "Did Chris call to be picked up?"

Jeff answered, "Not yet, but Dad called! He said, 'Tell your mother, thanks!'"

"What?"

"Yeah, I think you're in trouble."

"I'm in trouble ... for what?"

"I don't know. Maybe you'd better call him."

"I will!"

"Hi, Mom," Ally chirped. Then her tone darkened. "Oh,

did Dad get ahold of you? He's furious! He came home to change his clothes 'cause when he was in court and he crossed his legs, ya know?"

"Yeah?"

"His skin showed."

"And that's supposed to be MY fault? Your father needs new clothes ... but he hates to go shopping! Is it my fault that he doesn't have much to choose from?"

"I don't know, Mom. I just know he's real mad."

"Yeah, well, I'm mad, too!"

The look on Ally's face made me feel guilty for dragging her into something that Danny and I should have settled privately.

"Never mind, Ally. I'll call Dad and we'll get this ironed out."

I jabbed out his number on my cordless and waited for the phone to ring. He answered.

"I understand you have a problem with me!" My enunciation was crisp and cool.

"Yes, I do. Is it too much to ask to have clean clothes in the closet?"

"Yes! Right now it is. I think your timing stinks! You know I've been out of town, and I've been working on a deadline. Things are a little behind."

"A little behind? The place is a pit! You've been home for three days, and you still haven't unpacked. You haven't been to the store; the yard is a trash hole from the dogs running wild.... I don't know what your problem is, but you sure seem to be spinning your wheels."

"You're right, Danny. You don't have a clue about what my problem is, because part of the problem is YOU!"

"Oh, sure. Blame YOUR disorganization on me! That's right. It's all MY fault!"

"I didn't say that. You're not listening!"

"Great, now I'm deaf! I'm tired of this conversation. The fact is, you really don't care. You let everything go until I can't stand it any more and I blow up. The kids are in their own little world, too. They know they're supposed to clean up after the dogs, but do they? You just try to walk across the lawn without slipping in one of the piles! Nobody cares. For days I've stepped over a styrofoam meat tray in the driveway, wondering how long it would stay there. If I didn't bend over and pick it up and put it in the garbage can myself, it'd be there forever." (I held back from telling him how much I'd LOVE to have been there when he bent over!)

"Danny, you say we're in our own little world, but you don't realize what that means. We've all got pressures beyond the garbage in the driveway. You act like the kids and I are a bunch of no-good, lazy, shiftless slackers!" (I dried the mouthpiece with my sleeve, took a deep breath, and continued.) "You're oblivious to what we all do while you're at work. Give some credit where it's due! You've always said, 'Homework comes first!' and they're on the honor roll. So the piles on the lawn don't always get attention. Well, evidently they've learned to prioritize between dog poop and good grades!

"Chris works five days a week at the pizza place; he swims on the team and plays tennis, and he goes to Civil Air Patrol once a week. And Jeff works weekends mowing lawns, and answers the phone at our office, and he practices with the diving team five nights a week.

"Now Ally, she's not old enough to get a job yet, but she helps me with dinner every night and does anything I ever ask her to do! She's student body president; she plays the piano and takes horseback riding lessons in Battle Ground two days a week—and who do you think carts them all over the place? When I'm not chauffeuring them to all THOSE places, I'm hauling them to the orthodontist or somewhere else they have to be, or I'm here at home trying to keep things up! If we missed the meat tray, we are sorry! But we are NOT a bunch of bums!"

"I didn't say you were bums. I'm only pointing out that the house is filthy."

"No, it isn't! It's very clean, and you know it! It's just a little messy."

"Okay, it's messy then. Call it what you want, but there isn't one room that looks clean. That's the way it goes. You let it keep getting worse until I explode, then you run around cleaning things up, and for a while you have the house in order, but then you get sidetracked and things are right back where they were."

"Excuse me? I get sidetracked? I get sidetracked because there are too many tracks, and I can't be on all of them at once! You think you're the only one who wants a clean house? Right now it's probably bothering me more than it's bothering you! I just have a longer fuse and more tolerance ... and I DON'T blame YOU for the circumstances that have led to the mess. That's where we're different! You hold ME responsible. Well, it's too much! I can't do it all any more!"

"Then figure it out and cut back."

"Cut back on what? The laundry, maybe? I think that's how this whole argument got started. What would you have me cut back on?"

"That's for you to figure out. I don't know your schedule. Just quit playing games and take care of it."

"Playing games ... that's wonderful!"

"You are. It's the poor-me game. Get serious and figure out some kind of a work schedule and then stick to it."

"Fine!" I swallowed back the tears. My throat hurt so much that the ache went deep into my chest as I mustered my last stand. "Danny, one more thing. The next time you have a grievance with me, DON'T deliver it through the children. It's certainly not fair to them, and it shows absolutely no respect for my position!"

I was proud of the way I had stood up for myself in

spite of the lump in my throat. I had spoken as articulately as William Buckley.

It was quiet.

"Yes ... I'm sorry about that. I was wrong."

I couldn't talk. The lump had my voice box in a squeeze.

"I'll see you tonight." His tone softened.

"Yeah." I slammed the AT&T into its cradle and let the tears burst.

How could he be so insensitive about my feelings? Quit playing the "poor-me game!" Humph! How could he put so little value on my efforts and my time? Why didn't he recognize my contribution and see that I'm not able to take care of the house and his needs the way I did before I started my business? He was acting like he thinks I don't care. Does he really believe that, or was it just a cheap shot? All HE seems to care about is "how does this affect me?" It affects him because I'm not there to cater to him, feed him, and wash his clothes! I don't expect HIM to wait on ME. I'd never think to call to him from the shower to see if he bought shampoo. I wouldn't dream of asking him to lay out an outfit for me to wear to a speech. I'd love to see the look on his face if I hollered from the bathroom, "Hey, Babe, lay out my burgundy suit, and put a shine on my black pumps. Oh, and I'll need my off-black pantyhose, and pick out a scarf while you're at it." Hah!

He knows the subject of organization is a touchy one with me, and how dare he throw the word "sidetracked" in my face? He knows that's the theme of one of my books! Figure out a work schedule and stick to it! Yeah, but don't figure him into it! I should have said, "How dare you even suggest that this is MY problem!" I should have told him to mind his own business! No, that's a cliché. I should have said, "Until you are ready to be reasonable, there is no point in discussing this any further."

Yeah, I should have used words like "perhaps" and "occasionally."

"Perhaps I am occasionally dilatory in my responsibilities, both in my business and at home. However, I am endeavoring to maintain a balance between the two and keep my mental, emotional, and physical vehicles intact."

No, he'd say, "Stop playing the pseudo-intellectual game." I can't believe he was so hateful. How could he attack me on my home front? He knows my family is the most important thing in my life. He just doesn't understand. That's all. Figure it out and cut back! Uh-huh! I oughta keep a time log of everything I do! Would he ever have his eyes opened!

I got a spurt of energy at the thought of making a list of my work load compared to his. I would make that list, and, at the next confrontation, I'd be ready! Meanwhile, I'd get the kids to help me straighten up the house.

In less than half an hour, the place looked terrific, proving my point that it was purely superficial clutter and not filth.

When Danny came home that night, we were coolly cordial. Polite, yet barely looking at each other, neither of us cared to take up where our phone conversation had left off. Both of us were overly pleasant to the children and obviously indifferent to each other. I was still fighting off hurt feelings and waves of tears. At the dinner table, I said I wasn't very hungry and excused myself. Sneaking a chicken leg from the platter in the kitchen, I took a paper towel, went to the bedroom, and ate the fowl in the dark.

It was only eight o'clock, but I was exhausted. The fight had worn me out. I positioned myself as far over on my side of the bed as I possibly could without dropping off the edge. I was determined to cling there all night. "Hmm!" I muttered to myself. "Cut back! I can think of ONE thing I'll be cutting back on, starting tonight!" I slept, but never so deeply as to risk drifting closer to the enemy. Danny kept on his edge, too.

In the morning, I got up without speaking. When I looked in the bathroom mirror, I scared myself. I noticed my cheek had what looked like a large, serious scar across it. (It was just an indentation from the cording on the edge of the mattress.) My eyes were puffy and bloodshot from crying myself to sleep, and there was a little bit of barbecue sauce from the chicken left on my chin.

I went into the kitchen to make coffee and noticed it was immaculate! *I'll bet the kids did the dishes for me. They'd do anything right now to ease the tension around here.*

"Are you and Dad still mad at each other?" Chris asked. He looked worried. Danny and I rarely argue, and our real fights are limited to about two a year: one in the spring when we launch the boat for the first trip of the season, and the other in the fall when we decide whether to sell it.

"Yeah, Chris, we're still mad, but we'll work it out. I could use your help, though. Dad seems to feel that no one cares about the house and the yard the way he does. I don't think that's true. I think we do care, but we're all so busy and we're going in so many different directions that it's hard to keep on top of everything."

"Yeah, I know."

"I'm going to talk to Jeff and Ally and get them to be more aware of picking up their things and helping with the laundry and dishes, but it's going to take all of us."

"Dad, too?"

"Yeah, Dad, too. But for right now, I think we should be concerned about our own habits."

"Okay." We hugged each other.

"Start this morning by sorting your laundry."

"Where should I put it, in the hall?"

"Uh ... no. I'll set up a place in the laundry room. The puppies are getting too big to be in there. It's time for them to go outside."

Ally came into the kitchen with a little cloud of concern over her head. "Are you and Dad fighting?"

"Hmm ... I think we already fought. Now we're thinking

about what we said to each other, and probably for a while we're both going to be upset."

"How come?"

"Because we agree there's a problem, but neither of us knows what to do about it yet. One thing I can tell you for sure ... I love your dad and he loves me. On a scale of one to ten, if one would be a dirty look and ten would be a divorce, this fight would only be about a five." (She didn't need to know that, during our phone fight, we were hovering around fifteen!) "You don't need to worry, but it would help if you would be extra careful to see that the house stays neat." She agreed.

Next Jeff confronted me. "How come Dad was so mad yesterday?" he pried.

"Because he looked bad, and he didn't know who to blame. His hair didn't work because we were out of shampoo; he needs new clothes ... I don't know ... the house was a mess. I've been gone and he's had to be both mother and father ... I think everything just came to a head at once and we both exploded."

"What do you need me to do?"

"Just make sure that you take care of your own messes. That alone will make a big difference."

"I will."

I easily had the support and cooperation of all three of the children. I praised them and acknowledged what each was already doing to help. Then we talked about what they could do to make things better around the house and easier for their father and me. I had to wonder why I wasn't able to talk to Danny in the same comfortable way I could talk to the children. Our conversation had been accusatory and hostile. Maybe it was because our egos were involved, but all we had succeeded in doing was to create bad feelings.

Ten

Less Than Friendly Persuasion

From Pam:
When I left our office (we'd had to Federal Express the article to meet the deadline), I thought about the fight Peggy was going to have. Getting cooperation from her unsuspecting spouse of twenty years could be tricky. I was glad I didn't have to deal with that problem. Being single for ten years, I had promised myself that any man I became interested in would have to know, or at least be willing to learn, basic homemaking skills, before I would ever consider marriage.

It was true that most of the men I'd encountered were pathetic in that area. (Peggy and I had considered teaching a beginner's homemaking class for men only, after I'd gone through a string of retarded male homemakers. We agreed, however, that most men wouldn't come to a class like that unless we held it in a tavern, served beer and pretzels, and had wide-screen sports at the breaks.)

Terry was the new man in my life, and he was certainly no exception to the domestic retardation I'd seen in my previous dates. I liked him a lot and was seriously working on improving his skill level, because I could see his potential.

I had invited him over for dinner, and, because it would be his first meal in my home, I had decided to be extra careful that the evening's work load would be equal. I even called him at his office and told him we would be going to the supermarket together before we made dinner. He was pleased with the pronoun "we," and he agreed to take off a little early to allow time for the shopping.

We had fun together at the store, though I felt a bit as if I were taking a kindergartner on a field trip. Here was a forty-four-year-old man who had been single for two years and was feeding primarily on canned soup and peanut butter sandwiches.

The produce section was as foreign to him as the underside of a car would be to me. Interestingly, he soaked up every bit of information I gave out as we passed the colorful variety of fruits and vegetables. He was pleased to know that he could buy just one or two potatoes instead of a ten-pound sack. When we came to the bananas, I chose a nice yellow bunch and tore it in half, putting three in the cart. He had a look on his face as if he'd just witnessed a bank holdup.

"You can do that!?" he whispered, as he wielded a guilty glance around the produce department to see if anyone had seen me.

"You mean rip a bunch of bananas apart?"

"Yeah ... that's really okay to do?" He was still nervous, as if he'd been an accomplice in a crime.

"Of course it's okay to do that. What did you think would happen: sirens, loudspeakers: 'Guy in produce, rippin' off bananas?'"

He liked what I had told him and stripped off one more banana to test the validity of what he had learned. No sirens ... no loudspeakers ... no irate produce manager ... It really WAS okay!

With the bananas behind us, I asked him to get some carrots, celery, lettuce, and a couple of pounds of broccoli while I finished getting the fruit. He took the shopping cart and headed for the greens.

When I was finished with my selections, I joined him. He looked anxious for my approval as he cocked his head sideways a couple of times, motioning me to check the cart. "I got everything you told me to." He beamed.

I beamed back and turned to put my fruit with his vegetables. I was mortified to see what he had done! He had torn a head of romaine lettuce in half, severed four stalks of celery from the rest of their family, and decapitated all the broccoli florets from their stems, leaving the heavy stalks next to the scale. It was so unbelievable that my mouth started moving before my ability to edit what was coming out could take over. A flurry of superlatives hit Terry in the face.

When my social-awareness alarm caught up with my tongue, I was embarrassed, and Terry looked like a dog that didn't know why he was in trouble. He needed more hands-on training ... but not in public. I wondered if I could get him a video on grocery store etiquette that he would view in the privacy of his own home.

Leaving the spoils behind, I reluctantly rolled him into the meat department. I rang the bell for the butcher.

"What does that do?"

I hate sarcasm, but I couldn't resist. "It rings the butcher, who lives in the back with all his little barnyard friends. When he hears the bell, he'll come out and we'll tell him that we want this chicken sawed in half."

"In half? Why?" he winced.

"Well, because we are going to barbecue it. After it's in

half, we'll take it home and put the halves on the grill. Then the meat will cook from the inside out." I was beginning to feel the superiority of my vast culinary knowledge.

The butcher appeared, looking as though he'd been on the front lines. I was amused that he knew I was the one who had interrupted his work, even though Terry had the chicken in his hand. "What can I do ya for, ma'am?"

Terry held the chicken out as if he were holding a dead possum he'd found on the freeway, and gestured, with a slicing motion, to cut the bird in half. "We'd like this cut in two pieces, please." His voice was definite and authoritative.

"Whoa! You want it cut that way?" (Terry's cutting motion had divided the hen's top from its bottom.) "Which one of you guys is gonna get the butt and the two legs?" The butcher laughed. "I'm a breast man, myself! How 'bout you?"

Terry laughed, too.

I interrupted their obnoxious fun over the chicken parts, took the package out of Terry's hand, and instructed, "Just cut it right, please."

We were in the store much too long.

At home, I had Terry light the charcoal. (I made a mental note of the time it took.) When he was through watching the flames and was sure the briquettes were going to burn, he went out to the street to get the newspaper.

I let him sit down long enough to get comfortable. "Terrrrry!" I called from the kitchen.

"What?" He sounded as if he were responding to a lilting request.

"Will you please make the salad?"

It was interesting to find out that his idea of a salad was chopped lettuce. I was stunned to discover that his idea of salad dressing was mayonnaise. Not even mayo and catsup; just mayonnaise. I enlightened him. We made Caesar salad together.

I saw to it that the meal preparations were absolutely equal. By the time we were ready to eat, I was hoarse from the cooking lesson, and he was much more aware of what goes into fixing a good dinner. The paper was never read, but we set the table together and took turns basting the chicken. Terry snipped half the beans and learned how to clarify butter. I cut up my half of the strawberries, and, while he sliced his, I showed him how to make the roux. We shared in the preliminary cleanup, and when we sat down to eat he was exhausted and had almost lost his appetite.

After the meal, he was ready to throw himself back on the couch and relax. That's when the flare-up occurred.... There were still dishes to do.

The next morning, I called my sister. "I think a class to get men to do half is a generation away. Terry left last night with the look of a freed slave, and I don't think he'll call for a while, either; at least not until he recuperates from the big dinner! You know what? I hate being demanding. I get help with the housework only because I resort to screaming and nagging. The kids oblige, but it's always a big fight. And now Terry ... I'm sure I'm listed in his little black book under 'B' instead of 'Y.'

"The darned thing about that is I love to cook, and I would've rather done it myself. It's relaxing to me. I feel creative. I love the appreciation for a fabulous meal ... but I was afraid if I let him sit there and read the paper, he'd get the idea that HIS place was in the LA-Z-BOY! Isn't THAT interesting? They don't make a LA-Z-Girl recliner!"

"Oh, brother!"

"I don't want to end up with a man who's unwilling to do his share. Maybe I was wrong to insist we do everything together. It would have been all right if I had cooked alone, as long as he helped with the cleanup. I hate to do the dishes after I've cooked. But who doesn't? I mean, do you know anyone who finds 'cleanup' fulfilling? I'll bet the women's liberation movement was started by a bunch of homemakers who got sick and tired of cleaning up after everybody.

"I hope I didn't scare Terry away with my equal rights crusade. Do you think he'll call me? ... Hello? ... Sissy, are you in there?"

"No, I'm not! Here I've been in love with a man for two decades, and I found out his devotion is only as deep as a pile of dirty laundry! You're asking me if I think Terry will call you? Quite frankly, Charlotte, I don't give a rip!"

"Well!"

"Oh, I'm sorry, Sissy ... I'm just upset. Danny and I had a huge fight last night."

"Ohhhh ... right, I forgot about you guys! Did you win?"

"No. But neither did he. We're at a stalemate. We're speaking, but there is definitely a chill in the air!"

"What are you going to do?"

"I don't know yet. We'll have to talk it out sooner or later. I'm not looking forward to it. Have you ever had to argue with a policeman?"

"No."

"It's a losing deal! Danny puffs up and his lips disappear."

"I think all men do that when they're mad."

"Well, it's very intimidating."

"I know it!"

"I'm not going to get into any arguments until I have all my facts. I'm going to keep a log to show just exactly how I spend my day, compared to his. He may put in three or four more hours at his office than I do, but when he comes home, that's it! It's rest and relaxation. I come home in time to chauffeur the kids all over town, make dinner, clean up, do some laundry, and then it's bedtime!"

"Oh, Sissy, it'll be obvious that you do way more than he does."

"Yeah. But, you know, Danny is a hard worker. I don't mean to sound like he doesn't do anything, because that's not true. He has totally remodeled the house, and his flowerbeds are impeccable. What gets me is that he leaves all the little day-in and day-out responsibilities to me. It's the things that SEEM insignificant but collectively keep everything working that he takes for granted. He doesn't notice until one of the 'little' things doesn't get done, and THEN it gets his attention. Maybe he'd be more appreciative if he was responsible for some of those little things himself. Before I confront him, I'm going to have a list of changes to negotiate."

"Like what?"

"Like I don't want to make his sack lunch any more. On the weekends, I don't want to make breakfast both mornings. I want him to make it on Saturday and I'll do it on Sunday. I don't want to make the bed after he gets out of it, and I want him to clean his own tub ring and wash his whiskers out of the sink.

"I think we should take turns taking and picking up the kids. I want him to do his own dishes and supervise the kitchen cleanup while I relax from cooking the meal. I want him to share the laundry responsibility, take turns going to the cleaners ... and I don't EVER want to wrestle the German shepherds, trying to get them to the vet again. They're just too big!

"I'm going to have all of this in writing. It's going to be in black and white so there's no misunderstanding."

"Do you think you'll cry?"

"Yes."

"Darn. Men hate tears!"

"I know, but I'm not going to worry about it. In fact, I'm going to plan the talk so that I can cry hard if I feel like it."

"Whoa!"

"Yeah, but I don't cry very often, so if I need to cry over this, I get to. It'd be different if I was sloppin' all over the house in tears every day. THESE tears will mean something."

"Good luck!"

We hung up and I sat at my desk, so grateful that I was single. I had to admit that in my middle years, I had become very cynical about men. My son, Mike, had recently warned me that I had more of a chance of being sniped by a terrorist than I had of ever remarrying! (Peggy told me I should start dating terrorists.) Quite frankly, I was in no hurry to do ANY knot-tying! I thought about Terry. *Wouldn't it be great if, when you got married, the guy came with a written guarantee stating that, if he didn't work out, you could take him back and get a new one?* The thought of it made me laugh and prompted me to specify my spousal requirements in a poem.

WARRANTY MAN

You can bet that my next husband
Will come with a warranty.

Thirty years on parts and service,
He'll be trouble-free.

I will read that operator's manual
To figure out how he'll work.

I'll find out how to turn him on
And disconnect him when he's being a jerk.

I won't have to jump-start
His worn-out battery,

And if he starts to smoke,
He's going back to the factory.

I'll take all the extras,
As far as options go.

He's gotta have a nice size trunk
And be equipped with booze control.

I'll take him in for tune-ups;
They'll check his plugs and points.

They'll test his shock absorbers
And grease up his ball joints.

And when his road of life has ended,
I'll tow him faithfully,

Back to where he came from,
With a money-back guarantee.

Eleven

Infraction's the Name of the Game

From Peggy:
My warfare with Danny was far from over. Underneath the dirty laundry, there were deeply rooted male/female issues that needed to be weeded out and done away with forever.

I'm not sure when women got stuck with total responsibility for the home. I have my own theory that it goes back more than six million years. I think that in the beginning there was equality; male and female in perfect symmetry. Harmonious, even, and well-balanced, the two were distinct without difference. Like two pieces in a jigsaw puzzle, opposite yet perfectly matched, the equivalents were complete ... and then came mealtime. The dialogue went something like this:

"Great night's sleep! I'm hungry. Are you?"

"Yeah, I guess so. My stomach feels kinda funny. Maybe I just need to eat."

"Do you want me to go out and get something while you keep the fire going?"

"It doesn't matter. I could go."

"Nah, your stomach's acting up. I'll go."

"Okay, you go get it, and I'll cook it when you get back."

"Sounds fair to me."

"Good. I'll clean up around the cave and set the table."

"Great!"

He left in search of food, and she stayed home and kept the cave warm. Outside, there were all kinds of scary, scaly beasts and giant flying vegetarians, and food wasn't that easy to find. Meanwhile, back at the cave, the fire started to smoke, the queasy stomach got worse, and cavern-to-cavern solicitors kept the pregnant entity from getting a nap. Returning exhausted, the huntsman with the food was annoyed. He felt that she didn't appreciate all he'd been through out in the world. She also felt aggravated. The cave was boring and smoky, he was later than he'd said he'd be, the food didn't satisfy the craving, and the firewood was almost gone.

"How was your day?"

"Oh, just terrific. It's one big party out there."

"Yeah? Well, it wasn't that great being stuck here all day, either!"

Day in and day out, the couple woke up, got the food, cleaned the cave, cooked, ate, argued, and turned in for the night. Soon they were blessed with a child. The mysterious birth thrilled the co-creators, but with the added mouth to feed, the designated food-finder felt pressured to bring back even more. He began to leave earlier and stay out longer in search of provisions. After a tough day, he would often stop at a popular watering hole to enjoy the company of his fellow hunters. Commiserating over losses or swapping tales of brave victories, he'd usually lose track of time. Staggering home, dragging the catch of the day behind him, he would be greeted by his less than festive spouse.

While the father was out foraging, the mother nurtured the little cavette, teaching her right from wrong and the art of homemaking. The child tore around the cave, making messes, noise, and trouble. Every year there was another child. When it became clear what was causing the pregnancies, the stretch-marked female and the hairy-chested male had to cut back on their only form of entertainment (except for an occasional game of Pictionary).

When the cave got too crowded, the mother said to the father, "Take your sons with you today. The girls and I will clean the cave." Before anyone realized it, the roles were established ... the male went out into the world and the female kept up the cave. The balance didn't start shifting until "Family Ties" and "The Cosby Show" were in the top ten.

Thursday, March 26, 1987, was a beautiful, fresh, sunny spring morning, except at the Joneses'. I was gray. I hated the way I felt. I was bitter and hurt, fragile and confused. I wanted to get out of the house. I borrowed Chris's Walkman, plugged myself into something classical (leaving Def Leppard on Chris's desk), and Rosie and I went for a walk. She needed to get away, too.

I live on the edge of a canyon, overlooking a lake and wildlife refuge. There is a paved path around the lake that winds through maple and evergreen trees and peacefully leaves the world behind. It's a perfect place to listen for answers to prayer. (I know you probably didn't buy this book in a religious bookstore, and the last thing you want to hear is a sermon, but if I don't say that I prayed for an answer to the problems I was having at home, there will be a hole in the telling of what happened to make things right.)

I let Rosie off her leash, and she ran ahead to drink and flounce around in the creek. Then I sat down on a big rock, and I prayed. "I don't know what to do, God. These feelings of bitterness and anger are choking me. I feel heavy and dark in my spirit. I can't see any light in this situation. I can't even look at Danny without getting mad!

I've gone over and over the phone fight, and his words are more piercing every time. I need peace and a simple answer. I want us to understand each other. Please help me, God."

"Hey, you! Is that your German sheperd?"

"Huh?" I opened my eyes and saw Rosie in the distance. She had treed a jogger! I ran to rescue the terrified man. "Rosie! Heel! Heel! Rosie, heel! She won't hurt you; she's just smelling you! Rose! Bad dog!" The man was frozen to the tree and speechless. "There, see, she's back on her leash. You can come down now. I'm so sorry she scared you! Are you all right?"

"If you ever walk this trail with that wild animal off his leash again, I'll call the cops so fast you won't have a prayer!"

I felt like Jimmy Stewart did after he'd prayed on Christmas Eve in *It's a Wonderful Life.*

The naughty dog and I walked back home, and although my heart was even heavier, the exercise and fresh air had felt good. The only answer I had seemed to hear was one word: "Rest." I hadn't slept well since the fight. He was right; I needed a nap.

Later that day, I was on my way to the store, still preoccupied with thoughts of my forty-eight-hour domestic battle. The kids were being extra careful to see that their things were put away, but I knew it would last only as long as the cold war Danny and I were waging. Once the smoke cleared, things would pile up again, and I'd go right back to nagging and policing.

Just as I was thinking that it was a shame nobody was accountable without a fight, I noticed an abandoned car alongside the freeway. The highway patrol had tagged it. (Danny told me once that they tag cars before they tow them. The bright ticket is a signal to other circling troopers that the vehicle has been checked out, written up, and earmarked for the hook. I think he said the owner has something like twenty-four hours to retrieve the lemon before Speedy's Tow Masters get it.)

I wondered what it would cost the guy. *Hmm ... too bad we don't have some kind of house patrol. Stuff left out would get tagged, and the owner would have just so much time to retrieve it without paying. Not a bad idea ... make it official just like the state patrol does. Make the rules and then enforce them.* I got excited. There was the simple answer I had asked for in my prayer.

While I was in the store, I bought a package of bright, fluorescent adhesive dots the size of a nickel. When I got home, I couldn't wait! I went through the house and put a dot on anything I found that had been left out. (Anything of mine I found I quietly put away!) I was delighted that, since the children and I had made tidiness our life's work for the last couple of days, most of the stickers appeared on Danny's things! I loved it! His tennis bag was in the entry hall, his shoes were under the coffee table, the newspaper was on the couch, his coffee mug was on the bathroom counter, his sunglasses were on top of the dresser, his Thermos was by the sink, and his sport coat was hung on the back of the kitchen chair. With pleasure, I tagged him in every room. The children watched me.

"What are you doing with those stickers, Mom? Are we going to have another garage sale?" Jeff was puzzled. "How come Dad's selling his good coat?"

"He's not. I'm just tagging it for being on the chair." As I made my final rounds, my inquisitive kids followed me.

"See all these things your father left out? I have decided to play a little game with him. You can play it, too. The main rule is, if it's not decorative, it shouldn't be out. If it's out, I will consider it abandoned and tag it as an infraction!"

"What's an infraction?" Ally asked.

"You know, it's like a ... violation."

"What about your stuff?"

"Huh?"

"Won't Dad tag you for your stuff?"

"Uh ... sure, that's only fair. However, as you can see, all of mine is put away." There was arrogance in my tone.

"Mom?"

"Yes, Chris."

"I don't think your purse is a very good decoration on the piano."

"Well, no, but it's my purse, and I need to be able to leave it out. You understand."

"Not really. If the main rule is that junk left out has to be a decoration or be put away, I think you'd better find another place for your purse or you'll get tagged for it." (I put my purse in the hall closet on the shelf. It was the last time I would ever have to look for it again!)

The kids and I talked about the new game in more detail, making up the rules as we thought of them. Infractions would be counted for laundry and dishes left in bedrooms or any place else (one infraction per item), beds unmade, lights left on when the room is empty, tub rings, toilet seats left up, and coats, purses, books, and anything else left out that shouldn't have been.

Since I had more time in the morning than anyone else, I said I'd empty the dishwasher first thing, so they could put their breakfast dishes in there. If they left them in the sink when the dishwasher was empty, they would be counted as infractions. The owner would have a reasonable amount of time to retrieve his or her belongings without penalty. We would write the time on the dot so there would be no arguments about how long items had been left out.

When the time limit expired, the infractions and the amount charged would be written on 3 × 5 cards (one for each person in the family) and posted on the bulletin board in the kitchen. We decided that twenty-five cents was a fair amount to charge for each item and agreed that, for one week, we would be on probation, adding up the money but not actually collecting it. It would give us a chance to be aware of how much our actions would cost us, once the game really started.

INFRACTION CARD FOR _____		
DATE	INFRACTION	BALANCE
	TOTAL _____	

Then we discussed what we should do with the money. I thought it should go toward something decorative for the house (with all our junk put away, I could see the need for some tasteful knickknacks).

"What's the object?" Chris asked.

"To have the house neat," I said.

"I think the object oughta be to win the money by having the fewest infractions. The clean house would just be a by-product," Jeff proposed.

I wasn't sure I liked the logic of my brilliant offspring. I wished that he cared more about a clean house and less about the money, but the other kids loved his idea.

We decided that we could all act as watchmen and tag each other. We called the game Infraction! (I opted not to explain this new idea to Danny for a while. Wicked as it may have been, I wanted to infract him as many times as I could. It would be evidence of his contribution to the mess and I would have it in black and white ... and fluorescent red.)

During the next two days, we filled our 3 × 5 infraction cards with violations. (In one week, there would have been $19.75 in our kitty if we had actually collected the money.) The first day, Ally had eleven bathroom infractions alone. After that, she rarely left anything out that we could tag. Chris left ice cream bowls in his room, and Jeff couldn't seem to get his backpack out of the hall each day after school. I was repeatedly tagged on my car keys, which soon joined my purse in the closet, and I also got penalized for leaving my watch on the windowsill. (My watch is pretty, but they ruled that it was personally decorative rather than publicly decorative.)

Unbeknown to him, Danny was racking up the most violations. The times that he noticed dots on his things, he unconsciously peeled them off with no more concern than he'd have about picking a cat hair off his coat. He was guilty of whiskers, tub rings, toilet seats, damp towels, dishes, mugs, mail, and more. Since he was such a substantial contributor to the pot, we all looked forward to the day he'd find out he was a player and have to cough up the cash. I was second in line for the clutter crown; Jeff and Chris were tied for third (and eventually formed a union whereby they agreed not to infract each other and split the money, should they ever win it), and, after the first day, Ally was the neatest.

For the short time that the kids and I had been on the new system, the house had never looked so consistently tidy. The impact of something so simple was shocking. It had been so easy to enforce, yet its power was incredible. I wished that we hadn't created it out of desperation but instead had run into it happily, in some how-to book, without having to go through the fire.

Danny was still in the dark about the dots. I'd seen him pick one of the colored tattlers off of the seat of his pants (which had been carelessly tossed over a chair), and I thought that he must surely be puzzled by its conspicuous grip on his backside. He had no idea what the little fluorescent dot meant or how much it would cost him in the future. I loved it!

It was Saturday morning, and Pam and I were supposed to give a luncheon speech on "Home Is Where the Heart Is." My heart wasn't in it. When a couple doesn't usually fight, a blowup like the one Danny and I had had was especially debilitating. We both wanted a truce.

"We need to talk," Danny finally said. (Since I had suffered the most injustice, I felt that it was appropriate that he made the first advance toward peace.)

"Yes, I know we do, but when we talk, we need to have time to get everything that's bothering us out in the open. I know I'm going to cry hard, and I need to be able to do that without worrying about wrecking my makeup."

"All right."

"If it's okay with you, I'd like to postpone the talk until after my speech."

"That's fine. When will you be home?"

"About two."

"I'll be here."

I had had time to think, and so had he. We were both prepared for the confrontation. At two o'clock we met in our bedroom, closed the door, sat on the bed, and squared off. (I was glad that I was dressed up and looked my best. He didn't look that good.) It's hard to argue with a policeman, but it's probably just as difficult to have a talk with someone who earns her living giving speeches and writing books. The "talk" took two hours.

"I'm sorry for the things I've been thinking about you," I confessed.

"So what's going on?"

"I've given it a lot of thought and I've really prayed about it, because I want to understand both sides. I think there are several things happening to us right now."

"Like what?"

"I feel like you take me for granted. It doesn't seem like you appreciate all the things I do for you and the family. You're quick to point out what I haven't done and slow to notice what I have."

"So are you."

"What? In what way?" (It was news to me!)

"Last Saturday, for instance, I spent all day in the yard on my day off while you were shopping, and you came home and didn't even notice."

"I did, too! I told you it looked real nice."

"Yeah, well, maybe I would have felt like you really meant it if you'd taken a minute to walk around and really look at it."

"You're right. I should have, and I was going to come back out as soon as I took my packages in, but then I got busy and forgot. I'm sorry. I guess we both do that. The other day I was so proud of myself for hemming your new jeans right away and I said, 'Guess what, Danny! Your new jeans are hemmed and ready to wear!' and you said, 'Good. Did you sew up the pocket in my jacket?' I needed way more points for that!"

"I'm sorry. I'll try to be more appreciative."

"So will I."

"So what else? He took out his pipe and started his tamping ritual (a sign that he was vulnerable and needed the motions to give him time to think).

"I want you to lighten up."

He stared at me.

"You're always finding what's wrong." (I countered his tamping with some nail filing.) "Like Saturday, after you and the boys worked so hard all day in the yard, you stood back and looked at what you'd done and Chris said, 'It sure looks good, huh, Dad?' and you said, 'Yeah, but it needs barkdust.' I saw Chris and Jeff just look at each other."

"Really? Well, I didn't mean that I didn't appreciate

how much they did. I could just see what else we still had to do."

"You do it a lot. Someone will say, 'Dad, the pool sure looks great!' and you'll say, 'Yeah, but we need to scrub the tiles!' If you could just stop yourself before you say, 'Yeah, but ...'"

"I don't mean to do that. It's just that there's always something that needs to be done."

"I know, and that's the point. When you say, 'We can't play until the work is done,' you forget that the work is NEVER done! So where's the time for fun?"

"Hmm ..."

"I watched you last summer with the pool. You scrubbed it, vacuumed it, chlorinated it, backwashed it, and tested it constantly, but did you ever swim?"

"Not very much."

"You need to kick back and play more."

"Sometimes it irritates ME that you can play no matter what needs to be done. Remember when the McLains called and asked us to go on a picnic to Lewisville Park? You were right in the middle of wallpapering the little bathroom, but you said, 'Sure! We'd love to go!' I couldn't believe it! I wish you would take things a little more seriously."

"We're so different from each other, aren't we?"

"Yep. That's probably why, after twenty years, we're still intrigued with each other."

We were making progress, but there was still the issue of work loads to be discussed. I had abandoned the idea of throwing a time log in Danny's face because I decided I didn't have to prove my value that way, to him or anyone else!

Initially I had divided a piece of notebook paper in half lengthwise, with his name at the top of one side and mine at the top of the other, but, staring at the blank college rule, I changed my mind. I wasn't afraid to align my day with his, hour by hour; I just hated the nitpicky thought of, *Okay, let's see, it's 6:15. I'm making the coffee and what is HE doing? Ah ha! Still in bed, I see. LOG IT!*

I also hated it because of the ramifications of the hourly comparison. I could just hear what he'd be thinking: *It's 12:45 and I don't have the time to stop and eat! I wonder what SHE is doing. I think I'll call her at the office. "Hi, is Peggy there? She's at the Chat 'n' Chew? When did she leave? ... 11:30?"* (*Very interesting!*) *"Would you have her call me when her lunch hour and a half is over?"* I'll log in exactly how many minutes she spent eating!

Danny has no idea of how often I take a long lunch, spoiling my appetite and allowing me to give the impression at dinner that I eat like a bird. Depending on which day was being logged, the work load scale could tip in my favor or not. Some days, Danny works overtime or goes out of town, and he doesn't get home again until the next day or even the next week. That is the nature of his job. Other days, I'm the one who has to work late or travel. It would be very difficult to determine who is working the hardest, because we both work hard.

Apart from each other, we live completely different lives. He deals with all the ugliness in the world, and I'm a humorist. We couldn't be more opposite. If we were totally honest with each other, we would admit that neither of us really knows what the other's day is like. We do know that we wouldn't trade places with each other for anything!

Danny can't imagine how I can get up in front of a thousand people and give a speech, or go on television and not faint. He says it would scare him more than raiding an outlaw biker's party. (One time when he had to give the crime report on the local radio station, he said it was ninety seconds of hell! Unable to think of the word *deceased*, he said, "We are investigating the identity of the ... ah ... dead fellow." He was embarrassed!)

On the other hand, if I had to do the things Danny has

had to do, like wade through the filth of a drug dealer's house, wrestle a vomiting drunk into my car, hold a dying man's hand, break up a fight between a man and his wife, rescue a baby from a burning house, shoot a hit-and-run bank robber, go to an autopsy, or investigate a murder ... I couldn't!

One thing we do have in common is that we both know the feeling of working our faces off, with no rewards or applause. I have seen Danny's frustration at the end of a day when he has nothing to show for all of his efforts. He can work a case for months, finally arrest the crook, do all the paperwork, and, on the way home, pass the prisoner on the freeway because he's been released on bail or the jails are too crowded. Like homemaking, police work can be a thankless, losing battle.

I was sure that Danny admired my work from a distance, the same as I respected what he was doing. Still, I didn't think he would appreciate all the time I spent visiting with my sister. On a time log, it wouldn't look that good. I was afraid Danny wouldn't recognize the value of those "visits," even though they inevitably earned us a substantial amount of money. When we were together, we came up with our most profound thoughts, humorous viewpoints, and creative ideas, which turned into books, speeches, and television appearances. Was it our fault that we had so much fun while we worked? Maybe some things just weren't fair. Back home, at least, they weren't, and I was about to show my husband my new ideas for changing things on the home front. Perhaps what I wanted, almost more than a fifty-fifty deal, was appreciation for what I was doing to make our home an oasis from the world outside. I was doing more than Danny realized, and in his unknowingness he had been insensitive. We continued our talk.

"So what else?" he said.

"Have you noticed how neat the house has been lately?" I asked.

"Yes, I have, and I've wondered how long it will last."

Wanting to rip his tongue out, but containing myself for a more incisive victory, I deliberately put down my nail file, folded my hands, and proceeded to explain our new infraction game. With a feeling of importance, I presented him with his personal list of infractions for the last couple of days ($9.75 worth), then graciously reassured him that it was merely a probationary week, so he needn't actually pay.

I showed him, in writing, how his messes contributed to the conditions he so disliked. It was the first time he was aware that HIS stuff was cluttering the house as much as my unpacked suitcase had. He had to admit that the object of the game (lowest infractee takes all) was a most brilliant money twist, and the by-product of a clutter-free house was even more appealing.

"So, Danny, do I have your support?"

"Sure, I'll play."

With clutter out of the way, we moved on to the more delicate issue of his contribution to household responsibilities. I got to say all the things I had practiced on my sister and rehearsed in my mind. I didn't leave out a word, and I had his complete attention when I said, "It's no longer men's work or women's work! It is people-who-live-in-the-house work!" At one point, I had to ask Danny to relax his lips from an angry line and unfold his arms. He asked me to stop pointing at him and to contralto my voice.

"Can I read something to you?" I was holding some papers in my hand. "It's about Christmas." He had a pained look on his face, as if he were about to listen to an Edgar Allan Poe poem.

"Sure."

"It's a list of all the things that, traditionally, fall in a mother's lap." He listened as I read all the things that had to be done:

- Make a list of the holiday and family traditions to be followed
- Take the children to see Santa Claus
- Go caroling
- Find out what children and family members want for Christmas
- Make gift list for family, friends, neighbors, col leagues, employees, children's gifts to family, friends, and teachers
- Select gifts that must be mailed early
- Buy gifts that must be mailed early
- Take children shopping so that they can pick out their presents for each other, parents, grandparents, and teachers
- Mail the gifts
- Buy remainder of gifts (including extra gifts for those you forgot who might drop in)
- Buy stocking stuffers
- Buy wrapping paper, ribbons, gift cards, and tape
- Wrap the gifts
- Make card list (save for next year)
- Buy cards
- Address cards
- Buy stamps
- Mail early
- Rearrange furniture
- Order tree
- Pick up tree
- Buy and hang wreath
- Check decorations (crèche, tree stand)
- Check tree lights (replace bulbs)
- Make decorations (string popcorn and cranberries, make tree ornaments)
- Buy decorations (bulbs, tinsel, hooks)
- Trim the tree

- Clean the house
- Buy and arrange holly, mistletoe, flowers, and pine boughs
- Set up the candles
- Decorate the house (yard and outside the house)
- Place gifts under the tree
- Hang and stuff stockings
- Leave a snack for Santa near the tree
- Give tips, gifts, thanks, and appreciation to special people (milkman, mailman, paperboy, employees, garbage collector, hairdresser)
- Check after-holiday sales on Christmas gifts for next year.
- Remember the needy and donate to your favorite charity

"And now, Danny, you're finished, unless, of course, like last year, we're going to have another Christmas party. Then you need to:

- Decide on the date and the time
- Plan the guest list
- Write out directions to the house and duplicate it
- Call the guests
- Buy the stamps
- Send out the invitations and directions
- Plan the menu
- Make shopping list
- Order special holiday food (goose, seafood, plum pudding)
- Assess the need for a caterer or other help and hire
- Borrow/rent/buy tables, chairs, coatrack, bar, cof feemaker
- Wash/borrow/rent/buy dishes, cups, serving dishes, and punch bowl

- Wash/borrow/rent/buy glasses (wine, champagne, eggnog, punch)
- Polish/borrow/rent/buy silverware
- Polish trays and silver items (candlesticks and candy dishes
- Clean table linens, dish towels, and aprons
- Take out the napkin rings
- Refill salt and pepper shakers
- Prepare an outfit to be worn
- Check recipes for procedures to be done in advance
- Buy ingredients for special holiday treats (fruitcakes, candy, and cookies)
- Buy holiday candles
- Buy the beverages
- Replenish the bar with condiments and supplies (onions, olives, cherries, lemons, limes, oranges, and stirrers)
- Buy mixers and juices
- Buy film and flashbulbs
- Buy paper goods (paper towels, napkins, and toilet paper)
- Shop for the food
- Get money to cover all the expenses
- Make the ice
- Chill the beverages
- Make a list of cooking and serving chores
- Make holiday drinks (eggnogs and toddies)
- Prepare foods that can be made ahead of time
- Put out the guest towels
- Clear out the closet and set up a coatrack
- Prepare a place for boots and umbrellas
- Check outdoor lighting
- Load the camera
- Put out ashtrays and coasters
- Buy last-minute perishables

- Buy the flowers and make a centerpiece
- Cook
- Set the table
- Put out the ice bucket, tongs, condiments, and snacks
- Make the juices for the drinks
- Decant the wine
- Set up the coffeemaker and the teapot
- Prepare the sugar bowl, creamer, lemons, and teabags
- Put out the ice
- Heat up the toddies
- Set out the hors d'oeuvres
- Warm and prepare the serving dishes
- Serve and clean as you go
- Return the rented/borrowed items

"See, I do Christmas every year, and your part is licking envelopes! That's not fair."

"I guess not, but I can tell you, we'll never have another Christmas party! That's insanity!"

"And listen to this. There's another list in here for packing for a summer vacation...."

"Okay! Okay! Okay! I get the picture. What do you want me to do?"

"I want you to do your half."

It was the beginning of new awareness for my husband, and from that time on things were very different. In the next weeks, we redefined the game to cover gray areas, such as personal bedrooms. In the name of relaxation, the resident needed to be able to kick back and leave out a little, but we agreed that no laundry, dishes, trash, or unmade beds would be allowed.

To keep the children from nosing around each other's bedrooms and our own, in search of violations, we added an invasion-of-privacy clause, whereby minors were not permitted to infract anything in another person's bedroom. Only parental tagging in those rooms would be permitted.

We learned, in time, that if the infraction cards came down, so did the house. As embarrassing as it was, the degree of neatness in our home depended on the 3 x 5s on the bulletin board. We were accountable because of cash, but at least we were accountable.

(We also discovered that, if the losers didn't fork over the money within twenty-four hours, they got away without paying, because everybody was concentrating on the next week's game. We made a new rule to stop the boys from cheating their sister out of her due. If payment, in cash, wasn't received within twenty-four hours of the verified tally, players would owe double the amount, compounded daily.)

With Danny's input, the game was even more fun. We continued to make new rulings, like time-outs for illness, holidays, and vacations, and seventy-two-hour amnesty for schoolbooks left out during finals. A shower lasting more than seven minutes was declared a misdemeanor, stopping hot water hogs cold!

After playing the game for several weeks, we added the car and the yard ... and Styrofoam meat trays in the driveway were a thing of the bitter past.

Twelve

Keeping Up with the Joneses

From Pam:

Before I decided to try the infraction cards at my house, I watched Peggy and her family for more than four months. It was amazing how consistently tidy her house was. Each person had taken responsibility for his or her own belongings, and Danny had assumed a good portion of the household tasks. The yard, which had always looked good, was even neater because the whole family was doing their part.

It was summer now, and I was back to being a single mother with three children in the house. Mike and Peggy Ann were home from college and busy with their summer jobs. I knew if I didn't get control soon, I would once again experience a summer full of stress. I'd barely made it through spring break with a voice.

Terry did call me back after he had rested from dinner at my house, and we started seeing each other almost every day. We had met when we were thirteen. We'd gone through junior high school and high school together, and although we had never dated, we had always been good friends. We were cheerleading partners for three years in high school and spent hours with each other, practicing our routines with the rally squad. We were together every Friday night because there was always a game. Our scrapbooks have many pictures of us together ... because we always were. Now we were spending wonderful hours, remembering our happy days and planning new ones.

One night we were having dinner in a very romantic setting, discussing how compatible we were, when he said something that abruptly changed the tone of the evening. "I can see that there is a little difference in the way you live and the way I do." He looked as if he hoped I was listening.

"Really, and what is that?" I could feel a judgment coming my way, and I silently reminded myself that I take criticism very easily.

"I have noticed that you and your kids leave quite a bit of stuff out at your house." Mysteriously, he seemed to look like my mother for an instant.

Even though I knew it was generally true, I wanted him to be specific. "Like what, for instance?"

"Oh, like the blanket Joanna took when we went to watch the fireworks. It's August. The blanket has been in the entryway for over three weeks."

I suddenly knew how my sister had felt when she and Danny had had their huge fight. "Terry, that blanket is 100 percent wool, so I have to take it to the cleaners. I keep telling myself I have to go there, and then I get busy and forget. Since it's been out so long, I don't see it any more, and besides, Chelsea Marie is using it for a bed now." He seemed to understand.

I told him I really didn't think that the messy house would be a problem between us, because it had been bothering me for a couple of months and I intended to change things. I explained, rather defensively, that our book *Side-*

tracked Home Executives was wonderful for organizing household cleaning chores. I pointed out that my house was immaculate as far as floors, windows, bathrooms, woodwork, and everything else was concerned. He agreed that was true, and he seemed to be relieved I was aware of the other problem. Grateful that the discussion was over, we let the flickering candlelight and music regain their hold on us.

Spurred by the stimulating dinner conversation the night before and impressed with my sister's successful cleanup campaign, I decided I'd try the infraction game on MY family. Since Peggy had told me that during the first week they played the game she hadn't really charged the money, I decided to do the same thing.

I went through the house with four infraction cards (one for each person) and about fifty bright red dots. Instead of tagging something, putting the time on the dot, waiting an hour, and then writing the infraction on the card, I decided to dot and infract at the same time. I figured that, since I wasn't going to charge money for the first week, there was no need to give anyone an hour to put his or her things away.

In fifteen minutes I had filled up all the cards and had to write on the back of Mike's and mine. I put a dot on everything I could see that should be put away.

I discovered during the dotting process that, like the Fourth of July blanket, many of my belongings hadn't seemed like clutter to me. I had become oblivious to the fact that they contributed to the overall messiness of the house. The rule in Peggy's home—"If it isn't decorative, it isn't out"—didn't seem to apply to me. I had to be very careful to be objective. Did my pocket calculator really look that pretty on the kitchen counter? Was the world globe that attractive in the bathroom? (That room had the best light in the house, and Joanna and I had taken the awkward ball in there to examine Indonesia with my magnifying glass.) Were my shoes an accent under the lamp table? Was my purse a nice touch, hanging on the dining room chair?

When I finished dotting everything, the house looked as if somebody weird lived there. At twenty-five cents each, the infractions added up to a total of $14.75 that we would have had to pay if this weren't a probationary week. I didn't put away any of my stuff, because I wanted the kids to know that this was a problem we all needed to work on, including me. I couldn't wait for each of them to get home from work so I could show them what I'd done.

When I get a new idea in my head, whether I think it up myself or get it from somebody else, I lose all sense of timing. Invariably, I prematurely jump into sharing before the sharee has had a chance to think. Like the time I came home from Weight Watchers and shared the water rule I had learned with my sister. Marilyn, the group leader, had told us that she had lost 120 pounds in fourteen months, and that in the few weeks she didn't have a weight loss, she could directly attribute it to NOT drinking eight glasses of water. Peggy said she and Danny would try to follow the rule. Later she told me that Danny had bucked at the idea because he said he'd feel like a fool, filling an eight-ounce glass at the drinking fountain in the police station.

I knew there had to be a solution. A couple of weeks later, as I was drinking one of my waters, I got the idea to count the gulps it took to finish the glass. It took fifteen gulps. I immediately called Peggy and passed on the information. She called Danny and he said he'd try out my idea. It wasn't until the next day that I found out he was mad at me. She said that he had had trouble the day before, drinking so much water. He had called her from work and complained that he couldn't leave the station for very long, because he had to keep going to the bathroom. Peggy had told him that I said that, when you first start drinking the amount of water you need, it will seem like too much because you aren't used to consuming the proper amount.

The next morning while he was standing at the sink, drinking his first glass of the day, Danny had inadvertently started counting his gulps. It seems it only took five swallows and the glass was empty! How was I to know that people's gulps are different? We figured that Danny must have drunk about forty glasses of water that day. It was no wonder he couldn't leave the police station.

This new game idea was far more exciting than gulping water, and I could hardly wait for the kids to get home. As usual, my enthusiasm for a new idea caused my timing to be terrible. Mike came home first. I nailed him just as soon as he was through the door. I didn't give him a chance to unwind and cool off from the summer heat; I slapped the infraction card in his face like a ticket-happy cop and started in on him. "Mike, things are going to change around here, and I'm starting with you. This is what you call an infraction card. It's got your name on the top, and your sisters and I each have one of our own. I went around the house today and I found twenty-seven clutter violations on you alone! That comes to six dollars and seventy-five cents!"

"What? Why?"

"Each infraction costs twenty-five cents, but I'm not going to charge you anything yet. You'll have a week of probation. But just look at this." I handed him the official-looking infraction card. "There are dish, glass, spoon, and fork infractions, some dirty underwear violations, and some miscellaneous messes, like the shaving stuff you left out. That one mess alone would have cost you one dollar and twenty-five cents!"

"Mom, chill out!"

"Do what?"

"Chill."

"Don't get sassy with me, Michael. This is my house, and if you are going to stay here, you will have to live by the rules! From now on, nothing will be left out unless it's decorative. That means your briefcase and backpack are out of the living room. That also means if you eat a piece of pie and you don't clean up after yourself, it will cost you a dollar and a quarter. A quarter for the knife you used to cut the pie, a quarter for the plate, a quarter for the fork, a quarter for the glass of milk you drank to wash the pie down, and a quarter for the crumbs you left when you cut the pie.

"See, what you'll do is, when you cut a piece of pie, you'll put the knife in the dishwasher. Then when you pour yourself a glass of milk, you'll put the milk carton away. Then you'll eat the piece of pie, drink the milk, and put the dish, fork, and glass in the dishwasher with the knife. Then you'll brush the crumbs off the kitchen counter into your hand and throw the crumbs into the garbage can under the sink. No, on second thought, you'll clean up the crumbs BEFORE you eat the pie. Oh! And if the bag under the sink just happens to be full, you'll empty it in the garbage can in the garage." I was out of breath.

"Mom, is there pie?"

"No, that was just an example of a typical mess I end up cleaning up. I'm not going to do it any more. I'm sick and tired of being everyone's slave. Oh, I almost forgot. If you have friends over, you will be infracted for their messes. I can think of one particular night of entertainment that would have cost you about eleven thousand dollars!"

"Mom, it's a hundred two degrees outside. Could I get out of this suit before I clean up my stuff?"

"Yes, but after this week there will be a time written on an infraction dot. The rule at Aunt Peg's house is that you have an hour from the time you are dotted."

Peggy Ann came home next. She had been working at Super Tan as a receptionist.

"Peggy, this is called an infraction card. On it is a list of items you've left out. It adds up to five dollars and fifty cents."

"Mom, I'm sunburned, and you know I don't have five dollars and fifty cents. Besides, you didn't give me any warning!"

"I won't start charging for a week."

"How am I supposed to pay after a week is up? I have to save my money for college!"

"Well, maybe you'll have to quit school."

I explained the rules in detail to her, and I had one more kid to go. Like a spider, I waited for Joanna to get home from her babysitting job. She was the least guilty of messes. She came in around 5:30 and plopped down on the couch with a growl. "Oh, those Hinds kids! What a couple of brats! Mom, you wouldn't believe how awful they are! The parents don't believe in saying 'No!' Jamie got mad at me because she wanted to watch cartoons and I was watching 'Days,' so she went over and pulled the cat's tail. Sometimes when she gets mad at me, she takes it out on the cat. So I go, 'Don't be mean to the cat!' and she goes, 'She likes it,' and I go, 'I'm sure! She does not.' Then Mark comes in and he flicks the TV while we're arguing. Oh, Mom, I don't know how I'm going to last the whole summer over there."

"Joanna, I'm sorry, but I have to change the subject for a sec. This is an infraction card. Notice your name is on it. So far today, you owe one dollar and fifty cents. You left out your manicure stuff, and you need to take the blanket that's in the hall and put it out in the car. I'm going to take it to the cleaners."

"Mom, that's not fair. Mike and Peg have junk out all over the house."

"I know that, and from now on it's going to cost them." When I explained how the new system worked, I could see the money light go on in her little blonde head. Her natural ability to keep things neat would now pay off in cash.

The system soon worked wonders in our house, and if it hadn't been for the fact that I jumped on my kids before they had a chance to relax after work, it would have been an almost perfect transition. It was not surprising that in that first week of playing the game, I was the one with the most infractions. Mike was a close second, Peggy Ann was third, and, of course, Joanna would have won the pot.

I have to say there were quite a few fights at the refrigerator, where the infraction cards were taped. When you are guilty, it's very hard to find out that you have been written up for something, but it makes you nuts to be written up when you are innocent. A good example was the time Mike wrote Peggy up for leaving a cereal bowl in the sink. Peggy was innocent, so she crossed through the infraction notation with a bold line and wrote, "NO WAY!" Then she turned her vengeful pen onto Joanna's infraction card and wrote her up for the bowl. By the end of the day, the children's cards were severely defaced by the dueling pens, and the cereal bowl was mine.

We had to make a rule that NO ONE was allowed to cross off an infraction without a group hearing. We decided to have a question mark infraction card so that, if there is doubt about an item, it can be written up and investigated later.

I discovered that, just as at Peggy's house, if the infraction cards were not posted every week, the house would fall back into a state of chaos. It was maddening to think that a few stupid little 3 × 5 cards and some fluorescent red dots stood between clutter and order, but it was wonderful to realize that those simple tools worked to change things drastically.

One morning, while we were talking to our agent, John Boswell, discussing the proposal for this book, he asked, "Why do you really think the game works so well?" We both said it was the money that spawned such enthusiasm. He laughed. "Do you mean to tell me that you think a forty-year-old man is inspired by a pot of change at the end of a week?" We had to admit that that did sound a little stupid.

"You guys really don't know, do you?"

"Well, then, smartypants, why DOES it work?"

"Competition. It's plain and simple ... COMPETITION!"

We had to think about that for a while. It was true that competition was half of it, but we realized that there was more ... the other half was GOOD SPORTSMANSHIP!

From the time men are little boys (and we know this from rearing three of them ourselves), they are taught to be good sports, and they will do nearly anything to prove that they are. Competition is inherent in the genes of every American male. It's the sport of it, and in any competition "good sports" play by the rules.

Ice hockey is a perfect example. We went to a game once and thought it was hysterical that tough, aggressive athletes would be willing to sit in a naughty box for breaking a rule by being too wild. There isn't a man alive, in his right mind, who would consent to sit somewhere in a pen as a punishment for being unruly, unless it was one of the rules of the game.

Call it good sportsmanship and you can get eleven tough men to stop frantically grappling for an elusive football ... just by throwing a hanky into the air. Call it good sportsmanship and nine giant men will stand with their toes exactly on the line, while the player who was roughed up gets one or two chances to throw a ball through a ring without anybody messing with him.

Call it a game and a man will pay thousands of dollars to be part of an elite club, wear special clothes, and drive a popsicle-type truck all over several hundred acres of grassland, smacking a little dimpled ball toward designated holes in the lawn. In the name of good sportsmanship, the same man who leaves his dirty tracks across a newly waxed kitchen floor will actually stop his game and rake his footprints out of a patch of sand he's had to walk through to whack his ball out of the grains.

Sportsmanship at home! That was it! It was competition and being a good sport that motivated each person in the family, especially the man of the house, to play by "the new house rules of order." We think that, on the playing fields, competition motivates athletes to win, because they hate to lose. We also think that the rules for good sportsmanship were invented because the athletes wouldn't play fair without them. If we were right, our home Infraction game would work with anyone who loves that "Wide World of Sports."

We all know that women are not going to get the cooperation they need from men by using the old feminine tricks of whining, manipulating, conniving, and nagging. Butting egos with the opposite sex doesn't work, either. It's time to try a fresh approach, one that includes LOVE and LAUGHTER. One with a united motive: more time to spend with each other, loving, laughing, and living in a home where there is peace, joy, and order.

Thirteen

The 50/50 Family

Once your husband realizes how important HE is to the success of a messless house, you are on your way to a 50/50 family.

Our definition of a 50/50 family is one in which the husband and wife stand together as an example of cooperation. To be that wonderful example to the children, the mother and father, if they both work outside of the home, must spend an equal share of time and energy on household maintenance and childcare. That doesn't mean that one week the husband cleans the toilet and takes the kids to ballet lessons, and the next week the wife does it. It means that the couple is more aware of the time and energy each spends working at home, and there is a sincere attempt to share the enormous burden, equally.

Today about 50 percent of all marriages end in divorce. Statistics show that it is usually the woman who throws in the towel, along with all the rest of the laundry. Judging by most of the people we know who have divorced, we think that almost all of those marriages probably could have been saved. Perhaps the truth behind courtroom scenes is that the couples aren't as overwrought with each other as they are with their SITUATIONS. When a situation gets out of hand, it's easy to lose your perspective and confuse the two. If the house is a mess and all you do is complain and whine, pretty soon no one listens to you. Everyone knows how long you'll nag before you explode, and they'll ride your fuse to the wire. If you choose to keep quiet and pick up after everyone yourself, you end up feeling like a martyr. Your resentment escalates, and before you know it you are a gritchy, exhausted lump of nagging humanity. You feel as if nobody cares. You look at your husband and children in anger instead of understanding. You feel a sense of futility.

The good news is that being upset with a situation is far less critical than being upset with a person, because you can change situations. Homes CAN become neat and stay that way. When a house is orderly and the woman is no longer solely responsible for making it that way, she will then have more energy to be fun-loving, kind, and nurturing.

With everyone working together, housework is not the giant bore it used to be. Even the kids do their share of the action cards. Through the years, as we improved our system, we came up with a great way to compensate them.

Each action card has a time estimate on it. That number is the key to our point system. We assigned a point value to every job in our homes, according to how long the job takes. We made each point equivalent to one minute of help. For example, if one of the cards says it takes twenty minutes, that job is worth 20 points. We keep track of points on charts that are posted in a central place.

A chart (see an example of one of our charts on page 195) has a place for the person's name and columns for the description of the job; the point value (20 points for twenty minutes); parent verification (each job must be inspected by a parent and initialed); the date; and the balance forward. A running balance is kept so that at any time it is very clear how many points a person has. The points are worth money, merchandise, or special parental services.

No matter what the age of a child, there are things he or she wants. Young children may want to have a friend spend the night or play at the park, go to the show or visit the zoo. Older children want the keys to the family car. Since children are always going to want SOMETHING as long as they live in your home, you have a perfect opportunity to teach them to help, in trade for what they want. This barter method impresses upon kids that life isn't free. There is a price for everything.

A value must be previously assigned to all of your services so that when one is needed your child knows how many points he or she must collect to afford that service. We post a list of services and their price. We charge 250 points for one of our children's friends to spend the night. (That service includes popping popcorn, renting a movie, and fixing a midnight snack.) To go roller-skating is 175 points. Charging points for using the car was inspired by Hertz—and the teen is charged by the mile. You need to set your own value on services, based on how valuable they are to your children, and it is very important to have it in writing!

If the points are cashed in for money, we decided that one cent per minute was sufficient payment for simple jobs. Sweeping the deck would be worth twenty cents if the sweeper wanted to convert his or her work to cash. Bigger jobs for bigger kids, such as washing the car, fixing dinner, mowing the lawn, or cleaning the fireplace, would have a greater value than a penny a minute. You decide.

We have thought of several other ways children can rack up points. We give them for grades (As are worth 500 points, Bs are worth 300 points, and Cs just mean that the child has the privilege of living in the home through the next semester). We also give bonus points for compliments our children get from adults. For instance, if someone says one of our children was kind and gracious on the telephone, that compliment is worth 25 points. If we ever catch one of our kids being nice to his or her sibling, we give bonus points.

Any jobs that are performed voluntarily are worth double-point value.

If you are like we are, you hate the idea of keeping track of information, but once you post these charts (and you stand strong against requests without earned points), your children will begin to see the value in keeping track of the information on their own.

This chart idea has several uses. We have a friend who decided to use it to track the behavior of the guy she had been going with for three years. She loved him, but the man was a workaholic, and the relationship seemed to be stuck in the waist-deep piles of his work load.

She decided to keep a running balance of what he contributed to the relationship, the same way we keep track of our kids' job contributions. In time it was clear that the beau wasn't committed to the relationship with the same quality of caring that our friend was. After charting him for several months on paper, she could see, in black and white, that the man spent very little time and energy enriching their relationship.

He received 250 points for remembering her birthday and another 100 points for giving her a card with a puppy on the cover, since she loved dogs. She gave him several hundred points for just being great company (the one day a week they saw each other). He lost 200 points when Valentine's Day came and he gave her a scraggly potted geranium with the PayLess sticker still on the bottom of the plastic flower pot. (This man was not cheap. He had just run out of time and opted for a quick stop at any open store he could find.) He gained 350 points for fixing her dripping sink and 400 points whenever he said "I love you," rather than "Me, too." Because she was usually the one to say it first, the courter only picked up 800 points.

He lost 2,000 points for not being with her when her dad had open-heart surgery and 500 points for not calling to see how he was doing. He got docked another 1,500 points for letting her think he had gone to Germany for three weeks when, in fact, he had stayed home and caught up on back work that all workaholics always have. He lost points every time he waited until Friday to call for their one week-end date. Every time he was late, it cost him 100 points (which totaled 1,200 points over the three-month period she charted him). The chart went on and on, and in the end, even though she loved him, she broke up with him.

Life has a way of slipping away, and if it is not going in the direction you want it to, you could end up wasting your life in the hopes that someday things will change. Charting what is happening will put your life in a different perspective.

Pam ... er ... our friend didn't show the man his point chart, because she fell in love with Terry and ceased caring if the man changed or not. The gray flannel suitor went away without the slightest clue that he was 3,550 points in the hole. Perhaps if he had seen his behavior in writing, he would have had a desire to change, but as far as our friend knows, he is probably repeating the same neglectful behavior in his current relationship.

We think one of the reasons that sports are big all over the world is because of the word "point." If points were not bestowed in games, no one would care much about the activity taking place on the field or court or table or any other surface. If you think about it, points are really silly. Yet everybody keeps score. We ask the score, argue the score, boast the score, celebrate the score; and the only way to have a score is to keep track of points. What is a point, anyway? A point is a unit of value in the eye of the beholder.

We learned early in our business career, working together almost every day, that points were valuable to the two of us. We are always giving each other points for remembering things, for knowing something the other one doesn't know, for working longer than the other one. We never keep track of them on paper, and we wouldn't know what to do with them if we did, but they have given us a real, tangible energy that mysteriously accompanies appreciation.

It is not easy for some people to give and receive compliments. Maybe they don't know what to say or how to say it. It is also socially unacceptable to ask for compliments, even though most of us would love more recognition. For us, the points have turned into a wonderful way to recognize each other's value. Whenever either of us feels we have not received enough credit for something we have done, it is so much easier to say, "Hey, I need some more points for that" than to say, "I need to be told how great I am for doing what I did."

We suggest that you take the chart on page 195 and make several copies. Give one to each of your children and explain how the reward system works. If you are going to start infracting the people in your house, you might as well get them all started helping more with the housework at the same time.

Previously, we instructed workshoppers, "Establish order yourself first, and your family will follow your lead." That's a crock! Well, it's partly a crock. It is true that if you want to have things change in your house, it will help if you change some of YOUR messy habits before you start involving your family. (Chances are good that you are one of the major contributors to the havoc in your home.)

We suggest that you spend at least a week watching yourself. Before you get a bunch of colored dots and start slapping them on everything that isn't decorative, start mentally infracting yourself, and you'll end up becoming very aware of some of your careless habits. You might as well get a jump on your family. In that week, think about the changes that are going to take place in your home, and watch your husband and children to observe their infractibility.

With a week of self-observation on your side, you'll be ready to present this new plan to your family. But one word of caution. Positioning is crucial, and just as our government spends years positioning itself for Mideast peace talks, you need to be very careful about the timing for yours. Your FIRST shot is going to be your BEST shot! Prepare for it. Have it in writing when you talk to your husband. Then the two of you can present it to the children as a united front.

We know that a 50/50 deal is a little unreasonable to expect, at least at first; but the trend is far more important than instant results. (A potato baked in the oven at 400 degrees for an hour is so much better than a russet nuked for ten minutes in the microwave.)

People really do not like change, especially if it means more work. Be patient and praise every bit of improvement you see in your family. There is nothing more effective than appreciation in speeding up the trend of cooperation.

The change that will take place in you will be especially wonderful. The time and energy you used to spend trying to get cooperation will now be there for you to use for more positive things. Your family will be amazed at what a different person you are. You won't be nagging anymore. You'll have leisure time to nap, play, and relax, and you will be so surprised that at the end of the day you will actually have energy left over for romance.

Family values are in a transitional time right now. The new direction must be toward more cooperation. If each member of your family can clearly see that the changes will benefit everyone, then a 50/50 family is definitely a possibility in your home.

POINT CHART FOR:

DATE	ACTIVITY	VALUE	BALANCE FORWARD	✔

Fourteen

A Mother's Day That Really Was

From Peggy:
   A few days before Mother's Day last year, Danny said to me, "This year we're going to do something different for Mother's Day! We're not all gonna go out for dinner and stand in those long lines, waiting for a table, like we do every year." I stared at him suspiciously. Surely he wouldn't DARE suggest that I prepare the meal! So what did he have in mind? "I'm going to take care of the dinner myself," he boasted. My suspicion turned to concern.

   Danny is not renowned as a chef. Over the last few years he had learned a few basics, but a galloping gourmet he was not! True, he'd made great strides since that first Saturday breakfast he'd fixed and brought to me on a tray. I had been given hot coffee and a bowl of chili with onions and cheese sprinkled on top. (My niece, Joanna, was spending the weekend with us and later she told her mom, "There's no place like Aunt Peg's on a Sunday, but you never want to be there on Saturday!")

   Being careful not to show my true feelings, which I feared would discourage Danny's efforts, I was falsely delighted with the breakfast. "Mmmm ... chili ... with onions, too ... I'll bet this'll hit the spot!"

"Yeah, I couldn't control the onion very well, though, so some of the chunks might be a little too big. How do you keep it from rolling around while you're chopping at it?"

Now, just a short time later, he was a chop-o-matician. He'd learned the correct way to chop onions, slice mushrooms, cut potatoes, dice tomatoes, and cube cheese; but prepare a whole dinner for company?

"Really? You're going to do the whole thing yourself?"

"No, I don't think I'll do it all myself. I'll make it a potluck. I'll call my dad and your dad and Terry and get them to bring filler, but I'll do the main dish."

"Filler?"

"Yeah, you know, baked beans and stuff."

"Mmmm ... baked beans and stuff ... I'll bet that'll hit the spot!"

"I'll call everybody and set it up. Just give me the phone numbers and you won't have to lift a finger." Danny called the greenhorn trio, and each one agreed to bring the assigned "filler." Meanwhile, I made three follow-up calls to the mothers. I asked them to refrain from taking over, even if the food contribution was an embarrassment. The women agreed to sit back and let the men culinate.

Terry was the baked-bean man, but he hit a snag at the grocery store, trying to pick out dry beans that were the "right color." He called Pam for help. "The brown ones say 'kidney beans,' but aren't those what you get at a salad bar?" My sister advised him to go to the canned goods section (he knew the aisle number from his premarital days) and pick up a couple of B&Ms and then "doctor" them with just the right blend of sautéed onions, crumbled bacon, Worchestershire, Grey Poupon, garlic, and chili powder. He seemed semirelieved.

Dad was in charge of providing the salad, and as a

pleasant twist he chose a recipe called "Tropical Fruit Festival," the makings of which cost about thirty-five dollars. He elected to peel, pit, and prepare the fruit the night before (a decision that made Mom get out the Mylanta). Reading from the red-checkered cookbook, Dad was at an impasse. "Mom, where do we keep the bias?" "What?" "The bias, where is it? I'm supposed to cut this kiwi on the bias."

Danny's dad was assigned the dessert. He "U-picked" and finely sliced an entire flat of strawberries, purchased those packaged, yellow Styrofoamlike shortcake replicas, and a spray can of whipped aircream, and he was ready for the party!

The Mother's Day celebration was to commence at 2:00 P.M. on Sunday. At noon, Danny (the "entree"preneur) was still chaised out in his robe with the morning paper. As the stove's digital advanced, I couldn't stand it any longer! I didn't smell anything cooking, the table hadn't been set, hors d'oeuvres were nonexistent, and I broke.

"So, Babe, what're you going to serve for the main dish?"

"I don't know ... I thought I'd go to the Food Pavilion and see what looks good."

"Mmmm ... that should work."

"Yeah. Maybe I'll do a chicken."

"Uh-huh. Chicken's always good."

"Yeah. Do you have a recipe for that Veal Pavarotti stuff you make?"

"Veal Scallopini?"

"Yeah."

"Gee, Babe, do you really want to get that involved? It's past noon."

"Nah, I better not chance it. I guess I'll barbecue."

"Uh-huh. Good idea. You might want to be gettin' over to that Food Pavilion pretty soon now. I think you're gonna be losin' your light here before too long."

"Yeah, I'd better get my shower and head out."

I was a nervous wreck! Danny seemed oblivious to the fact that, in less than two hours, fourteen people would be sitting down at a blank table.

Returning from the store with an assortment of poultry parts, he went to work. He carefully scrubbed each one, as if preparing it for surgery. He made barbecue "dip." He said that he didn't want sauce; he wanted to dip the parts in the goop, not mess around having to paint them with a brush. I explained that the recipe would be the same, whether he dipped or painted. He was pleased.

He took the raw chicken outside to the cold Weber as if he expected to turn a knob, like on the stove, and the coals would be glowing. He brought the chicken back into the house and asked me where I kept the charcoal lighter fluid. The next time I looked outside, flames were high above the grill, threatening to torch the bill of Danny's baseball cap, and Danny was standing back, with new respect for the container of Squeeze-A-Flame. I had to look away.

It was two o'clock. With singed eyebrows and red cheeks, Danny greeted the hungry guests. The proud culinarians carried their efforts to the kitchen, like 4-H-ers bringing their entries to the fair. Each one eyed the other's exhibit, anxious for the judging to begin, but I reminded them that we couldn't eat until the table was set. They all looked disappointed.

I turned to the other mothers and asked them if they would like to join me in a game of pool while the men set their table. Although pool is nothing any of us would ever want to play, they all accepted the invitation.

Downstairs at the pool table, we realized that no one knew the rules, so we made them up. We called the game "Ball in the Pants," and it went something like this: We would all use the same pole and take turns hitting whichever ball looked good. If the ball went into one of

the pockets, the hitter had to take it out and put it in one
of her own pockets. If her pockets were full, she could put
the ball any place in her clothing as long as it would stay
there without dropping. (Mom was actually so good at it
that she got to put two balls in her bra because her pockets were already full.) We were having a great time when
Danny announced over the intercom, "Come on, everybody, dinner's on the table!"

"Okay," my sister lilted, "we'll be up as soon as the game
is over." I covered my mouth to keep the gasp from trans-
mitting into the kitchen, and we all got hysterical at the
thought of turning the tables on our mates.

The table was set! The guests of honor had special
plates, covered with shiny aluminum foil. (I learned later
that the purpose of the foil was more functional than
decorative. It was to save the men from having to wash
the dishes!) We each took our places at the feast table.
Everything looked delicious! We were quite amazed. In
their preparations, the men had only neglected one small
thing ... the children.

"Looks real good, Dad. Where are we supposed to eat?"
Chris looked around for more plates. Danny grabbed a stack
of paper plates for the six starving outcasts and let them
serve themselves from our table. Reaching over the seated
guests to fill their wobbly plates, they seemed like partakers
of a hot meal at a soup kitchen. They took their pitiful por-
tions and went off somewhere to eat by themselves.

The meal was delicious! The proud men traded recipes
and watched to see whose dish was the most popular.
When we were finished eating, I said, "Great dinner, Babe!
How 'bout another game of Ball in the Pants, ladies?"

We left the men to their kitchen cleanup and retired to
the family room. We found it interesting how fast they
were able to finish their work. They didn't chat or nibble
on leftovers; THEY CLEANED. They were janitorial team-
mates, there to do a nasty job and do it fast!

There was only one casualty that wonderful Mother's Day ... my ceramic turkey platter. (Danny had put the barbecued chicken on it and put it in a 400-degree oven to stay warm while he set the table.) We don't know how the men will outdo themselves next year, but we're going to let them try!

Fifteen

A Critical Message

From Peggy:
As you already know, we totally understand the problems connected with being disorganized. Mail comes from sister slobs who scrawl page after page on odd tablet paper they borrowed from their kids or motel stationery they brought home from a vacation. The envelopes seldom match, and often the paper and envelope are marked with a coffee cup ring, crayon, or some unidentifiable stains, which the writer apologizes for, explaining that if she rewrites the letter it'll never get mailed. The dates on the letters are usually several weeks earlier than the postmarks, indicating that lack of stamps probably held up the mailings.

Our pen pals aren't interested in the seven (or even three and a half) habits of highly effective people. We've already established that those books are for people who already are effective. Our readers aren't in the Superwoman syndrome; they're on a merry-go-round. One woman begged, "Please write a book on how to just get by!" We wrote back to her and gave her seven secrets of minimally effective people. Hints like: "Sleep in your jogging suit. It's better than hanging around the house all day in your nightgown. If you have to run to the store, spritz your hair with a bit of water, slip a sweat band around your forehead, smooth a little Vaseline on your face, over some blush, for an exercised look, and step lively down the aisles as if you're still in cool-down. If you've slept in the suit more than one night, you'll look just like a marathoner."

To the woman who had a critical, condescending husband who wondered what she did all day (besides raise three children under the age of four), we wrote, "Just before Mr. Tudball gets home from work, dab a bit of Pinesol behind your ears and around the doorjamb, get out the ironing board (put the dog out so he won't bark at the two-legged intruder), hang a bunch of clean shirts on several doors, and scratch your fingers across a chocolate candy bar so it goes underneath your fingernails. Meet him at the door with a kiss, show him your nails, and say, 'Are these working hands or what?' "

People who are born organized do not understand us. They would never think to tell somebody to fake organization. Ordell wouldn't dream of using our recipe for "the smell of apple pie."

Purchase an apple pie from your favorite bakery. Remove the pie from its cardboard box. (Burn the box or discard it in the neighbor's garbage can.) Place the pie in your own pie tin. Note: Bakery pies are usually eight inches, while most household pie tins are nine. If the store-bought pie is smaller than your tin, simply press the pastry down until it fits, giving it an even more "genuine" home look. Meanwhile, combine the following:

one tablespoon flour
one tablespoon cooking oil
one tablespoon water

one teaspoon each: cloves, nutmeg, and cinnamon
one apple core

Mix ingredients in a disposable tin (chicken pot pie size). Shove the apple core into the center of the dough and bake at 225 degrees, all day. (For the smell of pumpkin pie on Thanksgiving, substitute a chunk of the jack-o-lantern on the front porch from Halloween.)

Once in a while we get a letter from an "Ordelly" who is irritated by our orderly accomplishments. One woman typed a quick note to us on lovely bond with a matching envelope and wax seal. She said, "I just completed reading your book and found it very interesting. Little did I know, my natural knack for organization could bring me dollars. I regret not having been as clever as you, as I too could have marketed my skills."

Over the years, we have been intimidated by born-organized people. We are always defending ourselves against their condescending observations and remarks.

Ring, ring, ring ...

"Hello?"

"Ooooooooo, Sissy, that Lillian Buckflank makes me sooo mad!"

"Who?"

"She's so smug! I was at the Urgency Treatment Center today and she's a receptionist th ..."

"Sissy, what happened?"

"Nothing. Ally just needed her sports physical. But anyway ..."

"How come you didn't take her to Dr. Ruiz?"

"I found out you have to have an appointment way ahead, and I couldn't get her in before volleyball practice starts, so I had to take her to one of those walk-in places."

"Ooo. Where is it?"

"Over by The Sink & Shears."

"I've never been there."

"You know that place where they wash your hair and cut it and you go away wet, but it's real cheap and you don't need an appointment?"

"I know where you mean. I hate their commercial."

"They've got a commercial?"

"Just on channel 52."

"You watch channel 52?"

"Yeah, once in while I like to watch Dog Court, where the dog-control people catch dogs at large with no licenses. Then the owners have to claim 'em and tell how they got out."

"So how come you hate the commercial?"

"Huh?"

"The Sink & Shears commercial."

"I don't know. It just makes me mad."

"Oh, yeah, speaking of mad, back to Lillian Buckflank."

"I don't know her, do I?"

"She's Larry Buckflank's mom. You've probably never met her, but she's irked me ever since we were room mothers for Chris's kindergarten class. The first time we met, I was in that huge dog costume you made and I was late to the Halloween party because I'd run out of gas and had to walk all the way down Hazel Dell Avenue to the school. You know how heavy that dog head is!"

"How come you didn't take it off?"

"I was carrying three dozen melting Dixie Cups, and, anyway, at that point I thought it was better to keep it on as a disguise. I was embarrassed. I had to pass a street crew by the Grange and it was humiliating."

"Lots of grown-ups wear costumes on Halloween."

"Yeah, but it was Friday, and Halloween wasn't till Sunday. I was a hit once I got to the school, but Lillian, in her black skirt and white blouse, just stared at me and pointed out how late I was. The teacher had told us to wear costumes, but Buckflank's idea of a costume was to wear

Larry's Mickey Mouse ears with a red polka-dot bow pinned to 'em."

"Whoa, that's pretty creative."

"Yeah, really. Since we got organized, it's bugged her to death! Today she really rubbed it in about where I had to take Ally for her physical. She smirked, 'Why, Peggy, I thought you were supposed to be so organized.'"

"She's just jealous."

"But you know how it makes you mad when you get accused of being disorganized when it doesn't have anything to do with organization. We didn't know when practice was going to start, and when the school sent the letter home, it was too late to go to our family doctor. It was the school's fault. Then you show up as a desperate walk-in and YOU look like the one who didn't plan ahead."

"Yeah, and somebody like Buckflap ..."

"Flank."

"Whatever ... would just tell her kid, 'Volleyball's out!' She couldn't handle the curve."

"Yeah, that's probably true."

"I think that the truth is, Lillian would probably like to be more like you. I'll bet she doesn't have a playful bone in her body."

"Maybe you're right. Once when we were doing the hearing tests on all the kids, she said, 'Oh, Peggy, you'll appreciate this. I did something the other day that made me think, *That's something crazy like Peggy would do!*'"

"I hate it when people use words like 'crazy' instead of funny."

"Yeah, like you're nuts or something."

"So what'd she do?"

"I was hoping it would be something like the dog suit deal, but she said, 'The other day at the bank, I made my deposit like I usually do, and when I got home I realized I had forgotten to get my deposit receipt. Well, I went straight back to the bank and told the teller that I'd forgotten to get my receipt and she said she knew I'd be back! Well, we had our little joke, but when I got out to the car, I checked my receipt against my check stub and I realized that I had accidentally put my paycheck in checking instead of savings!! I laughed so hard I thought someone was going to hear me.'"

"HO, HO, HO, what a riot!"

"Yeah, I wish you could have seen my face, listening to her."

"I can picture it. It's the same face I've had listening to you tell the whole thing."

"You want to go over to Mom's?"

"Yeah, what time is it?"

"Five to four."

"FIVE TO FOUR? I was supposed to pick up Ally after practice at 3:30!"

The truth is, as Sarah Lee says, "Everybody doesn't like something." If you get accosted or get put down by some humorless ho ho when you know you are doing your best, don't forget who the accostee is. That person probably vacuums indoor pets and is so knotted up inside that personal validation can only be found in someone else's turmoil. You are the heartbeat of your home! You'll never be so rigid that you can't change directions. You'll never put things before people. You'll never give up having fun. Although it is the most demanding, complicated, and mind-boggling of life's commissions ... you are a HOME-MAKER!

FROM PAM:

If you have read any of our other books, you know that I had an extremely unhappy marriage, but today I am remarried and happy beyond anything I could imagine! My first husband was cantankerous, cranky, and critical, and I have tried to help other women who have chosen to live with a person bearing those difficult three "C"s.

We know, from reading our mail from people all over the country, that most of the homemakers who are getting their acts together have husbands and families who are supportive of their desire to get organized. The hundreds of success letters we receive yearly usually express appreciation for supportive spouses. It doesn't surprise us to hear of the great and wonderful changes that happen when loved ones nurture and sustain the one who is challenging a major problem like being disorganized. It also doesn't surprise us when we receive letters asking for help from those who do NOT receive encouragement and even receive criticism from the people closest to them.

When I was a slob, my husband and I fought daily over the mess. He was frustrated with me and rightfully so. After all, I was a full-time homemaker and he worked very hard in the business world. Today, I can put myself in his place and feel how powerless he was to get me to change something that affected both of us. I know people can change, but they do it when they are ready. There is a wise saying: "No one can make anyone do anything they don't want to do."

In my case, on June 16, 1977, when I really decided I wanted to change, we had three children, ages twelve, nine, and three. For fourteen years we had struggled with the effects of MY problem. However, when I began to get control of things, my husband did not support me. He subtly put me down with comments like, "I wonder how long this kick is gonna last?" or "I told you that's what you should do, years ago. Now you're acting like it's your big idea." He would shake his head and point out all the things that were still out of control, instead of acknowledging the changes that were gradually taking place.

We keep telling you that climbing out from under the rubble takes time. It's the trend that counts. No one gets into a mess overnight, and no one will get out of it in twelve hours.

In the beginning, the person desiring to change has a lot of self-doubt. Criticism only confirms that self-doubt and prolongs the time it takes to truly change. I know from experience that criticism took its toll on my energy level, back when I was getting organized. Energy I could have used to chip away at the problem. My sister and I are very thankful to have been raised by wonderful parents who taught us to allow no one to cause us to doubt our ability to succeed. I used that idea over and over again when faced with my husband's negativity, and I won the battle in spite of him.

If you are married to a critical person, you have two options. One, you can let him win and you both lose, because you'll eventually give up and quit. Or you can get stronger! (The person with a supportive husband doesn't have the benefit of that negativity.) It takes an extremely strong person to take flack from another individual and still win. When you win, so will the critical partner (at least, as far as your problem is concerned). Remember, people who are critical have a much bigger problem than people who are disorganized. A person who criticizes was usually criticized when he/she was a child and consequently has extremely low self-esteem, which usually messes up relationships, not rooms in houses.

You have your work cut out for you. If you are married to a critical husband, he has his work cut out for him. Do not let anyone, husband, sister, mother, mother-in-law, friend, ANYONE, cause you to doubt your ability to succeed! You will succeed if you want to, with or without the support of someone else; and when you have accomplished your goal, it will be of little consequence that someone in the background was less than a mature person about his/her part in the picture.

If you are married to someone like my first husband, this is my advice from experience: do not waste your time and energy defending yourself, but convert both those commodities into tangible progress on your road to organizational freedom. Refuse to indulge in any form of defense. Instead, let his criticism be a trigger for you to clean out a drawer, iron a skirt, fold clothes, etc. Just make sure you are busy heading toward your goal every time you feel the pressure of the critic. Depending on how critical your spouse is, you could be triggered into getting much more accomplished than the person with a supportive husband.

Post 3 × 5 cards in a few strategic places with these words on them: I WILL NOT ALLOW ANYONE TO CAUSE ME TO DOUBT MY ABILITY TO SUCCEED. Also, remember that the critical person can change, too ... if he or she wants to.

Recently, I sat with a man (I'll call him Mark) on a flight from Chicago to Portland, and now I have new insight for those of you who have a critical spouse. Mark had been married for nineteen years and was very much in love with his wife, whom I'll call Sally. When I told him that my sister and I help the organizationally impaired and that we think it's genetic, he listened with great interest.

He told me his home was always a mess and he had tried everything to get Sally to keep it nice. As I guessed the kind of person she was, because I assumed she had the same wonderful attributes that all of you do, he was amazed that I could accurately characterize her. He was even more astonished when I could describe the condition of their home and know some of the things he was doing to try to get her to get organized. I'm sure he thought I was clairvoyant.

It's a four-hour flight from Illinois to Oregon, and in the air I realized for the first time how helpless a husband can feel when his home is out of control and yet he knows his wife is such a wonderful person. As I listened, I saw in this man utter desperation on one hand and total appreciation for the kind of person his wife was, on the other.

Mark raved about what a wonderful mother Sally was, how she had such a great relationship with their fifteen-year-old daughter, how close she and their eleven-year-old son were, how much fun she was at parties, how she loved to decorate, how happy she was most of the time ... the raving went on and on and on. When I said that you can't buy a good mother, a great hostess, a flexible, creative, spontaneous, and happy person, but you can pay for housecleaning help, he totally agreed. Yet he felt so powerless to have his home be the peaceful, clutterless place he craved it to be.

Then Mark told me something that I promised I would share in this book. He said that Sally really did not care that the house was a mess, or that she had gained forty pounds, so he had more or less given up any hope. When I told him she really DID care, he argued with me. I argued back. "Oh, she cares all right, but for nineteen years she has heard both your subtle remarks and blatant fits, and she is not about to let you know how she really feels about this problem, especially when she thinks there is no solution. She has pride, and to admit that she needs help, especially to another adult of equal value, would be too hard for her to do." He stared at me in disbelief. I told him that when I was a slob, I was very defensive because when I would decide to clean up the place, it never lasted. I'd get discouraged and go one more step backward in self-esteem. If you have acted as if this problem we share is no big deal, let your pride down and confess to your mate how it is affecting you. Mark was grateful to hear that Sally really was concerned, and he was eager to support her in any way.

Of course, he wanted to get all of our books and the card file, but I told him he couldn't have them. I said that Sally or her sister or a close friend would have to be the one to discover us. I made him promise not to go home and tell her that he had sat next to an author who writes books on how to get organized. He looked like a little boy who had just had his new bicycle run over by a garbage truck. I felt sorry for him.

You have the information, regardless of how you got hold of it. Now, the rest is up to you. We have great expectations for you. We know you can get your act together. If we could, so can you.

God bless you and your family.

Nativity Cross
800- 693- 7755